Sh

THERE was a hint of dawn in the sky when they reached a rough shelter. Denver got down from his mount and looked inside and around it.

Then he came back to help her down. "It's empty and waiting for us," he said. "We need to rest a few hours. We can make better time in the daylight."

Clare looked back along the murky trail apprehensively. "Do you think we'll be safe here?"

"I'm almost sure of it," he said. "This is off the main trail. A hiding place for gunmen like me when they are in trouble."

"Don't call yourself that!" she protested.

He smiled at her bleakly. "That's what they call me."

"They're wrong! Oh Denver, I love you so!"

"I know," he said quietly and embraced her again. Then he walked with her to the shelter and they made their way in. He lit a candle and set it out so they could arrange a comfortable bed from his blankets. Their lips met once more in a lingering, caressing series of kisses. And as she stretched out beside him and studied his handsome face in the candlelight, she was taken over by a strong desire to give herself to him...

Denver's Lady

Clarissa Ross

POPULAR LIBRARY

An Imprint of Warner Books, Inc.

A Warner Communications Company

To Frank and Dee Ervin
Friends and neighbors.

Chapter One

Tempestuous, auburn-haired Clare Thomas sat tensely in the large, expensively furnished office of the Intercontinental Railway Company located at the rear of the ground floor of the famed Pembrook Hotel in Denver, Colorado. The year was 1876 and it was late in the month of May. Across the room from her were her father, engineer Milton Thomas, and Jefferson Myers, the Denver representative of the railway company. Her father faced the railway executive, who dominated the room from behind his wide, mahogany desk.

Caught up in their discussion of the plans for continuing the building of the railway, neither man seemed to be aware of her presence in the room. They were smoking long, black cigars and the room was rapidly filling with nauseous, blue smoke. Clare could barely see the opposite wall with its ornate gray wallpaper and framed photographs of railway officials.

1

Her father had insisted on her being present for the meeting as he relied on her opinions a good deal. From him she'd learned a good amount about engineering and actually worked beside him on his various jobs. Thinking wryly that she was a woman born ahead of her time, she decided the moment had come for self-preservation. She jumped up from her chair and crossed determinedly between her father and the other man, found a window, and opened it.

"With your permission, gentlemen," Clare said with a smile. "My lungs have never been able to cope with solid cigar smoke. I require just a little air."

For a moment the men stared at her in silence. Then Jefferson Myers put his cigar in an ashtray on his desk and boomed out with laughter. His huge body—rumor had it he weighed close to three hundred pounds—rippled with his appreciative guffaws, and his heavy, gray side whiskers vibrated from his merriment.

"Good girl!" he finally managed to wheeze through his laughter, his high-pitched voice issuing from the massive body in striking contrast.

Her father rose, cigar in hand, faced her apologetically. "I'm sorry, Clare. I entirely forgot how much you dislike cigar smoke."

"I'd think it would fog your thinking," she told him.

Myers nodded with amusement. "You are quite right, my dear. I dare say it has clouded the issues."

Clare went on, "With a rival company planning to complete a line from Denver to join the Union Pacific in Cheyenne before us, I'd call this a moment for clear-cut decisions!"

The fat man at the desk waved her to a chair near him. "Sit down, Miss Thomas. You are completely right. And as you work so closely with your father, I want you to contribute something to our discussion."

She smiled again, looking charming and most un-businesslike. "Thank you, Mr. Myers, but I doubt if I have much to contribute."

Her father said, "Clare, along with my assistant, Harris Trent, has been a tremendous aid to me. I always seek her opinion and value it."

Myers gave her a questioning look, his heavy jowels floating over his hard collar. "You've heard our discussion, my dear. What do you have to say?"

She hesitated and then told him, "This new Great West Company seems dangerous. Especially since they plan to take a shorter, more direct route to put down their tracks, while we have much more mileage because of our pledge to take the line through the mining towns along the way."

"Which was the proper decision, to serve the towns," her father said. "We did not know of a rival company then."

Clare asked, "How do they intend to serve these communities if they bypass them?"

Myers sat back in his chair. "They claim they will build spurs from the main line to the largest of the mining towns. That will be costly and might not work, but it could give them the edge in completion time."

"And we cannot change our route?" she asked.

"No," her father said. "That is all firmly agreed on."

"Then we'll have to find our own means to get the

line through as quickly as possible. It will depend on what engineering shortcuts we can produce to get through the mountains."

Her father nodded. "I agree. But there is a problem."

"What?" Jefferson Myers demanded.

"Harris Trent, my assistant engineer, is a most cautious man," Milton Thomas sighed. "I spend far too much time arguing with him about procedures. He makes it difficult to take the risks which may be needed."

Clare spoke up. "You are the senior engineer, Father. Your decisions ought not to be questioned by Harris."

"Aha," the fat man behind the desk said. "What is your answer to that, Mr. Thomas?"

Her father frowned. "Perhaps I do need to be more firm. But Harris Trent is my friend as well as Clare's fiancé."

Myers offered her a congratulatory smile. "My best wishes, Miss Thomas!"

Clare felt her cheeks crimson and burn. Almost sharply, she told her father, "That is most unfair! I do see a great deal of Harris Trent because we are working in the wilderness together where there are few other people. He has proposed to me but I've not accepted him."

Her father asserted, "He has told me he means to marry you."

"I hope I may have something to say about it!" she declared. "I find him terribly dull!"

"Good! A young filly with spirit!" Myers said. "I

like her thinking and I'd say you should listen more to this young woman than to Harris Trent."

"So it would seem," Milton Thomas said, looking embarrassed.

Clare felt a pang of hurt knowing she had caused the father she adored an awkward moment. But she had grown up independent in mind. She had been only sixteen when her frail mother died and she had lived entirely with her engineer father since then, following him into whatever wild outlands his railways had taken him. He had also become her teacher.

He had lectured her by lamp- and candlelight in the rough camps on the intricacies of engineering, and he had also enriched her mind with readings of the classics. Wherever they travelled he still brought along a huge, wooden box with volumes of Shakespeare, Swift, the Greek and Roman classics, and their favorite novelist, Charles Dickens. His teachings had worked well; she'd grown up strong in mind and body as well as attractive and feminine.

"What are the hazards in this area from the Indians?" she asked Jefferson Myers.

Myers clasped his hands over his mountainous stomach. "The Utes have signed a peace treaty. They do not like the railway going through, but they will keep their word not to interfere. This does not rule out occasional groups of renegade Indians who have broken from the tribes and prey on whites and Indians alike."

Her father said, "I fear renegade whites more than the Indians. There are many ex-soldiers still roaming the country, some of whom have become outlaws.

They'd like nothing better than striking at a rich construction company."

"The worst threat," Myers said solemnly, "could come from such men hired by the Great Western to impede our progress. It is a ploy that could gain them more time."

Clare's father reached over and stubbed out his cigar in an ashtray on Myers' desk, then pointed out, "Ever since the Civil War ended, the West has had more than its share of killers for hire. Men such as Kid Curry, Ben Thompson, Wild Bill Hickok, and John Wesley Hardin."

Jefferson Myers' small eyes gleamed knowingly as he said, "We have one of the breed here in Denver. No one knows his real name but he calls himself the Denver Gent."

Clare smiled. "I doubt if he conducts himself like a gentleman."

The railway executive eyed her with interest. "As a matter of fact, he has a gentleman's manners and looks and dresses like one. But cross him in a deal or a gambling game and you're faced with a different man! They say he's killed more than a dozen men in a trail that covers almost as many states."

"What is his business here?" Clare asked.

"Gambling," said Myers. "He operates a fast poker game here in the bar of this hotel. I gather it is a most profitable operation."

"No doubt," she said dryly. "Since he probably kills anyone who dares to win from him."

"On the contrary," Myers said in his squeaky voice. "I have played at his table and I believe he operates an honest game."

Clare's father cleared his throat, "Aren't we getting away from the main subject of discussion? I shall be leaving day after tomorrow. Plans for completing the line should be decided on before my daughter and I go back to the main construction camp."

"Our board of directors will back you in any reasonable plan, Mr. Thomas," Myers promised. "I say it is up to you and Mr. Trent, along with your most enterprising daughter, to come up with some plans to speed the finish of construction."

Clare told Myers, "Some of the risks might lose us men and materials. Are you prepared for such losses?"

He nodded. "We want our line completed before Great Western gets to Cheyenne ahead of us."

"I will do my best," Milton Thomas said. "I promise that. But I have no new plans formulated as yet."

"Plenty of time to think about such matters on the stage ride back to construction headquarters," Myers said.

Clare's father rose. "It would seem useless to waste further time in discussion at this moment. With your permission, I'll get back to checking the supply wagons."

"I quite agree," Jefferson Myers said raising his huge bulk up from his chair. He smiled at Clare. "May I have the pleasure of showing you around the lobby, Miss Thomas? Denver is justly proud of the Pembrook Hotel."

"You're very kind," she said, returning his smile.

As they moved towards the door to the hallway, she told her father, "After we've looked at the hotel I'll return to the Wentworth House and see you there."

"Take your time," her father said. "I shall be busy

going over the wagons and checking on supplies for at least a couple of hours."

As soon as her father left them, Myers led Clare out to the ornate lobby of the hotel. Its leather chairs and potted palms were the latest in hotel decor and had been brought to Denver from the East. The prim man behind the desk recognized Jefferson Myers as they went by and gave him a quick nod, one so brief that many might not have noticed it.

"This happens to be Wild Bill Hickok's favorite hotel," Myers said, gazing around the busy lobby with satisfaction. "He's done a lot of guard duty for our company. I wish he were here now, but he's working for another railroad company at the moment."

"I hear he's a wonderful marksman and Indian scout."

"The best," Myers wheezed. He gave her an amused side glance. "So you're not going to marry Trent?"

She blushed again. "I'm sorry the matter was brought up."

"But you won't marry him, will you? Even though it's what your father wants?"

"I think not," she said carefully. "Father is carried away by his friendship with Trent. I have never thought of him as more than an older male friend."

Myers chuckled. "Stick to it, girl! I like your spirit! And from all I hear you've got some good ideas about engineering as well. Make your father listen to you."

"That isn't always easy," she said. "Even though he treats me more as an equal in business than most men would."

"Keep showing him you've a mind of your own, and you'll manage him!" Myers chuckled again. "Now

I'm going to take you to a spot where less venturesome young ladies than yourself would never dare show themselves."

She raised her eyebrows. "And where is that?"

"Room on our right," he said. "Headquarters of the Denver Gent's gambling business and the location of the small private bar that caters to his customers."

"It must cost him business not operating in the regular bar," she said, indicating the open entrance to the crowded hotel bar on their left.

"Wrong! He does better in his own room," Myers replied. "Gets the best of the local and travelling trade. Come along and see for yourself!"

She hesitated. "Are ladies welcome?"

"I don't know about ladies," Myers said, amused. "But females have always been a weakness of the Denver Gent's. He is always happy to welcome a pretty face!"

Clare followed with some misgivings, worried that she might be making a mistake. But the fat man had more or less challenged her to join him in the gambling den and she had a dislike of turning down any challenge.

Myers opened the door for her, and Clare stepped into a room with crimson flowered wallpaper, a short oak bar at the rear with a display of exotic bottles, and a big bartender in shirt sleeves. In the exact center of the room was the round poker table and conducting the game was one of the most attractive men she'd ever seen.

She hadn't a doubt this was the Denver Gent. He was taller than anyone else in the room and his body was lean. He had a handsome face and black hair and flashing black eyes; a deep red scar ran down his left cheek, and his white teeth flashed in a smile of greeting as he noted her entrance. His skin was tanned and there were weather lines about his eyes and at his mouth. He wore a perfectly tailored black frock coat, checkered trousers, a gleaming white shirt with a black string tie, and a flat, black, broad-rimmed hat on his head. A diamond ring sparkled on one of his fingers.

"Afternoon, Denver," Jefferson Myers called to him. "Brought a friend to see your place!"

The gambler smiled and bowed. "You are most welcome," he said in a low, pleasant voice. Then he returned to the game.

"You see!" Myers gloated. "A real gent!"

"Yes," she said, taking in the scene. A coal-oil lamp hung from the ceiling to spread a yellow, smoke-glazed glow over the room. There were only one or two cowpokes in the place; most of the patrons were town dudes or travelling men in eastern city suits. Scattered among the men draped about the sides of the room and at the bar were several loudly dressed, heavily made-up women whom she could only assume were from one of the local brothels. They regarded her with some surprise and whispered to their male companions, undoubtedly about her.

She pretended not to see them and moved closer to the gambling table to watch the Denver Gent at work. He handled the cards with dexterity and coolness, and the other players never let their eyes leave his hands and the cards. Myers stood behind her, peering around her shoulder and murmuring encouragement to the various players.

The Denver Gent at last raked in the pot, then said, "Time, gentlemen! We will resume play in a quarter hour!"

Several of the players voiced annoyance, but in the face of his adamant decision they drifted away. This left him alone and smiling as he faced Clare and Jefferson Myers.

"We seldom have a guest as attractive as yourself," the dark-haired man said, hat in hand. "May I enquire your friend's name, Myers?"

"Sure thing!" Myers said happily. "This is Miss Clare Thomas, daughter of Milton Thomas, the famous railway engineer. And she's done some engineering as well."

His black eyes met hers with mocking light in them. "I'm delighted to meet you, Miss Thomas. I have heard of your father and his work."

"And I have heard of you and your accomplishments," Clare replied.

"May I invite you to join me in a drink?" the Denver Gent asked. "Sarsaparilla or perhaps a glass of sherry?"

Mischief gleamed in Clare's green eyes. Coolly, she said, "I'd prefer a shot of whiskey, straight."

"You see!" Myers chortled with delight.

"Let me escort you both to the bar," the gambler said, "and you shall have the best whiskey in the house." They moved up to the bar where places were quickly made for them by the awed onlookers.

When the drinks were served, the Denver Gent raised his glass and made a toast, "To you, Miss Thomas, and to the success of the Intercontinental Railway line."

11

"Thank you," she said and downed the powerful drink in the manner she'd learned from the workers in the construction camp. She noted that the gambler watched her closely to see if she coughed or gasped.

He said, "You must find Denver very tame after working out there in the wilderness. Quite risky, I'm told."

"We've been fortunate," Clare responded. "We've had few incidents that were threatening."

His eyes met hers again. "But you do have a powerful rival group in the Great Western people."

She showed interest. "You know about them?"

"All sorts of people come in here to gamble," the Denver Gent said. "I hear many things."

Jefferson Myers spoke up. "I know those fellows have been spreading the word around that they're going to destroy our camp and scatter the construction crew. But they won't ever manage it!"

"I hope not," the gambler said quietly.

Clare asked him, "Did you hear any specific threats of what they might try to do?"

The Denver Gent smiled. "Their main theme seemed to be to get to Cheyenne first."

"I think we can win that race," she said stoutly.

"After meeting you, I grant you might well do that," he said. "Another drink, Miss Thomas?"

"Thank you, no. I must leave in a moment or two."

"Will you be in Denver long?"

"Another day and night," she said. "Then we go back to the camp."

"I would very much like to see you again," he said with some sincerity. "Perhaps I may recall something

I overheard when the Great Western people were here."

"If you do, I'm sure my father would be interested," she told him with a small smile.

At that moment a flashily dressed blonde with heavily rouged cheeks came striding up between them, a tall glass in one hand.

"My name is Mame Burke," she said in a voice with a slight Irish brogue. "I'm the Denver Gent's woman! Who the hell are you?"

Clare stared at the indignant young woman and said, "I don't think it really matters to you."

The Denver Gent placed a hand on the blonde woman's shoulder and in a reasoning voice said, "Mame! Don't be a fool!"

Mame flashed him an angry look and said, "You're the fool! Falling for every simpering female who turns up here!" And to Clare she said, "If you need experience I run the best house in town. You're a new face and I can use you."

"Thanks," Clare said coolly. "I have other plans."

"They better not include the Gent," Mame Burke warned her. "I make a specialty of carving up pretty faces. The Gent didn't get that scar on his face in a duel, he got it from me!"

"I think you're a little overwrought," Clare said.

"My, we use fancy words!" and with her free hand Mame slapped Clare hard on the cheek.

The blow came so unexpectedly that it sent Clare reeling back for an instant. Then she quickly reached out, took the drink from the blonde woman's hand, and poured the liquid down the front of her low-cut dress. Mame howled and sputtered in surprise as Clare took Jefferson Myers by the arm and marched with great dignity towards the exit. In her wake came shouts of delight and applause from the other men and women in the gambling room.

When they reached the hotel lobby, Myers halted to take a huge, white handkerchief from his trousers pocket and wipe the beads of perspiration from his bald head. "Never saw anything like it," he declared. "You were wonderful!"

Clare smiled thinly. "A little less than that. And probably that poor woman does have a good claim on the Denver Gent. One can't blame her for trying to protect her rights."

"Her rights!" the fat man scoffed. "She has no rights in the Gent. She runs the best house in town and happens to know him as a friend. The Gent is careful with females like her. If he goes to any of the houses he takes up with one of the girls, not the madam. It makes for less problems."

"Still, he seems to have a problem with Mame."

"He'll deal with her," Myers promised. "Not treat her bad or anything like that. But he'll quietly put her out of the room and tell her not to return."

Clare looked amused. "Our little adventure turned out to be more exciting than I imagined."

"I certainly wasn't looking for anything like that," Myers said ruefully. "Don't tell your father what I did."

"I should!" she teased him.

"He'd never forgive me for taking you in there to meet the Gent."

"I'll spare him the news then. But you must tell

him what the Gent said about the Western Railway crowd making threats."

Myers nodded worriedly. "Yes. Bad news."

"At least it makes us aware of possible danger."

"That it does," Myers agreed. "I'll walk you back to the Wentworth House."

"Thank you," Clare said. "But I'm sure I can manage it on my own."

"I'd rather not take risks," said Myers. "I'll escort you."

And he did. When they reached the Wentworth House, the rambling, three-story hotel in which she and her father had rooms along with the wagon men, Myers said goodbye to her in the lobby.

"This is a nice, quiet, family place," he said, glancing around.

Clare smiled. "Not anything like the Pembrook Hotel!"

"Don't go out alone while you're in town, or take any other risks. We don't want anything to happen to you."

She laughed. "After what just took place it's a little late to tell me that."

Jefferson Myers winced. "Be a good girl. Just forget it ever happened!"

She promised that she would and left him to go upstairs to her room. It was next to her father's with the connecting door her father considered necessary for her safety. It was a small room with an iron-frame single bed whose chief feature was a lumpy mattress. A calendar from a mail-order house in Chicago was the only decoration on the faded floral wallpaper. There was a commode with a washbasin and a single chair. Looking around her, Clare realized with rueful amusement that her room at the construction camp was much more comfortable.

Moving to the single window overlooking the street, she pulled back the worn curtain and glanced down. A heavy wagon rolled by leaving a cloud of dust in its wake and was followed by a mangy dog barking wildly. The houses in the street were nondescript, faded, wooden affairs of one and two stories. Directly across from the hotel was a barroom with a false front. Needless to say, it was doing a land-office business, with a large group of cowpokes standing on the wooden platform outside it.

It was a depressing view contrasted with the majestic snow-capped blue mountains which greeted her every morning at the construction camp. The shops in Denver were not all that exciting, either; she longed to one day go east to New York and really catch up on her wardrobe. But how many new dresses did she need working in the wild lands beside her father?

Her thoughts turned to the railway, and she frowned. They could have done better if Harris Trent had not always protested against taking risks. He was a very solid engineer, but too cautious for the sort of job they were doing. Removing her hat, she left the window to stretch out on the bed, and after she'd adjusted the thin pillow, she began to think of the man she'd so recently met whose handsome face kept intruding on her thoughts.

The Denver Gent! Almost the instant she'd seen him, she'd felt a magnetism between them. By all the standards of her class, he was the type of man she should not even engage in conversation, yet here she was wondering what it would be like to be clasped in his strong arms. Even his soft, deep voice had thrilled her! And it didn't matter that the flamboyant madam, Mame Burke, felt she had a prior interest in him; Clare knew she would like to win his love for herself.

This pleasant, romantic dream lulled her into a light sleep, despite the hardness of the bed. She did not waken until she heard the door from her father's room open, and a moment later he came to stand silently over her.

She looked up at him and saw his face was shadowed by worry. "Is something wrong?" she asked.

"We've lost Nick, one of the wagon men," her father said. "And a wagon full of supplies as well. He simply loaded up and went off with them."

She sat up on the side of the bed, coming fully alert as she ran a hand through her rumpled auburn hair. "How could he do that? Didn't anyone try to stop him?"

"No," her father said grimly. "They all trusted him and assumed he was going ahead on my instruction."

Clare stood up. "He's likely on his way to the Great Western camp now."

"Probably they put him up to it. They'll buy the provisions and give him a job."

Her eyes showed anger. "Did you notify the sheriff?"

"Yes," her father sighed. "But he didn't hold out much hope for recovering the provisions or Nick. The Great Western people will post him someplace with the work crew where it will be almost impossible to find him."

"Are the other wagon men trustworthy?"

"I'd say so, but I thought Nick was all right."

Clare kissed her father on the cheek and said, "I guess it's another reverse we'll just have to overcome."

Milton Thomas nodded. "How did you make out with Jefferson Myers?"

She was standing before the mirror of the commode, fixing her hair back in place. She smiled into the mirror as she told him, "He's a funny man! I felt I should humor him by allowing him to show me around."

"He likes female company," her father advised. "And it's mighty important that he doesn't lose faith in what we're trying to do. He is our main link with the eastern investors who are bankrolling us."

"I realized that," she said, turning to her father with a smile. "We had a very pleasant time and he walked me back here."

"That was wise," Milton Thomas said. "I'd prefer you not go out alone."

She smiled. "You know I can protect myself."

Her father shook his head. "That tiny pistol you keep in your handbag is some insurance. But not enough. Suppose someone suddenly attacked you, knocked the bag out of your hands, or took it from you?"

"I doubt if that's going to happen on the Denver streets in broad daylight!"

"It happens more often than you think."

"I still must go to the millinery shop tomorrow," she said. "And there is a dress store I want to look in at as well."

"Perhaps Jefferson Myers can find some lady to accompany you," her father suggested.

She shook her head. "I prefer to be alone and I'm not worried at all."

"I hope you are right," her father said with a shake of his head. "I'm not convinced. Are you ready for dinner?"

"Yes," she said. "We can go down now."

The dining room of the Wentworth house was as drab as the lobby. But the tablecloths were clean and the food was good, if plain. The tables were set out in boardinghouse-style and one might find oneself at a long table with perhaps two dozen strangers. Clare and her father located two seats at a table near the entrance to the kitchen.

Hank, one of their wagon men, an old-timer with a bald head fringed with gray hair and a drooping walrus mustache, was seated directly across from them. On seeing Clare, the elderly cowboy offered her a smile, revealing many missing teeth and one or two yellowed survivors.

Hank paused in his meal to say, "Heard you put Mame Burke in her place today! Didn't surprise me at all!"

Milton Thomas frowned at the old wagon driver. "What are you talking about?"

"It's nothing!" Clare protested, blushing and realizing she should have known the incident would one way or another reach her father's ears.

"I wouldn't call it nothing!" Hank said gleefully. "Mame came up to stop Miss Clare talking to the Denver Gent. She slapped Miss Clare across the face and Miss Clare took a glass of bourbon out of her hand and poured it straight down her cleavage!"

Clare's father gave her a sober side-glance. "Is this true?"

"In a way," she said in a small voice.

Her father turned to Hank. "Where did this happen?"

"In the Denver Gent's gambling room. Where else?"

Her father turned to her again. "How did you happen to be in there?"

Clare knew she could protect Jefferson Myers no longer. With a small smile, she told her father, "Your friend took me there."

Milton Thomas frowned. "That was most indiscreet of Jefferson. And I'd expect you'd have better sense than go there."

Hank attempted to come to her aid, saying, "The Denver Gent's gambling place is real classy! And so is the Gent!"

Her father shot a cold glance across the table at the mustached Hank and snapped, "If you please, we shall have no further discussion of the matter!"

But Clare knew this would not be the end of it. And a little later when they were both in her bedroom upstairs, her father gave her a stern warning about visiting such a place again.

"I blame myself for keeping you here in the wild country with only rough males as your chief companions. But you must hold onto some standards!" he argued.

Clare sat primly in her chair and told him, "You're making far too much of this!"

Her father stared at her with concern. "Your mother was a fine lady. I want you to grow up to do her credit.

Make a good marriage and live a happy, protected life."

"I'm not sure that's what I want," she said.

He frowned. "It should be. It appears I've led you along the wrong paths. Perhaps we'd better change it right now. Suppose you take a train back East and live with your Aunt Patricia. I'll see you have all the money you need to be launched on society."

She replied to this with laughter. "Boston society! Can you imagine me standing in line meekly in my silk gown, my eyes lowered as I wait for some scion of an old Boston family to invite me to dance? You have to be joking!"

Her father's frown vanished as a smile came to his pleasant face. "Hard to picture my tomboy daughter, who rides the trail regular-saddle like a man, in a silken gown at a Boston ball. But maybe you're cheating yourself."

Clare got up and kissed him on the cheek. "If I am it's not your fault! I'm perfectly happy being with you, and right now what concerns me most is getting that line to Cheyenne finished before that Great Western gang."

Her father held her in his arms and beamed at her. "Just the same, no more ventures into gambling dens."

"We'll be leaving day after tomorrow," she pointed out without giving him any real promise.

They talked for a while, then he went down to the bar while she sat in her room rereading *David Copperfield.* When her eyes became weary she changed for bed and put out the lamp. Now she was aware of the sounds of drunken revelry coming up from the bar below. There was also the tinkling music of a player piano which was the central attraction in the oversized saloon. It made it difficult for her to sleep.

And once again she pictured the handsome Denver Gent, standing in the middle of his own gambling room and bar. She kept wondering about him. What sort of person was he? Had he killed a dozen men as people claimed? What had made him decide to be a gambler and gunman? Was Mame back at his side tonight? Or had he dismissed her from his gambling place forever? Crossly she punched her pillow and tried to change the direction of her thoughts. She knew, whether she wanted to admit it or not, the Denver Gent was the first man who had ever set up such stirrings within her.

After breakfast the next morning Clare went down to watch her father supervising the further loading of supplies for the camp. She pointed out some items which she had missed and paid her respects to the wagon drivers.

Old Hank of the drooping gray mustache came up to her on the sly and whispered to her, "Going back to gambling again?"

She gave him a pretended look of anger, then laughed and said, "You nearly caused me a lot of trouble!"

Hank chuckled as he kept a weather eye out for her father who was busy somewhere else at the moment. "Hear the Denver Gent is a devil with the ladies. Sure would make that Harris Trent jealous to know where you'd been!"

Clare pointed a finger under the old cowhand's nose. "Don't you dare ever talk about it at the camp or I'll see you're shifted from the wagons to the shovel brigade!"

The old man raised a protesting hand. "You don't need to worry about me, Miss Clare. I ain't going to mention it again!"

She then went on to the main shopping area looking prim and proper in her lavender suit and frilly shirtwaist, her wide-brimmed straw hat decorated with violets. No one could have guessed this demure lady walking delicately with parasol and pocketbook was the same mannish beauty who rode astride in rawhide breeches with a regular cowboy hat on her head.

Her destination was the store of Madame Ouida whose window bore a sign, "Latest Imports From Paris." Madame Ouida was presiding over her small shop alone. She proved to be a tiny woman whose flowing skirt seemed to dominate her. Her thin, graying hair in a pompadour did nothing for her wizened, small-eyed face. There was no hint of Paris in her speech.

"I'm from Kansas," the petite woman said proudly. "All this Paris stuff is to help me sell my hats and dresses."

Clare gazed around at the many hats set out in the window and on counters around the tiny shop. She said, "You do have some very nice styles."

Madame Ouida studied her and then said, "I make all my own hats. Copy them from the designs in the eastern mail-order catalogues. And I have just the thing for you!"

"I don't want anything too fancy," Clare told her. "I don't really like the hat I have on."

The little woman came back displaying a hat in a

much neater style without any wide brim. "This is the one for you!" she said.

She took it in her hand. It was a pretty blue with white trim. "What is it called?" she wanted to know.

"That," Madame Ouida said, "is a Shirred Capote. Everyone in New York has at least one. It's surah and lace and the box-pleated brim is raised at a point in the front. The edge of the crown is shirred in a wide band to have the fullness form a large puff. And there's a triple velvet bow at the front of the crown with strings of the same style on the side."

Amused by the woman's long description, Clare sat down before one of several mirrors and tried the hat on. It was youthful and actually looked very good. She made a decision at once. "I like it," she said. "I'm going to wear it because I don't have much chance to wear such hats when I'm home."

"Of course, my dear," a pleased Madame Ouida said. "I'll put your other hat in a box and you can carry it with you."

Clare paid the woman and left the shop in a happy mood. She started back for the hotel, having to wait a moment for a carriage to roll by before crossing the street. The dust made her cough a little, and she had to hold her skirt up a trifle on the side to keep it from dragging on the wooden sidewalk.

Suddenly two drunken cowboys came staggering out of an alley and took a stand directly in front of her, barring her way. They laughed and jeered at her as they weaved drunkenly back and forth. With dismay, Clare realized she could not get by them; she decided to turn and go back the way she'd come, but one of the cowboys danced around so that she was caught between them.

"Missy, been shopping?" the taller cowboy leered at her and, snatching the hatbox from her, took out the hat and let out a loud howl. Then he doffed his sombrero and put on her hat and did a little jig.

"You look sweet, Joe!" his partner shouted drunken support.

Clare let this all happen for a brief moment as they had taken her by surprise. Then she whipped out the small pistol from her pocketbook and shot at the feet of the posturing Joe!

The tall man screamed with pain, stopped his dancing, and reached for his foot where the bullet from her pistol had grazed the toe. The hat fell from his head, and he let out an oath and ran off. His drunken pal shouted something to him, cursed her, and then staggered quickly down the street after his pal.

From behind her as she watched them flee came a familiar, pleasant voice. "I was hurrying to rescue you but you did very well on your own!"

Chapter Two

Clare turned around swiftly and found herself face to face with the Denver Gent. He looked as handsome and assured as he had when dominating his gambling room.

"I don't think the hat is harmed," he said, picking it and the box up and carefully putting the hat inside.

"Thank you," she said, replacing her pistol in her pocketbook. "I appreciate your concern for me."

He looked at her as he stood there holding the hatbox. "I guess I should have known that any girl who could down a whiskey neat the way you did would know how to use a weapon and have one."

"Your coming along as you did was what really sent them running," she said with a smile. "Otherwise I'm sure they'd have attacked me."

"Sorry that happened," he said seriously. "Gives Denver a bad name. And we're actually quite a law-abiding town."

"I'm sure that is probably true," she said. "For myself I prefer the wild lands."

"Not much good for my business," the Denver Gent smiled.

"I can see that," she said, a little at a loss at what to do next. All her instincts made her wish to keep talking with him and get to know him better, but she recalled her father's concern about seeing the gambler again.

"I'll walk you back to your hotel," he said.

Clare protested. "No need. I'm sure I'll be safe now. There seem to be people in the streets. They won't try anything again."

"I'd feel happier if you'd let me escort you," the Denver Gent said. "Actually, I was on my way to your hotel to ask for you."

She stammered, "You were? Why?"

"I wanted to see you again."

She was blushing like a schoolgirl and hated herself for it. She said, "I didn't think you'd give me a second thought. That by now you wouldn't even remember me."

He shook his head. "I don't meet that many ladies like you."

"I'm sure you have lots of female friends. Mame Burke as an example!"

The Denver Gent winced. "Sorry! The fact is Mame is, and has been, a good friend of mine, but nothing more. Every now and then she gets the idea she owns a big share of me. And I have to set her straight."

"Oh, that's how it is," Clare said, pretending cool sophistication. "I'm sorry if I caused any trouble between you."

His sharp black eyes met hers as he said, "Whatever trouble you caused, I'm glad of it. I've waited a long while to meet someone like you."

"I think we should start walking," she ventured, aware of the glances they were getting from passers-by on foot and in wagons.

"By all means," he said, taking her arm and carrying her hatbox as they strolled along. "I know you are Clare Thomas, the daughter of engineer Milton Thomas. But you don't know my name."

She smiled, "But you are the Denver Gent."

"My real name is Jack Bruce," he said. "I came north after the war. I was an officer in the Confederate army."

"That explains your air of authority, the way you deal with people," she said.

"Perhaps. I wasn't that good a soldier. But I believed in the cause. When we lost I felt I had no personal future. I drifted along and then found I had a talent for cards."

She glanced up at him as they walked on. "Wasn't that settling for too little? I see you as a lawyer or perhaps a doctor."

"I might have been a lawyer but for the war. My father was one. He died at Bull Run."

"I'm sorry," she said. "But I did pick out what you're suited for."

"I'm best suited to be a gambler," he said. "I'm not ashamed of my career."

"What about the men you're supposed to have killed and the banks you robbed?"

He laughed softly. "How legend builds! For your information, I was never involved in any bank robbery

29

or any other sort of robbery. I have never been a renegade gunman. The few men I killed were killed in self-defense. In my line somebody often draws on you quick and if you're not quicker, you're dead."

"So you have killed men to stay alive yourself."

"That's the truth," he said. "And not as many as they say. And only when I had no other choice. My hand is as good with a Colt as with cards."

"Then you must be an expert gunman. I saw the way you handled cards yesterday."

They had arrived at the entrance to the Wentworth House. The Denver Gent doffed his hat and stood there looking even more handsome than she had remembered him. He said, "This has been a pleasant encounter."

"It has for me," Clare said.

He handed her the hatbox. "I understand you are leaving Denver in the morning."

"Yes."

"It would give me great pleasure if you would dine with me in the private dining room of the Pembrook Hotel tonight. A sort of occasion for us to get to know each other better."

Embarrassed, she said, "I think not. I usually dine here with my father."

The Denver Gent smiled. "He'll not lack for company at the boardinghouse tables in there."

She looked down. "I would like to dine with you but it might cause talk."

"Surely this is not the same girl I've seen drink whiskey and shoot straight," he protested. "Worried about what a few old gossips might say."

She smiled up at him. "I'm usually not so cautious."

"Why be now?"

She hesitated, a mixture of emotions buffeting her, then on impulse, she said, "All right, Denver. I'll accept your invitation."

"Wonderful! But the name is Jack."

She shook her head. "Denver suits you better. Let's leave it that way."

"Denver it shall be, if that's what you want," he said with a warm smile. "I'll come for you in a carriage at seven o'clock."

"I'll be waiting," she said, smiling in return.

He nodded. "Wear something real pretty. I'll have to live on the memory of tonight for a long while."

She shrugged. "I'll do my best. What about your gambling table?"

"The game will start late tonight," he said. "After I see you safely home." And he bowed, put on his hat, and strode back down the dust-ridden street.

Clare watched him go, incredulous at what she had done. There was no doubt that the Denver Gent robbed her of the ability to use her head; where he was concerned, it was her heart which ruled her. Yet all in all she wasn't sorry, and she wasn't going to back out. As she went inside, she was already trying to decide what gown she would wear. Her wardrobe was limited but she would find something.

She mounted the stairs and made her way to her room. When she unlocked the door and went inside, the adjoining door to her father's room opened. There was her father, looking stern. Behind him stood Jefferson Myers, looking frightened.

She knew at once what this meant. "You've been spying on me!"

31

Milton Thomas' pleasant face was shadowed with concern. "Not by intention," he said gravely, "Mr. Myers happened to be here conferring with me when I looked out the window quite by chance. I could not help seeing you and that gambler!"

Jefferson Myers wheezed, "Has that fellow been bothering you?"

"No," she said evenly. "As a matter of fact, he saved me from being tormented by two drunks just a little while ago. Then he was kind enough to see me home."

Her father looked pained. "Clare, you don't have to defend him!"

"What I say is true," she insisted.

"All my fault," Myers mourned. "I should never have exposed you to that man!"

"You need not apologize, Mr. Myers," Clare said. "I've profited by knowing him."

"You were talking together very intimately," her father said. "Do you intend to see him again?"

She shrugged. "How much chance is there for that? We go back to the camp tomorrow."

Her father's eyes fixed on her. "You have not answered my question."

Clare let a moment pass and then admitted, "He has asked me to join him at the Pembrook House for dinner this evening."

Myers' jowels trembled. "Of course you refused him!"

"No," she said coolly. "As a matter of fact I told him I'd enjoy it."

Her father raised his hands in despair and exclaimed, "Clare!"

32

Myers stepped forward and, with perspiration showing at his temples, begged her to reconsider. "Send him a message you can't join him."

"No," she said firmly.

Myers looked miserable. "We have reason to believe the man may be in league with the Great Western crowd."

"Because they happened to patronize his gambling salon?" she suggested.

"That and other things," the fat man said. "He has been a gunman for hire in the past. He may be again. He could plan to work for them. Lead raids on our camp and construction crews. He may be looking to get information from you which he can later use."

"I don't believe that," she said. "And what makes you so sure he has been a hired gunman?"

Her father came back to Myers' side and said, "Be sensible, girl. Ask anyone in Denver. They'll tell you. The town is full of stories about him!"

"Stories, yes!" she said. "But how many people know the truth? That he was an officer of the Confederacy, the son of a fine gentleman who died in battle."

"I'm sure he told you that," her father said. "But what about the banks he's robbed and the men he has shot down in cold blood?"

"Name some of the banks." she said.

There was another short silence as the two men exchanged urgent looks. Then Myers said, "We don't know the names of them. But everyone talks about the banks he held up."

"None," she told him. "And the men he shot were in self-defense."

33

"Useless," Milton Thomas said, shaking his head dolefully. "You have accepted all his lies and made up your mind."

Clare nodded. "If you wish to think that, Father. I can't work at your side like a man, making judgements every hour, without developing some faith in my own opinions. You can't depend on me as an assistant and at the same time treat me like a frail creature in crinoline!"

"I've never seen you declare yourself so for a man before," her father said, amazed.

"Perhaps because I've never felt before as I do now."

"Harris Trent loves and trusts you. He has asked you to be his wife," her father reminded her. "Do you think this is fair to him?"

"I told you earlier that I have no romantic notions where Harris is concerned," she said. "It seems you forget easily!"

Jefferson Myers groaned. "I feel so completely responsible for all this. Is there anything I can do?"

"Yes," she said. "Try to make my father understand that the Denver Gent is not the monster he seems to think. And persuade him that a quiet dinner in the dining room of the Pembrook Hotel is not the equivalent to my entering a house of ill repute."

Her father stared at her a moment and then sighed and told Myers, "We may as well leave her alone. She has made up her mind. And when she does there is no changing her." With that he shepherded the stout man back to his room and closed the door behind them.

Clare stood staring after them, aware that she had

won a small victory and desperately hoping her trust had not been misplaced. She knew her father had read her and decided she'd fallen in love with the Denver Gent. It was dangerously close to the truth.

She decided on her ottoman velvet in dark green with a brocade trim of lighter green and a high collar which arched around the back of the neck but fell away revealingly at the throat and bosom. Then she donned the pearls that had been her mother's and were kept for special occasions. She stared at herself in the cloudy mirror of her hotel room and made a few final adjustments to her auburn hair. Her green eyes sparkled. As she reached for her evening purse in which she'd stored the pistol, there was a knock on her father's side of the door which joined their rooms.

She hesitated a moment, hoping that there would not be another scene at this last moment, that he had not come to plead with her again. Then with a small sigh she went and opened the door. Her father, in a subdued mood, entered the room.

He stared at her and then said, "I've never seen you look more lovely."

"Thank you, Father," she said. And she went close and kissed him on the cheek as she so often did. "I must go down now or I'll be late."

"I've made a decision," her parent said.

Her eyebrows lifted. "What?"

"I shall accompany you down to the lobby and see you safely to his carriage," her father said. "In that way I will protect you as best I can. Let him know I'm aware of what is going on."

She felt her throat tighten and her eyes moisten at

her father's words. His decision was so typical of his fairness and his love of her that for a moment she almost wished she could cancel the dinner date and not cause him any worry. But the moment passed. He had risen to the occasion and was giving her freedom with dignity. She must accept it.

"I'll be happy to have you see me downstairs, Father," she said with a warm smile for him.

When they reached the lobby it seemed that every eye was turned to stare at her and the stern, good-looking man at her side. Several of the older ladies murmured in admiration of her gown, and the cowboys, young and old, forgot their manners and simply stared at her. Even the elderly desk clerk offered her one of his rare smiles.

Carriages rolled by the humble hotel's entrance but few halted. Then one with two fine bays came to a stop by the door and the dapper Denver Gent alighted from it and came inside. When he saw her standing there with her father he removed his hat and bowed.

"You look lovely, Clare," he said to her. "But then I knew you would." And to her father, he offered his hand, "My name is Bruce, Jack Bruce."

"Good evening, Mr. Bruce," her father said rather stiffly, shaking the younger man's hand. "Is it not by the name of Denver Gent that you are best known?"

Denver smiled. "That, sir, is my professional name. We gamblers must have our brand names as other businessmen do. Mine serves me very well."

"So I have been told," Clare's father said dryly. And to her, he said, "Have a pleasant evening, my dear."

Clare left the lobby on the arm of the gambler,

aware that there would be a buzz of speculation after they'd departed. The carriage was an ornate one with a driver and a lamp up front. Denver helped her up into the comfortable rear seat and then took his place beside her.

He said, "Your father is quite a person. But then I'd expect that when he has a daughter like you."

"He wasn't exactly happy about tonight, but he made the best of it."

"For which I give him credit," the Denver Gent said. "I think we could be friends."

Clare made no reply to this, knowing that it would take time for the gambler to win her father's trust. The Denver Gent pointed out local places of interest and talked of the town's growth as they made the short drive to the Pembrook Hotel.

The Pembrook lobby meant a repeat of the curiosity which had been shown by the occupants of the Wentworth House lobby. In this case, the difference was that many of the men knew the Denver Gent and called out a greeting. Denver was charming but kept his dignity and escorted her upstairs to a small private dining room he had arranged for the occasion.

The room had a window overlooking the street and walls papered in a gold pattern. There was a table set for two with a gleaming white tablecloth, shining silver, and sparkling cut glass. The gold-rimmed dishes were clearly for a special affair only. Two comfortable chairs graced the table and there was a large sideboard with an open bottle of champagne in a bucket of ice and glasses.

The Denver Gent went to the sideboard, poured

two glasses of champagne, and handed her one. He raised his. "A toast to our meeting, and to meeting many times again!"

"I can drink to that," Clare said, sipping the champagne. "Whoever arranged this table has exquisite taste."

His face lit up. "It was done under my supervision. I like to look after all the details of anything I'm engaged in."

Her eyes fixed on him teasingly. "Including your poker games?"

"Even them. Do you have any idea of the care I have to take? The danger in my sort of life? How long the average gambler continues on successfully?"

"You should know all those answers better than anyone."

"Probably I do," he said as he refilled their glasses. "Let me tell you that few gamblers last more than five years before they come to a violent end."

"And you stay with it knowing that?"

"I like the risk," he said with a smile. "Guess how most of them meet their sudden deaths?"

"By shooting, I'd expect."

He nodded. "Shooting, yes. But not on a fair basis; most of them are shot in the back without any sort of warning."

The idea was sobering. Clare asked, "Why not give it up when you can?"

"I'm making a great deal of money and have a sort of fame. It's not easy to give that up," he answered.

"It means giving up many other more important things."

The Denver Gent sighed. "I know. It stops me from

38

asking you to be my wife, which is what I'd like to do."

She gave a small, startled laugh. "You hardly know me."

His eyes met hers over his glass. "I know we could be happy together."

Clare turned her back to him to escape his probing eyes. "You could make a fine husband for any girl if you'd stop gambling."

"Would you marry me?"

"I don't know. I might."

"Give me your word and I'll think about it."

She turned. "You're relatively young. You might still become a lawyer. What a waste to have you shot down."

"I'm very careful," he assured her. "The others all became careless. I can't afford that. When I enter a room I never walk straight in. I step to the right or left and stand by the wall until I can size it up and see if there are any enemies present. Then I work my way around and take a chair with a view of the main entrance."

"So you can watch new arrivals?"

"Exactly," he said. "There is one other important rule."

"What?"

"Never let yourself be seated with your back to any door; that is how most of my contemporaries met their deaths."

She studied him sadly. "You're clever. But are you clever enough?"

"A lot of it is luck," he replied with a small smile.

At this point there was a knock on the door. Clare

exchanged a glance with him and at once felt fear. Suppose this was it! When the door opened, would a gunman run in and shoot them both? Was she to die with this man she felt she could love before she knew the truth?

Something of her fear must have shown on her face, for he grinned. "It's just the waiter." He opened the door and said, "You can begin serving in five minutes. Be sure the soup is hot!"

The dour waiter nodded. "Yes, sir."

As the Denver Gent closed the door leaving them in privacy again, she said, "So that's how you must live!"

"What do you mean?"

"Fear," she said, staring at him wide-eyed. "I was frightened the moment I heard the knocking on the door. I was certain some outlaw would burst in here and kill us both."

He laughed. "I might have been more cautious if I hadn't known the waiter was due."

"Suppose it hadn't been the waiter when you opened the door?"

"I would have had to think and act quickly," he admitted.

She shook her head in despair. "I couldn't live with it! The constant threat!"

"Isn't there any danger in your work?"

"Yes. But the odds are a good deal better."

The Denver Gent said, "Don't let us spoil what is for me a unique evening by talking of death and danger."

The waiter returned and served them hot turtle

soup, venison, partridge, and a flaming brandied dessert followed by coffee.

Clare sat back from the table. "I never have so huge a dinner."

He smiled at her. "Then you'll remember this one. That is what I wanted."

"You've managed better than you realize," she said. "If I'm to keep my figure, it's a good thing I'll be riding the trail tomorrow."

The handsome face of the man across the table went into shadow. He hesitated and then said, "I think I must warn you. When you return to your construction camp, things are going to be more hazardous for you."

"Why do you say that?"

"I have been told," he said. "The Great Western people have to slow you down or end your operation."

"You seem to know so much about them. Are you in their hire?" She shot the question at him directly, remembering her father's suspicions.

"They approached me," he said coolly. "I refused them."

"I see," she said. "And now you're warning me?"

"Your welfare has become immensely important to me."

"Thank you," she said. "I'm afraid I can do little more than you do to protect yourself. We must go ahead with our work, taking all the precautions we can manage."

His tone was serious as he said, "Please tell your father what I've told you."

"I will," she promised.

"I want to see you safely lay those twin ribbons of metal to Cheyenne and do it first."

"The last big rail link," she said. "Once it's done you can move on to Cheyenne and open a gambling salon there. Civilization hand in hand with progress."

"The Indians don't see it that way," he replied. "And I feel some sympathy for them."

"At least the Ute tribes have signed a pact not to interfere with the railroads," she said. "If they keep to it."

"They'll probably do better than our side," the Denver Gent promised her. "We invariably wind up betraying them."

She stood up. "And it is time for me to leave."

He left his chair and came around to her. Taking her by the arms and gazing deeply into her eyes, he said, "You may stay as long as you like. The night if it suits you. I will remain with you."

A little breathlessly, she said, "My father will be waiting. I cannot stay longer."

"I love you, Clare," he said in a low voice. "If only we'd met before. Now it is too late."

"Not if you really care," she told him. "You have free choice."

He made no reply but drew her close to him. His lips were hot on hers. Her knees seemed to weaken and her arms tightened around him as if they had a will of their own. She had never felt this way before, and wanted the kiss to last forever. Why had fate ordained that he be someone outside the boundaries of her kind of life?

As he released her, she felt dizzy. His eyes glittered

as he whispered, "Don't forget me!" And then he went to the door and held it open for her.

Little was said between them on the drive back to the hotel. The Denver Gent seemed to be in a silent, melancholy mood, and she was too bewildered to properly put anything into words. So she sat quietly beside him, though their hands were entwined. They parted in the lobby of the Wentworth House, empty now except for the ancient night clerk, and the Gent's only sign of emotion was his holding onto her hand for longer than might be expected.

"The best of luck," he said, his eyes fixed on her.

"And to you," she replied.

He nodded, then released her hand and walked slowly back to the dark street and his waiting carriage. She listened to it roll away and then went up the worn stairway to her room. There was no sound from her father's door so she assumed he was either asleep or out somewhere.

Slowly she changed and prepared for bed. She sat in her nightgown before the murky mirror and spent a long while braiding her lovely hair. And at last she knew that while she would be leaving Denver in the morning, her heart would remain there. For the first time in her life she was in love.

When she appeared downstairs for breakfast the next morning, few would have recognized her as the beauty of the night before. Her hair in braids down her back, wearing a work shirt, leather jacket, and gray riding breeches, she could have at first glance been taken for a boy.

Her father had a seat at the end of a long table

which was otherwise empty. She sat by him and ordered her breakfast from the sleepy-looking female in charge of the room.

Then Clare turned to her father and said, "I think you were asleep when I came home last night."

He shook his head. "No. I was in bed, but I didn't go to sleep until after you returned."

"I hope you didn't worry needlessly about me."

Her father made no reply to this but instead asked, "Did you have a pleasant evening?"

She smiled. "Splendid."

Her father cleared his throat. "Well, today we hit the road again."

"Denver gave me a message for you."

Milton Thomas scowled. "What sort of message?"

"The Great Western crowd is trouble. They are determined we shan't get to Cheyenne first."

"How does he know their plans?"

"They tried to hire him."

Her father glanced at her. "Are you sure they didn't?"

She gave him a reproving look. "Yes, I'm sure. He is our friend."

"I hope so," her father replied. Then her breakfast arrived and little more was discussed. After breakfast they packed and moved on down to the barns where the wagons were waiting fully stocked with provisions for the months ahead.

It was still cool when Clare reached the wagon train. There were nine of the covered wagons left with the desertion of Nick with his wagon. The horses were harnessed and impatient, while the drivers and extra men stood about and chatted.

Old Hank came forward to greet her and said, "Your dun is all ready. It's down by the second barn."

She smiled at him. "I love Nero," she said. "He always keeps calm. The bay used to panic over any little thing."

Hank nodded. "The bay dies while the dun will thrive wherever there is grass."

"You can't beat a coyote dun," Clare agreed. "And Nero is a very special one."

Hank looked around bleakly and then said, "We've got a fortune in supplies and only two guards. Ain't enough!"

"But all of us are armed as well."

"Another four guards would be a good investment," Hank said. "Protect the company's supplies."

"I'm sure my father has considered that and not found it to be necessary," she replied.

Hank dropped the subject and with a sly grin asked, "How did you make out at the Pembrook Hotel with the Denver Gent?"

She blushed. "What do you know about it?"

"Saw you going in," the old man said. "So did a lot of others. We'd made bets on whether you'd meet him or not. I won near twenty dollars."

"Then I hope you're satisfied," she said. "You'll not hear anything else from me!"

She turned and went towards the barns to get her horse. On the way she met her father and Jefferson Myers having a last-minute talk before the wagons moved off.

Myers removed his hat and bowed to her. "What a transformation!" he exclaimed.

She smiled. "Yes. I'm just another hired hand now."

"Had to see it to believe it," he said. "I've just been telling your father to keep a sharp eye out for renegade Indians, bandits, and the like."

"We had no trouble driving in here," Milton Thomas said.

"But you weren't loaded with supplies then," the fat man pointed out. Not much advantage attacking an empty wagon train. Now you'd make a rich haul."

Clare nodded agreement. "He's right, Father. Do you think we should have a few more guards?"

"Too late for that now," her father said. "We'll have to take our chances." He consulted his pocket watch. "Time we were under way!"

"Best of luck!" Myers said rather forlornly.

"I'll be at the head of the wagons," Clare's father told her. "You ride by Hank's wagon at the rear. The guards will work up and down the line between us."

She nodded and went down to the barn without a word. Nero was waiting; she patted his mane and said a few words to him and then swung up into the saddle. She circled around and held the horse by a taut rein until the wagons were moving and she could take her place at the rear. Then she rode up abreast of Hank's wagon. Behind her stood Jefferson Myers, his hat in hand, waving them a farewell.

Clare waved in return and took a last look at the town they were leaving. She had made many journeys like this before and said goodbye to many western towns but never with such a depressed feeling as today. She resolutely turned around and faced the road ahead with the mountains and wilderness in the background. This was her country and she must return to it.

She had hoped for a miracle. She'd thought that maybe in the space of a couple of days she could so impress the Denver Gent that he'd give up his career of gambler for her. But he clearly was not ready to do this. Foolishly, she'd allowed herself to fall in love with him. Now there would be the pain of remembering and the pain of losing him. Perhaps she was not meant to belong to any man, she tried to tell herself. Perhaps she was fated to journey through life alone, a solitary figure as she was on the dun right now. Her lips tightened with determination as she vowed that no matter what, she would not settle for a dull, prosaic partner like Harris Trent!

The road became narrower and more rutted and the frame houses and cabins on the outskirts of the city became less frequent until there were none. The gray sagebrush and the afternoon heat became her companions. Around her were the purple mountains which offered so many obstacles to the course of the railway line.

The road twisted and became little more than a trail almost overgrown in some places. A refuge for wolves, coyotes, prairie foxes, gophers, and such things. Occasionally there would be a glimpse of an antelope. No buffalo. But the air was good! The air was like a tonic!

The wagon train reached their first campsite as the sun began to sink. It was by the bank of a fast-running, narrow stream. They drew the wagons into a circle, built their campfire, fed and watered the horses. Soon the cook had a fragrant stew bubbling over the fire, and a pot of coffee going. Already the evening air felt chill, and they drew closer to the fire to eat.

Clare sat cross-legged beside her father with a tin dish of the stew, but her thoughts were far distant. Visions of the Denver Gent's handsome face kept intruding on her mind.

The surging flames of the campfire reflected on her father's face as he regarded her with some concern. "Better eat, my dear," he warned her. "We have three more hard days ahead."

"I know," she said listlessly.

"Denver's behind us," he said hesitantly. "I think it's time to forget all about it."

She looked wryly amused. "You probably think it strange but I enjoyed being a normal young woman for a change."

He sighed. "I gave you your chance to decide to go East."

"That's not what I want," she told him and began to eat a little of the stew.

"So many people don't really know what they want," her father said. "They think they do but they are confused. When you return to the camp and we start work putting down rails again, you'll feel a lot different from now."

"You think so?"

"I'm certain of it. You'll understand that the people you are with every day are more important to you than casual friends. That someone like Harris Trent is worth a dozen who might say they care for you one day and be gone the next."

She offered her father a weary smile. "I know what you're hoping, Father. But I don't love Harris Trent and I'll never marry him."

Because she was in an unhappy mood, Clare staked

out a spot for her sleeping bag away from most of the group, who were close by the remains of the campfire. She avoided Hank, who would have wanted to talk with her, and all the others as well. She saw the dun was properly tethered and then sank down to sleep, deep in the shadows, a distance away from the rest.

She looked up at the star-studded sky and the silvery moon and wondered why human lives were so often ordinary and unhappy. Why didn't people make the decisions they should with courage and not live with regrets? If she truly loved Denver, she should have accepted his offer of marriage and remained in the city at his side. If his work was to be gambling, she should be willing to stand beside him in the gambling salon. But she had chosen to run from the prospect, insist that he make the decision in her favor. And since he was even more strong-willed than she, he had refused to do more than acknowledge his deep love for her.

In this mood of self-reproach she sank into an uneasy sleep. She did not know how long it lasted. But she was wakened by a huge, rough hand clasping over her mouth and dragging her from the sleeping bag with an ease which suggested she must be at the mercy of some giant. She clawed at the hand and tried to scream but it did no good. Nor did her struggling as she was dragged up the bank and through the brush.

At last her captor halted in the darkness and her terrified eyes saw two other hulking figures loom out of the shadows. The man holding her whispered, "Got her, boys! Truss her up! She's a regular little wildcat!"

One of the other men chuckled. "What do you know? We have Denver's lady for ourselves!"

"We got our orders," her captor said harshly. "Don't get any sudden ideas!"

"I was aiming to have her shared all around," the other one replied.

"We ain't ready for any treats yet," her captor said. "Plenty of time to discuss that. Right now we want her bound up and as far away from here as we need to."

There was some more arguing among the three; then the rough hand was removed from her mouth and a filthy rag shoved in its place. This was bound tightly as were her ankles and wrists. She was limp and helpless as the big man lifted her up. She could only wonder where she was being taken.

Chapter
Three

The long ride lasted until dawn. Bound like a trophy in front of the rider, Clare felt mercilessly jolted at the movement of the horse over the rough trail. She moaned inwardly, every muscle and bone in her body aching.

After a while she hurt too much even to care which direction they might be taking. Then, as the sun began to rise, the three found a camping place on a hill high above the surrounding area. She was taken from the horse and dumped unceremoniously onto the hard ground.

The three men tethered their horses, lit a campfire, and started preparing their breakfast. The one whom she assumed was the leader sauntered over to her with an evil smile on his weathered face. She at once recognized the tall, lanky man—Nick Long, who had deserted the camp and stolen a wagon of supplies!

"You're a long ways from the wagon party now, Miss Clare," the renegade said. "There's no place for you to run! So I'm going to untie you for a little. How much freedom you get depends on how you behave." He removed the gag. She spat at him and in a hoarse voice, she managed, "Thief! Kidnapper!"

He paused in untying her and gave her a cool survey. "Callin' me a lot of names ain't goin' to help you a whit! We got you and we got you good. If you aim to keep healthy you better go easy!"

"Why?" she gasped as he untied her. She sat up and rubbed her wrists, trying to restore her circulation.

Nick stood back and warned her again, "Don't try runnin' off! You'll only die of hunger and thirst if I don't drop you with a bullet between your shoulder blades."

She started rubbing her ankles. They'd been abraded by the rope; as feeling returned they hurt. "Shooting someone in the back ought to be easy for you!"

Nick's smile vanished. "Careful what you say!" He jerked his head toward the others by the campfire. "Them two would have raped you straight off and slit your throat. I was the one who saved you."

"You kidnapped me!"

"Part of my job," Nick said. "You cause me no trouble and I won't cause you any!"

Clare awkwardly struggled to her feet. "Why have you done this?"

He grinned. "Some folks hanker to worry your pa a mite. They want to make a deal with him. Gettin' you back in return for his saying goodbye to his railway job and going back East."

"Great Western!" she said. "They're paying you for this!"

"Hard to get a grubstake just being a railroad hand. This way I can manage it easy," Nick gloated.

"You're being a fool, Nick," she warned him as they stood facing each other a distance from the two outlaws by the campfire. "The Intercontinental is a powerful company. My father is an important man. You'll pay for this!"

Nick offered her another of his sour smiles. "I hold the trump card in you and I ain't worried about your father."

"Then you'd better be!"

"This is a big, wild country," Nick went on. "As long as we keep moving they'll never be able to locate you. At least not until we have a deal and let you go free."

"It won't work!" Clare argued. "Let me go free now and I promise I won't say it was you. I'll give you a chance! Protect you!"

He shook his head. "Forget it! I have a deal and I'm staying with it."

Her eyes met his. "You won't win. I promise you!"

Nick jerked his head toward the two eating by the campfire. "Be glad I'm the one in charge. If Dummy or Swift was to have their way, they'd have their fun with you and leave you somewhere in a ditch."

"I'm thirsty," she said. "And I'm hungry."

"You come set by the fire with us and meet the boys," Nick said, taking her roughly by the arm and dragging her over to where the other two sat on their haunches. He poured her out a dark liquid from a large tin can. "That's coffee! It'll help!"

She took the tin mug of steaming liquid and gazed at it with distaste. "Thanks," she said, tautly, then warily sipped some of it.

Nick indicated a fat, greasy man with a half-grown black beard. "That's Dummy! Had his tongue cut out when he squealed on a pal in a Mexican jail!" Dummy leered at her.

"And that there is Swift," Nick said, pointing to a sly, blond, young man with blue eyes set too close together. "He's quick on the trigger and he's aimin' to be as well known as the Denver Gent one day!"

"Howdy!" Swift said, grinning at her appraisingly.

"You treat me and the boys right," Nick said, "and we'll not give you any trouble."

The coffee had revived her a little. She said, "That's mighty generous of you."

Nick eyed her with disdain. "Don't play the great lady with me! Everyone knows you were with the Denver Gent the other night! He ain't any better than the three of us."

"I'd argue that," she told him.

"Mebbe!" Nick said. "But you'd not win! So just take it easy, have some of that chow Dummy has cooked up. Pretty soon we'll be movin' on again."

"Where?" she asked.

"A good distance from here," he said.

"Don't truss me up like a bundle and make me travel that way," she said. "Let me ride along with you."

Nick was wary. "We'll see. Have some of that chow, then we'll decide."

It was a mixture of beans, chile, and bully beef. She'd eaten worse, but it was a struggle to get it down. Too far away for her to hear what they said, the men discussed their plans.

Finally Nick came swaggering back to her with a half-lit cigarette sticking to his lower lip. He said, "If you don't try nothin' I'll just tie your wrists. You'll sit ahead of me on my horse."

"Why must I be tied at all?"

"I know you. You're not that easy to handle. I watched some of the things you did at the construction camp. I'd feel better with you tied!"

She sighed. "So have it your way."

They put the campfire out, then Nick slipped a heavy thong about her wrists and tied it securely. After that he helped her up into the saddle before he swung onto the horse behind her. The giant, black stallion reared uneasily for a few seconds, but as the beast became adjusted to the extra rider on his broad back he settled down.

Nick led the party, winding through the pines further up into the rugged hills, making no attempt at conversation. Despite his earlier threats, she didn't think they'd kill her. She'd be the bait, instead—she knew the torture her father would be going through. And she was sure Great Western was promising her safe return on the condition that he resign from the Intercontinental project. Her mistake in choosing the site for her sleeping bag would bring an end to her father's dream of completing the railway.

It was inevitable that she should also think of the Denver Gent. He had been serious in his warnings that the Great Western meant to halt her father's work at any cost.

She had paid too little attention. The realization that she'd at last fallen in love had dominated her thoughts; his warnings had not had the importance she would otherwise have given them.

Now she knew how desperate the other railway construction company was and the lengths to which they were willing to go. She was to be a pawn in the game. Probably her father had been told the price for her return by this time. She knew the dilemma he faced and was once more angry at herself for being so careless.

At the moment she could think of no way out. Even if Nick continued to relax his vigilance, she hardly dared run off into the wilderness. She had no idea where they were, how far from other people. The mountains and forests could exact a terrible toll from anyone at their mercy, and she would be. She had little choice but to try and get along with her abductors.

The strange way in which Dummy kept staring at her made her uneasy, but Swift alarmed her a good deal more. Every so often he found a reason to bring his mount abreast of the stallion on which she and Nick were riding to ask some pointless question, using each opportunity to smile at her lasciviously. He was the one who made her tremble each time he approached.

Late in the afternoon they made another camp close

by the bank of a small, fast-running stream. Again
Dummy hunched over the campfire and prepared the
rough fare to sustain them. Nick left her hands tied
until she complained.

"What's the point of this?" she demanded, holding
up her bound wrists as they sat on boulders by the
campsite.

He gave her a sour smile. "Don't want you gettin'
any ideas about runnin' off."

"You know I won't do that!" she protested. "Where
could I go? I'd die in these mountains by myself."

He nodded. "Glad you have the sense to know that."

"So why keep my wrists bound?"

Nick got up, stretched, and came over to her. He
then began to untie the thin strip of leather which
bound her. He said, "Your daddy should soon be hearing from the Great Western people. They know where
I'm headin' and they may meet us tomorrow. If he
gives them what they ask, we'll send you back far
enough to get to your construction camp."

As her wrists were freed, she flexed them and said,
"My father will never give up his project."

"He thinks a heap of you."

"That will make no difference. He'll try and rescue
me somehow."

"No chance!"

"And if he can't manage that he'll hunt you down,
I promise you that, Nick!"

He grinned and, taking the makings from a rear
pocket, began rolling himself a cigarette. "I'm not
afraid of that. I want the reward and I mean to get
it. I'll be fixed for life."

She stared at him with disbelief. "You surely don't believe that?"

"Why not?" he asked, lighting the cigarette. "I may decide to be a gentleman gambler like the Denver Gent!"

Her smile was scornful. "I'm sorry, you don't fit the role."

He shrugged. "I ain't interested in your opinions. I know you are soft on the Gent. But don't make any mistake about him, he's as much an outlaw as any of us."

Dummy brought her over a tin dish of some blackened meat with hardtack alongside it. He shoved it in her hand and then lumbered back to the campfire as she stared at the dish in distaste.

Nick said, "Better eat it. It's all we've got."

She asked, "Where is Swift?"

Nick grinned. "You anxious about that blond boy?"

Her cheeks flushed. "No. I'm terrified of him!"

"Why?"

"Every time he looks at me he strips me with his eyes!"

Nick laughed softly. "Mebbe we all do a bit of that!"

"He's horrible!"

"He ain't too bright," Nick said laconically. "Neither is Dummy. But they're what I need for this job. They won't expect any big share."

"You haven't told me where Swift is."

He eyed her slyly. "You're thinking he's gone back with a message?"

"Why not?"

"Nope," Nick said. "He's out lookin' for some game

we can eat. That stuff you have on your plate is the last meat, if you can call it that." And he got up and left her to go over and sit with Dummy as he had his own meal.

She studied her plate with disgust, but knew she must force herself to eat what she could of it. It was tough and burned but she managed to get a little of it down. After eating less than half of it, she put the dish aside. She saw Nick was having his plate of meat seated by the fat man.

She watched the backs of the two men carefully and at the same time retreated back towards the brush. She had meant all she said about not trying to run away but there was a stream only a short distance from the camp and she wanted to wash up. Moving only a little at a time, she made her escape and then ran down the bank to the swift-moving, cold water.

Clare fully expected to have Nick come shouting after her as soon as he turned and saw she was missing, but she didn't care. She had been a prisoner for almost forty-eight hours and she felt filthy. Kneeling by the stream, she gazed down at her wan image for a moment and then began to rinse herself with scoops of the icy water.

The cold water was a shock but it made her feel better. So much so that after a few moments she unbuttoned her shirt and removed it, and then her undershirt. Naked to the waist she went on hurriedly bathing the upper portion of her body. So intent was she on completing this task that at first she did not hear a footstep behind her.

When there was another sound of a footstep on

the brush, fear shot across her face like a shadow and she clutched her hands to her bare breasts and glanced over her shoulder in panic. It was Swift!

His weak face was transfixed with lust as he dashed forward, grasped her by the arms, and turned her toward him.

"No!" she screamed.

Swift hit her hard across the mouth, temporarily stunning her. Then he threw her on the riverbank and sat astride of her as he tore at her breeches. She screamed, and fought back, trying to claw out his eyes. His hands closed around her wrists and she realized that if he succeeded in getting both wrists in one hand, she was doomed. Screaming with renewed terror, she bucked and struggled.

Then she was aware of someone else on the scene. And amid the struggle and clamor she saw a noose of rope dangle over Swift's head, drop around his throat, and tighten. She kept struggling as she saw the expression of surprise on his face, and then almost at once his hands left her to try and ease the rope from his neck. His eyes bulged and his face became purple as he struggled vainly to free the grim pressure of the rope.

She seized the moment to pull away from under him, draw her breeches together, and grasp for her undershirt. Now Swift was on the ground twisting and turning helplessly as Nick, on the hill above him, drew the rope ever tighter. She cried out in horror—the few seconds had brought Swift to unconsciousness and now he lay still on the ground. But she kept away from him with the same loathing she might feel for a snake, fearing he might be feigning subjection only to spring at her again as she came near.

Nick stood on the hill above her and shouted down sardonically, "That was a damn fool thing for you to do!"

"I was washing! He attacked me!" she quavered.

"What did you expect?" Nick asked and he dragged the unconscious Swift up the bank towards him. She watched in disbelief and new terror as Nick tossed the other end of the rope over the sturdy branch of a nearby pine tree, then hauled on the rope, lifting Swift from the grass until his body swung indecently from the branch. His neck stretched weirdly, there was a final jerking of his legs, and then he hung there limp and lifeless.

Clare turned away and retched. She was still gasping as Nick came and grabbed her roughly by the arm.

He was contemptuous. "You're supposed to be the equal of a man!"

She gazed at him with stricken eyes. "You didn't need to kill him!"

His hard eyes met hers. "You did that!"

"No!"

"You was bare bait, any coyote would have done that," he told her and led her stumbling up the riverbank towards the campsite.

"You could have stopped him without killing him."

"He'd be useless to me after what happened," Nick said. "Worse than useless, he might have tried to get at you again and upset the whole deal!"

Dummy was waiting for them and she knew by the

scowl on his black-bearded face that he was aware of what had gone on. Nick let her go so violently that she stumbled down onto her hands and knees. Then he turned to the other renegade and gave him some low, terse instructions.

As Clare continued to sit on the ground, she saw Dummy take a short-handled shovel which had been tied to his saddle and stride off in the direction of the tree from which Swift's body hung. Nick leaned down and poured himself some coffee from the pot on the fire.

She looked up at his grim face. "Is Dummy going to bury him?"

Nick nodded. "Any varmint rates that."

"Don't you see this is madness? It's all going to end in violence! Probably all of us dead!"

"I can look after myself," Nick assured her.

She closed her eyes and turned away, knowing it was useless to argue with him. It was a long while before Dummy came back; dusk was settling. She watched as the two sat together by the campfire. And she began in desperation to wonder if flight into the woods mightn't be preferable to meekly remaining their prisoner.

Nick could turn violent at any moment. If he thought the game lost, he'd worry less about taking her life than he had Swift's. The longer she remained with the two, the more danger she was in. And yet to venture into the wilds without food or any sort of a weapon would be almost equally dangerous.

She would remain docile, she decided, and try to ease their suspicions. Then when they were asleep, she would try to steal some of their provisions and at least one weapon, if only a sharp knife. Thinking about the plan gave her some courage. She knew the odds of escaping successfully were much against her, but she had at least to make an attempt.

Nick gave her plans a setback when he came to her a little later with the familiar leather thong in his hands. "Put out your wrists!" he ordered.

Her hopes sinking, she protested, "Not again!"

"I can't take any chances with you."

"But you agreed earlier there was no need to tie me up!"

His look was cold. "That was before you started your tricks by the stream and made me finish off Swift."

He tightened the thong around her wrists, then threw her blanket over her and went back beside the blazing campfire. It was unpleasantly cold now and would grow more so through the night. She stretched out and gazed up at the stars and wondered how long she could survive.

Swift was dead and buried. Whose turn would it be next? She tried to decide what her father might be doing on her behalf and knew he was certainly pursuing some plan. But would he reach her in time?

She fell asleep at last, a nightmare-beset slumber. She was wakened from the middle of one of these dreams by a hand touching her on the shoulder. Her eyes opened quickly and she was about to scream, when she recognized the Denver Gent bending over her. He touched his fingers to her lips for silence and at once went about severing the thong at her wrists.

Suddenly it was all changed. Hope surged up within her. How had he found out? Someone in the dark underworld of the renegades must have known and talked out of turn. Denver had heard and set out to find her.

Still signalling her to remain silent, he quickly drew her up to her feet. Then he began leading her away from the campfire towards the protection of the bushes. They'd only gone a few steps when she saw Nick sit up and stare around in their direction. In an instant he reached for his gun.

But the Denver Gent was ready for him and much faster on the draw. The gun at his hip blazed and the bullet caught Nick in the chest, toppling him back. Clare saw Dummy scrambling away from the campfire in an effort to escape. Denver fired in his direction but there was nothing to indicate he had been hit.

Denver spoke crisply. "Let's get the horses!" And he ran across to where the horses were tethered by a large tree. As he was untying the big stallion, Clare suddenly saw Dummy rise up from the shadows with a gun aimed at Denver. She screamed out in warning.

Denver ducked behind the stallion just as the fat man fired and missed. Then he returned the fire, and his shot was true. Dummy was downed by a bullet in the middle of the forehead. He fell forward on his face and lay still.

"There's no one else," she told Denver as she ran to him.

"There were three," he said. "Where's the other one?"

"Dead and buried," she told him without offering any details.

He took her in his arms and gave her a long kiss. Then he said, "Let's get going!"

She looked around in despair. "What about them?"

"There's a Great Western man coming to meet them," Denver said. "Let him look after the bodies. We want to be far away from here!"

"How did you know?" she asked.

"Your father sent a rider back to tell Myers and the town marshall," he said. "I looked up one of Nick's friends from the Great Western, got him drunk, and learned enough about the plan to guess you'd taken this route."

"Is Father also searching for me?"

"I don't know," he said, saddling the stallion. "The marshall is out with a posse. Your father may have gone on to the construction camp to organize a search party there." He tightened the cinch. "All right, you take him. I'll lead. There's a deserted shack a couple of miles from here. Let's move."

As he helped her up on to the horse, he handed her Nick's Winchester. "In case the Great Western crowd shows up."

She looked down at him anxiously. "Do you think there's a chance they will?"

"Yes," he said. "They're after you. And I doubt if they fully trusted Nick."

With that Denver went to his own horse which had been tied a distance back in the woods. He returned in the saddle and led the way along the woodland trail, with a skill Clare thought miraculous. But everything seemed miraculous just then. So much had taken place in the hours just passed. Here she was, free, and riding to meet her father in the safe company of the Denver Gent.

The trail was winding and rough and she was deadly tired, but she rode steadily behind Denver trusting him and her horse. There was a hint of dawn in the sky when they reached a rough shelter, thatched with branches and situated on a hillside by the trail. It looked too small for a person to stand in, but no doubt it was adequate for protection against a storm. Denver got down from his mount and went over to the shelter, looking inside and around it.

Then he came back to help her down. "It's empty and waiting for us," he said. "We need to rest a few hours. We can make better time in the daylight."

"How far are we from construction headquarters?" she asked as she stood with him.

"About a half-day's ride," he said. "We should get there by midafternoon."

Clare looked back along the murky trail apprehensively. "Do you think we'll be safe here?"

"We should be," he said. "This is off the main trail. With any luck we'll be at the construction camp before they realize they've lost us."

A wave of joy swept over her, and she whispered, "Oh, Denver, I love you so!"

"I know," he said, quietly and embraced her again. His arms around were all the happiness she'd ever need, she thought.

Then he walked with her to the shelter and they made their way in. He lit a candle and set it out so they could arrange a comfortable bed from his blankets. As she stretched out beside him, he studied her face in the candlelight. "Clare?" he whispered. "Are you sure?"

Not trusting herself to speak, she nodded, then reached out to trace the scar on his cheek. He kissed her deeply, passionately, then drew away.

As if by mutual agreement, they divested themselves of their clothes and there was a feverish moment when their naked bodies were exposed in the flickering candlelight and this time their embrace was the ultimate one. She gave a deep cry of joy as he penetrated her and they became one in a delirium of frantic lovemaking.

She cried out again when the glorious climax came between them. Then she relaxed and nestled close to him with a small smile on her lovely face. He reached over and extinguished the candle and drew the blanket over them and they slept.

When she wakened Clare was in the shelter alone. She quickly dressed and went outside. A smiling Denver already had a campfire built and was preparing their morning meal. He came to her and taking her gently in his arms kissed her once more with a fierce ardor.

She smiled up at him. "You should have made me get up."

"Why?" he asked. "You needed more rest."

There was a spring close by and she washed and then returned to have a breakfast of beans, bacon, and coffee. It was the best food she'd ever eaten, she decided.

Denver laughed as she polished her plate. "I gather you didn't have any decent chow while you were prisoner."

"That was the smallest part of it," she said. "But the food they had was awful!"

Denver sipped his coffee and studied her. "You look fine in spite of it!"

"I doubt that!"

"You do," he assured her. "When I first met you I thought you were the loveliest female I'd ever set eyes on. I see you the same way this morning." Then looking awkwardly down at his coffee mug, he asked, "About last night. I hope you have no regrets."

Her eyebrows raised. "Whatever made you think I might?"

"I hope I didn't take an unfair advantage of you!"

She laughed softly. "Denver, I wanted you to take me more than you can ever guess."

He looked at her soberly. "As soon as I get you safely back to your father I'll ask his permission to marry you."

"What if he says yes and I say no?" she teased him.

"You wouldn't, would you, Clare?"

She was touched by his almost boyish sincerity. "No."

They stood a little longer before breaking up the campsite and riding on through the woodland. The sun was rising, going about its job of warming the world. The trail wound crookedly through forests of pine, sometimes up steep inclines which led to open areas of boulders, then down from the hills again to the brush and the dark of the forest. Every so often they could glimpse a view of the blue mountains around them.

At noon they halted by a brook, looked after the horses, and drank some of the sparkling, clean water.

They had travelled for miles without any sign of another person.

She asked, "How far now?"

"We're actually only a few miles from the construction camp," the handsome gambler said, smiling at her. "Getting anxious?"

"I am," she admitted. "I'm afraid Father will be almost out of his mind with worry over me."

"I would imagine so," Denver said. "Well, with any luck we will soon set his mind at rest."

They rode on and it seemed to her the country had a more familiar air. She almost felt she recognized some parts of the trail.

The trail widened so they were able to jog along on their mounts, side by side. In spite of her anxiety about getting home to her father, Clare felt a relaxed happiness in riding beside the man she loved. And every so often Denver would smile at her proudly.

Then without warning a bullet whistled over their heads and a sharp voice called out, "Stop and put down your weapons!"

They reined their horses and exchanged troubled looks. Then he told her, "Whoever it is has the drop on us! Better obey!" And he dropped his rifle and handguns while she let the Winchester slide down to the ground.

Then from the woods all around them there appeared armed horsemen and directly before them a man came riding with a rifle aimed at them. Clare almost fainted when she saw who it was—her suitor and her father's partner, Harris Trent!

The thin, stern-faced young man was in a deadly

serious mood. His brown eyes glowered at Denver and he seemed ready to shoot him down without any further delay.

Clare cried out, "Harris! You have it all wrong! He rescued me!"

Harris Trent frowned and demanded, "What are you raving about?"

"I'm trying to tell you what is going on," she said, riding close to him. "This man rescued me from Nick and his henchmen and was bringing me home when you challenged us."

"Why are you trying to protect him?" Harris Trent asked.

Exasperated, Clare said, "Harris, don't be so dense!"

The other horsemen had all moved in close now, and she saw they were mostly composed of members of the camp construction crew. It was a search posse sent out to find her.

Harris Trent's face was an angry crimson. "You seem in a very buoyant mood for someone who's been kidnapped and held prisoner for days!"

"I'm trying to explain. Denver rescued me yesterday!" she protested.

Denver spoke up, "I think you should take the lady's word."

Harris glared at him. "I don't need talk from you."

"Where is my father?" Clare asked.

He shrugged. "I don't know. Out with another group looking for you. He can't be too far away."

"Someone should try and find him and let him know I'm safe," she said.

Nodding in an annoyed fashion, Harris asked, "Am I to understand this Denver chap, the gambler, somehow heard what happened and came to your rescue?"

"Yes," she said. "Nick and the other two are dead. Denver was escorting me back to the camp."

Harris Trent compressed his lips, then told Denver, "In that case you can retrieve your weapons."

"Thanks," Denver said with a thin smile as he dismounted and armed himself again. He picked up the Winchester Clare had been carrying as well and told her, "You won't need this now."

"No," she said. And to Harris she went on to say, "I'd like you to meet Jack Bruce, he's an ex-officer of the Confederate army."

Harris gave Denver a cold stare. "Aren't you better known as the Denver Gent, gambler and gunfighter?"

"I operate a room in Denver," came the quiet reply. "They know me there by that name."

"I should think that's the name you're best known by," Harris said in his precise way. "Hardly the type you'd expect to be rescuing ladies in distress!"

Clare reined the stallion, whose mood was becoming as restless and angry as her own. She said, "We became friends in Denver. That's why he came to my aid."

"Indeed," Harris said.

"Enough of this!" Clare cried. "Let's be on our way. And do try to get word to Father I'm safe!"

Harris Trent looked discomfited. He said, "Very well. I'll ride alongside you on the way to the camp."

"Thank you, no," she said, her cheeks flaming. "I shall continue to ride in the company of my rescuer."

"I see," Harris said sharply and then turned and rode away to give a message to one of the other riders. The entire company was soon following the route which would eventually bring them out at the construction camp.

Clare let the stallion fall in step with Denver's horse. "I'm sorry Harris Trent behaved so rudely."

"He was pretty upset," Denver ventured.

"He had no right to talk you as he did," she went on angrily.

"He was bound to be suspicious. I could have been the one he was after."

"But I told him you weren't! He never listens and he never wants to believe me!"

Denver gave her a knowing smile as they rode along. "He's your father's choice for your husband?"

"Yes," Clare said grimly. "But I think that's settled."

"Probably that's why he wasn't so happy to see you with me," Denver suggested.

It was Clare's turn to smile at him. "You think he may have heard of our dinner together in Denver?"

"Those cowhands working for your father are a lot of gossips," Denver warned her.

"I know," Clare agreed. "I can bet old Hank would relish giving Harris that bit of news."

They continued on with Harris Trent riding imperiously at the head of the group of horsemen. Soon they came to a regular roadway and then a clearing in the woods and directly ahead of them were the shacks and buildings which comprised the main construction camp of Intercontinental.

Clare's throat tightened with emotion at the sight of the gray buildings and the construction equipment, the railway cars on the siding with the work train. She had never expected to be feeling sentimental over this rather drab scene. But after what she'd been through it was a warm homecoming for her.

She rode a little faster and Denver followed her so that they edged up to Trent and past him. He gave them a disgruntled glance and refused to encourage his horse to go faster. As a result they were the first to reach the two-story building which housed the main office and the first to greet Clare's father who came rushing towards them with arms outstretched.

Clare jumped down from the stallion and ran to him. "Father!"

"My dear!" He embraced her. "I was afraid I might never see you again!"

"It's over!" she told him. "And I'm safe!"

Denver had also dismounted and was now standing there facing Clare's father with a smile, which was returned with a stare of confusion.

"What are you doing here?" Milton Thomas asked.

Clare spoke up. "He rescued me, Father. He's the one who really saved me!" And she linked her arm in Denver's.

Her father's face was grim. He said, "This is most unexpected." And he said it in a way which let her know he wasn't pleased despite her miraculous rescue.

Chapter
Four

Clare took a special delight in showing the railway construction camp to Denver. The construction train, which moved forward as tracks were completed, consisted of seven cars, some of them three stories high, some of regular height. In the multilevel cars were the dining and sleeping quarters of the workers, with more spacious living quarters in one such car reserved for the engineers. Other cars contained equipment, explosives, drills, and all the other materials used in such a project.

Clare, her father, Denver, and Harris Trent sat down to dinner that evening in the small but pleasantly decorated dining room of the executive car. Above this room were located the more spacious, preferred sleeping quarters. There was a thick tension at the table which had started with Clare's arrival with the Denver Gent and had not lightened since.

Clare had bathed and put on clean clothes, wearing a favorite blue gown especially for Denver. She was happy to have him there at the camp and it was her hope that she might persuade him to remain as one of the guards. So far the prospects for this seemed poor. Both her father and Trent were cold and aloof towards the handsome gambler.

Struggling to keep conversation going, she asked her father, "When did you first get word I was being held a hostage?"

Milton Thomas frowned. "I received a note from a cowpoke on his way back to his ranch. He told me a fat man with a beard met him along the trail and gave it to him."

"I think I know who it was," she said. "A mute man called Dummy by the other gunmen."

Her father nodded. "The cowpoke said the fellow couldn't talk but the instructions were written on the envelope holding the letter with terms for your release. Up until then I'd supposed you'd decided to return to Denver for some reason."

She asked, "What were the terms?"

"That I abandon the construction project and return East. You were to be released when I arrived in Denver and had arranged for my passage."

"Then Nick expected to get a money ransom for me from the Great Western people," Clare said. "He was waiting for them to contact him."

Harris Trent spoke up. "The entire scheme was to halt our work and give them a better edge as regards getting to Cheyenne first."

The Denver Gent, who had been silent until now,

said, "I talked with one of the Great Western crowd and he confirmed it was a plot."

Clare's father stared hard at the handsome gambler and said, "I find it odd that you have been on such good terms with these people and yet you have elected to give us your support."

Denver shrugged. "In my line you meet all sorts of people and make some strange friendships."

"I'm certain of that," Harris sniffed as he took a sip of his coffee.

"I don't think Denver's loyalty need be questioned," Clare said sharply. "The fact that he saved me from that gang should be proof enough."

Her father looked down at his empty plate. "I give the gentleman full credit for that. But you will admit he has been personally involved with both the Great Western crowd and with us."

She said, "He operates a gambling salon. He meets many people."

"Yes, of course," her father said, with a slight sigh. "I was at the point of giving up since you mean more to me than any project. Now that you're back safely we must buckle down to getting the railway construction moving at full speed."

"I agree," she said.

Denver again addressed himself to her father. "May I enquire why you used wagon trains to bring the material here when you have tracks laid from Denver to this point, and brought the work train here over them?"

Clare's father looked embarrassed. "You make a good point. But the sad fact is we've had a collapse in one of the small tunnels along the line. It is impassable at the moment, but we have a crew repairing the damage, and hopefully the next time supplies are needed they'll come quickly and safely by rail."

"The whole purpose in the building of the railway," Harris said stiffly.

"I didn't know about the damage," Denver said. "Was it the result of some natural weakness or perhaps sabotage?"

Milton Thomas shrugged. "I'm not sure now. We didn't suspect sabotage, but knowing what lengths our rivals will go to, it seems possible."

Clare said, "I think there should be more guards all along the route until the race to Cheyenne is over."

Harris' reaction to this was prompt. "We can't afford such costs."

"Nor can we afford to be without protection," Clare replied.

Her father intervened, "I believe your suggestion worthy of consideration. But I don't wish to make any rash judgements. I will think about it."

"I hope you have time," Clare warned him. "We don't want any more collapsed tunnels or damaged lines."

Her father said, "This is something that we may discuss better at another time." His comment left no doubt he did not want to continue the discussion with the Denver Gent present.

The dinner group left the table and Clare and Denver went outside to stroll in the twilight. The air was pleasant and the camp was settled down for the night. Squares of yellow were starting to show in the windows of the boarding cars as oil lamps were turned on. A group of the workers lounged on an embankment by the last of the cars and were being entertained by one of their party skillfully playing a mouth organ.

They walked a distance from the construction car before they halted and Denver took her in his arms. Their lips met with the hunger of their long hours of wanting each other. Clare clung to him fiercely.

He looked down at her with a sad smile. "I'm afraid I'm not exactly welcome here."

She grimaced. "You might expect Harris to be hostile to you; he sees you as a competitor for my attentions."

Denver smiled. "I believe he really thinks you will become his wife."

"Blame Father for that," she said unhappily. "He's the one who has given him encouragement."

"You might do worse," the handsome gambler said, still holding her in his arms. "He's not bad looking and he has a career ahead of him in engineering."

"I don't care for him," she said. "He's too cold and precise. I adore you."

"Because I'm neither precise nor do I have a suitable career," he teased her.

"I love you for yourself alone," she said. "And I'm going to talk to my father about taking you on as leader of the guards."

He released her and held up a hand in resistance to the suggestion. "It would never work out. Even if they felt I wasn't on the payroll of Great Western."

"I think I can persuade them," she insisted.

"I don't want that. A day or two and I'll move on."

"Back to Denver and your gambling?"

The Denver Gent smiled. "It's what I do best!"

"Until someone shoots you in the back and you go the way of the others. Don't throw your life away!"

He kissed her again gently on the lips. "Let's not spoil our time together with arguments."

"May I at least mention your staying here as a guard to my father?"

"If you wish," he said. "But remember, I make no promises."

"I'll worry so about you if you return to Denver!"

He smiled. "It seems to me that you are the one who is in danger."

"Nothing like that will happen again!" she protested.

"Don't be too sure."

She stared at him in surprise. "Why do you say that?"

"The Great Western people are desperate to get their line to Cheyenne before you people," Denver said. "I think they will try to focus on you to frighten your father off the job."

"It will never work."

"They don't know that," he warned her. "And maybe it might have if you hadn't turned up safely."

Her eyes were still fixed on him. "You give me the impression you know a lot more about this than you're telling me."

His eyebrows raised. "Do I?"

"Yes."

He linked his arm in hers and they started back to

the camp in the gathering darkness. He said, "So you also have suspicions about me."

"Not in the way Harris and my father do," she said. "I don't think you are a spy or intend us harm. Or you wouldn't have rescued me."

"I might have done that to be sure of your faith in me."

"No," she said. "There was more than that to it. Whatever you know, you feel it is best to keep it from us. Perhaps because you think it to our benefit."

Denver looked at her admiringly. "You really do think straight. I like that!"

Their conversation was interrupted when they met another couple at the edge of the camp. Clare recognized them at once. The girl was Dora Lee, the sharp-tongued sister and helper of the camp cook, Big Tom Lee, and the good-looking, young, dark-haired man with her was one of the work crew. She was going to introduce Dora to Denver but before she could manage this, the coarsely attractive redhead had thrown her arms around him.

"Denver!" she exclaimed happily. "The Denver Gent! I haven't seen you since Mame's!" This statement seemed to confirm the rumor around the camp that Dora was no stranger to working in brothels.

Looking slightly embarrassed, Denver kissed her on the cheek and disengaged himself from her embrace. "What are you doing up here, Dora?" he asked.

Dora said proudly, "I'm up here helpin' my brother, Big Tom. Got tired of being shoved around in those houses, though I must admit Mame treated me fair."

"Mame is usually fair," Denver said. "I saw her in Denver. She's still running the place as usual."

Dora suddenly was aware of the smiling, dark man at her side and belatedly introduced him, "Miss Clare, this is Larry Brand, he's one of the crew and my gentleman friend."

Clare smiled and said, "I'm happy to meet you."

"And this is the Denver Gent, the most famous gambler in the area," Dora told the dark man. "Be proud to shake his hand."

Denver gave the dark man a sharp look as he held out his hand to him, saying, "Seems I've seen you before. Were you by any chance in the army?"

Larry Brand shook hands with him and spoke in the manner of an educated man. "I was in the army. An officer. When I came out I had to take what work I could find."

Dora chimed in, "He's a real gent! Reads all those big books!"

Denver said, "Perhaps that's where we met. I was an officer in the Confederate army."

A mocking smile appeared on the other man's face. "I rather think not. I was in the Union forces."

"Well now that's all behind us," Clare said. "We're all working together to build a new West."

"May I say, Miss Thomas, I'm delighted you're back safe. I know how much work you do here and how your father depends on you," Brand said.

"Thank you," she said. And to Denver, she added, "It's time to return to the railway car; it will be dark in another five or ten minutes."

Dora nodded. "We don't aim to go much further. What with Indians and renegades lurking around, it doesn't pay to go far from camp."

"I know that better than anyone," Clare said as they

parted and she and Denver walked on to the car where their sleeping quarters were located.

When they were a distance from the others, she said, "So Dora is a friend of yours?"

"Acquaintance would be a better word," Denver replied.

"She was one of Mame's girls?"

"Yes," he said, adding quickly, "I've never enjoyed her charms. I was more interested in a Mexican girl Mame had brought in."

"I'm glad it wasn't Dora," she said quietly, realizing how jealous she'd been of the other girl.

"That Larry Brand," Denver said worriedly. "I'm sure I know him from somewhere."

"But where? You were in opposing armies."

"Probably some time since the war. Or I could be mistaken." There was doubt in his tone.

They reached the car and Denver saw Clare to her quarters and kissed her goodnight again. She went inside to prepare for bed and worry about what the future might hold for them. From all that Denver had said, he was determined to return to his gambling career. She wasn't going to give up easily. She would fight for her man, even if it meant trouble with her father. With this decided, she settled down to sleep in the first comfortable bed she'd known for some time.

She overslept and by the time she wakened, her father and Harris Trent had finished breakfast and were out on the construction site. There was no sign of Denver. She questioned the elderly waiter and he told her Denver had also eaten a while back and gone out somewhere.

She ate a hearty breakfast and then went over to the horse corral and asked Hank to saddle up the stallion.

Hank greeted her warmly. "Sure good to see you back," he said. He jerked his head towards the many horses in the corral. "You goin' to use the stallion instead of the dun from now on?"

She shook her head. "No. I'll probably use both of them. But today I want the stallion."

"He's got lots of spirit," Hank said.

"I know," she agreed. "Did the Denver Gent pick up his mount?"

"Yep," the old man said. "Mebbe half an hour ago. He said he was going out to see where they was layin' rails."

"Good," she said, relieved. She had been fearful that he might have taken it into his head to ride back to Denver.

It took Hank only a few minutes to saddle the stallion and lead the restless animal out. Clare quickly mounted and began riding out to the point about two miles ahead where rails were being laid. It was a sunny, warm day and by the time she reached the workers it was midmorning.

She reined the stallion on a hill overlooking the work. All the men were bare to the waist, sweating under the blistering sun. Far ahead was the shovel crew digging out and creating the flat, solid earth-surface on which the wooden ties were to be placed. A second group followed, putting down the ties, and behind them a supervisor and assistants directed the rail crew in removing the rails from the flatcar and putting them on the ties. Huge bolts attached the rails to the ties and each rail had to be expertly fitted.

Bare-backed men swung heavy mallets to bury the spikes so that they would hold. The sound of the metal rang in the air at each heavy stroke. There was a small derrick used to help transport the rails and all manner of other equipment scattered about. And this was a simple area of work with no special problems.

Clare saw her father on horseback moving up and down the line of workers, and Harris Trent was by the derrick talking to one of his assistants. It was a typical, busy day of the construction. As she watched all this, the Denver Gent came riding out from the nearby brush.

As he came up by her, he smiled and said, "I thought I'd see this for myself."

She returned his smile. "I'm glad you're interested."

"They seem to be doing a great job," he told her, staring down at the active scene.

"This is an easy section," she told him. "It's when we come to tunnels, bridges, gorges, and sharp bends that we have most of our problems. You can be held up for days."

"The Great Western crowd are solving that by taking the short and easy route," he said.

She nodded. "Stranding the towns they're supposed to serve. And even at that they can't get ahead without resorting to criminal acts."

Denver gave her a curious glance. "Do you honestly think you can win the race?"

"We must," was her reply.

They rode down the hillside and joined her father, a dominant figure astride his white mare. He greeted Denver warily. "You came out to see things for yourself?"

"Yes. I think you're doing great," Denver told him.

Milton Thomas nodded. "We are right now. But there are troubles ahead—mountains and a wide river. Both directly in our way."

"Can't you take an alternate route and find easier terrain to deal with?" Denver asked.

"We could do that," Clare's father admitted. "But it would mean miles of extra rails, a twisting road, and it would almost certainly put us way behind schedule."

"So you will try to forge on directly?" the gambler ventured.

Clare's father frowned slightly. "If you're planning to make odds on our getting to Cheyenne first, I think you'd better understand that."

Denver smiled. "The idea of making odds on the two construction lines isn't bad. I might pick it up from you."

Clare said, "Father, why don't you make Denver an offer to remain here as a guard?"

Her father reined his uneasy horse. "Are you interested in that kind of post, Denver?"

The handsome man shook his head. "No, sir. I aim to get back to Denver in a few days. But I'll gladly keep my eye on things while I'm around."

"That is most kind of you," Clare's father said stiffly and then moved on to stop his mount by Harris Trent and discuss something with him.

Clare turned to Denver and said, "I won't give up that easily."

Denver laughed, "I know."

They rode on ahead where a crew was clearing a path through brush and forest for the other workers to follow. Then they headed back to the work train for lunch. Clare's father remained at the work site, but Harris Trent had returned to get extra supplies and so was at the table with them for the noon meal.

He gave Denver a shrewd look of appraisal. "I saw you taking in the scene of our labors."

"Yes," Denver said politely. "It looks like you are doing well."

"Too well to please our rivals," Trent said in his sharp way. "I think we have spies in camp and they report on our progress."

"But you hired the crew," Denver said. "You must know a good deal about them."

"Only the old hands," Clare said. "We lose men every week and others come on the gang. We have to take whom we can get since it's not all that easy to find laborers."

Harris Trent said, "If your father had taken my suggestion and tried to use some Indians other than the few half-breeds we have now, we might have had a better crew."

The Denver Gent shook his head. "I think you are wrong in that. Basically the Indians fear the railway and there is word out among the tribes to do nothing to help it."

"So you are a specialist on Indians as well as gambling," Trent replied sarcastically.

The Denver Gent said quietly, "I know the country better than most."

"Your reputation as a gunman is certainly well established around here," Trent said and touched his napkin to his lips. "If you will excuse me." He got up and left the small dining area.

"Don't pay any attention to him," Clare begged Denver.

"I won't," he promised. "But I hope he doesn't waste time and money trying to hire Indians. It won't work."

"I'll tell my father that," Clare promised. "And this afternoon," she went on, "I want to ride a distance ahead with you and show you some of the obstacles we face."

"Great," he said.

Clare and Denver rode through the virgin forest to a mountainous area with a deep gorge running through it. Clare reined the stallion on the edge of the mountain trail and pointed out below, "There is where we have to run our line or else spend a fortune and too much time blasting a tunnel through."

Denver gazed down the dizzying depths and said, "But there is no natural ledge. Or at least only sections of one. Where do you propose to place the rails?"

Clare smiled at him. "Engineer's problem. We'll level and use the existing ledges and join them by building up walls from below on the mountain slope to form a support at the proper level; in other places we'll carve ledges out of the face of the mountain. When it's done they all will fit neatly."

"You see things with an engineer's eyes," Denver said.

"I've had enough training from my father to serve as an engineer in this kind of construction," Clare agreed. "But none of our ability is of any use if we haven't protection while we work."

Denver looked amused. "Bringing it back to me?"

"Exactly," Clare said, feeling that this time she might have caught his interest. She was far from giving up hope that somehow she'd get him to remain there and work with her. "Why not?"

Denver looked away towards the mountain peaks on the other side of the gorge. "You don't understand. I have things to wind up before I can leave Denver. I went out from there in a wild rush when I heard about your being kidnapped. I left everything behind in a shambles."

"I see," Clare said in a low voice which let him understand her disappointment.

"Let's find a spot where we can sit for awhile and rest before we start back," Denver said, changing the subject.

"Up above here," Clare said, heading the stallion further up the trail.

They tethered the horses by a spread of boulders, careful to leave them in the shade. Then they walked out onto the rocky surface, arm in arm. Suddenly Clare heard a sound and, alerted, looked down to see a coiled rattlesnake almost directly in their path. She let out a cry and Denver quickly pulled her aside, tossing a rock at the snake which slithered away.

Still startled, she admonished him, "You missed a chance to use your markmanship."

"Kill the rattler? Why? He was here warming in the sun first. We disturbed him."

She gave him a quizzical look. "You reserve your skill to use on other humans only?"

"You could say that," he answered.

"How good are you?"

He smiled. "I can place a ring of holes in and around a silver dollar at a neat distance. And I can do it fast—that's most important."

She moved on ahead where they could see the gorge below. "And you waste all that in a gambling parlor?"

"I don't see it as waste."

"I do," she said, facing him. "You told me you loved me?"

"I told you the truth."

"Then why aren't you willing to do as I ask?"

Denver shrugged. "Would you respect me for that?"

"In these circumstances, yes. You know I love you."

"I'm troubled by it."

She frowned. "Troubled?"

"I don't think it's right for you. In a way I'm on the side of your father and Harris Trent."

"Please!" she said with annoyance. "Things are bad enough without that. If you desert us, leave me here, I may decide to marry Harris after all."

Denver's face was solemn. "That might be wise."

Clare gasped in anger, "Sometimes I hate you!" And she slapped him hard across the face.

Denver accepted the stinging blow and calmly took her in his arms. As their lips met she felt all the pent-up frustration and rage ebb away. He held her close and she clung to him, not ever wanting to let him go. No words were needed now.

Then it was time to ride back. Her father was more friendly with Denver at dinner that night and her hopes rose. Especially when a discussion about the future construction came up and her father seemed not at all reluctant to discuss the different alternatives they faced before the gambler.

She remarked as they lingered over coffee at the table following dinner, "I took Denver out and showed him the gorge today. He thinks we'll have a difficult time making a passage along the face of the mountains."

"Difficult!" an angry Harris Trent exclaimed. "It's more than that. I call it impossible."

"I don't," Clare's father replied. "We can't take the time to tunnel through that rock. We have to find a way around it."

Denver pointed out, "The workmen will be taking wild chances. What protection can you give them?"

Her father explained. "We drop the men down on ropes and they keep themselves tied safely until they have a decent ledge to support them. Rope ladders are used as well and boatswain's chairs."

"Some of them stay down there for days rather than take chances ascending the cliffs," Clare explained further. "Food and water and the things they need are lowered to them."

"It's risky," Harris protested.

Milton Thomas' pleasant face was stern. "The time has come when we must take risks, my friend."

"All right," Harris said. "You try that for the Kerna Gorge, but what happens when we reach the Kerna River?"

Clare laughed. "What can happen? We have to build a bridge to span it!"

"Do you realize the height above the river that

bridge must be?" Harris asked her. "The only sensible solution is to bring the line gradually down and then over a low bridge across the creek."

"A viaduct is the only solution," Milton Thomas told him. "We can skip the marshy land around the creek, working across at three hundred or so feet high."

Harris Trent looked ashen. "To span that distance would mean a viaduct at least twenty-four hundred feet long! How can we manage it?"

Clare's father smiled and invited her, "Tell us what you think, my dear."

Clare hesitated a moment, then suggested, "We should do the skeleton piers first, erecting them by means of their own posts, and afterwards the girders can be placed on a travelling scaffold on top, projecting from sixty to say eighty feet. No staging of any kind need be used. The men can climb up the diagonal rods of the piers as if they were climbing up a tree."

"You see!" Her father said with a smile of approval. "Not impossible at all!"

"Not in theory," Harris said angrily. "But I say quite impossible to construct!" And he got up from the table and rushed out in a rage.

Clare said, "Well, I surely said the wrong thing."

Denver smiled at her. "I'm not sure I understood all you said but you made the project sound feasible."

"She has an engineer's mind," her father said proudly. "Did she convince you today that we could use you here?"

"You could use extra guards," Denver said. "But I'm not sure the job is right for me."

"I'll pay well," Milton Thomas told him. "Frankly, I was not sure about you when you arrived. But after talking with you and watching you since you've been here, I've decided I was wrong."

"Thank you," Denver said.

Clare looked at him anxiously. "Well, what do you say?"

"I'm grateful," the gambler said. "I'll think it all over. Perhaps I should help open up this country to the benefit of us all."

"The Great Western crowd are building a cheap line that won't stand up any time," Clare's father said. "We are building a fine railway of which the state can be proud."

Following dinner Clare and Denver went down to the horse corral. She sat on the top of the rough fence and he stood leaning on it close to her.

He smiled and said, "One good thing that came out of your kidnapping is the stallion. A great mount!"

"Yes. I imagine one of those three stole him from some ranch. He's not the sort of mangy animal they'd buy or rent from a livery stable."

"You're right," the gambler agreed. And after a moment he asked her, "What do you want from your life?"

The abruptness of his question startled her. She offered him a half-smile and said, "I'm not sure I know how to answer that. Will you phrase it differently?"

Denver chuckled. "You sound like a schoolmarm!"

"That doesn't worry me. Your question does."

He waved in the direction of the construction train. "I mean when you've done with all this. You can't go on building bridges with your father forever; he'll be too old to work on railway construction one day. What then?"

Clare said, "I have never intended to stay with this sort of life always."

"So what do you want after that?"

"I suppose a husband, a home, and children like most women," she said.

"This isn't the best preparation for that sort of life," he warned. "Do you think you'll be able to settle down as a wife and mother?"

She smiled at him. "Ask me!"

"To marry you?"

"Yes."

The handsome faced showed amusement. "I wouldn't dare. You might accept."

She eyed him coyly. "And what would be wrong with that?"

"We've been over this," he said. "I am a gambler. The wives and families of gamblers live a special kind of life, with the shadow of it always over them and never knowing when the man of the house will be carried home on a wooden door."

"I'd give up railroad construction," she said. "And you could give up gambling."

Denver said. "I don't think either of us would mean it or stick with it."

"I could!" she promised.

"I wonder," he said. "You know you have the reputation of being a wildcat! All Denver was talking about the way you shot the toes of those gunmen who tormented you."

She raised her chin. "I say females should be able to protect themselves."

"And you can, better than most," he conceded. "That's why I think you're fooling yourself with this marriage-and-a-little-home talk."

"You'd rather spend your time at the gambling tables and places like Mame's," she told him hotly.

He took it good-naturedly. "Mame is good company when she likes."

"I'm sure of it," she said, sliding down from the log fence. "And I suppose I'm not?"

"I didn't say that!"

"Well, I said it for you," Clare stormed. "Frankly, Mr. Denver Gent, I'm losing all patience with you!"

He laughed and said, "Now the wildcat is showing!"

She was speechless with anger and so walked away from him and went directly to her sleeping room. It was close to dark and she could not stand him in the mood he was in. As she prepared for bed, she began to regret her sudden rage and wish she had not let him goad her on as he had. She knew she still loved him, but he was making any future between them seem hopeless.

He had clearly started the line of talk to make her angry. She should not have let him. She decided in the future to handle him differently. It was humiliating to hear him joke about her wildcat nature. She'd been brought up to look after herself. She was in her nightgown and about to put out the candle and go to bed when there was a knock on her door. Her heart began to beat a little more rapidly as she went and placed her ear against it hoping it might be a repentant Denver, come to ask her pardon.

"Yes?" she said, listening at the door.

"Clare, I must speak with you!" It was the unwelcome voice of Harris Trent.

"I'm just going to bed, Harris," she told him, at once let down.

"Please, it's important," he insisted.

"Wait a moment," she told him, picking up her robe and putting it on. She opened the door and Harris Trent gazed at her with a warm admiration. "You look so lovely with your hair loose around your shoulders."

She eyed him sternly. "Is that the important thing you had to say?"

"No."

"Then what?"

"Please, Clare," he lamented. "I haven't had a single moment alone with you since you got back."

"I've only been back a few days. There's plenty of time."

"Let me step in for just a moment," he begged and at the same time he moved into the small cubicle.

"This is my bedroom!" she said, anger rising in her tone.

"Forgive me, Clare, I'm desperate," the young man said miserably. "That is why I gave such a bad showing of myself at the table tonight."

"You surely did," she agreed.

"I would never have thought of crossing your father so strongly if I hadn't been under a strain," he said. He looked at her unhappily, "Ever since you returned with that Denver Gent there's been a change in you."

"That's nonsense."

"You've treated me more coldly than ever before!"

"That's in your mind," she said wearily. "And what has it to do with your battling with my father over the construction?"

"Because when I think I've lost you I lose all my judgement," he said, looking into her face, his eyes troubled.

She drew her robe closer around her. "Harris, you and I had an understanding before this ever happened."

"What do you mean?"

"I told you I wasn't ready to commit myself to anyone. And surely not to you!"

Harris Trent seized her by the arms. "I don't recall that!"

"Please!" she said, trying to free herself of his fierce grip. "You're hurting me!"

He relaxed his hold a little but did not let her go, saying, "You've fallen in love with that gambler! That renegade!"

"Don't talk about him in that way!"

He thrust his face close to hers, perspiration streaming from his temples, his expression one of rage. "Isn't that so?" And he shook her. She now was aware of the liquor on his breath.

It was too much! She broke away from him and stumbled back to where her purse was. She opened it and drew out the small pistol she always carried.

"Get out!" she said tensely, the pistol pointed at him.

He crumpled at once. "You don't need to do that!" he said plaintively.

"Go!" she said. "And don't try to talk to me again until you are sober."

"Clare, I love you," he said in a near moan. And then seeing that she was not going to relent, he turned and stumbled out. She closed and bolted the door and leaned against it, weary from the scene.

She was up early the next morning, but again she found herself having breakfast alone. The old waiter told her that the Denver Gent had had his breakfast with her father and Harris Trent. She wondered if he might have gone ahead to the construction site and as soon as she could, she went down to the corral.

Old Hank was there to greet her. "Morning, Miss Clare."

"Have you seen the Denver Gent?" she asked.

The old man nodded. "Yep. He was here."

"Do you know where he's gone?"

Hank tugged his long, white mustache. "Yep, Miss Clare. He told me to tell you he was riding back to Denver."

Chapter
Five

In the month following the Denver Gent's sudden departure, Clare tried to comfort her hurt feelings by throwing herself into the construction work. She helped her father make the required new plans and remained with him on the job for long hours. Yet the hurt of Denver leaving was never far from her. This was complicated by her worries about him. The life of a gambler and gunman was always in danger and most of them were dead before thirty.

The tiny bunk in the construction car was airless and hot much of the time, even with the window left open. Summer had come to the rugged country with full force so that the driving sun singed the pines to fill the air with their perfume and the thick dust which rolled up from behind the loaded wagons seemed to smell of heat.

But it was an ideal time to push ahead with the

railway line and they took full advantage of it. Unhappily a series of attacks by vandals held up the project at several points. So much so that Milton Thomas and Harris Trent began to discuss the addition of more guards once again. Clare thought this was ironic since she and Denver had urged them to do this earlier but their pleas had fallen on deaf ears.

Harris Trent had been behaving better since the Denver Gent's departure. He was attentive to her but also showed some restraint, not pressing himself on her. She began to hope that he finally understood that while she liked him, she did not care for him enough to ever want to be his wife. But he did go on bothering Milton Thomas with his refusal to take the risks Clare and her father felt were a necessity.

The dispute in proceedure between the two engineers was brought to a crisis point when backer Jefferson Myers arrived at the construction camp for a few days. The tunnel between Denver and the campsite had been repaired and a work train was going back and forth on the line now. A caboose was added to the train and the fat man made his visit to them in style.

One morning after a particularly hot night when Clare had enjoyed little sleep, there was a conference in the drab building which had been constructed to house their office. Milton Thomas, Harris Trent, Jefferson Myers, and Clare gathered around a circular table on which several maps and plans were set out.

Myers mopped his brow with a large handkerchief and declared, "Denver is as hot as Hades these days, but this place isn't much better."

Clare's father showed a resigned expression. "I agree. It is the workers doing the digging and placing the ties and rails who take the brunt of it."

Harris Trent shrugged. "Most of them are from this area and hardened to the extremes of weather."

"And doing a good job," Clare spoke up. "Otherwise we wouldn't be getting anything done."

Myers flattened out the map before him and stared at it with a frown. "I see you have clearly marked the gorge route rather than attempting tunnels, and then you expect to cross the marshlands and the river at its narrowest point by means of a viaduct."

Clare's father nodded. "It will save us weeks of work."

Harris turned to address Myers. "Let me point out that this route is being taking against my judgement," he said.

Myers glanced up at him with a hint of irritation. "We must take risks. The Great Western are prodding us."

"They are doing more than that." Milton Thomas spoke up. "In the past three weeks we have had five or six incidents of vandalism and thefts of supplies. The attacks have come at night and at various spots along the line."

"All of them since the Denver Gent was here," Harris said. "He was here long enough to size up our entire operation."

Clare turned to him and said angrily, "That is no reason for your blaming him. I think if he could have been persuaded to stay here and head the guards, we could have coped with the raids."

"That is pure speculation," her father warned her. "But I do think we should have a leader of the guards who has no other duties."

"Create a new post?" Myers asked.

"Yes."

"Well, if these raids are truly serious, and it seems they are, we should enlarge our present group. It is unfair to ask a few men to guard miles of rail."

"Then you have my word the owners will back the move," Myers told him.

"Who to get?" Milton Thomas mused and then he looked Clare's way and cast his eyes down. He knew she still blamed him for not acting more friendly towards Denver and inviting him to command their guards.

"My choice would be in favor of a lawman, not a gunman," Harris said spitefully, as if reading her thoughts also.

"I think my father and Mr. Myers can be trusted to find the right man," she said.

Jefferson Myers smiled appreciatively. "I shall do my best, my dear. Now back to the plan. You are sure it can be managed?"

Harris Trent thrust his annoyed face at Myers and said, "I will personally not work, or supervise any work, in the gorge. I refuse to risk my life and the lives of my men!"

Clare's father gave him a look of reproach. "There is no need to worry about that. I have already agreed you should work on the main line while my daughter and I supervise the work in the gorge and on the viaduct."

Myers looked at the young man with surprise. "I'd

say that settles the dispute." And studying the map again, he continued, "About the viaduct, you cannot count on it being fully of iron or steel. We do not have enough promised."

"Father and I went over our needs," Clare told him. "For at least seventy per cent of the construction, good, dried timbers will suffice."

"Excellent," Myers said. "Well, I see a good chance for this shortcut to land us in Cheyenne first, in spite of that gang of ruffians operating the Great Western."

Milton Thomas nodded. "Even if they reach there after us they will find their line has little value since they have skipped the small towns along the way instead of going through them as we have." He smiled and continued, "So tomorrow my daughter will head a crew going to work at the gorge; and I shall begin foundations for the viaduct, while Harris looks after the camp here and the construction leading up to the gorge."

"I will do my fair share," Harris insisted. "But I can not work on projects I think foolhardy."

Myers chuckled, his chins rippling, "Well, no harm in having one cautious chap in the camp. But I'm afraid the rest of us must go along with our own hunches. Now, I shall be pleased to accompany you, friend Thomas, on a tour of the proposed route."

That ended the meeting. Clare and Harris Trent remained behind while her father and Jefferson Myers rode ahead in a suitably stylish carriage.

As they drove out of sight, Clare turned to Harris and said, "You mustn't keep arguing with Father. It will not change our minds. If you so disapprove of what we're doing, why don't you resign?"

His prim face turned crimson. In a stifled voice, he said, "I think you know that as well as I do. I'm fearful for your safety here."

Clare's lively eyes teased him. "Yet you're not concerned enough to venture into the gorge with me?"

"I think it's madness," he replied. "Your father should never have allowed the line to be detoured through such an impassable place."

"I disagree. I think we can do it successfully."

"With the price being the lives of you or your men falling to their deaths, to make an unsafe line."

Clare walked away knowing it was useless to argue with him. She made her way down to the horse corral, and the black stallion, which had become her favorite by now, whinnied at once and came over for her to fondle his muzzle. She gradually lost the tension she'd felt at the meeting and knew it was useless to let Harris Trent upset her.

Old Hank, who cared for the horses, came loping up to greet her, dragging his injured leg after him. He'd broken it in a fall and, not having been properly set, it gave him a peculiar gait.

He tipped his cowboy hat to her and said, "That animal sure has a fancy for you, miss!"

Clare smiled. "Yes. I found him under grim circumstances but I'm not sorry now."

The old man glanced up toward the construction train and said, "I see the big boss is visiting."

"Yes."

"Any more changes to be made?"

"He's authorized more guards for us."

"That's bein' smart! I worry a heap about this cor-

ral. I can't stay awake twenty-four hours around the
clock. There's just a boy here now when I leave."

"I'll speak to my father about that."

"Wish you would." Hank paused, then asked,
"Heard any word from Denver? I mean about the
Gent."

Clare blushed. "No. Not since he left."

"There's one marvellous shot," the old man said
with awe. "But it's the same with all gunmen. They
come to bad ends."

"I don't consider Denver a gunman," she protested.

The old man shrugged. "Well, he's got that name."

"I know," she said disconsolately.

The old man sighed. "I hope he fares better than
most of them do."

"Yes," Clare said in a small voice. "Let's hope so."

She patted the horse farewell and then strode up
towards the construction car. It was terribly hot and
she decided she needed a bath and a change of fresh
clothing. So she went on to the cook's quarters where
she found Dora Lee lolling on the steps fanning herself with a piece of old newspaper. The attractive redhead was perspiring freely and clearly troubled by the
heat.

"I'm going to the pond for a bath," Clare told her.

Dora's eyes showed interest, and she stopped fanning herself. "Do you want me to keep you company,
miss?"

Clare smiled. "You look as if you'd enjoy the cool
water as well."

"I would that!" Dora exclaimed standing up. "Are
you going now?"

"Just as soon as I get a towel and fresh under-things."

"I'll meet you outside your car," Dora promised.

So it came about that a little later on they both walked through the woods to a pond about a half-mile from the construction site. It was surrounded by woods and huge boulders but was fed by a cold spring.

When they reached the pond they stood on the highest boulders.

"A lot of the men come here at night," Dora said. "I hear them talking about it."

"No wonder," said Clare. "After suffering all day in the heat!"

"I couldn't find soap," Dora lamented.

Clare smiled. "Don't worry about it. I brought two cakes of some scented soap from Chicago."

"Scented!" Dora said eagerly. "I ain't had any of that since I left Mame's place."

"Well, we have it today," Clare said rather shyly. It seemed that Dora had no feelings of shame at all about her having been a prostitute.

Nor did she worry about concealing her body from others' eyes. "May as well get on with it," she said, and began removing her clothes rapidly until she stood in the sun in all her lithe nakedness.

Clare followed but divested herself of her clothes more slowly and carefully. She tried not to stare at Dora but could not miss redhead's well-rounded body with her lovely, full bosom and fine, womanly hips. When Clare at last stood nude by the other girl, she said, "I wish I had a figure like yours!"

Dora gave her a friendly appraisal. "You've got a lot better body than a good many I know who make

106

their livings selling theirs. Maybe an ounce or two more fat wouldn't hurt you!"

"I'll keep that in mind," Clare said as they made their way down to the water's edge.

Dora went in first with a splash and then cried out, "Oh, it's good! So good!"

Clare followed her into the water and when the initial shock of the coldness was over felt better than she had for days. They remained in the water for the best part of an hour, soaping and scrubbing each other and swimming back and forth. When they had had enough they came back to the rocks, toweled themselves, and dressed. Once in their clothes they sat under the shelter of a wide-branched pine.

"This has been a lovely afternoon," Dora said. "It's hot in the cook's quarters."

"It must be," Clare sympathized.

Dora smiled pertly. "At least I get out at night. Larry comes for me."

"The nice, dark man I saw you with?"

"That's him! A true gent! He was an officer! I'm in love with him, miss."

"Do you think you might marry him?"

Doubt showed in the redhead's eyes. "There are things to be settled first. Things I know about him and things he knows about me."

Clare stared at the girl, who sat with her hands clasped about her knees. "You mean you'd allow your past to interfere with a chance of a happy marriage?"

"Like I said, I have to get some things settled first," Dora said firmly. "I never loved a man before I met Larry. I sold myself to a lot, but not one of them meant anything to me."

"As long as he understands that, why should there be any problem?"

"I can't explain everything," Dora said cautiously. "But I think he will marry me."

"You really want him for a husband, don't you?" asked Clare sympathetically.

"I'll die if I lose him," Dora said.

"Then I hope you two do marry."

"Thank you, miss."

Clare smiled and touched a hand on Dora's. "I think we know each other well enough by now for you to call me Clare."

"You mean that?"

"I surely do."

"Well, miss—Clare, I wish you good luck as well. You're in love with the Denver Gent, aren't you?"

Clare was caught unawares by Dora's frank question. She felt her cheeks burn as she stared out at the lake and said, "I do find him interesting."

"I think more than that," the other girl suggested.

She glanced at Dora. "You're probably right. But what good can come of it? He's gone back to Denver! I'll likely never see him again."

"He takes a lot of risks," Dora agreed. "Once when a crazy man was gunnin' for him, he hid out at Mame's for near two days."

"A gambler and a gunman, he's a target for anyone," Clare said bitterly.

"I don't know whether he'd give it up or not," Dora deliberated. "I've seen some do it, but it was like they got religion or were too old to shoot straight."

Clare gave a small, bitter laugh. "The Denver Gent

has neither of those problems so I doubt he'll reform."

Dora eyed her with admiration. "He should with a beauty like you caring for him."

Clare got to her feet and tried to hide the confusion she felt. "Time to return. The men will be coming here from work soon."

"And my brother will wonder why I'm not there to help him with dinner," said Dora.

They hurried back through the woodland to the construction camp, Dora joining her brother in the cook's quarters and Clare going on to her own room. She sat for a while on her bunk bed and thought about all she'd heard. None of it had made her happy, and she was more afraid for Denver's safety than ever.

A pink linen dress was her contribution to the pleasant atmosphere of the table in the railway car dining room. Jefferson Myers was weary from his afternoon adventure and did not have much to say until he'd downed several whiskies. Harris Trent was subdued and sulky. Milton Thomas looked as if the tension was beginning to get to him. So Clare tried to ease things with a description of her afternoon's outing with Dora.

As she told her story, Jefferson Myers came alive and his chins rippled with amusement. "Both of you out there as naked as Eve and me wasting my time looking at some foolish gorge!"

Clare laughed. "We'd have run for cover if we saw you coming."

"I can move fast when I need to," Myers warned her. "I doubt if you'd have managed to get far ahead of me!"

After they left the table, Clare's father and Harris Trent went to the office to settle some problem of supplies. Clare and Jefferson Myers went out to stand by the car in the twilight and watch the workers who had gathered in a circle on the ground a distance down the track. A fiddler had joined the camp and he was standing in the center of the group, playing some lively square-dance tunes. The men sang and applauded.

Then Larry Brand and Dora moved from beside the fiddler and began dancing to the music. The other workers loved it and encouraged them with cheers, whistles, and clapping.

"That the girl you took a bath with?" Myers asked.

"Yes."

"She's a looker," the fat man said. "If I weren't going back to Denver tomorrow I'd try to get to know her better."

"She used to work at Mame's," said Clare.

"Then I'd certainly get to know her."

"She's not doing that anymore," Clare informed him, feeling a slight disgust for his attitude. "She's in love with that man she's dancing with and she hopes he'll marry her."

Myers removed his cigar from his mouth and asked, "Does he know she was a prostitute?"

"He knows something about it."

"Then they'll never marry."

Clare stared at him. "Why do you say that?"

"I know I wouldn't!"

"Perhaps not! But you're not in love with her."

"You think this dark-haired man is?"

"Yes," Clare said. "And from what Dora has suggested, he has some things in his past she has to overlook."

"I still say the chances are against the match." Then Myers gave her a shrewd glance. "Now what about you and the Denver Gent?"

Clare smiled bleakly. "Your friend."

"Sure he's my friend. And I introduced him to you. You ought to be grateful."

Coolly she said, "You think so?"

"Most women would, why not you?"

Her eyes met his directly. "For one thing, his way of making a living is not to my liking."

"It's dangerous," Myers admitted. "Fellow got in a fight with him last week and Denver had to shoot him."

"Did he kill him?"

Myers looked amused. "He killed the outlaw's gunhand by drilling right through with his Colt. I'd say the hombre is through being a crack shot!"

Relieved, Clare said, "Then no one was killed."

"Not that time!" Myers said putting the cigar back in his mouth.

Clare knew this was all too unhappily the truth. And she feared her love for the Gent could not stand up to such a siege. But she would never forget him.

She found herself asking, "Have you seen him lately?"

The fat man nodded. "Yes," he said.

"Did he know you were coming here?"

"He did."

Clare's voice wavered a little. "Did he ask for me?"

Jefferson Myers smiled broadly. "I was waiting for you to ask me that!"

"What did he say?"

"That in his opinion you were just about the perfect female!"

"He wouldn't say anything as preposterous as that!"

"Well, he used different words but that is what I took from them."

"Did he say he might come back here?"

"No."

"I suppose his gambling room is busier than ever," she said bitterly.

"Nothing like a shooting to liven business up."

"No, I suppose not," she said, looking down.

"But he did give me a message for you."

She turned quickly, eyes wide. "What?"

"He said you weren't to forget any of the things he told you. Does that make sense?"

"Yes," she said happily. "Yes, it does. At least he remembered me!"

"When he got my attention he talked about you most all the night," Myers complained. "At last I had to drag myself away from him."

"When you see him, will you give him a message from me?" she asked.

"Delivering messages is just my style."

"Tell him I want him to return here. That we need him. And I'm sure my father will welcome him, this time."

Jefferson Myers raised his eyebrows. "You think that's the truth?"

"Yes. All of it," she said, anxiously. "You will tell him what I've said."

"If you like, my dear," he said. "But I sort of feel responsible in this. Maybe I've gotten you into a heap of trouble."

"No. I'm glad I met Denver. He's the most exciting man I've ever known!" she said warmly.

"I'm not able to deny that," said Myers. "And I will tell him what you've just told me."

That night Clare could not sleep for the heat and for her many visions of the Denver Gent. She relived what it had been like to be in his arms again. She thrilled at the news that he was thinking about her and had asked Jefferson Myers to bring her a message. He could well have forgotten her. There were plenty of girls in Denver and most of them were available to him.

So he did truly care for her! But not enough to return and help them with the railway. It tortured her to think that one day some raw youngster with an itchy gunfinger and a yearning to get his name known would walk up behind the Denver Gent and put a bullet in his back. Not Denver!

At last Clare fell into a restless sleep in which she had a series of wild dreams. In the last of them, the Denver Gent was presiding in his gambling salon and Buffalo Bill Cody was at the bar watching him and telling everyone Denver was the best shot and best poker player he'd ever met. Then someone entered the salon and stood in the shadows for a moment before drawing a gun and stepping out into the middle of the room, walking towards the chair in which the Denver Gent was sitting.

It was Harris Trent and he was pale and wild looking. He pointed the gun directly at Denver's back and then fired. A stain of dark spread across the back of Denver's khaki shirt and he stood up and turned around to face the coward who'd attacked him. Harris shouted out an oath and shot Denver again, this time in the shoulder. Denver staggered towards him and then Clare came running into the room and he called out her name and fell forward onto the floor!

"Denver!" She called out his name so loudly that it woke her from her tortured dream. She sat up in her bunk bed flooded with perspiration. The dream had been so real! She prayed it had not been a glimpse of the future. The memory of it would haunt her.

Early the next morning Jefferson Myers left on the supplies train for Denver. Clare said nothing more to him aside from bidding him goodbye. Then she went back to getting ready for the conquest of the Kerona Gorge. It was not going to be an easy task and they would spend some nights camping on the mountains above their work.

Old Hank led the wagon train with the supplies and workers. Clare rode along with the wagons, astride the stallion. Her father had said goodbye and was heading for the spot where the viaduct was to be constructed. It was hoped that both jobs would be completed about the same time. From that point on the problem of laying rails to Cheyenne would be over comparatively even country.

When they reached their campsite it was sundown. Clare walked over to the edge of the cliffs and looked down to the area of partial ledge about 300 feet below and the huge drop beyond that to the narrow river in the depths between the mountains. She had never seen more forbidding ground on which to try and erect a railway line.

"A big drop down there, Miss Thomas," a voice at her elbow said.

She turned and saw it was Larry Brand, the former Union army officer whom Dora was in love with. She smiled and said, "I didn't know you were on the work team."

"I volunteered," he said with a charming smile.

Clare could not help but feel flattered. "I hope you don't regret it."

"I've respect for any woman who would attempt a task like this," he said, glancing down into the dizzying depths of the gorge again.

"Thank you. Railway lines like this have been built before. My father constructed one in South America. I have all his plans for getting the work underway."

"I have a good head for high places," Larry Brand told her. "What about you?"

"Fair," she said a little grimly. "At any rate we'll soon find out." She noticed that he was dressed very well, better than any of the other workers. No doubt with savings from his role as a Union army officer. It was unfortunate he hadn't been able to find a more suitable occupation than construction worker.

He leaned forward again and said, "I see there are natural ledges about halfway along the gorge. But how will you link them?"

"Bite into the cliff wall in places and slice out a ledge protected by its own umbrella of stone. In other places the linkage will have to be built from below with suitable props. Eventually it will all be in one piece and ready for the rails to be put down."

He shook his head in awe. "I wonder if the folk who ride the railway years from now will think of the impossible things you had to accomplish to make their easy journey possible."

She laughed. "I doubt it. Just now I'll settle for a good evening meal."

They sat around the campfire and were a happy company that night, all on edge with the expectation of embarking on the wild adventure facing them the next day. Clare sat between Hank and Larry and found herself listening avidly to the young man's lively stories of his adventures in the army.

She said, "The war was really just a giant adventure for you!"

"I hope I was patriotic as well," he said. "But I did enjoy most of it."

"What about the killing? The suffering?"

"Aren't such things always part of wars?" he said. "At least I had nothing to do with the war being declared. When I was called upon to serve, I did."

"I see," she said. "Do you always respond to duty without any question?"

"I think so," he said seriously. "When there is a job to be done I will do it."

"I'm glad. We need such determination here."

"That's what attracted me to the project," he said, the flames of the campfire highlighting his strong face. "I like risk and adventure."

"Dora is very much attracted to you."

He hesitated, "The cook's sister."

116

"Yes."

"Poor creature," he said. "I hope she hasn't started to get any ideas."

Clare gave him an accusing look. "You have been in her company a great deal. I've seen you together."

"Yes," he acknowledged. "I find her amusing. I have spent a lot of hours in her company. She's the only female in the camp aside from you."

"And you must have female company?"

His smile was embarrassed. "Don't misunderstand me. I like the girl. But she has been a prostitute. You must have heard of that?"

"She told me she is through with the life."

"The taint remains."

Clare asked, "Have you ever discussed this with her?"

"It's not the sort of thing one discusses with a young woman," he said.

"Not even when you both happen to be in love?"

"I don't love her. I pity her. But I don't love her!"

Clare frowned. "She told me she loves you."

"Probably she did," he said worriedly. "I see now that I haven't been too wise in my relations with her. When I go back to the camp I'll be careful. I'll avoid her."

"She won't understand," Clare warned him.

"It seems to me she doesn't understand now," Larry said firmly. "I think she is a pretty creature. But I am an officer and a gentleman. I could never think of her in any serious way."

"I see," Clare said. "That's too bad."

"Do you blame me?"

"Not entirely," she told him. "But you are the more worldly of the two. You should have been more wary in leading her on."

"I see that now."

"Since she has come to believe you love her, I think you owe it to her and yourself to be gentle with her. To let her find out the truth gradually and in the easiest way possible."

He looked at her soberly. "Thank you for the advice. I'm sorry I didn't get it sooner."

"So am I," she said. "I'm fond of Dora."

"You would be. You're a kind person."

"None of us are as kind as we might be," she said quietly. "I hope you remember that when dealing with her." She rose. "Now it is past time for me to get some sleep. We begin early tomorrow."

In the tent which Hank had set up for her, Clare lay awake a long time worrying about the conversation she'd had with Larry Brand. She felt him to be a decent person, and yet he'd been selfish in allowing the unfortunate Dora to think that he was truly in love with her. Probably he'd reasoned that in possessing Dora he was only one in a long line of men. But Clare knew this time it was different; this time, Dora had given her body because she loved. To be discarded after such a relationship would be devastating for her.

And yet Clare didn't know what she could do or say to help the girl beyond her frank appeal to Larry Brand. She had let him know how she felt and she hoped something would come of it. But he had sounded determined to not ever marry Dora. She could not help but bring Denver into her thoughts and believe that in a similar situation, he would be much kinder. With this confusion of thoughts she fell asleep.

Early the next morning her feminine concerns about romantic matters had to be put aside as they began Operation Gorge. In the most difficult sections no ledge existed and one had to be drilled out of the rock with supports built up from below. The men were swung over the cliff in two cages about three by six feet, open at the top and at the side next to the rock. They took construction tools and food with them and were not drawn up until their working hours were over.

For the places where sections of ledge already existed, the men clambered down to work on rope ladders; one of these was over sixty feet long and more than a hundred feet wide and served many men. After some experience, an active worker could walk up and down the cliff surface simply keeping a grasp on the rope ladder. When working the men wound a rope from above around them so they had their hands completely free.

Clare gazed over the edge into the steep valley and watched the men hundreds of feet below her scurry and strive across the face of the rock like so many ants. It was both frightening and amazing. The risk they were taking could mean the difference between success and failure for Intercontinental.

Old Hank came up by her and squinted over, then stood back. "I'm sure glad I'm an old wagonhand," he said grimly. "I wouldn't want any part of down there."

"They're fairly safe if they don't get careless," she told him.

"When you fall down there, the bottom is a long way off," Hank said.

She smiled at him. "Some day we'll have railway trains running along tracks on the ledge we build down there."

"Don't sound safe to me!"

"Many railroads have the same sort of tracks in mountain areas," she explained. "With the new advances in engines they can manage the steep grades and curves."

There was a call for additional drills to dig into the rock and she saw Larry Brand, naked to the waist and holding two of the drills, get into a boatswain's chair, a wooden seat six inches wide and two feet long with ropes at each end, knotted overhead at the top and attached to a pulley arrangement to be gradually lowered. She saw him being swung out over the edge of the cliff and gave him a wave of encouragement. He smiled back in reply, then vanished as he was lowered to one of the working areas.

There were no accidents the first day, though one man had a near brush with death when the rope holding him broke. Another man working with him saw what was happening and grasped him before he could fall, then held onto him until the boatswain's chair was sent down to tie another rope around him.

Clare felt that fairly good progress had been made. But she received conflicting reports about the kinds of rock the various work crews were encountering. She examined some samples sent up and could see that there was great variance among them. She decided that the only way she could get a clear picture of what was happening was to make a descent.

When Hank heard this he was in a state. "Your father would never agree to anything like that," he told her.

"It's part of my job!" she argued.

"Ain't no fittin' job for a lady!" Hank declared.

"I'm not a mere lady. I'm the bossman on this project," was her reply. "And tomorrow I'm going down to see things for myself."

"It ain't safe!" Hank continued his objections.

"I'll use the boatswain's chair," she told him. "I'll be perfectly safe in that. There's a seat and I can hold onto the ropes on either side of me."

Hank was not impressed. But she had made up her mind and was determined to go through with her plan. She felt she had no right to ask the men to take risks she would not take herself.

She was also careful to avoid any direct contact with Larry that evening. She was still feeling depressed by the things he'd said about his affair with Dora.

The next morning an early rain made the face of the rock slippery and more dangerous. But as the sun appeared it became safer. Clare waited until almost noon and then, with Hank standing by sputtering with rage, she settled onto the wooden chair, grasped the side ropes, and gave a nod to be lowered. As soon as she swung out over the cliff, the whole world took on a different aspect. She seemed to be suspended in space. As the seat was lowered it swayed rather frighteningly, but she gripped the ropes and refused to look down.

When she reached the level where the ledge was

being worked on she felt less afraid. Gripping the ropes of the chair tightly, she asked to be lowered a little more. Then she was able to step out onto the ledge where the workers were and let the chair swing out into the air. They cheered her and she smiled and began the inspection of the rock wall which had brought her down.

She finished one section and decided to move on to a more narrow point. Just as she stepped out, there was a shower of small stones from above. In an instinctive step back to avoid them she lost her footing! With a shrill cry of alarm she felt herself toppling back to drop into the deep gorge below!

Chapter
Six

Clare was poised in an eternity of space for a terrifying second and then felt herself drawn towards the chasm hundreds of feet below. Then there was a wrenching of her body, and she was dimly aware of voices shouting somewhere near. Her leg seemed to snap and burn, and with this pain there came an end to her falling. Hands were clinging to her and drawing her up to safety. Then she was on the ledge and saw the shocked face of Larry Brand hovering over her; after that she lost consciousness.

When she came to, she was in her tent with old Hank and Larry standing by her. Almost at once she felt the pain in her knee, and when she tried to move it the hurt was worse.

"My knee," she murmured in vexation. "My left knee!"

Larry knelt by her. "I had to grab you by the ankle as you fell back or you'd have gone down to your death."

She gazed up at him vaguely. "Yes, now I remember, some gravel came down, I lost my balance."

Hank shook his grizzled head. "Dang near done it this time!"

She closed her eyes and opened them again. "Was anyone else hurt?"

"No one," he said. "May I examine your leg?"

"Please do. I know it's painful but I have no idea how bad the injury may be."

Larry lifted the blanket from her, removed her boot and then her stocking, and with a pocket knife slit her breeches down the side so he could see the injured knee. He carefully examined the area and even moved the leg so that she cried out in pain.

When he had covered her again, he said, "I may be wrong but I don't think anything is broken. I believe your knee is sprained badly."

"How long will it take for it to get better?" she asked.

The young man sighed. "Hard to say. You might be a lot better in a week, it might take months!"

"But what will I do?" she wailed. "I've only just begun the work here."

"Always was too dangerous for you," Hank said indignantly.

"I agree with Hank," Larry said. "In my opinion someone else had better take over as supervisor. Your best bet to recover quickly is to return to camp and rest."

124

"Who will take my place?" she asked.

"I could send a messenger to your father," Larry suggested. "He will know what to do."

"He's busy with the viaduct," she reminded him.

"I'm sure he'll have a plan," Larry said. "Why shouldn't Harris Trent take over here? The work he's doing now could be supervised by a foreman."

"He's not in favor of the route we're taking."

"If he's still working for the company he'd better do all he can to further the project," Larry said bitterly. And rising, he asked Hank, "Who can you best depend on to get a message to Mr. Thomas?"

"Myself," the old man said promptly. "Tell me what you want me to do and I'll go right off."

Larry asked Clare, "Do you want to write the message to your father?"

"Please, would you do it?" she said. "My knee is throbbing."

So Larry quickly wrote an account of what had happened and gave it to Hank to take by horseback to Milton Thomas. By evening Clare felt well enough to sit up and have some tea and a plate of toast and beans. Larry brought her the food and drink and sat by her in the candle-lit tent.

"I'm a little late, I fear," she said. "But thank you for saving my life."

"Too bad I couldn't have managed it without wrecking your knee," he replied.

"A small price to pay for being alive," she said with a smile. "My father will be most grateful for what you've done for me."

Larry smiled back shyly. "I did what anyone close

125

by would have done. I didn't take time to think about what was happening—I just reacted instinctively and grabbed your ankle."

"I remember the moment I fell back. It was awful!"

"I thought we'd lost you."

"You took a terrible chance, you might have been dragged down with me."

"I didn't worry about that."

"Many would have," she told him, her eyes meeting his. "I'll not forget what you did."

"The main thing is to get you on your feet."

She nodded. "I imagine Hank reached Father before dark. We ought to get some word by morning."

"We should," he agreed. "We could start you back to the main camp whenever you like."

"No, we'll wait for word."

Larry hesitated a moment and then said, "You won't like me saying this, but this is no job for a woman."

"Now you're starting to sound like Hank," she said.

"Hank is a rough diamond. He just wants what is best for you. I know what I'm talking about; I did some engineering work when I was in the army."

Her eyes widened. "You didn't mention it before."

"There wasn't much point."

"You should have," she protested. "We've been short of trained help from the start."

"I'm by no means up to your standards, not to mention those of your father and Harris Trent. But if the work is laid out for me I can read a plan and carry out instructions."

"You must tell Father when you see him," she said. "Or I will."

"I think if someone came by every two or three days to solve special problems I could carry on here," Larry said.

"Somebody will have to take over until I'm on my feet again," Clare said.

"I'm used to handling men," Larry continued. "I think I could manage the crew."

"I'm sure of it," she agreed. "They are all impressed after your rescuing me today. Hank told me before he left you're a kind of hero in camp."

Larry shrugged. "We did those things and took such chances every day in the war."

She said, "Well, good comes out of bad. At least this has brought your talents to our attention."

"I don't mind being one of the work crew."

"You deserve better," she said quietly. "By the way, have you had any thoughts about Dora?"

He frowned. "Yes. I was troubled by thoughts of her all last night."

"Have you reached any conclusion?"

"I'm afraid not."

"The ideal thing would be your marrying her."

"No," he protested. "I can't do that. I don't care for her in that way."

"She has been building on it," Clare warned him. "Dreaming of it."

He looked unhappy. "I realize now that I've behaved badly. I'll try to let her down as easy as possible. I don't know why I allowed myself to get into such a situation."

"The camp is lonely," she said. "She offered you a kind of company."

"That was at the bottom of it," he agreed. "I didn't dare approach you, or even talk to your father or Harris Trent as an equal."

"But you were wrong in that. You are their equal in most ways. You've been doing yourself an injustice."

"Perhaps," he sighed. "I'll find some way to make it up to Dora. And I thank you for setting me straight in so many things."

She smiled. "I've done very little, considering my debt to you."

Larry's reaction to her words was completely unexpected. He stared at her intently for a moment, then leaned forward and took her in his arms and kissed her. It happened so swiftly she put up no struggle and was left startled as he finally released her.

Shamefaced, he mumbled, "Forgive me. I shouldn't have done that."

She regained her poise and said, "Let's forget about it."

He gave her a troubled look. "I'm afraid I can't. That's the bad part of it."

"What do you mean?"

"I've been in love with you for weeks and didn't dare show it," he said.

"I'm sure that isn't true. You mustn't say such things!"

He rose and stood staring down at her solemnly. "I'm afraid it is true. But I promsie you I'll keep my place in future. I would not want to lose your respect. I value it far too much." And with that he left.

This new complication on top of the pain in her knee was the last thing Clare had expected. She had watched him court Dora for weeks and assumed she was his love. Now, according to him, it was not Dora he loved but Clare.

Larry was attractive and had the manners and education of a gentleman, but he had been working in a job which was below his ability and so she had barely noticed him. Now, in one day, he had saved her life and announced his love for her!

Not knowing what to make of all this she slept little that night. And early in the morning Hank returned to camp with her father riding at his side. Milton Thomas came directly to her, and after he had carried her out gently they had breakfast together on a blanket outside the tent. Hank provided them with a fine mixture of bacon, eggs, and hash, and despite her ordeal she now felt hungry and ate most of the generous service Hank provided.

Over coffee, Milton Thomas said, "I shall forever be indebted to that Larry Brand. I must seek him out and personally thank him."

Clare smiled. "I'm sure he'll appreciate any commendation you give him. He's probably with the work gang now. But he's much too well educated to be doing such work."

"An officer in the Union army, wasn't he?"

"Yes," she said. "And he did some engineering tasks so he knows how to read plans."

"Excellent," her father said. "We must put his abilities to work."

"I think you should," she agreed. "How is the viaduct coming along?"

"The barest of beginnings."

She tried to move her injured leg and winced. "I don't know how long I'll be held up by this."

"You mustn't worry about it," her father said. "By the way, we had a raid on supplies at the main line camp the other night. Lost a lot of dynamite which we need badly. I'm sure it was the Great Western crowd."

"Is there no way of stopping them?" she asked angrily.

"More guards," her father said. "Harris Trent and his crew fought the raiders off after they were alerted." He paused. "Harris got a glimpse of some of them."

"Oh?" She had a troubled feeling that there was more behind her father's words.

Her father at once proved this by going on, "Harris is almost sure one of the raiders was the Denver Gent, and that he may even be the gang's leader."

"That's preposterous!" she cried.

Her father shrugged. "The Great Western people are spending large sums of money to hire such people to harass us."

"Denver doesn't need or want that kind of money," she said hotly. "Why should he play raider in the hills when he is making a fortune comfortably operating his gambling room in the city?"

"You make a reasonable point," her father agreed. "I was only repeating what Harris said."

"Harris Trent is so jealous of the Denver Gent he's seeing him behind every bush. It's his imagination! I don't believe it at all!"

"You're probably right," her father said. "In any event he will soon be here. I elected that we hold a council of war before you were taken back to camp."

"Why not let me remain here and work as over-

seer?" she argued. "I'm certain I can manage somehow."

"It would only hold you back," her father said. "No,
you return to the construction camp until you're able
to use that knee! You can work at keeping the plans
up to date."

"I'll gladly do anything," she said. "I want to stay
on the job."

"Just hope we won't have to take you and that knee
all the way back to Denver City."

"After Larry examined the leg, he felt sure it's nothing more serious than a severe strain."

Her father stood up. "I'll go find this Larry. I want
to talk with him. Harris Trent ought to be here shortly.
Then we shall have a full-scale debate."

Clare felt frustrated and useless sitting in the tent.
But every time she moved she suffered hideous pain,
and while she was in this state she could not concen-
trate properly on her work. In the distance she could
hear the shouts of the workers as they climbed about
on the face of the cliff.

It was humiliating that she'd only been in charge
of this camp for a few days when she'd had her accident. She hoped it would not hold things back too
much. She wondered whether she shouldn't let her
father take her back to the city for treatment—at least
that way she'd see the Denver Gent again. And now
there was the further turmoil of Larry Brand, insist-
ing that he was in love with her.

Hank came by every so often to chat. "I'm taking
good care of the stallion," he said.

She smiled. "Thank you. Any other news?"

"Just that dang raid! Trent managed to send them running but not before they stole all that dynamite."

"That was too bad."

"And he thought the Denver Gent was leading the raid."

"So I've heard," she said. "I consider that utter nonsense."

"Yep. You're right," the old man said tugging his mustache. "I reckon the Denver Gent is takin' in all the cash he needs back in that gambling room."

She nodded unhappily. "I was impressed by him. I felt he was on our side and wanted to help us. Then he rode off in the night and we haven't heard of him since."

"He's a loner, Miss. Most all those gunmen are!"

"He probably felt he was doing the right thing," she said with a sigh.

"If I know the Denver Gent that's most likely true," Hank agreed.

She rested for a little and then she heard a horse come up. Hank talked with someone outside and a moment later a tense Harris Trent appeared in the tent.

"My dearest Clare," he exclaimed, kneeling down and kissing her tenderly on the temple.

"Please, Harris," she said, embarrassed. "I'm all right. I'm going to be fine."

"I heard about your accident. You're lucky to be alive."

"I know."

He stood up. "I came as soon as I received your father's message."

"I have no idea what Father has in mind," she said.

"Nor I," he replied. "You heard about the raid on our section?"

"Yes," she said. "You did well to fend that gang off."

"Whoever set the raid up knew the workings of the camp. They knew where to strike and when. I think it was the Denver Gent—he sized us up and came back with that gang."

"Never!"

"I expected you'd say that. But I *do* think I saw him."

"I'm sure you didn't," she said firmly.

"Well, I've reported it all to your father. We'll see what he decides."

She did not encourage Harris to stay with her longer and he went out in search of her father. She lay back and tried to rest but found her nerves too on edge to allow anything like that. She wished she could walk out and take on her task of supervising again and ride the black stallion. But her injured knee did not give any sign of a miraculous recovery.

It was more than an hour later that her father returned and told her the council of war was at hand. He again carried her out and they all sat in a circle. She was surprised to see that Larry Brand had been included in the emergency meeting. He smiled at her as she gave him a startled glance.

Clare's father presided as usual. He began with, "Due to my daughter's accident I have no alternative but to place someone else temporarily in charge of construction here."

"I don't expect to be an invalid long," Clare interposed.

"While you are," her father went on, "someone else must be responsible here." He turned to Harris Trent. "I know you are not in favor of this project but you are my best substitute for Clare. Will you take over?"

Harris' face was shadowed for a moment as he gave the matter consideration. Then he said, "Whatever my personal views, the good of the company comes first. I'll take on the job."

"Thank you," Clare's father said.

"But if we have many other serious accidents I reserve the right to leave the site and present my objections to Jefferson Myers," Harris continued.

Milton Thomas accepted this with a curt nod. "I'll agree to that," he said. "Just remember it is your responsibility to prevent accidents."

"I don't think the accident rate here should be worse than at the viaduct," Clare said.

"We've only had one minor injury there so far," her father told them. "But it is early in the game. We have the first supports up but we've gone only a little way in the projection of the bridge itself."

Harris asked, "Are the supports complete on both sides of the marsh and river?"

"They are finishing the other side now," Clare's father said. "We'll work from each side until the arch of the bridge is completed in the central section high above the river."

"That is the biggest gamble," Clare said.

"Quite true," Milton Thomas agreed with his daughter. "So I shall remain at that site until the viaduct is completed. Which brings us to the question of who will look after things at the construction-car head-quarters and who will see to the daily track-placing along the line leading to Kenora Gorge."

Harris Trent said, "I have been in charge. We are well up to schedule, in fact a few days ahead."

"I'm pleased," Thomas said. He now gave his attention to Larry Brand who had remained silent up until this moment. "I wish to introduce a new person to the engineering staff of our project. Captain Larry Brand, formerly of the Union army, and one of an engineering team during the war years. He joined us as a worker without revealing his abilities until he rescued my daughter from what surely would have been a fatal fall."

Harris Trent eyed the dark man with some hostility. "Why didn't you come forward with your qualifications before?"

Larry Brand spread his hands. "I did not think anyone would believe me."

"Well, we believe you now," Clare's father said. "And I'm placing you in charge of the camp and the or-dinary rail laying. You will work out of the car head-quarters and return each evening to the construction train. Your crew will also live on the train and travel back and forth every day."

Larry Brand said, "Then I shall be responsible for the track building on the level ground and the safety of the construction camp?"

"That is it exactly," said Milton Thomas. "My daughter will remain at the camp drawing up plans and doing general supervision until she is able to get around. Then we will study assignments once more."

"It gives me very little to do," Clare complained.

"Enough," her father said. "We are behind with our stock taking and in a lot of other areas. Complete rest should put you quickly on your feet."

Harris smiled and promised her, "I shall visit you whenever I can get a free moment."

"You mustn't neglect your work," she said.

"I propose to take my daughter back to the construction car at once," her father said. "And we shall all get on with our various jobs." Then he stood up and began talking to Harris.

This left Larry free to go to her side and kneel, saying, "I thank you for the opportunity you've granted me."

"I had little to do with it," she replied. "You drew attention to yourself by your courageous action."

"I know you spoke for me," he insisted. "And I shall not forget it."

"You'll be heading a construction crew but it will be the one with the fewest problems," she told him.

"That's a good thing," the young man said. "It will give me a chance to renew my engineering experience without having too much responsiblity."

"Well, my congratulations," she said.

"We'll be bound to see a good deal of each other," Larry went on. "Since we'll both be living at the construction train."

Somewhat tensely, she agreed. "Yes, that is true."

His keen black eyes fixed on hers. "I look forward to that," he said quietly. Then he rose and joined her father and Harris Trent.

She studied the three men who played such a large part in her life and wondered what the future might hold for them and for her. Harris Trent had indicated he was still romantically interested in her and Larry Brand had startled her by telling her of his love. She doubted that her father would favor either of the men, though he had once been confident she would choose Harris Trent for a husband. She felt he knew better now.

It was ironic that the man she cared for most and yearned for now was not even present. It appeared that he had renounced her for her own protection. She fervently wished the Denver Gent would appear again so she could tell him there were no longer restrictions on her love for him. She would follow him anywhere no matter what road he might decide on. If he was determined to remain a gambler she would even endure that.

But Denver was not there and she was crippled and unable to do anything but remain a prisoner at the construction train. The days ahead would be anything but bright unless her knee healed a lot faster than seemed possible.

On the way back to the construction camp, it was Hank who drove the buckboard with her nestled in her sleeping bag and the black stallion hitched on at the rear. The "road" hardly warranted being called such. Every so often a rut or washed-out area would cause the wagon to bump and send excruciating pain through her.

By the time they arrived she was sick from pain and weariness. Hank and a helper carried her into her bunk and Dora was there to help her undress and wash up. Clare had never been happier to see the kind-hearted redhead.

When Clare was safely tucked in bed, Dora said, "Now I'll go get you some broth. My brother has prepared it just for you."

Clare sighed. "I'm not sure I can manage anything."

"You must try some," Dora told her. "It will do you good. You have to gain strength while your knee is healing."

Clare gave in to the girl and actually found herself feeling better after she'd had the cup of broth. She smiled at Dora who was seated by her bunk bed.

"You have been so good to me!"

Dora said, "You are my friend!"

"Indeed I am," said Clare. "And how lucky I am to have a friend such as you."

Dora's face was radiant. "It is a good-luck time for us all. I have heard from Hank that Larry is to become a boss."

Clare at once felt a small uneasiness. Quietly, she said, "Yes. He is."

"He's a real gent," Dora said. "I knew he'd get his chance one day. And he saved your life."

"Yes," Clare said. "He surely did that."

Dora said, "There's a few things I know about him which are best unsaid. And I guess what he did to save you wipes the slate clean."

Clare was confused. "I'm not sure I understand about his past."

The redhead said, "It really isn't important. Not any more."

"I see," Clare said, wondering what Larry's secret might be.

Dora's eyes shone with hope. "Maybe now we can be married."

"You and Larry. Has he asked you?"

The other girl nodded shyly. "He told me he'd marry me if he could find a decent job. I told him I'd marry him anyway. But he wanted no part of that."

"So he actually didn't say he would marry you."

"He said when he was doing better and now he's a boss," Dora said eagerly. "I know it will be different now."

"I hope so," Clare said sincerely.

Dora stared at her. "Don't you think he wants me for his wife?"

Clare said, "I have no idea what is in his mind at all. And I don't think you do either. So I deem it wise that you not count too much on anything he may have said. See what he has to say now."

Dora said, "You are right. I know that. But I'll still go on dreaming."

"However it goes I wish you happiness," Clare told her.

"Larry will be back in camp later. And I know the first thing he'll do will be look me up and tell me the good news!"

But that was not what happened. The first person Larry Brand called on when he returned was Clare. He was excited and filled with plans for his new position. She found herself listening in a troubled frame of mind and wanting to ask him about Dora.

He paced back and forth in the small confines of her compartment. "I need a foreman," he told her.

"And I've chosen one. He's been a chum of mine. Half-Mexican he is. Pedro Reilly."

"Did you consult my father about this?" she asked.

He showed mild surprise. "No. But I'm telling you now."

"I'm not really in authority over you," she warned him. "Any decisions you make should be approved by my father."

Larry smiled warmly. "I'm sure he'll approve of Pedro. He's a first-rate worker."

"Just tell my father about the appointment at the first opportunity," she advised him.

He halted his pacing to sit and gaze at her. "You look good. You survived the ride well."

"I'm not feeling too badly," she said. "Dora was kind to me when I arrived."

He ignored the mention of the name and said, "I've got some ideas on how to save time transporting the rails."

"Good," she said. "You must tell Dora about your plans."

His eyes met hers. "You know I'd rather tell you."

"Larry!" she protested. "I'm grateful for your saving me. But I'd hardly noticed you before my accident and we're still almost strangers. You can't fancy yourself in love with me."

Larry's sober face stood-out against the growing shadows in the small cubicle. He said, "But I do love you!"

"I can't possibly love you!"

"You will!"

"I don't even know you!" she protested.

140

"When you do you'll feel differently towards me," he said. "You'll find me more dependable than the Denver Gent."

"How dare you bring up his name?!"

Larry Brand smiled. "Why pretend? Everyone knows you were swooning at his touch."

"Go!" she said.

He rose. "I didn't mean to offend you."

"I need to see you only when we have some business to discuss," she said.

"That will be almost all the time," he promised.

She gave him an accusing look. "I hope you seek out that poor girl and deal with her kindly."

"Ah, yes, Dora," he said. "That is a problem."

"She cares for you."

"I know," he said. "All the wrong people care for each other. But we can surely straighten things out somehow." And he bent quickly and managed to brush his lips across hers before she drew back. He laughed at her gesture and went out.

Clare was stunned by it all. His manner had changed in a not-too-subtle way and now he was acting almost as if he was in power over her. She began to worry that her father might have made a mistake in giving him so much authority.

In the week which followed her knee improved greatly and by the end of it she was able to get about with a cane Hank found for her. It was exhilarating to have even this amount of freedom once more. She was able to go to the shack where the office was located and work on the plans. She also made a hard journey to the corral to pet a delighted black stallion.

141

Hank chuckled. "That one has missed you!"

She said, "I'll soon be riding him again."

"Sooner the better," the old man said. Then he leaned forward and confided, "I don't think all that much of the new boss."

"Larry Brand?" she asked in surprise.

Hank swallowed hard. "I know he saved you from being killed but I think he's using it for his own benefit. Making that critter his foreman!"

"What about Pedro?"

"Bad card!" Hank spat into the dust in anger. "Smiling all the time, but carries a knife a foot or more long which he'd just as soon stick into you as not."

"You're telling me he's a criminal?"

"If I ever met one, he's it," Hank told her. "The story is he escaped from prison in Cheyenne and made his way here. Rumor has it he was a bank robber and a killer."

"Larry Brand has made a friend of him," she pointed out.

"Which makes me wonder about that hero," the old man said with disgust. "I'm not sayin' anything. I'm just telling you what some of the boys think."

Clare heard this with some dismay. What Hank was saying might be true, but then again the old cowpoke resented anyone new who was assigned authority, and this could be making him say the things he had. But she did not approve of Larry appointing his own foreman without the approval of her father.

Her first meeting with the man came soon enough. She was working in the office when the fat, smiling Mexican entered and bowed to her. She put aside the plans she'd been drawing and gave him her attention.

"Do you have a problem?" she asked.

He nodded his head. "Si, Senorita," he told her. "I do not have a horse."

"Foremen generally aren't assigned one," she told him. "They are allowed to take one occasionally from the corral pool for some special purpose."

He made a gesture with his open hands. "I know all this, but I need my own mount to patrol the line. I have been given far too much territory to cover without one."

Clare did not want to make a precedent, so she told him, "I will discuss the matter with Mr. Brand. If he thinks you need a horse you'll be given one."

Pedro's broad face broke into a smile. "Si, Senorita!" And he left.

She assumed that he was satisfied with her reply because he was certain Larry Brand would back up his request for a horse. And Larry did.

With her father and Harris Trent living temporarily at their job sites, she and Larry were the only ones using the executive dining room. That night when he joined her at the dinner table she brought up the foreman's request.

Larry, with his usual assurance, said, "He does need his own animal. I've given him twice the ground to cover than foremen have had in the past."

"So he told me," she said, noting that Larry was carefully washed and neatly dressed for his meals with her. Now that he was holding a senior position he was behaving like a person of his class.

"Hank has some extra horses," Larry said. "I'm sure he can find one for Pedro. It would ease things all around."

"Very well," she said. "It's unusual but under the circumstances I'll back up his request."

Larry offered her one of his beguiling smiles. "You're an ace, Clare. You know you're doing a great job for the company."

"I'm not much use with my leg like this," she said.

"Is it improving?"

"A little. But it's slow progress."

"I saw you walking with your cane. You seemed to be doing a lot better."

She smiled. "You're observant."

"Where you are concerned," he said. "Can we sit outside for a little after dinner? There are some problems about the line I want to discuss with you."

She was a little surprised by this but said, "All right."

A half-hour later found them seated on a bench outside the executive car. Almost at once Clare realized that Larry Brand had no urgent questions about the rail laying; this was to be a discussion of a more personal nature.

He began with, "Are you angry with me?"

She stared at him. "What made you think that?"

He shrugged and glanced down at his polished boots. "I behaved a little too boldly towards you. I shouldn't have. I want to apologize."

She said, "It isn't necessary."

"I'm going to try and warrant your respect," he told her earnestly. "I want to make a success here."

"If you hold that attitude I'm sure you will."

He smiled at her. "Then we can be friends as well as co-workers?"

"Of course," she said. She wondered what he'd done

about Dora but did not think it a discreet thing to bring up at the moment.

Larry talked on for a little, mostly about his family and his time in the army. Then he excused himself and left to go to bed. She went to her own small compartment, filled with questions about the ambitious, attractive young man. He had all the qualities to attract a young woman, yet something about him made her wary, although she couldn't decide what it was.

Later, Clare came to the conclusion that it was his attitude towards Dora which prejudiced her against him. In addition, he was taking the greatest possible advantage of her father's gratitude for saving her life.

It was a troubled Dora who visited Clare at the office the following day. She looked as if she'd been crying and she stood before Clare's desk and told her, "I think Larry Brand is in love with you."

Clare was embarrassed. She said, "Nonsense! Why would you think a thing like that?"

"Since he rescued you and has been made a boss, he's around you all the time!"

Clare said, "That's because we're working closely together."

Dora shook her head. "It's more than that. He doesn't want me anymore. He hasn't said more than two words to me since he came back. And then only when a lot of other people are around."

Clare was shocked. One of the things Larry had promised to do was talk to Dora and let her down gently. She had even hoped there might be a recon-

ciliation between the two. But that looked most unlikely.

She told the upset girl, "Perhaps it's because he has
all this new responsibility. He's working hard for long
hours."

"He has the time," Dora said. "It's just that he's
used me and now he thinks he's too good for me."

Clare came and put an arm around her. "That would
be most unfair of him. If you like I will speak to him
about you."

Dora sighed. "It's no use. I know when a man is
through with me. But you better be careful!"

"Why do you say that?"

"He's working on you now. I can see it every day."

Clare said, "It won't do him any good."

"I hope you mean that," Dora warned her. "Don't
ever trust him! I know that now!"

"Do you still love him?"

The other girl hesitated and then nodded. "I wish
I didn't."

"I swear I'm not encouraging him," Clare told her.
"Be patient and I think he will come back to you."

Dora smiled sadly. "Thank you, but I doubt it."

After Dora left Clare pondered over all she'd said.
She could not blame her for feeling hurt and desolate.
And in view of what Dora said, she made up her mind
to lecture Larry on his behaviour at the first opportunity.

Chapter
Seven

Over the next two weeks Clare's knee slowly improved. Most of the pain vanished and she was able to walk without a cane. Twice she briefly rode the stallion, though Hank worried about her venturing this so soon.

When she returned from the second of the short rides, he told her, "The last thing you want now is to fall and get hurt again."

She smiled at him. "I'm really well enough to go back to work."

"Your father doesn't want that," Hank said. "He knows if you go back before that knee is properly healed it's liable to cause you trouble all your days."

She teased him, "Hank you never see the bright side of things."

"No bright side around here these days," Hank said

with a long, woeful look on his mustached face. "Now that Larry Brand and his pal, Pedro, have taken over."

"But they're doing a good job. Getting the track down faster than Harris Trent did."

"Mebbe," the old man said doubtfully. "I still don't trust him and that greasy varmint."

"My father is pleased with what they're doing," she told the old man.

The truth was that Larry Brand's devotion to his work and his helpful suggestions had won both she and her father to his side. The only thing she had against him was his callous attitude towards Dora now that he had become a boss.

She continued to think about the Denver Gent, and whenever the work train returned from Denver she was the first to get the newspapers, avidly reading all the news for any mention of his name. Most of the time there was nothing about the gambler, but occasionally there was a reference to him in connection with something else. Then one day there was a front-page headline about him.

She trembled with both fear and excitement as she read the account of a gun battle that had taken place in the gambling salon. It seemed that a gunman named Joe Gant had sat in at the poker table, and after a few hands he had accused one of the other players, a young man from Chicago, of cheating. Joe Gant insisted the young man was using sleight of hand to substitute cards.

The argument grew heated and Joe Gant jumped up and shot the young man through the chest. Then, covering the Denver Gent and the rest of the players, he and a henchman named Billy G. retreated from the room. By the time the Denver Gent and others in the salon were able to follow, the two had mounted their horses and made their escape.

The Denver marshall was offering a reward for them. The Denver Gent also had put up his own reward. Investigation proved that the young man, who died within a few minutes following the shot to his chest, had not been cheating. All of Denver was in an uproar about the crime. An editorial against private gambling salons hinted that this kind of violence would continue as long as such places were allowed to operate.

Clare read the article twice and it made plain that the man she loved was still surrounded by danger. It was only good luck that Joe Gant had not killed him rather than the youth from Chicago.

Another item in the paper also interested her. It said that the Great Western had forged well ahead with their direct line to Cheyenne and with good weather and no halt in operations would surely reach there before the Intercontinental Company. It quoted the eastern backers, who claimed Intercontinental was taking insane risks and creating a dangerous route in order to try and win the race. This, the eastern financiers solemnly claimed, would only lead to disaster both in construction and later on when the line was opened.

She was furious about the news story but said nothing about it until the following Sunday when her father and Harris Trent returned for their usual respite from work on the gorge line and the viaduct. She brought the story up when they were all seated around the dining table at noon.

After hearing the article, Milton Thomas looked mildly annoyed. He said, "I shall write a letter to the editor and refute their claims."

Harris Trent looked uneasy. "It is not far from the truth, if we're to be fair."

"How can you say that?" Clare demanded.

Harris said, "We are taking great risks and I see the ledge line as particularly vulnerable to falling rock and snow and landslides."

Larry Brand spoke up in a quiet, authoritative fashion. "But it would take us months longer to build tunnels rather than the ledge line."

Harris said sarcastically, "I had no idea you possessed so much engineering knowledge."

Larry reddened. "I don't but any laymen could see that tunnels are a much larger undertaking."

"He is right," Clare's father said, anxious to prevent any severe arguments between the two. "You are both right to a degree."

"I know I am," Harris said emphatically. "Any textbooks will tell you that tunnels are preferred in Europe where they've been building railroads a lot longer than we have."

"No question," Milton Thomas agreed. "But the United States is a vast territory. We have great distances to span in contrast to the European countries. So we have had to develop new methods. I'm now following the example of other American railways."

Clare interjected, "With the new engines capable of handling sharp curves and steep grades we can lay a different sort of line."

"That is my contention," her father said. "As to the dangers of rock fall and snow or mudslide, they are minimum in the areas where we are using ledge tracks. These are almost all places where there are formations of solid rock."

Harris Trent sighed. "I have lost three men to falls since we began. Clare was injured over the gorge. We're taking the risks but there is a high price to pay."

Larry Brand eyed him with a hint of disgust. "I'd gladly take on the ledge project and let you come back to the level line work."

Clare's father waved this aside. "You're both doing too well in your present positions. There will be no changes."

When they all left the table, Harris followed Clare outside and said, "I'd like to talk to you."

"All right," she said. "Let's stroll down to the corral."

As they began walking slowly across the sloping, grassy field, he said, "I've missed seeing you. I'm glad you're almost recovered."

"I could go back to work now but Father insists I wait at least another week."

Harris gave her a troubled glance. "I see I have a new rival here."

She stared at him. "What do you mean?"

"Don't pretend innocence," he protested. "You must know that Larry Brand is trying to court you."

"That's an incredible thing for you to say!"

"I'm certain it's true," he went on. "I was worried about the Denver Gent for a while. But I guess you won't see him again. He's having plenty of trouble in town."

"Trouble not of his making."

"I wouldn't say that. A gambling salon is bound to attract unsavory characters. That's the nature of the place."

Clare said quietly, "I hope you haven't asked to talk to me to give me a sermon on the Denver Gent's sins."

Harris winced. "No, but I'm just saying that now I'm the one you should most respect."

"I have always respected you, Harris."

"And just when I think I might be your husband, along comes this other stranger trying to make love to you!"

"You're imagining all this," she told him. They had reached the corral and she leaned against the log fence, whistling for the stallion to come over.

"I can see it better than you, not being here all the time," Harris insisted. "Brand is acting like one of us now."

Clare patted the black stallion on the muzzle and glanced at Harris, asking, "Isn't he?"

"He's come up in the world fast," Harris said indignantly. "To put it bluntly, he doesn't know his place."

Clare felt the familiar irritation which always came when she had to listen to the young engineer's platitudes. She said, "I think Larry Brand is behaving very well for the most part. And as for my being in love with him, that's foolishness."

Harris studied her soberly. "I want that to be true."

"It is," she said.

"I've only stayed on this job because of you," he continued. "I don't agree with what your father is doing and I don't like it."

"Then you *should* give up," she told him.

"I want to be near you," he reiterated. "At least it's good to know you're not thinking about this Brand fellow."

Clare patted the stallion for a final time and said, "I'm going back." With that she started up through the field once more.

Following her, Harris continued to plead his case. She felt it was pathetic and was grateful he was now working up at the gorge; she hardly saw him except on Sundays and although she was terribly lonely at times, at least she wasn't being constantly bothered.

But she was deeply concerned about the future of the Denver Gent. At the first opportunity, she cornered her father in the office away from the others and discussed both the Great Western article and the one concerning the brawl and killing in the Gent's salon.

"When are we making another trip back to Denver?" she asked him.

"Not until we have a lot more work done," her father said. "Why do you ask?"

"That story about the shooting terrified me. I get the feeling something will happen to Denver and I'll never see him again."

Her father pursed his lips and cupped his hands, his elbows on the arms of the chair. Glancing up at her, he said, "So it is the man you speak of, not the town."

She blushed. "I would welcome a return to the town for many reasons."

"Seeing the Denver Gent being one of them?"

153

"I love him, Father."

Milton Thomas frowned and looked at the plan on the desk before him. "I should have been firm and never allowed you to go to dinner with him."

"If you hadn't, he'd never had gotten to know me and come to my rescue."

Her father looked at her again. "You're in love with him because you think he saved your life?"

"Partly because of that."

Her father's eyes met hers directly. "If that's the story, you should also be in love with Larry Brand. Didn't he save your life as well?"

"You're trying to confuse me," she protested.

"I'd like you to forget the Denver Gent."

"I won't!"

"I'm trying to save you from heartbreak. He's going to be killed. It may be soon, it may be sometime in the future, but that's what's in the cards for him."

Clare knew all too well that it was true, but not wanting to hear it, she argued, "Not if he should change his ways."

Her father rose from his desk. "You think you can make him do that?"

"I haven't been with him long enough to make a good try!"

Her father shook his head. "Never marry a man who drinks or gambles with the idea he'll reform. Anyone can tell you that."

Again she knew his advice was wise but she turned away from him and said, "I wanted a father's help, not a lot of silly platitudes."

Milton Thomas came to her and gently placed a

hand around her, kissing her on the cheek. "My dear, people have marveled at how I've managed you over the years. You always do what you like, just the same as the wildest filly brought into the corral to be broken. If you are determined to spoil your life I doubt if I can stop you, but if you do find yourself broken by a misguided love, I shall, as long as I'm alive, be ready to forgive you and help you all I can."

The warmth of his manner and the generosity of his words brought happy tears to her eyes. Feeling much the little girl, she clung to him tightly.

Once during that weekend she saw Larry talking with Dora. She had no idea what the conversation was about, but Dora ran from him after the talk had gone on for a little. She made for the construction car where she had her room and Larry just stared after her without making any attempt to follow. It seemed to Clare that the two were quarreling and that Dora had fled from him in frustration.

Larry spent much of his time in the company of Pedro Reilly. The two made a most unlikely team but, because of their ability to make the workmen apply themselves to the rail laying, they were actually ahead of schedule.

As they worked further and further away from the construction camp, Larry Brand changed his routine. Instead of returning each day at sundown, he, Pedro, and a few of the crew now returned only every three nights to stock up on food and materials.

Clare was relieved by this new plan since she did not like being alone in the camp with Larry. It meant they shared the executive dining car alone which gave him every encouragement to try and gain in his courting of her. Unlike Harris Trent, whom she did not love but at the same time didn't fear, there were moments when her instinct told her Larry Brand possessed a sinster streak.

She was feeling better with each new day and intended to insist on going back to work the next Monday. She filled her time with some dressmaking, riding the stallion, and writing letters to be sent to town with the materials train. One of these letters she addressed to the Denver Gent care of the Pembrook Hotel.

She was completely indiscreet in the letter and told him that her love for him was still a burning thing which gave her no peace. She begged him to come visit her and promised that she would come to him as soon as she could. And this time she made it clear she would remain with him or go with him wherever he might choose, whether he remained a gambler or not.

She further made up her mind that if she heard no word from him, she would do what she had never imagined herself capable of—she would desert her father and the project. She would take the next supply train and join Denver. She knew how badly her father needed her help at this moment but she also knew she would hate herself for the rest of her life if she didn't try to save the man she loved.

Dora kept to herself a good deal, staying in the cooking car with her brother. But Clare made a point of seeking her out when Larry was away. They met on the grassy slope near the construction train.

Dora had a wicker basket of wash which she was

carrying back to hang up to dry. She nodded as Clare came up to her. Pale and sad-eyed, Clare was at once worried. "You look ill. Are you?"

"No," the redhead said resolutely. "I'm fine!"

"You are thinner and you have dark circles under your eyes."

Dora stood by the basket of wash and rubbed her hands on the sides of her print dress. "I haven't been sleeping as I should."

"I'm sorry," Clare said. "Is there anything I can do?"

Dora looked away. "No, nothing."

"Has it to do with Larry? I saw you talking to him."

Tears sprung to Dora's eyes. "He's rotten!"

"I had hoped he would be considerate of you."

"Considerate! That one!" Dora spat out the words, anger replacing her sorrow.

"I talked to him. Told him he owed you much."

Dora shook her head. "He wouldn't listen to that! The most he did was brag to me that he had won you over!"

Clare gasped. "Won me over?"

"That he had you, went to bed with you," Dora said, her green eyes meeting Clare's in a way that left no doubt Brand had indeed said this.

Clare touched her hands to her cheeks. "He had the nerve to say such a thing!"

"You don't have to be ashamed in front of me. Remember I was a girl in Mame's house!"

"It's not that," Clare protested. "If it were true I wouldn't hide it from you. But it's a lie!"

"He said you'd slept with the Denver Gent and then

157

with him," Dora went on. "And he claimed he was going to marry you!"

"He told you all that?!"

"Yes. He said he couldn't lower himself to be with me any longer."

"Heaven forgive him," Clare said fervently. "I'm sure I can't. I have never been intimate with him or even all that friendly!"

Dora said, "Then I'm glad for your sake!"

"You mustn't believe him!" Clare said again.

"Nor must you."

Clare frowned. "I won't."

"He isn't what he tries to make out. Not the great gentlemen he claims. I know some things about him," Dora said confidently. "And one day I will tell them!"

"What do you know?"

Dora picked up the basket of wash. "I won't say now, Miss. But I promise you'll hear it when it will do the most good!" And with that she went on towards the quarters she shared with her brother.

Clare was left very distressed; Larry had not only disregarded her advice to be kind to Dora but had actually lied to her and tried to hurt her. She was also puzzled by Dora's mysterious reference to knowing more about Larry than he would like to be told. She suddenly thought she knew what Dora meant. She had somehow had suspicions of it herself. She was almost sure that somewhere back East, Larry Brand had a wife whom he'd deserted.

If this were the case, no doubt he'd confided it to Dora in the first ardent period of their affair as an excuse for not being able to propose marriage. Now she was ready to use it against him.

But when? Dora would surely speak up if there was any indication Clare had succumbed to his wooing and agreed to marry him. Dora was waiting to savor and enjoy the moment when she could proclaim Larry Brand an intended bigamist. The more Clare thought about this, the more convinced she was that this was the meaning of Dora's threats.

It was an intolerably hot afternoon. Clare remained at her desk in the ramshackle office building on the edge of the clearing. Her father had asked her to make a new drawing of the bridge structure, allowing for some changes he had decided to make. She wanted to have this work completed before he returned at the weekend, so she kept at her task despite the sweltering heat.

She had left the door to the outside open so that more air would circulate in the dingy office, and as she bent over her drawing she heard approaching hoofbeats. At once she went to the doorway to see who it might be, and she saw a figure on a white horse coming down the makeshift roadway in a cloud of dust.

A moment later the rider dismounted and after tethering his horse to the hitching post, came towards her. She could hardly believe her eyes! It was the Denver Gent! She ran to him with a cry of happiness and he took her in his arms.

Denver held her close and said, "I was hoping you'd be here."

"I'm so glad you've come," she told him, smiling up into his handsome face.

His face took on a restrained expression. "First, I must tell you the truth about my being here."

159

She linked an arm through his and they walked back to the office together. "You must be exhausted from riding in this hot sun."

"I managed," he said. "I stopped at a water hole a way back."

They went inside and she faced him to ask, "What made you change your mind about coming here?"

"I didn't change my mind," he said quietly. "Something happened to bring me this way."

She felt some of her joy fading. "What happened?"

"It was in the Denver newspaper."

"You mean the shooting of the young man from Chicago?"

"Yes," the Denver Gent said. "Joe Gant accused him of being a cheat at cards. The charge wasn't true. Gant and his henchman got away and left me with a murder on my hands."

"I did read about it," she said. "But what has that to do with your being here?"

His eyes became hard. "I have to settle with Joe Gant. If I let him get away with that murder, I'll have more in my gambling salon. And that would put me out of business."

"And so?" she asked tensely.

"So I had a lead that Gant was heading this way. I decided to be here when he arrives."

"You've come here for a gunfight, not to see me!" she said in reproof.

He came close to her and, taking her cheeks between his hands, smiled down at her. "The thought that I might see you again made it all much more interesting for me." He kissed her gently on the lips.

She drew back a little. "I'm not a child!"

"I believe we have established that," the gambler said.

"Gant is not here. I know no reason why he should come to this place."

"Several people saw him after the shooting and he gave every one of them the same story. He was heading for Cheyenne along the railway line."

"Likely the line the Great Western is following."

"No, this way," Denver insisted. He paused and then added, "He also made threats against you."

"Me?" she said incredulously. "How would he know that I exist?"

"He saw you with me in the Pembrook Hotel. Heard the rumors that you were my girl. So you see how dangerous it can be to be close to me."

"Likely he was just bragging, talking wildly," she said, though she began to understand that it just might be true. It almost had to be since Denver had come the long distance from Denver to warn and protect her.

He shook his head. "I wish I thought that. But Gant is an especially nasty character. So is his henchman, Billy G. All the way here I had horrible visions of their arriving first."

"They wouldn't dare harm me," she protested.

"Based on the knowledge of what they've done in the past, they'd hold everyone in the camp hostage, rape you and Dora, and then kill you both! He's done things like that before."

She shivered despite the heat. "Don't tell me any more!"

161

"I won't," he said. "But I have to stay here until I'm sure there is no danger for you."

"What about the gambling salon?"

"It's closed until my return, if I return."

"Denver!" she said unhappily and clung to him.

The rest of the day proved uneventful except for the heat, but with the sunset the air became cooler fairly quickly, as it did in this mountainous region. Dora and her brother prepared a fine meal for Clare and Denver and they sat in comparative splendor at a candle-lit table in the executive dining room.

Denver held up a glass of the ruby wine and smiling at her said, "To our being together again!"

Clare raised her glass and looking directly at him, amended his toast to her own, "To our always being together!"

He nodded and drank. Then he said, "What about the others? When will they return?"

"They remain at their projects during the week," she said. "Father at the viaduct and Harris Trent at the gorge. And the man you saw with Dora while you were here is now a boss."

Denver looked interested. "The personable, dark-haired man?"

"The one you thought you'd seen somewhere before. He was a Union army captain during the war."

"I remember. Wasn't he just a workman?"

"He was until I almost had a fatal fall," she said. And she told Denver about her accident and Larry Brand saving her, and that after the attention drawn to him he'd been promoted.

"Is he doing well?"

"Very well. He's looking after the rail work in the flatlands. He has a man named Pedro Reilly as his foreman. They are actually ahead in their schedule."

Denver looked at her quizzically. "You must be extremely grateful to him."

"I am," she said. "I like him but sometimes I have a fear he may not be exactly what he seems."

"Why would you feel that way about him?"

She then told him about Larry's harsh treatment of Dora once he'd been promoted; of his boasts that he'd taken Clare to bed; and that he had tried to insinuate himself with her until she'd discouraged him.

Denver smiled bleakly. "I can see why you have ambiguous feelings about your rescuer. He appears to be a complex character."

"And his pal, Pedro, is said to be a convict who escaped jail in Cheyenne."

"Does your father know all this?"

"Only some of it," she admitted. "If I told him everything he'd dismiss Larry and we do need him if we're to complete the line on time."

"You know you're taking a risk."

"A calculated one," she said. "You'll remember I know something about taking care of myself."

He looked amused. "Spitfire and vixen were the first terms I heard used to describe you."

"I haven't changed all that much."

"I don't like seeing you here in an almost-deserted camp."

"Next week I'll likely join my father or Harris Trent at one of the sites," she said. "Unless you take me back to town with you."

163

"You wouldn't come," he teased her. "You don't approve of gambling."

"I don't care anymore," she said, leaning across the table toward him. "I just want to be with you, wherever you are and whatever you may be doing."

Denver made no reply. After dinner they walked under the stars and it seemed incredible there could be any danger in the restful peace of the nearly empty camp. Once again Clare knew that she would only know happiness when she was with him. She was even thankful for the threat which had brought him back to her.

She gave him her father's bed in the compartment next to hers. He kissed her goodnight and she went inside and quickly undressed, then slipped on her prettiest nightgown with its bodice of lace. She searched out her favorite perfume and dabbed herself with it. Then she went to join him.

Denver was already in bed, his naked upper body showing above the covering. Surprised when she stepped into the moonlit compartment, he sat up in bed. She smiled at him and with a deft movement let the nightgown slip from her. Then she slowly moved towards him, her nakedness highlighted by the cold, blue moonlight.

Denver stood up and took her in a passionate embrace that ended with them on the bed together locked as lovers. She felt the ecstacy of his strong maleness pressing hard against her and lost herself in the intensity of his loving.

When the peak of their passion had come and gone they lay for a long while in each other's arms. At last she heard his regular breathing as he settled into a deep, welcome sleep, and very cautiously she disengaged herself and made her way back to her own compartment. She stared up into the darkness for a long while and prayed the shadow of violence would not come between them.

Denver was restless the next morning. When Clare went down to the office he followed her to the ramshackle building. Every so often he went to the single window and looked out as if he were expecting someone.

She pretended not to notice his agitation and worked on at her bridge drawing. But she knew what was on his mind. And she hoped he would be wrong.

He left the window and came to her to ask, "Do you still carry that small pistol with you?"

She paused in her work to smile and nod. "Yes, I have it in my side breeches-pocket now."

"Don't be parted from it," he warned.

"I'll remember."

He went back to the window again. Over his shoulder, he added, "If there should be trouble and anything happens to me, don't hesitate to use that weapon. And shoot to kill."

"I will," she promised.

He seemed a little less anxious and came and watched her working on the plan. He even asked her some questions concerning it. For a little while Clare forgot they were waiting for the arrival of Joe Gant and his henchman.

Denver relaxed to the point where he decided to stroll over to the corral and see how Hank was looking after his horse. He promised to meet her back at the construction train for lunch. She worked on for a few minutes after he left and then went outside to return to the executive car.

She'd not gone a dozen steps when she heard the sound of horses' hooves approaching rapidly. She quickly turned and a terrified look came to her lovely face as she saw two horsemen rein up behind her.

The burly one wearing the flat-topped, black hat had cruelty etched across his coarse, weathered face. She recognized him at once from Denver's description as Joe Gant. And the younger, slimmer man in the Stetson with a scar running the length of one cheek was undoubtedly Billy G.

Joe Gant smiled at her in ominous fashion. "You don't look happy to see visitors!"

She used one hand to shield her eyes from the sunlight and with the other furtively reached for the pistol in her side pocket.

"What do you want?" she asked.

"What do we want?" Joe Gant echoed in a harsh voice and laughed raucously. "Billy, go fetch the lady!"

"Sure, boss!" The slim man on the piebald grinned and came riding up to her.

She was ready as he reached out to lift her onto the saddle with him. She presented the pistol point-blank and fired. A stain showed in his shirtfront, close by his heart, and his look of surprise was the last expression he'd ever show. He toppled over the saddle onto the ground and the frightened piebald raced away.

Gant let out an ugly oath and she saw that he had

her covered with his Colt. He said, "Don't try any of that fancy shooting with me. Drop it!"

She knew he was anxious to shoot so she put up no protest and dropped the pistol and raised her hands. Billy G. lay motionless on his side in the dust by her feet.

Gant rode closer to her. "They said you was a wild-cat! I guess I'll have to tame you!"

She stood there in the blazing sun not daring to move. She pictured the gunman lifting her up and attempting to ride off with her but before she could decide what to do the name "Gant!" came in a ringing tone from directly behind where he was seated on his horse. It was the Denver Gent standing ready with his gun in hand.

Gant wheeled his horse around and fired, but Denver's shot rang out first. Joe Gant rocked in the saddle for a moment and then slumped over, his Colt dropping to the ground and blood streaming from the wound in his chest.

Denver grasped the reins of the outlaw's frightened horse as Joe Gant's body slid down to the ground where his henchman lay. Then he let the horse go and came quickly to Clare.

"Are you hurt?" he asked.

She shook her head. "I did what you said. I shot to kill."

His arm came around her. "I should never have left you."

"Perhaps it worked out better this way," she said, looking at the sprawled bodies of the outlaws.

"I had a bad moment when I saw you facing them

167

alone. But I didn't dare rush out; I had to come around back of them."

Now a breathless Hank came limping up to them and surveying the two bodies, exulted, "Looks like we're goin' to have a fancy burial party!"

Denver nodded. "You take charge of the bodies, Hank. I'll help you dig graves later."

Clare couldn't really believe that the terror which had been shadowing them had so suddenly been lifted. In the grim world of the gunman, scores were settled fast. A half-hour earlier Joe Gant and Billy G. had been approaching the construction camp filled with their plans to spread pain and death. Now they were themselves dead, victims of their own code.

Back at the construction car, Dora and her brother waited for an explanation of what had happened. Clare told them tersely; then she and Denver went inside to sit down to a whiskey bottle. She drank the heady stuff straight the same as he did.

She said, "I've never killed anyone before."

"You had no choice," he told her. "If Billy G. had remained alive he might have finished me before I had the drop on Gant."

She shuddered. "His face! That frightened look! I'll think about it often! See it in my nightmares!"

Denver poured her another whiskey. "Don't waste any sympathy on them. They would have raped and killed you and finished off the others if they'd found you alone and not warned."

"What now?"

He downed another whiskey and considered. "I'll take some identification from the bodies for the marshall back in Denver. Then Hank and I will bury them."

"And?"

"I'll head straight back to see the marshall."

She looked at him soberly. "I'll go with you."

"No," he said.

"Why not?"

"I don't want you placed in danger again. These vendettas don't always end with the principals shot. Gant and Billy have friends. They may decide to come after me!"

"They wouldn't!" she protested.

"All too likely someone will try as soon as they learn Gant and Billy are dead."

"But that would make it endless. The murdering will just go on!"

"True," he said. "It will be like this until this country is tamed. The railway you're building will help take care of that."

"You'll be in even more danger back in town. Why don't you stay here?"

"I can't," he said. "That would be showing the white feather. They expect me to return and open up the game again. And I will."

"You wouldn't have if you'd been killed," she pointed out.

"No. But I wasn't killed," he said quietly. "I have no choice, Clare. These are the rules I live by. But you are not obliged to take the same risk. And I won't let you."

Tears filled her eyes. "It isn't fair!"

"I'm sorry, my darling," the gambler said, rising. He gently kissed her on the temple.

She looked up at him. "When will you leave?"

"Before sundown," he said. "As soon as Hank and I bury the bodies I'll hit the trail." And he went out, leaving her to bend her head and sob.

The two mounds were in the grass beyond the corral. Clare stood staring at them as Denver handed his shovel over to Hank.

The old man said, "I reckon we don't need to say any words over them two."

"I think not," the Denver Gent agreed. And then he came to Clare. "Feeling any better?"

"What do you think?"

He took her hands in his. "I think any girl who had the courage you showed this morning has the courage to face a parting."

"I may never see you again," she murmured.

Denver smiled. "I think you will."

"You won't let me go with you!"

"I've explained why," he said. "And your father needs you here."

"I won't know what happens when you reach town!"

He sighed. "All right. I'll send you a letter by the supplies train."

"You promise?"

"Yes."

"When can I join you? I mean to stay with you."

"We'll see," he said. "I'll tell you in the letter."

"I think you don't mean anything you're saying, that you'll vanish and never come back. Or some outlaw friend of Gant's will murder you."

"Not if I can help it."

It was midday when Hank brought Denver's horse

up to the construction car. The moment had come to leave.

He took her in his arms and said, "Don't forget me!"

"I wish I could," she said in a small voice.

He kissed her for a long moment, then swung up onto the saddle. Hank released the reins and Denver turned to smile and wave goodbye to her. Then he rode off with the dust trailing after him just as it had when he arrived at the camp such a short time ago.

Chapter
Eight

When Clare's father returned for the weekend, he was shocked to hear what had taken place, as were Harris Trent and Larry Brand and it was inevitable that the happenings should be the central point of their weekly roundtable.

An all-night rain had cooled the air and settled the dust. Clare's father summoned the meeting for shortly after the Sunday noon meal. He presided behind his desk in the office and Clare sat near him, with Harris and Larry on plain chairs near the door.

Clare's father began, "We must do all we can to avoid having incidents such as the one the Denver Gent was involved in take place here. We are already being accused of recklessness. If it becomes common gossip that we have notorious gunmen shooting it out here, we will lose all our credibility."

Harris Trent spoke up. "I say the Denver Gent is actually an agent for Great Western. Probably he was checking on our progress for them once again. If we have another raid we can put it down to his letting them know the main camp is largely unguarded."

Clare said, "Won't you ever get tired of that theory, Harris?! Denver came here for one reason and one reason only, to protect me!"

"So he told you," the young engineer said with derision.

Larry Brand said, "Whatever his reason for coming here, it was bad publicity to have a shootout within the camp limits. Especially as the Gent will take the news back to Denver."

Milton Thomas frowned. "I have already written the Denver paper in response to Great Western's accusation that we are taking too many shortcuts. I cannot very well write another letter apologizing for the camp being the scene of gunmen's battles!"

Clare said, "The best thing is forget it. Denver did what he came to do. Nothing like it will happen again."

Larry offered her a smile. "I assume he assured you of that?"

Clare was angered by his manner. "I happen to believe he is a gentleman and I'm ready to accept his word."

Harris said coldly, "This gentleman friend puts you in the position of joining him in a shootout. I would not thank him for that."

Clare's father raised a hand for order. "I believe Clare has the best advice. The event is behind us; let us hope there is not too much publicity. Our biggest problem now is to get on with our railway line."

Clare asked, "What are you worried about?"

"I need more help at the viaduct," her father said. "We are now moving out from the main supports, high above the river. I ought to have at least two key people, one to assist me and the other to supervise at the other side of the viaduct."

"I can join you tomorrow," Clare reminded him.

He nodded. "I know that. It still leaves me short an engineer."

Larry said, "I'm ahead with the track laying. Pedro knows enough about it now to proceed on his own. I could join you at the bridge."

"No," Harris protested, "I have all the main work done on the ledge through the gorge. There's no reason why Brand can't take that operation over and free me, a more experienced engineer, to help with the problems of the viaduct."

Milton Thomas considered this and asked Larry, "Are you ready to take on the ledge work?"

"Any time," Larry replied. "I know about it as I was there as a worker."

Clare nodded. "I think that is the best solution."

"In that case," her father said, "let us settle down to the particulars which each of us will be responsible for during the coming week."

The conference went on for an hour. When it broke up, Clare's father remained behind with Larry to advise him on some of the problems of the ledge work, and Clare found herself strolling back to the construction train with Harris.

He said, "I'm sorry if what I said about Denver made you angry."

She shrugged. "It was foolish and unfair."

"Still, he knows all the Great Western people. And we've had serious raids on our supplies after every one of his visits."

"I don't think there's any connection between his visits and the raids."

"Well, I won't argue with you. Did he try to make love to you along with shooting down those two outlaws?"

"Violent love," she said with sarcasm. "All the time he was shooting them down! I admire you for your vivid imagination, Harris."

The young engineer looked hurt. "I can't help being jealous. You're in my mind all the time. Especially when I'm away from you."

They had reached the entrance to her car. Clare halted and said, "Well, at least we'll be working together now. So your mind should be at ease."

He smiled. "It will mean a lot being with you every day. I know you despise me but I do care for you."

She smiled and placed a hand on his arm. "That's not true. I find myself liking you a lot of the time. It's only when you're possessive of me that I become angry."

"I'm awkward about such things," he admitted. "I'll try to behave better."

Clare could not help but be touched by his humble attitude. She gave him a warm look. "You will always be one of my trusted friends," she told him.

Early the next morning two wagon trains set out for the gorge and the viaduct, and Pedro oversaw the work train which proceeded to the point where the tracks were being put down. The work was thus divided into the three divisions they had agreed upon.

Clare tried hard to put her thoughts and concerns about the Denver Gent behind her. She knew she needed all her alertness and concentration for the job at hand. She consoled herself that Denver would take care of himself and that they would meet again. She was determined to see to that as soon as the railway work was completed.

Her father posted her on the opposite side of the viaduct from the one where he and Harris Trent were in charge. They were relying on wooden-trestle construction for this viaduct because they could not get enough iron in time. Her father was normally particular about the quality of this timber, never using any less than two years old. But because of the urgency now facing them, he could not even wait for seasoned timber. Instead he was relying on something called the Howe truss, with which they were able to adjust the joints with screws and nuts so that shrinkage could be taken up. In addition the parts could be concentrated in such a way that the viaduct could carry the heavy, concentrated weight of locomotives without being crushed. Although wooden bridges were susceptible to decay and fire, these were minor risks and had to be taken in this case.

Clare was impressed by the progress her father had made with the viaduct. It stretched out from a high point of land on either side and would eventually meet above the river which was narrow at this point. Much of the structure ran above the marshlands along either side of the river.

Her father and Harris Trent were on the spans far out while the work at her end was proceeding more modestly. She climbed up the supports along with the men and supervised the new construction from the surface where the rails would eventually run. She was continually amazed by the dexterity of the workmen as they moved out into space with very little protection.

By the end of the first day, Clare had become more familiar with the methods and had a better idea of how she might perhaps improve them. She lived in a tent near one occupied by her father and Harris Trent, and they all gathered at the campfire at night to have dinner and discuss the work.

Harris sat beside her and said, "This span is too wide for all-wood construction. We should either have used tunnels and a short bridge or somehow found the iron and steel we needed."

Milton Thomas gave his young associate a troubled glance. "If I could have arranged for the steel and iron we'd be using it. It simply wasn't available to us. We've been lucky to get a sufficient supply of iron rails."

Harris sighed. "As long as we understand the risks."

His words meant little to Clare then, but she would have cause to remember them later. The following morning they returned to their stations and the building of the viaduct continued. Clare was standing at the top watching the work on the other side; it was projecting far out now and a crane was hoisting a heavy load of timber sections into place.

Without warning it happened! There was a strange, wrenching sound of wood breaking and giving away, and like a toy, the crane dumped down into the river hundreds of feet below, the workers dropping with it, pygmy figures doomed to die on the rocks beneath.

All work on the bridge ceased, and Clare clambered down to the ground as quickly as possible, all the other workmen making the steep, swift descent along with her. On the opposite shore the wreckage of the crane lay in the shallow water of the river and the limp, lifeless bodies were strewn along the rocks.

Two of the workmen quickly rowed her across the river in one of the small boats and she raced across the uneven, marshy land to where the workers were gathered. She saw her father holding onto his right arm, his head cut and bloody, and she raced across to him.

"You're alive!" she cried.

"Yes," he said slowly, still in a partial daze. "If only all the others had been as lucky."

"What about your arm?" she asked.

"Broken, I fear," he said.

"What caused the collapse?"

"I'm not sure," her father said, staring vaguely at the place where the huge section had torn away. "Most likely a weakness in the timbers."

"Harris warned there was a great risk," she recalled.

Her father looked at her strangely. "Yes, he did."

And it was only then that she sensed it. She said, "Where is he? I don't see him anywhere!"

Her father said, "The men are out there now trying to find him. He went down with a half-dozen others."

Her throat tightened and in a stifled voice she said, "Then he is surely dead!"

"Let us hope not," he said. "There may be a slight chance."

She shook her head, and with tears in her eyes she went down to the riverbank.

The rescue crew were returning in several small craft. But they were not bringing back live men, they were bringing limp bodies. In the first of the boats, she saw Harris stretched out, showing no marks of his fall, with his eyes closed and his face strangely peaceful. She turned away and knelt on the grass, her body wracked with sobs.

Eight men, including Harris Trent, died in the accident. And it was decided that it would be wisest to bury them on the riverbank near where the tragedy occurred. The rest of the day was spent preparing the graves, and one of the men who was an expert at woodcarving began at once placing the names of the victims on wooden crosses. Each grave would be identified in case someone wished to transfer the remains later.

It was a grim picture, the eight rough coffins with the bodies of those who'd died in the crash, each coffin beside a freshly dug grave. With his arm in a sling, Milton Thomas moved from coffin to coffin offering prayers. As he finished, the coffin was lowered and buried. It was late afternoon when it was over.

Clare urged her father, "We must get back to camp. Let them know the news."

He nodded. "And Tom Lee can set my arm properly. He was a medical aid during the war."

"What about Harris Trent's family?" she asked.

"I'll write his mother," her father said, "and send her the items I found on him."

"I can't believe it," she said, turning away from the graves.

"I know," her father sighed. "I'm sorry you were here to see it."

"That couldn't be helped," she replied. "But such a waste of lives."

"I shall always feel guilt for Harris Trent's death," her father admitted.

She thought about the last time she and the young engineer had talked privately and, though she had never wished to marry him, she knew she would always feel a great loss.

Clare also recognized that now there would be a great deal of extra responsibility on her shoulders and on those of Larry Brand. They were the only ones left to take charge with her father. She was willing to work much harder, but she worried about Larry being given more power. The promotion was proving difficult for him to handle. He had turned his back on Dora and made an almost outright proposal to Clare.

As long as Harris Trent had been around as a balance, she had felt fairly secure. Now she was worried and a bit frightened. Things were happening too fast. Larry was still in many ways almost a stranger to them, yet he was now being accepted as a trusted partner. She recalled Dora's threatening to reveal some things about his past and felt the redhead might offer a means of keeping him under control.

Her father organized a crew to begin clearing up the mess and hopefully to salvage the derrick. The point of the collapse would be examined and new timbers placed at what appeared to be the weak spots. Clare told the foreman she would return the following day to supervise.

The wagon ride back to the construction camp

seemed interminable and the jolting tormented her father whose unset arm rested in a rough sling. But eventually they arrived and Tom Lee was called on to set and splint the arm. Clare's father had several strong drinks and went to bed at once.

Clare had a quiet cry in her own compartment and then made an attempt to eat something of the excellent meal which Dora brought her.

Dora said, "You mustn't blame yourself for what happened."

Clare looked up at her. "I realize that. But Harris warned us about the bridge."

"He was always the careful one," Dora recalled.

"Yes," Clare said with a sigh. "I don't know what effect this will have on us completing the line."

"I don't see your father ever giving up."

"I don't either," Clare agreed. "But this is a bad setback. We've lost good men and our crew was short to begin with."

Dora looked at her questioningly. "I suppose *he* will be having a lot more to say now?"

Clare knew who the other girl meant. "Larry?"

"Yes."

"I imagine he will by the nature of things. Perhaps my father will go back to Denver and see if Jefferson Myers can get him a rush replacement for Harris."

"I'd like to see that happen."

"You're afraid of relying too much on Larry?"

"There's no secret about what I think of him," Dora said.

"He's done well so far."

"There's a long way to go still," Dora warned. "He won't be easy to handle."

"I've thought of that," Clare said. "I've decided to speak to my father about it in the morning."

Dora picked up the used dishes. "I think your father should be warned. Larry Brand cares only about himself. He can't be loyal to anyone or anything!"

Clare fell asleep pondering Dora's warning and when she wakened she decided to discuss it all with her father before she left for the viaduct site.

Milton Thomas was feeling well enough to join her at the table for breakfast. "My arm is much better," he said. "I think I might even go back there today."

"No," she said. "You'll stay here and give that arm a rest. Hank will ride with me for company and I can carry on alone."

Her father frowned. "Don't stay there. Just see what they have done and give them extra assignments to keep them working."

"I will," she promised. When they were nearing the end of breakfast she asked, "What about Larry Brand? No one has told him yet."

"I felt it wasn't urgent," her father said. "He has plenty to keep him busy."

"He'll likely be back tonight anyway," she agreed. "He usually returns for overnight midway through the week. If he arrives before I return you can tell him."

"I will," her father promised. "I'm also sending a special messenger to Denver informing Jefferson Myers of what took place. And I'm asking him to send us another engineer."

"Do you think there will be one available?"

"If there is, Jefferson Myers will know about him."

"I hope you do get someone," said Clare. "Even

183

with my being on the job full time, we'll have to depend a lot more on Larry if we don't get a replacement for Harris."

Her father gave her a startled glance. "Are you suggesting Brand can't be trusted with extra responsibilities?"

"I'm merely saying he has risen from the ranks fast."

"Which means something of the same thing."

She said, "I know that his success has made him less agreeable as a person."

Her father frowned. "I haven't noticed."

"Because he has been careful around you," she said.

Milton Thomas stared at her for a moment, apparently getting the message she preferred not to put into words. He sighed and said, "Then I'll stress to Myers that we badly need the replacement engineer."

"Do," she said, rising and kissing him on the cheek.

"There is the letter to Harris Trent's mother," he said. "I shall take some time with that today."

"Poor Harris," she said. And then she quickly left as a threat of tears surged up in her.

Old Hank made a good companion for the ride to the viaduct. He had saddled his veteran dun and she was riding the stallion. They knew the trail well and made good time.

"Who did your dad make foremen when he left?" Hank asked her.

"An older man," she said. "I think I've heard my father calling him Judge."

Hank chuckled. "That would be Judd. The boys allus jokes about his name and call him the Judge."

"Is he a good man?" she asked as they rode along.

"The best," he said. "Your father knows who to trust. Except with this Brand. I ain't strong on him!"

She glanced at him as he moved the dun a little ahead. "You and Dora haven't much use for him."

He spoke over his shoulder, "A lot of others feel the same way but won't say it out loud!"

Clare guessed this might be true. Some of the workers were veterans who'd worked with her father on various other projects over the years. Many of them would feel themselves entitled to promotion. Instead, her father had singled out Larry, chiefly because he had saved her life, and pushed him far ahead.

They reached the viaduct site by midmorning and were greeted with the sight of the derrick on the sandy riverbank with several workmen putting the rig in working shape again. Up on the bridge itself a small crew were removing some of the wreckage.

As Clare stood watching them, her hand shielding her eyes from the sun, the man her father had spoken to came down to greet her. He was medium sized and in his early fifties with a stern, lined face and gray hair.

"Miss Thomas!" He touched his hand to his hat. "I'm glad you got back."

"How is it going?"

Judd looked grave. "We've had a proper setback, no use to deny that."

"I know," she said. "What about the derrick?"

"The boys are fixing her now. She'll work again."

"Father will be pleased to hear that," she said.

"We'll get her back up there soon," he said, glancing

up at the partially completed bridge which loomed over them.

"And the damage to the bridge? How much has the accident cost us in that regard?"

Judd hesitated and he gazed at her with his somber, gray eyes and said, "It weren't an accident, Miss Clare."

"What?"

"I'm sorry to tell you this," he said. "Someone got to the bridge. The nuts and bolts holding whole cross-sections of supports were loosened."

"Sabotage?"

"A nasty job of it," the foreman went on bitterly. "Even some saw cuts made to weaken it all the way across."

"You have evidence of this?"

"Yes. You can take back some of it to your father. We made a mistake in just keeping a guard over supplies and the camp. Whoever did it just slipped by in the night and went up to the bridge and fixed it so that as soon as the derrick was moved it would collapse."

Clare listened in growing horror. "Then those men were deliberately murdered."

"You could say that," Judd agreed.

"The Great Western again," she said brokenly. "I didn't think that even they would go this far."

"They've set us back a week in supplies and in construction and lost us Mr. Trent and seven other good men."

"My father could easily have been killed as well," she said grimly.

"You had to hear the truth, Miss," the foreman said.

"I suppose we can blame my father for not having

a more secure guard over the site," she said, glancing around.

"We thought the man at the camp was enough."

"Have you talked to him about this?"

Judd nodded. "He swears he wasn't asleep. But he might have dropped off for a spell. I saw him sleeping on guard one night."

"Even so," she rationalized, "we can't entirely place the blame on him. The task was too large for one guard."

"We've been short of men. We'll be shorter now."

She went and inspected the damaged pieces from the bridge and saw that Judd had not exaggerated. There were clear signs of sabotage. She took several items and had Hank put them in a bag which he tied to his saddle.

Then she told Judd, "Because of the importance of your news I'm going directly back to talk with my father."

"That's a good idea, Miss," Judd agreed.

"In the meanwhile appoint some other men guards and see that the viaduct is protected at both sides of the river."

"I'll do that, Miss," he promised.

"I'm not worried by the loss of construction time for a few days but I don't want anymore of what we've completed wrecked."

"I understand, Miss," the forman said.

She and Hank then went to look at the graves. He had known several of the dead men. And they both stood respectfully by Harris Trent's grave for a few moments before they began the ride back.

When Clare reached the construction camp she went

straight to the office and found Larry Brand there with her father. She showed the evidence of sabotage to the two and they both were shocked.

"This criminal activity must be reported to the authorities," her father said angrily, pacing back and forth by his desk.

Standing by her, Larry said, "I doubt if you'll find anyone who can help us."

"But this is beyond law and order!" Milton Thomas raged.

"So are many things out here," Clare said. "And how can we link what happened to the Great Western people?"

Her father halted, facing her. "Who else would have a motive?"

"That's hard to say," she sighed. "But we must have definite proof before we go around accusing our rival."

Larry said, "I believe, like your father, Great Western hired thugs to do this. But I agree with you that unless someone breaks down and talks or we get some solid evidence, we can't say anything."

"I lost Harris Trent and seven other men," Clare's father lamented. "Aren't their lives worth anything?"

Larry Brand's good-looking face was clouded. "They'll tell you that was part of the risk those men took."

"And that is also true," said Clare.

"When sabotage is committed, it is beyond ordinary risk," her father said bitterly. "I shall send a full account of all this to headquarters."

"Perhaps you might make use of the tragedy to get

us a larger supply of iron and steel," Clare suggested. "We could use it on the viaduct."

"The design calls only for wood," her father reminded her.

"Iron or steel reinforcing would make it stronger," was her reply.

"I agree," Larry Brand spoke up. "The viaduct covers too wide a span to rely completely on wood. You should give that some serious thought, sir."

Milton Thomas looked angry. "I will see, but I'm not sure that anything can be done about it."

Clare gave her parent a weary look, "It seems, Larry, that my father thinks of the widest possible profit margin first," she said angrily and then left.

As she went to the construction car she heard footsteps following her and a perturbed Larry Brand came out to join her.

"Better not to quarrel with your father."

She glanced at him. "I couldn't help it."

"He has been wrong having too few guards," Larry said. "I don't see how he could have done anything about the rest."

"We've lost Harris as a result."

Larry gave her a surprised look. "I thought you didn't care for him at all."

"Then you're wrong," she said. "I cared for Harris very much. I said I didn't love him!"

They were at the entrance of her sleeping car and she halted before stepping inside. Larry remained on the grassy slope, staring up at her.

"I suppose it's still the Denver Gent you love," he said.

"That is not any of your business," she said and turned angrily and went inside.

Clare had little to say when they all gathered at the table in the dining car. She was indeed thinking much of the Denver Gent and wishing he might be there to help them. Larry talked more than usual, and every now and then he would smile at her in an effort to get into her good graces again. She ignored his smiles and let her father do the other half of the talking.

Following dinner she went to her room and began reading. She sat on the bunk reading *Hamlet* for perhaps a fifth time. She and Harris had read the play together in the early days of construction and they had each found different things in the tragedy of the Prince of Denmark whose life was cut short. Now Harris Trent was dead at an age when most young men were marrying and beginning a family. The tragedy had hit close.

She read until she was weary. Her father came by and said goodnight. Then she changed into her nightgown and went to bed. Her sleep, when it came, was filled with chaotic dreams in which she kept trying to cry out to Harris to be careful. High up on the viaduct, he paid no attention to her, and then fell to his death as the bridge collapsed. The dreadful sequence of events kept repeating itself in various ways in the nightmare.

Then she suddenly came awake to sounds of shots being fired. She sat up in bed and with trembling hands held back the blind at the window. Outside in the moonlight she could see riders circling around the train with rifles in their hands. She could not tell how many of them there were, but she could hear their shouts.

She was aware of gunfire being returned from the train and knew that the perhaps two dozen left at the camp were not taking the attack without fighting back. There was a loud knock on her door, and her father cried out to her, "Clare, are you safe?"

She left her bed and opened the door. He was standing there half-dressed with a rifle in his good hand. She said, "You mustn't go out there! You'll be killed!"

"I can manage this well enough to get at least one of them," he said grimly, balancing the rifle in his right hand.

She was about to go on pleading with him when a shot came through the window and imbedded itself somewhere in the wall of the compartment. Her father at once thrust her down on the floor and then crouched there himself.

"Don't stand up!" he ordered her. "It could be worth your life!"

"And don't you go out there," she said, holding onto him.

She could barely see his face in the shadows but she heard his moan. It was the distressed cry of an old man agonized by this new round of adversity.

There was movement somewhere along the corridor of the car, and she reached over for the pistol she always kept under her pillow at night. She faced the door of the compartment, weapon in hand, waiting. Suddenly a figure moved in the darkness. Her finger was on the trigger when the intruder spoke. It was Larry Brand.

"Are you all right?" he asked.

"Yes," Milton Thomas said, still half-crouched. "How is it going?"

"We're driving them off!" Larry said. "Stay where you are. I'll be back!" And he ran on down the corridor.

There was more shooting and sharp cries along with the frightened whinnying of horses and the thud of their hooves. Then capping all this came a tremendous explosion which rocked the car in which they lay huddled and lit up the outside with a false dawn. There were several more reverberations and rumblings and then an uneasy silence broken only by some moaning.

"The dynamite shed!" Clare's father exclaimed. "Someone set it off!"

Clare moved warily to the window and looked out. There were fires burning here and there around the grounds, lighting up the darkness, but the riders had vanished and no more shots were fired.

She stood up and turned to her father. "They've left!"

Milton Thomas weakly rose and stumbled along the dark corridor to the outside with Clare following him. The first thing she noticed was a horse stretched out, probably the victim of a stray bullet. She saw several of the workers wandering about looking dazed, still on a kind of patrol, their rifles at the ready.

A moan on her right led her along the grassy bank to a figure stretched out. Then a man came runing up with a torch to join her and she saw that it was Hank who lay there.

The old man's head was bloodied and he was deathly

pale. She knelt by him and called, "Hank! Can you hear me!"

There was a dreadful moment of uncertainty, and then he blinked open his eyes and stared up at her. He gasped and managed, "Miss Clare!"

"Your head," she said. "Is it badly hurt?"

The young man with the torch knelt and examined Hank's head carefully. "Near as I can tell he was grazed by a bullet just above the ear. It would stun him."

Hank responded with a groan and sat up. "You're right, young feller! That's where they got me! Cowardly rats!"

The young man helped him up. "I've got to move on," he said. "Some of the others haven't fared as well as you, Hank!"

Clare's father now came over and looked about him with dismay. "Another hit-and-run raid! This one the worst ever! It's too much to ask to recover from this!"

Hank was more himself now as he said, "I reckon we got a few of them as well."

"What about the corral?"

"One of those pesky varmints came down to open the gate but I winged him and he went ridin' off!" Hank said.

"Then you came up here?" Clare asked.

"Yep. I could see here was where all the action was. I'll go back and make a check on the horses now."

"Are you sure you're well enough?" she said.

"I sure am," Hank replied and wobbled off into the darkness.

Clare's father gazed down at the giant flames still shooting up from the area of the dynamite shed. "All the supplies in the sheds next to it will have been destroyed," he told her.

"We can worry about that later," she said. And she moved on to where more torches were glowing and she could see what was happening.

Larry came up to her, a torch in his hand and a look of desperation on his face. "A bad night for us!" he said. "Three men killed, two others wounded."

"What about the raiders?"

"We've got two dead Indians and a white man who's dying right now."

"Did you try to get any information from him?"

"Impossible," Larry said. "He's been unconscious since we found him. We got a couple of their horses as well."

"So we don't know whether it was just a raid by renegades or the work of Great Western," she said unhappily.

Larry looked bleak. "I can't see that they got much in the raid. It was mostly done to destroy. Makes it look like another Great Western try to stop us."

"This time they may have managed it," she said.

He stared at her and after a moment said, "I'm going to make a further survey of what has gone on. I'll meet you and your father in the dining car in a few minutes."

Clare turned and started back to find her father. Along the way she passed Larry's fat friend, Pedro. He had a torch and a rifle, and he grinned at her and said, "Plenty of action."

She was going to make an acid reply but bit her tongue and continued to look for her father who she found in conversation with Hank. The news in this case was good, none of the horses had been harmed.

Hank said, "I'm going back down there and stay for the rest of the night."

"I don't think they'll be back," Clare's father said.

"I ain't riskin' it," Hank told him.

"What about that head wound?" Clare asked.

"Just washed it in the spring," Hank said. "Feels a lot better now. It wasn't nothin' but a scratch anyway!" And he went off towards the corral.

"I wish I had his courage," Milton Thomas said watching after him.

"I just talked to Larry," she said. "He wants to meet in the dining car to give you a report."

"The loss of the dynamite alone will cripple us," her father said.

"He'll give us all the facts he's been able to collect about it all," said Clare as they walked back to the executive car.

Someone was coming towards them carrying a limp body in his arms. He was walking slowly and it took them a moment to get close to him. With a shock Clare saw that it was the big cook, Tom Lee.

"Tom!" she cried.

"They got her, Miss Clare, they got her!" the big man wailed, holding the limp figure protectively close to him.

"She's dead?" Clare's father gasped.

"Bullet through her head," Tom said, gazing sadly at his burden.

"Why did she go out there?" Clare asked, stunned and almost nauseated by the news.

"I don't know, Miss," the cook said. "I guess she felt she had to grab a rifle and go out there and fight."

"She would," Clare's father agreed.

"I'd have stopped her if I could," Tom said. "She was a good girl."

"Dora was a wonderful person," Clare said with a sob and ran up into the railway car.

She pressed a hankie to her mouth and tried to stifle her sobbing. She had lost two people she liked and who were close to her within hours. She felt completely shattered. She thought of Larry and his repudiation of Dora. He had wanted to be rid of her; well now he was.

Her father came and touched a hand to her shoulder in an attempt to comfort her. "I know how you must feel," he said.

"It's too much!"

"Tom says she died right away. There was no suffering. She didn't know what happened. We can only be thankful for that."

"Such a waste!"

"Six men and poor Dora, counting the losses on both sides," Milton Thomas said grimly. "The man or men who planned the raid have a lot to answer for."

They stood waiting in the soft yellow of the lamp set out on the table. Shouts continued outside and then Larry Brand came to join them.

All his jaunty manner had vanished. "A bad night's work," he said somberly. "I doubt if we can recover from it."

Clare gave him a scathing look. "Did you know that Dora was killed?"

He looked down. "Yes, I know. I talked with her brother just now."

Chapter
Nine

Dawn revealed the damage to the construction camp. It was worse than they had expected, and Clare had never seen her father more downcast. Larry Brand, on the other hand, had taken over command naturally and set about calmly restoring order and seeing that the graves were dug for those killed in the raid.

It seemed suitable that it should begin to rain gently as Milton Thomas stood by Dora's open grave and read the burial service. Clare felt as if the sky were weeping for the poor, lost girl. Larry Brand appeared saddened by the girl's death and Clare hoped he had at last come to regret his behavior towards her. Even his henchman Pedro stood close by the grave and gazed down at the body being lowered with an unusual gloomy intentness.

As the service ended and the workers went back to clearing away debris, Clare, her father, and Larry

Brand made their way to the office for a council of war.

Milton Thomas sat behind his desk with the other two facing him. His face seemed to have taken on new lines of age since the reverses, and Clare was touched by the signs of fresh gray hair at his temples.

He said, "I suppose the main blame for all this rests on my shoulders."

She protested, "That's nonsense! We were raided by paid outlaws. Sent here by the Great Western Company."

Larry glanced at her and said, "Again we are assuming this. We've found no definite proof of it."

"Did you search the clothing of the ones who were killed?" she asked.

"Yes. Nothing to identify them or link them with our rival."

"It was murder and sabotage," Clare's father sighed. "We are lucky to be alive. The question is, what are we to do now?"

Clare turned to Larry, saying, "Most of the supplies at the viaduct are safe, though they set us back there by damaging the construction."

Larry nodded. "That is true. We also have plenty of materials at the gorge and on the main line."

"So the chief losses were here," she said. "Mostly of material you'd be calling on in the weeks and months ahead?"

"Our stockpile was here," her father acknowledged. "That is mostly what we lost."

"Then the main thrust of work can go on if we have enough men?" she asked.

Her father frowned. "I suppose we can go ahead for a week or two at least."

She said, "We can take the work train back to Denver and try and get new materials and more men from Jefferson Myers."

"It's a chance, but I wouldn't count on it," her father said. "Myers and his supporters have dropped a lot of money into this project. And it's still as uncertain as ever."

"If they don't come up with more capital they stand to lose everything," she pointed out.

Larry Brand addressed Clare's father. "What Clare says makes sense."

"That would mean Clare and I would have to journey to Denver," her father said. "Who will keep things going on here?"

Larry said, "I can do that. At least for a brief period. You could leave any special instructions for me."

Milton Thomas' eyebrows lifted. "You actually feel competent to oversee it all?"

"With help," Larry said. "I can get Pedro to divide his time between the main line and completing the line at the gorge. And I'll stay at the viaduct and supervise the building of the bridge."

Clare said, "We have only to lay tracks ten miles beyond that point by our contract. The people in Cheyenne are working on that end."

"I wonder if they're having the same trouble with Great Western," her father said. "Probably not. They have only a relatively minor length of line to do and the success or failure of things rests on our shoulders."

Clare asked Larry, "Do you think Pedro rates such

trust? It is the same thing as making him a head foreman."

"Whatever his other faults, he's a worker. I couldn't get along without him. He's done well."

Clare's father said, "I'll accept him on condition you take the full responsibility for his performance."

"I won't hesitate to do that," Larry said.

"So we can go on for a little and maybe we'll get the extra support we need in Denver," said Clare. "Perhaps this tragedy will draw us together to work even harder."

Her father said, "I think we should lose no time. If at all possible, Clare and I should leave on the work train in the morning."

"That seems reasonable," she agreed. "Are you prepared to take over at short notice?" she asked Larry.

"Yes," he said. She was not surprised by his answer, given his hunger to improve his position with the company.

"Well that seems to be all we can settle at this point," her father said. "One of my chief pursuits in the city will be to try and round up a team of vigilantes who will come out here and protect us until we've completed our task."

"Perhaps if the Denver Gent is still there he might be persuaded to join us," Clare said.

Larry objected. "I don't see him in that role."

"I think he'd be excellent," Clare's father said. "We certainly ought to try him. I just hope we can talk him into it."

Larry stood up abruptly. "I'm sorry, but I simply can't see him as anything but an outlaw."

Clare looked at the angry young man and quietly said, "I'm sure we understand that."

The meeting broke up and she went down to the corral to check on the black stallion. He came over to the fence the moment she called to him. As a reward she gave him several lumps of sugar. She was still petting him when Hank came limping up.

"Everything in good shape here, Miss!"

"You did your job well."

He touched the injury on his head. "Just a mite from turning in my chips!"

"I'm so glad you're all right," she said warmly.

"And you and your father," the old man said. "Of course Brand and Pedro looked after themselves."

"They fought against the raiders as hard as the rest of us," she said. "And Larry is taking over while my father and I go to the city for more money and men."

"Well, I ain't goin' to cheer about that," Old Hank said and spat on the grass. "He sure backed away from Dora after he got to be a boss."

"I know," she said quietly.

"Dora may have had a past," Hank went on, "but she had a kind of decency about her. At least I always figgered she was a girl who deserved better."

"I couldn't agree more. I thought Larry looked pretty broken at the funeral. He may be truly sorry for the way he behaved towards her."

"Crocodile tears if you ask me," the old cowhand snorted. "Well, I'll just have to get used to him lording it over me and the boys."

"If you have any problems, let me know," she said.

Hank nodded. "Harris Trent may have had a stick

201

up his back but he was a proper gent! And he knew engineering!"

"That's true," she said. "In spite of his disposition, Harris was a valuable member of our team. But Larry Brand has done well in a short time. We mustn't cheat him of proper credit."

"It would be hard to cheat him out of anything," Hank said disgruntled. "He's as smooth as a grass snake!"

It made her think of Dora's same warnings.

After dinner that night Clare went for a brief stroll before retiring. As she walked towards the corral, she came upon Larry Brand and Pedro Reilly in earnest conversation. They stopped talking as she came by, and Pedro tipped his sombrero to her, grinning and moving off into the shadows.

Larry smiled for her benefit. "We were just discussing our work plans," he told her.

"You will have a lot of responsibility."

"I know. But I welcome it. It could give me an opportunity to prove myself to your father and to you."

She said, "My opinion isn't that important."

"I disagree," he said as he stood facing her. "It is as an individual I want your approval. Your approval of me as a person."

"I think I've made my feelings clear," she replied quietly.

He looked concerned. "You are holding that business of Dora against me, aren't you?"

She shrugged. "In my opinion you treated her badly."

"I was going to make up for that," he insisted.

"When?"

"Right away," he said. "I intended to talk to her and see what we could work out. You know the rest, they killed her before I could do it."

"It took you a long while to get around to it."

"I can be blamed for that, I'll admit. But I meant to do the proper thing. I swear it."

She sighed. "It's all history now."

"Except that you keep on holding a resentment against me," Larry said.

"I can't erase it from my mind. But I will give you the benefit of the doubt. Accept your word that you meant to at least let her down easier."

"That's all I ask," he replied. "All I can expect. Where are you going?"

"I'm just taking a short stroll before bed," she said.

"May I walk along with you?"

"If you like," she said in a noncommittal tone. She would have preferred to be alone, she had so many things to think out before she left for the city.

At her side, Larry said, "In Denver you'll be seeing the Denver Gent again."

"That's not a certainty."

"It's likely."

"We'll see," she answered, thinking it was none of his business and not wishing to give him any satisfaction. "I'd like to return now. We've gone far enough."

Larry began the journey back with her, and in no time he hit on the question of the Denver Gent's loyalty. "In my opinion he's been a spy for the Great Western crowd all along. He came here when your father and I were away."

"To protect me!"

"So he said. But he did get a chance to see all that was going on here and the general layout and I think he passed the word on."

Clare shook her head. "I'll never believe that."

"I know you won't, now," he said. "But one day I may be proven right."

Clare gazed ahead at the lighted cars of the construction train, so peaceful now. "Who would believe what went on here last night?"

"Things can change quickly. We were sitting ducks for that gang."

"Sometimes I wonder if all this violence has to be! Is the project worth it?"

"The West is being opened and such things will happen until it is. One day people will live here and travel through here and take it all for granted. It will be as uneventful as a trip from Boston to New York is today."

She halted at the entrance to the sleeping car. "I wish I could live long enough to tell them."

"Not likely any of us will," Larry said. "Last night was a lesson in the shortness of life in this section. But we're the ones who got here first and I guess we have to keep on."

Clare smiled up at him. "I didn't know you were such a philosopher."

He shrugged. "I am and have been a lot of things. You've not tried to know me well."

"I must remember that," she promised.

"I won't be around when you leave," he said. "I'll be heading for the viaduct. So best of luck!" And he took her in his arms and kissed her.

Under the circumstances she had almost expected

the gesture. But she had not guessed that his embrace would be so gentle and his kiss so meaningful. For a few seconds she was lost by the need to be safely in someone's loving arms. Then she easily pushed him away.

"Good night, Larry," she said quietly. "And good luck to you as well."

He nodded. She mounted the car steps, turned, and smiled at him, then went on in to her sleeping compartment in a rather confused state of mind. She had determined to keep Larry Brand at a distance, to ensure their relationship was strictly professional. But it was difficult; he had charm and he was assuming an increasingly important role in the project, which meant he was also more involved with her and her father.

As she prepared for bed, Clare considered what he'd said about trying to make up with Dora. She could only take his word now that he'd been serious in this. Poor Dora was not around to testify, but she had turned bitter towards Larry and warned Clare about him. This could have been expected when she'd been discarded by him so cruelly. If she had lived, perhaps Larry might have made things up to her. Unhappily, no one would ever know.

So now she must judge Larry on his performance in the future. She knew he was ambitious and could not be blamed for that, but there remained doubts about his strength of character. And his friendship with Pedro was a strange one, though he'd used the Mexican ex-convict to good advantage as a foreman. But overriding and coloring everything was her love for the Denver Gent.

The next morning Hank led a group of workers who'd remained at the camp to the rear platform of the supplies train, where Clare and her father stood waiting for their journey to Denver to begin. She was wearing her best dress, pale blue sateen and white lace trim at the throat and sleeves. A loose, black ribbon was tied pertly below the open neckline and a thin black band at the waist. With her matching parasol she would equal the best-dressed ladies in the town.

Her father was wearing a formal black suit and looked much more the businessman than when he wore his engineering garb of riding pants and multicolored flannel shirt. Both were touched by the small group who came to see them on their way.

Hank limped close, took off his Stetson, and squinting in the bright morning sun, said, "You let them folks in Denver know if they send us the supplies and men we'll get the line down, and done in time!"

This statement brought cheers from the other members of the camp's remaining crew and Milton Thomas cleared his throat to say a few words. "Boys, we've been through a bad time. We've had sad losses! None of us will forget our friends who died for this railway line in one way or another. My respect and thanks to those of you left who wish to carry on. And to do justice to your belief and courage, I cannot do less than face the investors and ask that they show the same qualities."

There were more cheers from the men and then the engine started up and the small, three-car train began to move out from the camp. Clare and her father remained on the rear platform until the men by the track and the camp itself vanished as they rounded a bend.

Travelling back to the car which had been fitted to serve the needs of up to a dozen travelling executives, Milton Thomas sank into a seat and Clare sat opposite him, looking worriedly at the recent changes in his face. It was lined deeper than before and his eyes had lost their brightness. He gazed ahead of him with a kind of resignation.

She leaned forward and patted his knee to encourage him. "I thought you spoke very well," she said.

He stared at her and then dryly asked, "Did my words have any meaning?"

"Of course they did!"

"I wonder," he sighed. "I expected this project would have its problems. But I wasn't prepared for the violence and bloodshed we've had to deal with. It never occurred to me that other so-called businessmen would resort to law breaking to gain financially."

Clare said, "I'll say again what we've had to admit many times. We have no proof the Great Western people organized the raids and the sabotage."

"It has to be them," her father said wearily. "No one else would benefit from the things that have been done."

"So?"

"I wish I could interest the government and the press," her father said. "Perhaps turning the full glare of publicity on the Great Western would halt them in their attacks on us."

"You can try that when you reach Denver."

Milton Thomas gazed out the window. "So easy now

to make this journey. Yet every length of rail we've laid has taken its toll on us. I doubt if head office realizes that."

"Try to make them understand."

"We've lost thousands of dollars in supplies alone," he said. "And if it weren't for Larry Brand, no work would be going on in our absence."

"Yes, I know," she said evenly.

Her father caught the tone of her reply and gave her an appraising look. "You still don't like him, do you?"

"Let us say I have mixed feelings."

"He saved your life at the risk of his own."

"I know that."

"He has shown himself to have ability."

"True," she acknowledged.

"He has been loyal to us and helped fight off that gang the other night."

"I'm aware of all those things," she said, a little desperately.

"In many ways he's a better man than Harris Trent was."

She looked up at her father in dismay. "And in other ways he is much less a man. Surely much less a gentleman!"

Her father nodded grimly. "I forgot you have a weakness for so-called gentlemen. Especially one particular example, the Denver Gent."

Defiantly, she said, "I've never concealed that I like him."

"Yet he's done little but charm you and expose you to danger."

"That's hardly fair!" she protested.

Her father ignored this and asked, "Are you going to seek him out when we reach the city?"

"If he's still there I'll likely see him."

"We'll be staying at the Pembrook Hotel," her father said. "If he still has his gambling salon there I'd prefer that you not enter it except in my company."

She blushed. "I dislike making promises that I may not be able to keep."

"And I most emphatically dislike having to worry about you with all my other problems on my shoulders," her father said angrily.

"If you worry it's because you want to. There's no need."

"I curse Jefferson Myers for introducing you to that man! He may well be the spy who has repeatedly betrayed us!"

"You're merely echoing Larry Brand now," she said. "You must know we've no grounds at all to think that."

"Brand believes it!"

She smiled bitterly. "He's saying it loudly because he sees Denver as a rival for my hand. Not that I have ever thought of Larry seriously."

"Why not?"

"I'm not in love with him!"

"Love is sometimes infatuation and built on deceit. A deceit one practices on oneself. You always spurned Harris Trent because you felt he was not worthy of your love. But I warn you Larry Brand will not be so easy to handle. He may destroy your daydreams about this Denver Gent!"

Clare rose defiantly. "That is not at all likely," she said. And she went and sat as far away from him as she could.

Her father had both hurt and angered her. As she sat staring out at the wilderness she decided that she must not abandon her self-determination. No matter what her father said, she was going to manage her own life. And as long as Denver did nothing to alter her love for him, she would continue to try and have him become the one man to whom she would commit herself.

After a little her father left his seat and came up to sit at her side. He placed one of his hands over hers and said, "I'm sorry, my dear. I was unfair."

"It doesn't matter," she told him.

"You're all I have," he went on. "I'm concerned and frightened for you. It seems everything else in my life has crumbled. I don't want anything to happen to you."

She looked at him with a tiny smile. "Father, you raised me to know how to look after myself."

"I hope I succeeded."

"Don't worry, you have," Clare assured him. "Let me go on being called a spitfire and a vixen. And let me decide for myself about the men in my life."

He said, "I know you will do that."

"But always remember, Father dear, that I love you," she said and raised her lips to touch his cheek. "And I'm in this battle with you. Whatever happens, I'm at your side."

It was close to six P.M. when the train pulled into the busy Denver station. Other trains, larger ones from the East, were on the various tracks, some of them having just arrived and others waiting to get under way. They were using a siding where loading was easy and they would not interfere with the regular traffic.

In the pleasant early-evening weather, Clare and her father made their way across several tracks to the railway station and its platform looking over the town. They found a carriage there and her father instructed the driver to take them to the Pembrook Hotel.

As they were driven through the streets, Clare was impressed that Denver was more bustling and booming than when they'd last been there.

"There are so many more people here!" she said, turning to her father. "And everyone seems in such a hurry!"

"It is becoming a city," her father agreed.

The sights intrigued her. A beer wagon passed drawn by a big Clydesdale, and there were many fancy carriages with fine driving horses all neck-reined and prancing along. And the men had a more civilized look; hardly any of them were carrying guns where you could see them, though she had no doubt most had a holster under the arm or perhaps a weapon hidden behind a waistband.

As the Pembrook Hotel came into view, Clare felt her heart beat faster, and she could barely contain her excitement. She wondered if by some miracle she might meet Denver in the lobby, that he would be the first person she encountered. She was already rehearsing in her mind what she would say to him, picturing his strong, handsome face and the touch of his hand.

They reached the entrance to the hotel and she saw a group of men lolling around, talking and watching the new arrivals. They all appeared to be in western clothes and then she noticed an easterner in a checked gray suit and black bowler hat smoking a long, thin cigar. He was tall and well built with jet-black hair which was long enough to show beneath the bowler at the sides and rear. His face was on the narrow side and his shrewd eyes fixed on her as her father helped her down from the carriage. From the corner of her eye she caught him quietly smiling to himself.

So this stranger was to be the first man who paid any attention to her or whom she noticed. So much for dreams! At the desk her father ordered them rooms side by side, as usual. The bald clerk recognized them and gave them a friendly greeting.

"Mr. Myers left a letter here for you," he said, rummaging under the desk for an envelope and passing it to Clare's father.

She glanced in the direction of Denver's gambling salon and was startled to see that this area had all been opened up and made part of the lobby.

"What happened to the gambling room?" she asked the clerk.

The bald man smiled. "You've noticed, miss. We don't have it here any longer."

"Did you find it a problem?" Milton Thomas asked.

"One shooting too many and the boss asked the Denver Gent to leave. Not that it was Denver's fault. We all liked him."

Trying to hide her dismay, Clare asked, "Did he leave town?"

The clerk chuckled. "Not Denver! He likes this place! No, he moved over to Mame's house. She let him outfit a room on the ground floor there and I hear it's been a big boost for her regular business."

Her father wished to hear no more of this and had the clerk summon a porter to take their bags upstairs. Their rooms were at the rear of the hotel and so likely to be quiet, although there was a livery stable there with a blacksmith shop.

Soon after Clare was settled in her room, there was a knock on her door. It was her father with the opened letter from Jefferson Myers in his hands.

Clearly perturbed, he said, "We've arrived at a critical moment."

"Really?"

"Yes," he said. "Jefferson wrote me this as a warning. Three of the Eastern money men are here. They've heard disturbing rumors about our progress and are seriously thinking of trying to sell out or amalgamate with Great Western."

"They can't do such a thing!" she exclaimed.

He sighed. "I'm afraid they easily can. In fact, by what this letter suggests, they may have already made up their minds."

"Then you must stop them!"

"Jefferson wishes us to have dinner with him this evening so we may discuss this privately before I have to face the three bankers. He's coming here to meet us at seven."

"It's almost that now," she said. "Are you sure you want me to be there?"

Her father frowned. "Certainly! You have been my equal partner in all this."

"Then I'll change to something suitable," she said. "And Father...."

"Yes?"

"After you and Mr. Myers have dinner and your talk, will you escort me over to Denver's new gambling salon?"

Her father gasped. "Absolutely not! Take you to a brothel? Have you lost your mind?"

"I see no harm in going to his salon. He is an old friend."

"He is a gambler and gunman, evicted from this hotel," her father stormed.

Her eyes met his. "I mean to see him, Father!"

Her father stood with his hands clenched at his sides. "If he is such a fine gentleman, he will call here to see you."

"He doesn't know I'm here."

"Denver is not all that large yet," her father said. "He will soon hear. Word will be out about the railway meeting."

"I see," she said quietly. "Well, I've told you my intention."

Her father moved to the door. "I trust you will show some sense in this matter. Please be ready to go down to dinner in ten minutes."

As Clare hurriedly fixed her hair, unable to make it look as she wished, she inwardly raged at her father's unbending attitude towards the Denver Gent. As she quickly undid the hooks and eyes in her blue travelling outfit and put on a white gown more suited to the hotel dining room, she made up her mind that one way or another, she'd see Denver before the night was over.

Jefferson Myers was waiting for them at a secluded table. He gave her a fatherly kiss on the cheek and when the waiter came by for drink orders, he said, "You still take your whiskey straight, Miss Thomas?" with an amused gleam in his eyes.

"I have not given up the pleasant custom," she said, with a smile.

Jefferson Myers laughed, his ample stomach heaving in unison. "This is a fine girl you have, Milton. She has plenty of spirit."

"Yes, she has," her father said dryly. After their whiskies were served Jefferson ordered steaks for all of them and then lifted his glass for a toast.

"To all the brave souls who have kept the Intercontinental Line from coming to a halt," he said.

Clare and her father joined in the toast and Milton Thomas added, "Some paid for it with their lives."

"Yes, I saw your reports," Myers said, frowning. "A pity about Harris Trent. I'm sure his death was a shock to you."

Clare felt her cheeks warm. "Yes. He was a good friend."

Myers continued to regard her. "I know that," he said.

Her father interposed in the awkward moment. "He was a great loss to us. Fortunately this Brand fellow has filled in for him incredibly well."

"Excellent," Myers said, "and..." He stopped talking suddenly as his eyes fixed on a figure taking a table at the other side of the room. He turned back to them and said, "See that man?!"

Clare looked and saw he was referring to the tall, narrow-faced easterner—the man who had smiled at her so mysteriously.

She said, "I saw him this afternoon when we arrived. He was standing outside the hotel."

"He's staying here," Myers said. "Take a good look at him! He's the enemy!"

"The enemy?" her father echoed in a subdued voice. "You mean he is with Great Western?"

"He's their chief representative out here," said Jefferson Myers. "More than that, he's a lawyer and he knows every trick in the trade."

"What's his name?" Clare asked.

"Carter. John Carter. He visited my office just once to identify himself. He'll be carefully observing what goes on here. Reporting on our meetings with the bankers from the East."

Milton Thomas eyed Carter, who was sitting with his back to them at the other end of the big room. He said angrily, "No doubt he knows who I am. Since he's so well informed."

"Without question," Myers said. "I just want you two to be aware of him."

"Would he be the one organizing those terror raids against us?" Clare wondered.

"It is quite possible," Myers said. "Be sure he had some part in them."

"I'd like to go up to him and call him a murderer!" she said indignantly.

"I understand how you must feel," Jefferson Myers placated her. "But that would do little good. The way to beat them is to get to Cheyenne first."

"I suppose they are almost there," she said.

"No," Myers said. "They have had problems finding workers—they pay poorly and treat them badly. They've been held up for several weeks."

"Then that explains their desperation," Clare's father said. "Why they've made the raids on us on the one hand and offered to buy us out on the other."

"I've already told the bankers that," Myers said. "But they are now concerned about whether you can finish the line you've started at all. The Great Western people told them the route was impassable."

"We've already conquered the worst of it," Clare said. "They mustn't back out on us now."

"It would be the worst sort of treachery," her father said with anger.

"Nothing has been settled yet," Myers said. "You will have your opportunity to try and sway them to your side tomorrow morning."

"Where is the meeting to be held?" Clare's father asked.

"In my office," said Myers. And to Clare he added, "I think you should be present also."

"Are you certain?"

"You know all about the project. You've worked on it. And a pretty face around won't do any harm," was the fat man's reply.

"We shall be there," Clare's father told him.

They settled down to an excellent steak dinner and Myers regaled them with all the gossip he'd heard. There was serious discussion of the recent massacre of Colonel George A. Custer and many of his troops by the Sioux Indians.

"Another famous figure of the West gone," Jefferson Myers said. "But he was a hothead and would listen to none of the warnings given him."

"He had a job to do," Clare said. "He was probably doing it the best way he could."

"I suppose there is a lot to be said for him," Myers agreed. "But it's too bad he had to lose his life and that of so many of his men."

"The tribes seemed docile here," Clare's father said. "The white renegades seem to be the chief threat. And they do sometimes drag in some Indians to help them."

"People back East don't understand our problems," said Myers. "At least the three bankers we have to deal with don't appear to have any idea of the risks we must take."

"I'd like the job of telling them," Clare said.

"You may do it tomorrow morning," Myers said with a smile on his broad face.

They finished dinner and on their way out of the dining room, Clare saw the tall, thin man glance up from his table and note their departure. She gave no hint she'd noticed him.

In the lobby her father held back and told her, "I need to talk some details out with Myers before we join the bankers. I suggest you go to your room. You must be very weary."

"Thank you, Father," she said. She bade Jefferson Myers goodnight and then went upstairs. But she had no plan of remaining up there. She changed into a dark suit and selected a small bonnet of the same dark hue with ties under the chin. It was an outfit she felt would cause little attention.

Then she cautiously made her way downstairs and out a side door of the lobby. She had a glimpse of her father and Jefferson Myers seated by a palm in the lobby, discussing their plans. When she stepped outside she was glad she'd worn the heavier dress. The air was chilly compared to the warmth of the sun during the day.

She had found the town busy during the day. Now that night had come it was equally exciting. Light poured out the windows of most of the houses. The saloons, and there seemed to be many of them, were crowded, and raucous laughter and song came through their swinging doorways. Cowboys rode straight down the streets, sometimes shouting at those who happened to be in their way, and often almost running the unwary pedestrians down.

In a ramshackle building on her right lights blazed from the windows of Doc Jenson's Tonsorial Parlor and Drug Store. A smaller sign by the door proclaimed Jenson to be a master mortician, providing "Speedy Funerals at a Small Price."

Carriages rushed by and for a while Clare was on a wooden sidewalk which served as a refuge if one didn't mind brushing by the occasional drunken cowboy or equally drunken Indian. She passed Johnston's Saddle, Harness, and Shoe Shop, and next to it was the Empty Saddle Saloon. She continued on, remembering the area from a drive through it with Jefferson Myers. On her right was the New York Hotel and Restaurant and next to it, with gold letters on its windows, was the Denver City Bank.

On her left and a few doors ahead was the three-story building known to all Denverites as Mame's House. Light blazed from its windows through discreetly drawn lace curtains. By its front door, on a chain, there hung a conspicuous lantern with a red glass shade. This was for the benefit of any stranger passing by who hadn't happened to hear of the reputation of Mame's House.

There were plenty of cowboys loitering around, some of them drunk, all of them in boisterous humor. They were shouting obscene comments to each other, and when Clare passed by them she attracted a number of stares and winks. She walked straight on, pulling the small jacket of her suit coat tightly about her with one hand and looking neither left nor right.

She was within a few feet of the entrance to Mame's House when she was confronted by a big, burly man with a cruel, gape-toothed smile. He was roughly dressed and none too clean.

He grabbed her by the arm and said, "You look pretty good. I'll try you!" He then began to drag her off towards an adjacent alley.

She fought and pulled back, crying, "No! Please! You don't understand! I'm not one of Mame's girls!"

Struggling with her, he chortled, "All the better! I'll take you in the alley and you won't have to share with anyone!"

"No!" she cried, furious now. She tried to open her pocketbook to get at her pistol and ward him off at the same time. Unfortunately she failed in both and to her horror, he grabbed her pocketbook and threw it into the street!

Chapter
Ten

The struggle between Clare and the burly hoodlum attracted attention. Passers-by halted to see what was going on. It was not unusual for one of Mame's girls to have a quarrel with a client so no one interfered. Slowly Clare felt herself being dragged towards the dark alley, despite her screaming and attempting to fight back. The man was just too powerful for her.

"Hold it!" She heard the words ring out sharply and prayed that at last one of the onlookers was making a move to help her.

The burly man paid no attention to the shout but in the next instant a man jumped between the bully and Clare, seizing her attacker by the throat.

The big man threw her defender off and as Clare staggered back, he snarled an oath and with eyes glistening made a rush for the slender man who had tried to help her. But when he closed in, the bully received a rain of quick blows to his face and the side of his head before he could more than land two body punches on Clare's defender.

The big man's face showed astonishment and anger, and blood dribbled from the corner of his mouth. He roared a threat and lunged again and this time landed some blows which sent the slender man reeling. The big fellow now moved in for the kill, but again his opponent seemed to revive and this time landed a heavy punch to the burly man's chin which made him halt and sway a little.

This was the moment for the slender man to become the aggressor. He went at the big man and landed two blows to the face area and a heavy one to the stomach. The burly man bent over and then crumpled onto the ground.

All the while this battle was going on, a crowd had gathered and was cheering wildly. They didn't care who won or lost—street battles were one of the most popular forms of entertainment offered free to the cowpokes. Only when the slender man dropped his opponent did Clare realize who it was. It was the narrow-faced, suave lawyer who represented the Great Western, John Carter.

As the bully's friends dragged the still-unconscious man off, someone handed John Carter his suit jacket. He very casually put it on and ran his hands through his long, black hair.

His bowler hat was at her feet and she picked it up and went to him with it. "Thank you," she said. "You interfered just in time." He retrieved her pocketbook from the ground and gave it to her, smiling. "I happen to have a belt for my boxing. I wouldn't have matched up with a man of that size if I didn't think my skill would outmatch his weight benefit."

"I still can't believe you managed so well!" she marvelled.

His hat still in hand, he asked her, "How about you? Did he harm you?"

"Just handled my arm a little roughly. I think I sprained it. It will probably ache for a day or two."

"My name is John Carter," he told her.

"And mine is Clare Thomas."

Amusement showed in his tone as he assured her, "I knew who you were and that you weren't one of Mame's girls as he inferred, or I wouldn't have come to your rescue."

"It was my great good fortune that you came along when you did," she said.

"You should not be out in this district alone," he warned her. "Certainly not at this time of night. No decent woman shows herself here after dark."

"I came to see someone," she said, feeling her cheeks burn. "I had no idea it would be so dangerous."

"Well, now you know," he said.

"Yes," she agreed. "You are the lawyer here for the Great Western, aren't you?"

"Correct," he said. "And you are the daughter of Milton Thomas, the engineer in charge of the Intercontinental group."

She nodded. "Which places us on opposite sides. Makes us enemies."

He smiled, showing little signs of the fight except for slightly rumpled hair. "Friendly enemies, I trust."

"You were surely my friend just now."

"I'm glad I could help," he said, studying her so closely it embarrassed her.

Most of the onlookers had left and the bully and his friends had piled into a carriage and rolled off somewhere. From inside Mame's place came the sounds of ragtime piano.

She indicated the house. "I was going in there."

"May I ask why?"

"I want to visit the gambling room. The Denver Gent is a friend of mine."

"I see," said Carter. "You should have found a man to accompany you."

"I know that now."

He hesitated a moment and then said, "If you like I will escort you into the gambling room. And if you need me, I'll wait and see you safely back to the Pembrook Hotel."

"I feel I'm imposing on your generosity," she protested.

"Not at all."

"Then I'll accept your offer gratefully," she said. "Thank you, again."

He went to the door with her and nodded to a big, grizzled man who evidently served as bouncer. He said, "We want the Denver Gent's room."

The bouncer eyed them both and then, with a jerk of his head, told them, "Straight down the corridor. It's the room at the back."

Carter thanked him and with Clare on his arm strolled down the corridor. Halfway down, they passed a door open to the room where the piano music was coming from. An ancient black man sat manipulating the keyboard with a sure touch. Seated and standing about the room were a number of young women, garishly dressed and heavily made-up; with them were a few cowpokes of various ages.

Carter halted for a moment so she could take in the scene. He said, "This is the waiting room where the boys take their pick. Mame takes the fee and they're assigned a room up above."

"Hello, John Carter," a raucous female voice said, and Clare turned to see it was Mame, the proprietor of the house.

Mame's heavily rouged face showed astonishment. "You're back!" she declared.

"Yes," Clare said. "I wanted to see the Denver Gent."

"I remember your interest in the Gent from last time," said Mame with a slight smile.

"I hope you don't mind," Clare said.

"I'm not one to hold grudges," Mame said. "And the gambling room is open to any one wanting to spend a little money. John, here, has given it all his trade and passed up my girls."

John Carter smiled. "I daren't expose myself to so many charmers. I'd be too bewildered to make a choice."

Mame tapped him on the shoulder with a big fan she was holding. "Any time you change your mind, let me know and I'll do the picking for you."

"I'll remember that," Carter promised.

"Will you be back in the town long?" Mame asked Clare.

"I don't know," Clare answered. "It all depends on how long my father's business takes."

Mame gave her a sly look. "From all I hear, John

Carter's outfit is going to be the first with a rail line into Cheyenne."

"We are far from accomplishing that," the lawyer said modestly.

"I think it much easier to talk about it than do it," was Clare's reply.

Mame laughed. "Not bad! Not bad at all!" And she went on into the parlor to join her girls.

John Carter continued to lead Clare down the shadowed hallway, saying, "Mame is not a bad sort. I think there was a time she hoped the Denver Gent might be her lover."

"So I understand," Clare replied.

"It didn't work out but she continues to be his friend and has given him a classy setup here."

They reached a black-painted door which he opened and they stepped into a long room with a bar at the far end. In the center was the familiar round table with a hanging lamp overhead, presided over by the Denver Gent.

In spite of her unpleasant experience and her unexpected escort, Clare could think of nothing but the pleasure of being close to Denver again. He was as handsome as she remembered and very cool and self-contained as he concentrated on the game, not noticing her entrance. But a lot of the cowpokes standing on the sidelines and by the bar made no attempt to hide their interest in her and her companion.

"Would you care for a drink?" Carter asked.

"No, thank you," she said. "But please don't let me stop you."

He smiled. "I can master my thirst for a little."

She studied the room and the elegant bar with the painting of a nude woman above it. She said, "It's much like the room he had at the Pembrook Hotel."

"Close to it," Carter acknowledged. "Do you want me to let Denver know you are here?"

"I'd rather not disturb him until he finishes his game."

"Whatever you like," Carter said.

She gave him a side-glance and tried to sort out her feelings about him. He had apparently come to her rescue with no thought of his own safety. He had known who she was and had not hesitated to help her. Yet, as Jefferson Myers had pointed out, he was surely their enemy. It could well have been he who had planned the raids on their various camps.

One thing was sure, he was no ordinary lawyer. The Great Western people had probably picked him because of special talents for this kind of situation. She must try to separate the man from the role he was playing with the rival railway construction company.

Carter lit one of his long, thin cigars and said, "I hear you are something of an engineer."

"I've learned a little from my father. I can read plans and take care of simple tasks."

"I'm sure you're being modest," he said. "Are you people being beset by the same problems we are?"

She gave him a direct look. "Our worst problem comes from outlaws raiding our camps. We've just had a serious attack on the construction train. Quite a few people were killed."

John Carter listened with interest, showing no sign

227

of guilt. "This is a wild country, Miss Thomas. There are many outlaw bands composed of former soldiers who are now desperate and jobless."

"I don't think the raids were the work of such men. I think someone cleverly directed a group of paid thugs and Indians to vandalize us."

Carter flicked some ash from the end of his cigar. "If things have come to such a state, it is very bad indeed."

"I'd say so," she agreed. And she decided he either knew all about the raids, and was an excellent actor, or he was only the company's legal representative with no knowledge of what had been going on. It was hard to decide.

He nodded towards the table. "The game is over. Now is your chance to speak to your friend. I'll be at the bar if you should need me to escort you home."

"You're very kind," she said and left him to cross to the table where Denver was standing in conversation with an older man.

When she presented herself before him, Denver showed both shock and pleasure. "My dear Clare," he exclaimed, taking her by the arms as if to make sure she was real. "I've been hoping for something like this, but I'd almost given up."

Her radiant face expressed the pleasure she felt. "I have been worried about you."

"And I about you!"

She smiled. "Yet here we both are, safe and together."

He nodded. "I've heard rumors of some trouble in your camp."

Her face shadowed. "We were raided several times. Harris Trent was killed in an accident caused by vandalism, and Dora Lee was shot and killed by the raiders."

"It's beginning to seem your game is more dangerous than mine," the gambler said. "Did you venture here alone?"

"I did and almost ran into serious trouble." And she told him about her being attacked and her rescue by John Carter.

"The Great Western lawyer," he said. "He's a regular at my table. So you were saved by the opposition."

"That's how it worked out."

"I must thank him," Denver said, glancing over at the bar where Carter was standing with a drink in his hand.

She said, "He's offered to see me safely back to the hotel."

"No need," the Denver Gent said. "I'll do that. I'll close the game early."

"Please don't let me interfere with the table," she said.

"I have the privilege of closing when I like," he said. "And I'll let the play go on another half-hour and then call it an evening."

"Very well," she said. "I'll go down to John Carter and tell him. I'll chat with him while I'm waiting for you."

"Good idea," the Denver Gent said with a smile.

He returned to the table while she walked the length of the long room, feeling the eyes of the cowhands watching her.

On reaching John Carter, she said "Thanks for your offer. But Denver will see me back to my hotel."

The slender man looked wryly amused once more. "I rather thought he would," he said. "Then I shall leave soon."

"I do appreciate your wanting to help me," she told him.

"I'm sure we will meet again," he said. "Perhaps we can have a meal together. I'm also staying at the Pembrook Hotel."

"Perhaps," she said, not wanting to make any promises.

He tipped his bowler hat and bowed as she left to rejoin Denver, standing near him while he finished what was to be the last poker game of the evening. When she glanced in the direction of the bar again, she saw that John Carter had apparently finished his drink and left.

The tension of the game now held her interest. She saw the chips moved to the center of the round table and the winner drawing them in as the game progressed. Now with the last hand in play the stakes were extremely high as evidenced by the tall stack of chips in the middle of the table waiting for the winner to claim them.

The big pot was won by an elderly man in eastern dress. He seemed not too excited about his good luck and he and the Denver Gent shook hands before he went to cash in his chips. Then Denver said goodnight to the others and joined her.

"I'll have a carriage made ready," he told her and gave some instructions to one of the helpers.

She smiled at him. "I slipped away from the hotel.

If my father learns I'm not there he'll be very worried."

"So he should be," the Denver Gent told her. "You must never do such a thing again."

"I couldn't bear waiting another day to see you!"

His face was as tanned and attractive as she'd remembered. "It's easy to forgive you when you say a thing like that."

"I mean it," she said. "I have missed you so."

"And I have missed you," he said sincerely.

"You left camp without warning. Without a proper goodbye." she reproved him.

"I didn't dare risk a goodbye. I knew you'd ask me to stay there and I'd find it hard to refuse you."

"Yet you left."

"You know why," he said, his eyes meeting hers. "I needn't go over it all again."

"But you're wrong," she protested.

The helper returned. "The rig is waiting out back," he said.

Denver nodded and then took Clare out by a door near the bar to a dark alley where the carriage was waiting. He helped her up into it, then got up himself. As he took the reins, the livery stable man released the horse's bridle and stepped back.

They rode out to the main street and she saw that all the shops and houses were in darkness, except for Mame's House which shone like a beacon in the gloomy night, and the various bars from whose fronts light and plenty of noise emerged.

He did not go straight to the Pembrook Hotel but drove the carriage out along a lane; there he tied the reins to keep the horses temporarily at a halt. Then with the moonlight shining down on them he gently took her in his arms. She responded with the pent-up hunger of waiting for this moment.

As he slowly released her from the passionate embrace, she looked up at Denver with pleading eyes and said, "I don't want to be separated from you again. Not ever!"

"My way of life is not for you," he said, still holding her in his arms.

"I don't care. I'm willing to live any way you wish!"

His smile was sad. "Before, you begged me to give up gambling. Why this change?"

"I've decided it's more important for me to have you than to have you merely on my terms."

He kissed her again and fondled her chin with his hand. "I want to hear you say such things and yet I know that it's wrong to encourage you."

"Why?"

"You have been brought up to lead a lady's life. Your father can give you all the advantages you should have."

"And I'd rather be with you!"

He sighed. "And associate with outlaws, pimps, prostitutes, and all the others who live on the fringes of gambling? You had a taste of it tonight."

"That was different. It wouldn't happen again."

"Don't be too sure," he warned her. "If you were living with me I'd not be able to watch over you all the time. And you'd be surrounded by a type of people you can't even imagine."

"You're trying to frighten me," she said bitterly. "I'm not that easily scared. I've fought at my father's side and done a man's work. I can shoot as straight as many men."

"I know all that," he told her. "And I still don't want to drag you down to my level."

"You don't have to remain here," she argued. "You can turn the room over to someone else."

"And if I did?"

"You could join us at the camp and take over the guards," she said. "If we don't have proper security we'll never finish the line in time."

He smiled. "I have heard all this before."

"But now things are more desperate," she said. "Do think about it."

"All right," he said with a sigh. "I'll think about it, but I make no promises."

Regaining some of her spirit, she warned him, "If you don't come to the camp I'll stay here. And even you think that will cause trouble."

The Denver Gent shook his head in despair and reached for the reins, saying, "You're a difficult lady!"

She smiled and linking her arm in his, said softly, "I'm Denver's Lady! And I will be always!"

Now he headed back to the main artery of the town and took her to the Pembrook Hotel. He saw her safely inside and kissed her goodnight in the deserted lobby as the elderly clerk pretended to be studying his ledger.

Denver said, "We'll have an early dinner here tomorrow night. I'll come at seven."

"You will think about what we discussed?" Clare asked.

"I will," he promised with a smile.

"And you must stop treating me like a stupid child," she warned him.

"I'll never see you in that light," he said and he waited to see her safely up the stairs to the door of her room.

There was no sound from her father's room and she was thankful. Apparently he'd gone straight up to bed and was now asleep. She was not in the mood for arguments or explanations; she was in a strange state, her joy in being with Denver again overshadowed by a fear he would somehow elude her. Even though he had promised to have dinner with her, she could not escape the fear that by tomorrow he might have vanished, thinking that this was best for her. There was little she could do but wait and hope.

After a restless night she met her father at breakfast. He glanced at her across the table and said, "You've seen him?"

She hesitated and then said, "You mean Denver?"

"You went to him last night," her father said with concern. "I checked your room and you weren't there."

"I had to go!"

"To that place, that brothel! I can't think the man has proper respect for you or he'd not encourage it!"

"He didn't. He was upset by my going there."

"Well, that speaks well for him, at least," said her father.

"I love him, Father," she said.

He sipped his coffee and stared at her with worried eyes. "We are facing the greatest crisis I have ever known and you add this worry to it."

"My caring for Denver should not be a worry," she protested.

He sighed. "So what do you plan to do?"

"He is having dinner with me tonight. I've tried to persuade him to return to the camp and organize our guards. I think he'll give me his answer at dinner."

"You didn't consult me on this!"

"We have discussed it!"

"The man showed no interest. He rode away last time without any warning. And we were raided just after."

"It had nothing to do with him!"

"You think what you like," her father said. "And so will I. You are expected to attend an afternoon meeting with the three Eastern bankers, Jefferson Myers, and myself. I hope you will get your wits about you and be there."

"I will," she promised. "When is it to be?"

"At two o'clock in Jefferson Myers' office. It may be the death knell of our project."

"They wouldn't do that!"

"Don't be too sure. We are stalled in our work and short on supplies. It looks as if the Great Western will win."

"They also have had setbacks," Clare reminded him.

He sighed. "Well, we will know this afternoon. And in the meantime, do try to get your wits about you."

She smiled. "I'll be there, Father. And I'll try to do my part."

He rose and kissed her. "While you're here you should see about buying some new dresses and bonnets. That should keep you out of mischief." And he left her.

Clare sat in the hotel dining room alone as she finished her coffee. It seemed there was a male conspiracy against her. Last night her father had flatly refused to accompany her to the house where Denver had his gaming room. When she had gone on her own, she'd been accosted by an outlaw and rescued only through the intervention of John Carter, the head lawyer for Great Western.

To cap it all off, when she'd finally reached Denver he had let his delight in seeing her be overshadowed by his concern for her. And he was continuing his threats to desert her for her own benefit. All this was so male and illogical she decided to do the only sensible thing in such a situation, go out to Madame Ouida's Shop and buy herself a new bonnet!

The tiny Madame Ouida recognized her at once and gave her a warm welcome. She studied her brown silk Watteau walking suit with interest.

"Now that is very smart," the little woman said. "And I like the small straw bonnet with its flowered top. It suits you."

"What are the new styles?" Clare asked her.

The little woman stood with her hands folded before her. "The high waists threaten to go even higher, though it's not stylish for some figures. And the bustle is definitely here to stay."

"Impractical for me, except when I am here in the city," Clare told her.

"I know that, my dear," Madame Ouida said.

"I have a fine practical outfit for you," Madame Ouida said. "A black velvet jacket that falls below the waist and a flowing brown skirt to match."

"Is it my size?"

"I'm almost certain it is, my dear," the little woman

said. "Step into the fitting room and I'll bring it to you so you may try it on."

A few minutes later Clare found herself standing before the mirror in the cubicle dubbed the fitting room, studying herself in the outfit. It suited her and seemed to fit very well.

Madame Ouida had gone outside and now Clare heard her talking to someone else. She decided she'd buy the outfit along with a new straw bonnet and changed back to her own dress. Then she went out with the outfit in her hands.

The first person she saw was Mame, very regal, in a stark black two-piece dress and black bonnet. She looked like the most conservative woman. With her was a pretty, young girl in a simple white dress full of flounces and a plain straw hat.

Madame Ouida smiled nervously. "Miss Thomas is one of my out-of-town customers," she told Mame.

Mame smiled wryly and said, "I know her. We've met before."

"Really?" Madame Ouida looked puzzled.

"Yes, we have met," Clare said at once. And passing the outfit in her hands to the little woman, she said, "I like it. I'll take it."

"I'll fold it and place it in a box for you," Madame Ouida promised and went to the rear of the shop to do this.

Mame took the opportunity to speak to Clare, "I hear you were manhandled last night in front of my place."

"A gentleman was kind enough to come to my aid," Clare responded.

"John Carter?" Mame said, unblinking as she studied her.

"Yes."

"From what I hear he did it very well."

"He turned out to be an expert boxer."

Mame smiled. "He's expert at a lot of things. Most of my girls would like to know him a lot better. For that matter, so would I. But then you only have eyes for Denver."

She blushed. "Denver is a close friend."

"You must be looking for trouble," Mame said. "Do you want your heart broken, giving it to a gunman and a gambler?"

"That is my business."

"Don't play the angry lady with me," Mame said casually. "I know you're ready to turn your life over to Denver. But have you thought about how it will end?"

She stared at the woman. "What do you mean?"

"I think you know," she said. "It will end with Denver with a bullet in his back or his head and you left to mourn him."

"You supply him with the gaming room." she accused.

"I'm in business," Mame said crisply. "If he wants to rent a place to gamble that's strictly a business proposition."

"Even though you know he may be killed there one day?"

Mame smiled grimly. "What you don't understand is that we know the risks, Denver and me. And we want to take them because that's what makes our lives worth something."

"I'm willing to take the same risks!"

"That's because you don't realize what it will be like," Mame said. "You just don't know."

"Thank you," Clare said firmly. "I don't need your advice. I've had enough from all sides."

Mame shrugged. "Well, I've tried, kid. Remember that!" And she turned and began to confer with the girl about a choice of gowns.

Madame Ouida returned with the box containing Clare's purchase. "I hope you enjoy wearing it," she said.

Clare paid her and said, "I'm sure that I will," and then left as quickly as she could to avoid having any further conversation with Mame.

She tried to put these personal problems out of her mind as she had a light luncheon and then proceeded to Jefferson Myers office. The men had all arrived before her and she hoped the new outfit from Madame Ouida's was severe enough that they would not think her merely a frivolous female.

Jefferson Myers' chins were wobbling with slight nervousness as he greeted her and introduced her to the bankers. The three were arrayed on one side of the room while her father sat on the other where there was an empty chair, presumably for her. Jefferson Myers would be seated at his desk between them in the role of referee.

Although they ranged in size from small to tall, the three bankers were much alike. They were all sober-faced with gray beards, none had an extra ounce of flesh on their spare frames, and they did not seem to have any interests beyond a melancholy concern for their investments.

Jefferson Myers strived hard to be cheerful, and when all the introductions had been made and they were all seated, he cleared his throat and began to go over the situation.

He finished with, "In short, Mr. Thomas needs more steel and more funds to complete the line."

The tallest of the bankers frowned and asked, "Does he also not need more time?"

Milton Thomas replied, "If I can get the steel to the construction camp quickly enough, I think I can guarantee to complete the line according to contract."

The small banker said, "We hear the Great Western has an advantage over you. That they will reach Cheyenne first."

"Exactly," the middle-sized banker joined his comrades. "I may as well speak plainly. The Great Western's lawyer has approached us and offered to buy us out."

The tall banker nodded gloomily. "And with all the mishaps and the problems still to be solved, that is perhaps the safest way out for us."

Clare could contain herself no longer. She said, "Gentlemen, I have worked with my father in the field on this project."

The tall man looked bored. "What importance has that to us?"

"I want you to understand that I can speak with some experience. Experience as an engineer," she said. "We have taken big risks and made good progress. Our setbacks have been caused by outlaw raids, instigated most likely by the Great Western or someone acting for them."

"That's a serious accusation," the small banker warned her.

"I understand that," she said. "And I also know I do not have the evidence to back up these suspicions."

Her father gave her a troubled glance and then said, "My daughter may have presented this somewhat emotionally but the raids have not only cost us materials but some friends very dear to us."

Jefferson Myers nodded soberly. "True."

"Sentiment should not enter into our considerations," the middle-sized banker contributed.

"It's a matter of losses," the tall banker went on. "We feel the most likely way out is to cut our losses by selling to Great Western."

Clare spoke up again. "That will be the final and most calamitous loss!"

"What do you mean?" the tall banker asked irritably.

"The figure Great Western will offer you for a half-completed line will be in direct value to it's worth. And at the moment it is worth very little," Clare pointed out.

The small banker glanced nervously at the middle-sized banker and then at her. "Perhaps you can think of a better way."

"Give us the money needed for extra men and materials. We will strengthen our security and with any kind of luck in the weather we can complete the line as promised. It will take only a little while for you to make up the extra money along with all you have thus far invested."

Her father nodded. "My daughter is telling you the

obvious facts. If you back down now, you lose most of your investment. The gamble is surely worthy of a fighting try."

Jefferson Myers' chins wobbled with emotion. "I must cast my vote with Mr. Thomas and his daughter."

The bankers looked at each other and there were some whisperings among them. Then the tall one said, "We will take all this into consideration and announce our decision tomorrow morning. We must leave for Chicago in the afternoon."

"Thank you for hearing us, gentlemen," Milton Thomas said, rising. "We will leave to allow you to talk more freely with Mr. Myers."

"Good afternoon, gentlemen," Clare said in a firm voice.

The three bankers rose and almost in unison bade them, "Good afternoon."

Outside, Clare fumed. "After all we have gone through, they are ready to sell us out!"

"I think we may have persuaded them differently," her father told her. "I thought you were excellent in stating our case."

"I merely told them the truth," she said, still angry.

"Jefferson Myers is on our side," her father said. "I'm sure he will do all he can for us." He studied her new outfit. "I like your new clothes. Did you get them this morning?"

"Yes," she said. "I wanted to attend the wake in a proper sort of dress."

Her father smiled. "You did well."

She said, "I'm having dinner at the hotel tonight with Denver."

He pursed his lips, then said, "that is certainly better than going to that brothel. I ask you not to go to there again."

"The gambling room is quite separate."

"It is under the same roof," her father said sternly. "I beg of you not to go there."

"Very well," she said quietly. She knew his advice was wise. She had not told him of her rescue by the lawyer of the Great Western and she did not intend to. It would only upset him more.

In the afternoon she went for a short stroll along the wooden sidewalk. She was standing with her parasol over her head staring into the window of a hardware store which was featuring a display of tall grandfather clocks. These were newly imported and apparently a token of status to ranchers in the area.

"Considering a purchase, Miss Thomas?" a mocking male voice said from behind her.

She turned and found herself facing the dapper lawyer for the Great Western. She smiled and said, "Not at all. We have little use for such a timepiece in a construction camp."

"I hadn't thought of that," he admitted. "But surely you and your father have a home somewhere."

"We lived in hired rooms in Chicago," she said. "My father has been almost constantly travelling from one project to another. I have chosen to travel with him, so we have no need for a home base."

John Carter said, "Not the ideal life for a young lady like yourself."

"But I love the open. And I'm thrilled by my father's work. He's helping to conquer the West."

"You interest me," the lawyer said. "I find you a most unusual person."

"Perhaps this country attracts individuals," she said. "You have to be one to survive."

Carter smiled cynically. "Even so, many of us loners don't survive."

"That is part of it."

"The challenge," he said. "Your good friend the Denver Gent must know that. He is not likely to have a long life."

She was shocked by his frank statement. "Do you think it proper to say that about him?"

The slender man shrugged. "I don't mean only him. I'm thinking of most of us. We all are taking risks."

"I don't see those who hire outlaws to do their dirty work taking much risk," she said bitterly.

Carter eyed her thoughtfully. "I have been told you accuse the Great Western of doing such things. And so you must be now referring to me."

"If the shoe fits," was her reply.

"I regret you have such a low opinion of me," he said. "But even if I am guilty, you couldn't expect me to admit it."

"I suppose not," she said.

A small smile returned to his face. "In spite of our being in different camps, I would like to continue being your friend."

Relenting a little, she said, "You left me in your debt last night."

"I wouldn't want our friendship to be based only on that," he said.

"I'm sure, given time, we'll find other mutual interests," Clare said.

"Do consider this, Miss Thomas. The Great Western is a large company. While I am the lawyer for it based here in Denver, I do not know everything that happens in the management of the company."

"I'm sure that is true," she agreed.

"Nor am I involved in all the company's decisions. Especially those made in the field. I'm instructed to act in certain matters. And this I do."

She looked at him directly. "Such as making an offer to buy out the Intercontinental project?"

"Yes," he said. "While you may question the offer, it is being made honorably so far as I am concerned. A pleasant afternoon to you, Miss Thomas." He put on his bowler hat again and jauntily made his way down the street.

Clare watched after him with a small smile crossing her face. She had only one good reason to be grateful to him and many reasons to hate him, but she surprisingly was finding herself beginning to like him.

Chapter
Eleven

The Denver Gent provided Clare with a sumptuous feast in the same private dining room they had eaten in before. He wore a beautifully tailored black suit much like evening dress, only his string tie conflicting with the image of a gentleman attending some fine social event. She wore her white silk dress and together they attracted the usual interest when they met in the lobby.

Upstairs in the privacy of the small, ornate dining room, they faced each other across a table decorated with the finest silver, china, and flowers. The waiter who served them was both efficient and unobtrusive. Clare felt that if life could go on in this manner, she would be forever happy. But she knew that it could not.

As they neared the end of the meal, she rather

shyly asked him, "Have you thought about our discussion last night?"

"Yes," he said, staring down at his half-empty coffee cup.

"And?"

He looked at her earnestly. "I love you. Let's not worry over that. But am I capable of being the sort of man you should marry?"

"I think you could be."

"I know myself better than you or anyone else." he said. "Give me a ranch, a loving wife, and a family, and I'd probably become restless in a year or two and run away from it all."

She smiled. "I wasn't suggesting you become a rancher. I know that's not possible."

"Then you partly understand."

"I do, Denver. And I want to save our love. If you go on as you are, we'll both wind up lost and unhappy."

He said, "That needn't happen to you."

"If you should be killed or sent to prison it would ruin my life," she told him.

"Another man would come along."

"Perhaps," she admitted. "I might even marry him, but in my heart I would still long for you. I would never be a truly happy person."

Denver offered her a crooked smile. "You are placing a grave responsibility on my shoulders. Your future happiness!"

She reached across the table and touched her small hand on his. "It's too late to change that now."

"And your answer to it all is that I take over as head of security for the Intercontinental line?"

"Yes. If the project doesn't collapse. Right now my father is waiting for a decision."

He said, "Let us assume they go on and can still use me."

"Well?"

"It would mean my moving to the other side," he pointed out. "I've the reputation of being a gunman. I doubt if I'd win much respect as a law-and-order marshall."

"Ben Thompson has done it," she said. "And he had a record far blacker than yours. He's a respected marshall now."

Denver looked surprised. "How do you know about Ben Thompson?"

"I've heard some of the cowhands talk about him."

"Ben is a special case," Denver said. "He and his brother Billy were reputed to be the most dangerous gunfighters in the West. Ben made it a rule to let the other fellow fire first. He also tried to argue whoever it was out of settling their differences with guns. Thus when he fired, he had a verdict of self-defense on his side. He gambled that the other man would be so nervous he'd miss that first shot. Then Ben would fire and he never missed."

"But he's a marshall now and all that is forgotten," she insisted. "They say he's a good one."

Denver looked grim. "Still, the chances are that some other gunfighter will kill him one day to settle some old argument."

"At least he'll die a lawman and not a gambler."

"Give me a little more time," he begged her.

"If we go on with the construction you'll have to make a decision soon."

"Mame set me up in the room. It's a big part of her business. I don't want to let her down."

"Someone else could take over."

He smiled. "You underestimate my special talents."

"I don't," she said. "But there are others who would be glad of the opportunity to run the room."

"We'll see," he told her. "Just now I'm due back there."

She looked at him with troubled eyes. "Suppose that there is an argument tonight. That someone draws a gun on you. Just one lucky shot and that would be the end for us."

He stood up and held his arms out for her. "The risk is small," he said.

Clare rose and went to him. "I pray that is so!" she whispered before his lips had found hers and he held her in a long, loving embrace.

When he released her, he said, "I'll be thinking of this moment all evening."

She smiled. "You'll be thinking mostly of a good poker hand."

He put an arm around her as they started to the door. "I like you for your frankness," he said.

"When will I see you again?"

He halted a moment. "I have the ideal time planned. Tomorrow night the new Denver Hotel is opening over on State Street. Just about everyone is going. There's a dance and plenty of food. I want to take you."

"What about your game?"

"I'm closing it down so we can be together and I can waltz around the ballroom and show you off to everyone."

"Will you call for me?" she asked.

"I think you'd better come with your father or Jefferson Myers. They are both bound to be invited."

"Then I'll meet you there?"

"Yes," he said. "I may be a little late arriving. There's a gambler in town called Blackie Mason. I've promised to play him in the afternoon. Big stakes! We might play right through until the evening."

Clare felt a chill at his account of the game and asked, "Do you have to sit down at the table with him?"

"Yes. A matter of honor."

"It sounds as if he's looking for trouble."

"He's after big money," Denver said. "He's had a strong run of luck in every town he's hit up here. He wants to make his big win here."

"And if he doesn't?"

"He loses."

She said, "A man like that won't lose without anger."

"That's why I'm giving myself plenty of time to play the game. If it goes against either of us, there can be no complaints that the loser wasn't given a chance to recoup. It might work to my advantage as well as his."

She looked up at him. "I'll worry until I see you at the dance tomorrow night."

He touched his lips to her temple. "You mustn't," he said and they went downstairs. She saw him to the door where a carriage was waiting for him.

When she went back inside, John Carter was standing facing her with a look of admiration. He said, "What a remarkable change that dress makes. Ordinarily you are just an attractive girl; now you're positively beautiful!"

She smiled at his flattery. "You are proficient with words, Mr. Carter. I can imagine you would do well in a courtroom."

"Thank you," he said. "May I buy you a drink? The bar is almost empty. I'm sure we can find a quiet corner."

She decided there would be no harm in accepting his invitation. Then she would go up to her room and read for a while. Her father was dining somewhere with Jefferson Myers, debating what might be done if the bankers withdrew their support.

She smiled at the lawyer and said, "I would enjoy a glass of sherry."

"They have some fine sherry here," he assured her and offered his arm to show her in. He led her to a table in a corner far from the bar.

After they had ordered their drinks she said, "Will you be here in Denver long?"

"I don't know," he said. "It depends."

"On whether the Intercontinental accepts your offer and closes down operations?"

With a small smile, he said, "So you didn't really have to ask me those questions. You know."

"Yes," she said. "But I don't know the outcome."

"I expect we shall, soon enough," Carter said. Their drinks were served and he raised his glass. "A toast to a lovely lady, whatever way it goes."

"Thank you," she said. "Considering the raids we've suffered, I should hate you for harassing us. But it's my misfortune to find myself liking you."

"My good fortune," he said, his face showing pleasure. "I pride myself in being a shrewd opponent, but

252

I can honestly tell you that these attacks you mention were instigated by people other than myself. I have heard rumors of them but I had no hand in them."

Clare smiled. "I want to believe that."

"Please do," he begged her. "I take it you had dinner with the Denver Gent?"

"Yes."

"He's a lucky man."

"I hope he always retains his luck," she said with a hint of uneasiness.

As she spoke two men entered the room and went up to the bar. One of them immediately attracted attention. A big man without fat on his frame and standing a foot taller than his companion, he was dressed entirely in black, including a black Stetson. With his small, black Vandyke beard and tiny mustache, the total effect was satanic.

John Carter noticed the big man had caught her attention. He said, "Just arrived this noon on the train. His name is Blackie Mason; he's a gambler."

She gave a small gasp. So this was the opponent Denver would be facing tomorrow. She had had grim premonitions about the game and they were only increased now that she'd seen the man, who was more menacing than anything she'd imagined.

She said, "Denver is playing a special game with him tomorrow."

Carter gave a soft whistle. "So that is why Blackie is here. You know he's been on a big winning streak?"

"So I've heard."

"He could clean the Denver Gent out."

"Denver has to play with him. He can't refuse."

"I know," Carter said watching the men at the bar. "And it's too bad. Blackie has an evil reputation, and he also has a gang of followers who travel with him. The sort who like to cause trouble."

"I'm sure Denver is aware of the risk," she said, not wanting to let her fears be known.

"Let us hope so," the slender man said. And then he changed the course of the conversation by asking, "Are you planning to attend the opening of the Denver Hotel tomorrow night?"

"I'd like to go," she said. "Denver can't take me. But I may be able to persuade my father or Jefferson Myers to escort me."

"You needn't depend on them," he told her. "I'm going and I'll be happy to see you safely there and back."

She smiled. "Denver has promised to meet me there."

The lawyer shrugged. "Then I'll take you over and you can join him when he arrives."

"That's generous of you."

"I'll be delighted to share your company for even a part of the evening," he assured her. "We should go about nine—that's when the festivities begin."

"Then I'll come down when I'm dressed," she said.

"And I shall be waiting," he promised. "If my enemies were always like you it would be a pleasure!"

They left the room shortly after it began filling. On the way out, Clare heard the giant Blackie ordering drinks for half a dozen or so who were gathered around him at the bar. His henchmen no doubt.

She had barely returned to her room when her

father came and wished her goodnight. She read a little but could not keep her mind on the printed pages; crossing her thoughts were terrifying visions of Blackie Mason. His manner at the bar had been bullying and unpleasant. Denver would have a hard time with him.

After breakfast the next morning she and her father made their way to the office of Jefferson Myers. The fat man showed them in at once and she could almost tell by his air of delight that all had gone well.

"Dear friends, we have been rescued," he announced. "Our bankers have decided against dealing with Great Western."

Milton Thomas sighed in relief. "I can only say they've acted wisely."

Myers smiled at Clare. "It was you, my dear, who did them in. You made it clear it was either gamble for the big stake or lose almost everything. They've decided to gamble."

"Wonderful!" she said. "When will the money and supplies begin to flow?"

"The money will come almost at once," the stout man said. "The supplies may take several weeks but no longer. We will get the steel we need!"

"Then the viaduct will become a reality," Clare's father promised.

"It was touch and go," Myers confessed. "Those fellows think only of profit."

"They can make plenty when the line opens," said Clare.

"The run to Cheyenne will be popular. No question," he agreed.

"So?"

"We shall have to collect what supplies we have on hand and send them to the camp," Myers said.

Milton Thomas nodded. "Yes. I shall remain here for a day or two longer and pick up every scrap of material I can."

"You won't find much," Myers warned him. "The Great Western people have been scrounging as well. They are tight for supplies along with us."

Clare said bitterly, "And we haven't made attacks on them."

"They lost this round," Myers pointed out. "I don't think John Carter was too upset. He gets paid whichever way it may go. But it's only a round in a fight that isn't over."

Clare said, "There's the added security force we need. I hope Denver will agree to head it."

"Do you really think he will?" her father asked.

"Yes. I feel I'm finally winning him over."

Jefferson Myers' chins rippled with glee. "That could be another plus for our side!" He pounded his fist on the table. "I say we are going to make it! We'll get to Cheyenne first!"

"We'll make a good try," Clare's father said. And he told her, "As soon as you have definite word from the Denver Gent, send him to me."

"I will," she said. "I expect to see him at the opening of the new Denver Hotel tonight. They have a dance scheduled with special food and drink."

"Is he taking you?" her father asked a little tautly.

"No," she said. "I'm going with John Carter. Unless either of you gentlemen wish to escort me?"

"Not with my injured arm," her father said, indicating the sling in which it still rested. "I've been moving about too much as it is."

"I shall be there," Jefferson Myers told her. "But as a major stockholder I'll be going early for a special dinner."

"Then I'll go with John."

"You astonish me," her father said. "You're making a close friend of the Great Western's lawyer?"

"I like him. The quarrel we have is not a personal one, it is between the two companies. Let us keep it at that level."

"An excellent thought, my girl," Myers said. And he told her father, "You are to be congratulated, Milton, for having a daughter with such intelligence and spirit!"

As the day wore on and the time for the poker game between Denver and Blackie Mason arrived, Clare felt tense and depressed. From the start she'd worried about this confrontation, and now it was at hand. She wished she could go stand by the table with the man she loved. But she knew this wasn't possible; she could only wait and hope.

Later on, dressing for the party provided a diversion. She chose to again wear the white silk—few people had seen it and those who had were strong in their praise of it—and she spent some time arranging her hair in a series of ringlets. Finally she put on a black velvet shawl and made her way to the lobby.

John Carter, elegant in a pale gray suit, was waiting for her. He tipped his matching top hat and offered her his arm. "On to the party!" he said happily.

257

The Denver Hotel was composed of brick and wood and stood four-stories high. Supposedly the latest thing in hotels, it boasted two special suites and some fifty rooms. The lobby had many glass windows and was large, carpeted, and imposing. To the left of the lobby was the bar where many of the locals and visiting cowpokes had gathered, and to the right was the ballroom.

The elaborately decorated ballroom was filled with dignitaries, top-level businessmen, and their guests meeting to mark the occasion. An orchestra was already playing on a small stage, but dancing had not yet begun. People were lined up at the long buffet table selecting from an astounding array of fine food.

When Clare had divested herself of her wrap, she and John Carter joined the line and afterwards took their plates to a table not far from the orchestra.

"Lobster!" John Carter said, lifting up a claw. "It must have cost them a penny for all this."

"It's a lovely hotel," she said gazing around at the well-dressed men and women. "They'll get all the plush trade."

"That's the idea," Carter agreed. "And if their food stays at this level, they'll have no problems."

By the time they finished their meal, the dancing was underway. So Clare found herself having the first dance with John Carter. Though he was an excellent dancer, she found her mind wandering as she worried about Denver's absence.

Suddenly spotting Jefferson Myers standing on the sidelines with his wife, she said, "I must speak with Mr. Myers for a moment."

They went over and Myers introduced his wife to

Clare and John Carter, saying, "This is truly the event of the season! Your father ought to have come, arm or no arm!"

"I agree," she said, smiling. And glancing towards the entrance she said, "The Denver Gent promised to meet me here. I'm surprised he's so late."

Myers leaned close to her and in a conspiratorial tone, said, "I can explain that."

"Please do," she begged, leaving John Carter to entertain the buxom Mrs. Myers.

"You know he was playing the notorious Blackie Mason this afternoon," Jefferson Myers said.

"Yes. I've been worried."

"I don't blame you. Blackie is a vicious type. The game went against him today and he and the Denver Gent had a fight across the table."

She gasped. "Gunplay?"

"No, just words, but the wrong kind! Blackie accused Denver of cheating. But he could prove nothing, so after a while he sat down to play again. The game should be over by now."

"Unless they quarreled again and it developed into a gunfight," she said in a tense voice. "Something told me he ought not to have played with that Blackie."

John Carter touched her on the arm and with a smile, said, "You need worry no more. Denver just walked in."

Her spirits rose at once and she turned to welcome Denver who, elegant in a black evening suit, was marching across the room towards her. He looked as assured and handsome as she'd ever seen him.

Coming up to her, he apologized. "I'm sorry I'm so late."

"As long as you got here," she replied. "John has kindly seen me safely through the buffet and the first dance."

John Carter bowed and said, "And now that Denver is here, I shall turn to the pursuit of some of the other lovely ladies."

As Denver watched him walk away, he said, "I like him."

"So do I," Clare said. "Do you want some food?"

Denver shook his head. "No. But I would like to dance and this is a waltz," and he guided her onto the floor.

He led her around swiftly to the fast-moving music, his large, graceful steps and strong lead making the dance easy and pleasant for her. They moved about the floor more quickly than most of the other couples and she was exhausted by the time the dance was over.

"The Viennese waltz can be too tiring," she said, still breathing heavily from her exertions.

"We'll rest for a little," he said and led her to a spot where they could talk. Then he admitted, "Things went badly."

"I heard about it," she said, studying him with concern. "That Blackie accused you of cheating."

"No good came of it," the gambler said. "He half-apologized and I agreed to go on with the game again."

"And?"

"It wasn't his day. He lost heavily."

"He must have been in a rage!"

"He was. We only stopped playing about an hour ago. He walked out without saying a word, and he left a tidy lot of money behind him."

Her eyes were anxious. "Do you think he'll make more trouble?"

"I doubt it," Denver said. "The game was on the square. He's a bad loser."

"He always has a crowd of followers," she said worriedly.

"Most of them are harmless," Denver said. "But Blackie is not to be trusted."

"I knew you shouldn't have played with him!"

His handsome face broke into a smile. "They're playing a fast-step. Let's not miss it!"

So they went out onto the floor and began dancing again, and for a time it seemed that all was going to go well. Then as they finished a mazurka and came off the floor, Clare saw the evil-faced Blackie standing with two other men in the doorway of the ballroom, gazing around as if he were looking for trouble.

Denver saw him at the same moment and with his eyes on the door, told her, "You stay here for a little. He may be looking for me."

She clutched his arm. "You mean gunning for you?!"

"Maybe," he said, his eyes fixed on Blackie as his hand went inside his tailcoat to touch the holster under his left arm and make sure all was in readiness.

"Not here!" she gasped. "He wouldn't dare!"

"I'll have to find out, that's certain," Denver said. "You stay a distance from me."

"Denver!" she said, frightened as she'd never been before.

He escaped her hold and slowly marched across the dance floor to the entrance where Blackie was standing. All in the big room were now aware that something was going on between the two men. Some hurriedly left with their ladies by a side door. But at least a third remained to watch, though keeping a healthy distance away from the spot where the two would meet.

Blackie now decided to come forward and meet Denver. Clare felt she might faint, when a supporting arm was placed around her and she heard the voice of John Carter. "It will be all right," he said softly. "Blackie is no match for Denver when it comes to handling a gun."

Blackie and Denver were now facing each other with perhaps three feet between them. Blackie curled his lip in disgust and said, "The great Denver Gent who's down to being a pimp and a card shark in a brothel!" He spoke loud so his words rang around the room.

Denver's handsome face paled. "You're drunk, Blackie," he said. "You're spoiling the party."

The big man sneered. "I want everyone to know you cheated me today!"

There was a ripple of shock at the accusation. Denver said, "No man has ever called me a cheat and lived!"

"I'm calling you one now."

Denver stared at Blackie for a long moment. Then he said, "I think this can best be settled outside.. You have a second?"

Blackie shook his head. "We won't settle this with guns; that would be too easy for you!"

"I want satisfaction," Denver told him. "Either apologize or we settle it another way."

"I was the one cheated," Blackie told him. "I'll call the terms."

"I don't care who calls the terms," Denver said. "What are they?"

"A duel in the dark in one of the upstairs rooms. With bowie knives!"

This again caused a murmuring in the room. Clare could not believe what she was seeing and hearing. She whispered to John Carter, "That Blackie is insane!"

"No, but he is an expert with a bowie knife. He's left a trail of dead man in his wake, all of them knifed," John said tensely. "He's tricking Denver into using his weapon."

Denver nodded slowly. He said, "A fight to the draw in the dark with bowie knives!"

Blackie called one of the men with him over. "Show him the knives," he said.

The henchman unwrapped a cloth from them and Clare could see the fifteen-inch long, gleaming steel weapons. The thought of what they could do sickened her.

Denver turned and called John Carter over. "You go with Blackie's man and select the room. Make sure it's empty and no other weapons are stashed in there."

John nodded and went off with the man who'd produced the knives. Blackie moved back to the entranceway and stood talking with his other henchman. Jefferson Myers, who had remained in the ballroom through the incident, now rushed up to the orchestra stand.

"Play, boys!" he commanded them in his high-pitched voice. "And keep on playing!"

The orchestra, who had been huddled together, slowly took their proper places and at the signal of the leader began a lively polka. Myers was the first to lead his wife out onto the floor and gradually others followed. Clare went up to Denver who had moved over by the door.

"You mustn't let him taunt you into this madness," she pleaded, tears in her eyes.

"There's no other way," Denver said bleakly. "I wish I could have spared you this."

She glared angrily at the nearby Blackie arrogantly smoking a big cigar and declared, "He'll murder you! That's the revenge he wants for losing all that money."

"I realize that," Denver said. "But I can't back away from him."

"At least it should be a duel with guns!"

"The bowie knife is his weapon," Denver said, his tone grim. "That's why he wants it this way."

"Will he listen to me?" she asked.

Denver smiled down at her sadly and took her hands in his. "You know better than that! You warned me something like this would happen. You were right."

"It's like deliberately allowing yourself to be killed," Clare said brokenly. "Give him back his money! You don't need it!"

"It's beyond the money now," Denver said. "I have to prove myself. He's left me no choice."

The music continued but the dancers grew fewer. Jefferson Myers came over to where they were standing, his many-chinned face wet with perspiration.

"I've done all I can to keep things moving," he said. "Is the fight on?"

Denver nodded. "Yes."

The fat man glanced fearfully in the direction of Blackie. "Be careful with him. He's full of trickery!"

"I know all about Blackie," Denver said.

John Carter returned with the other man trailing him. He looked pale as he said, "We've settled on a room. Head of the stairs on the second floor. I've gone over it. There's nothing hidden there. We've moved the furniture to the walls."

Denver nodded. "I'm ready whenever he is."

Carter hesitated. "Why not toss for weapons? It's not too late. You'd be better off to stick with guns."

"He called the terms," Denver said. "I'll meet them."

"As you say," the lawyer said and conferred with Blackie's second.

Clare was numb with terror, aware that she was a participant in a macabre ritual which had been repeated many times before. An accepted form of murder in which two men fought to the death, the law turned away and pretended not to see, and the frightened spectators and those close to the principals retreated to the sidelines.

She had always been fearful of what might happen to Denver. But she had never visualized it happening in this fashion. Her nightmares had been of someone stalking him at the gaming table. But this was different! The mere idea of two men attacking each other in a dark room was madness! Blackie had tricked Denver into this insanity by publicly insulting and taunting him. Such was the code of these gunmen that Denver could not ignore the obvious move to lure him into an uneven struggle. For Blackie was a known master of the bowie knife!

Denver turned to her and said, "Wait for me!" Then he took her in his arms and kissed her gently. When he let her go he and John Carter joined Blackie Mason and his second, and they all proceeded up the stairway to the second floor.

Jefferson Myers had left his wife in some safe place and now remained at Clare's side to support her. They, along with about a dozen others, all men with the exception of Clare, followed the duelists up the stairs. They halted partway as the door of the room facing the landing was opened. There was another brief conference among the principals in the hallway.

Clare whispered to Myers, "Can't you get the marshall to stop this?"

"Too late now," he told her. "The law never interferes in these things anyway."

She gazed up again and saw that Blackie and Denver now had the knives in their hands. Holding a lamp, Carter led the way into the room and the two duelists followed him, taking their places on opposite sides of the room. Then Carter came out, and placing the lamp in the hall, he closed the door and stood waiting with Blackie's second, a sober look on his face.

Clare closed her eyes and pressed close to Jefferson Myers. "He'll be murdered!" she sobbed. "And for what?"

"A code, my dear," Myers said. "This is what they live by."

"And die by!"

"Easy, Miss Thomas," he placated her. "Denver is

supple and younger than Blackie. He'll make no easy victim!"

"How long does it last?" she asked, her eyes blurred with tears.

"Until one of them is so seriously injured that he can't continue," Myers answered.

There were mutterings among the rough men gathered waiting on the stairway; some of them gave her curious stares. It was not the place where they expected to see an attractive, young woman. John Carter had turned and was staring anxiously at the door. The ugly henchman of Blackie Mason had his hand on the gun in his hip holster as he also watched.

"Why doesn't John Carter throw open the door and stop it?" she exclaimed.

"No chance," Myers said. "A single flash of light might give Blackie the advantage he needs to slit Denver's throat!"

She bent her head and gasped, "Don't!"

"Sorry," he apologized. Then he said tautly, "I think I saw the door handle turning!"

Clare looked up, every nerve in her body strung out to the point of pain. Jefferson Myers had been right. She saw the door handle move and then very slowly the door opened and it was Blackie who slowly stepped out!

The big man had a strange, triumphant look on his face and he stood there very steady for just a few seconds before he fell forward onto the carpeted floor and the knife could be seen protruding between his shoulder blades.

Then Denver appeared, his cheek slashed and bloody, supporting himself by leaning against the

267

doorframe as he gazed down at the prostrate Blackie.

John Carter at once went to Denver's side and checked him for injuries, while Blackie's henchmen bent over and examined the motionless outlaw.

He looked up and announced, "Blackie's dead!" And he stood and glared at the still exhausted Denver saying, "It wasn't an even fight and it ain't over for you yet!" With that he callously left Blackie's body to push his way down the stairs through the onlookers.

There were no shouts of pleasure at Denver's victory. No outward signs of approbation. Two of the onlookers rather reluctantly came forward to pick up the body and take it downstairs to some more private place.

Except for Jefferson Myers and John Carter, everyone went back down the stairs to the ballroom. Sounds of people returning and the orchestra playing again announced that the crisis had ended.

Clare rushed up to Denver, accompanied by Myers. "Are you safe except for that cut?" she asked.

Denver nodded. "Yes."

John Carter said, "Well done! I wasn't sure you could manage him."

"He was overconfident and half-drunk," Denver said. "After the first few minutes he was stumbling around like a frustrated bull."

The lawyer said, "You must get that cut looked after and then get out of here."

They all went down to the manager's office off the lobby. The manager, an agitated, bald man in evening dress, brought them hot water, a bandage, and some tape.

"I must ask you to leave the hotel, Denver." he said.

"We cannot tolerate any more violence here!"

John Carter, who was cleaning up the cut on Denver's cheek, gave the irate manager a bleak smile. "Don't complain, Crombie. The story of this fight will be on the wire services tomorrow and every paper in the United States will be running a yarn on the new Denver Hotel!"

"We do not wish to be known as the center for outlaw duels," the manager said angrily. "You will not be welcome on the premises again. Any of you involved in this affair." He gave Clare an ugly glance.

Clare, angered by his manner, said with some spirit, "Denver did not look for this quarrel. A drunken Blackie Mason was allowed in here to threaten him. Your help should not have allowed him in."

The manager scowled. "I do not care to argue with you, whoever you are!"

Denver's cheek was clean and the bleeding had been staunched. He now seemed much his regular self as he thanked John Carter and then told Jefferson Myers, "You'd better look after Clare. I'll be on my way."

The fat man held up a hand. "You mustn't go out there alone. You heard what Blackie's man said. His gang are going to be shooting for you!"

The manager exclaimed, "Well, he certainly can't stay here!"

Myers' chins wobbled with indignation. "I happen to be a shareholder in this hotel and I say he can remain here as long as he pleases!"

The manager gaped at this and said nothing more.

John said, "I'll go ahead to the livery stable and get a horse for you, Denver. You and Clare leave by carriage from the front door. The outlaws won't challenge you there; they'll wait until you're driving through the dark streets."

Denver said, "What is your plan?"

"Instead of driving Clare to the Pembrook Hotel, go straight to the stable just across the street. I'll have a saddled horse waiting for you. You can get out of town before they guess what you are up to."

Denver nodded. "It sounds good!"

Clare called out to John as he started out, "Have two horses ready and saddled. I'm going with him!"

The lawyer hesitated. "You'd better not! You're not even dressed for it!"

"I can manage," she promised him. "I'm riding with Denver!"

Jefferson Myers looked at her in despair. "How will I ever explain this to your father?"

Chapter
Twelve

Denver spent a few futile moments arguing with Clare against going with him. But he was no match for her now; she had been through too much and was in her most reckless mood. Jefferson Myers quickly called a carriage for them and Denver made a show of driving it to the Pembrook Hotel.

"See any sign of Blackie's crowd?" he asked her.

"A single horseman is staying behind us," she said. "It could be one of them."

"We turn here," Denver told her and quickly reined the horses and guided them down an alley.

She looked nervously behind them and said "I don't see anyone following now."

"We'll be at the livery stable in a minute," he said. "If John has done his work the horses will be waiting."

"Then we can move more swiftly!"

He gave her a pleading look. "Please remain here with John. You shouldn't go with me!"

"Sorry," she said firmly. "I'm taking no more orders. I'm going with you!"

"You'll be a target in that white gown," he warned her. "I expect Blackie's men will be after us."

"I have money with me," she said, resolutely. "I'll buy one of the stablehand's clothing!"

Denver couldn't resist laughing in spite of their danger. "I don't believe you!"

She was absolutely serious. When they reached the stable, John Carter was there with two horses saddled and ready. As they jumped out of the carriage, Clare approached the smaller, thinner saddleboy holding a dun mare and said crisply, "I'll give you ten dollars for your clothes!"

The boy's freckled face showed disbelief. "For this old outfit?"

"Yes! Make up your mind fast!"

The boy looked at the other stablehand doubtfully and said, "I ain't got nothing else to wear!"

"Your friend can find something," she urged him.

The other lad holding a chestnut horse nodded eagerly, "Sure, Buck, I can get you something from my place."

"I ain't got on anything underneath!" the smaller boy lamented.

"Don't worry about it, I'm not modest," Clare told him. "Come around back and we'll change. You can wear my petticoat until he gets you other clothes!"

Denver and John Carter heard this with stunned amusement. The only thing to spoil the humorous side of it was the knowledge that somewhere out in the dark streets, Blackie's gang would be waiting to shoot them down.

Clare literally pushed the surprised youth into one of the nearby stalls and began divesting herself of her clothes. They stood back to back and he handed her his things and she passed him the petticoat. In a few minutes she was transformed into a stablehand in loose woolen trousers, worn boots, a dirty flannel shirt, and a brown floppy hat which hid her face very well. She turned and saw the unhappy stableboy standing there naked to the waist and wearing her petticoat.

She picked up her purse, handed him the ten dollars, and stuffed her money and the jewelery she'd been wearing into a trousers pocket. With a smile, she told him, "You can have the pocketbook as well!" And she ran out to join Denver.

"You look wonderful!" John Carter said, amazed at the transformation.

"I still would like to go alone," Denver warned her.

"I'm going," she said. And Denver helped her up onto the dun and then mounted the chestnut.

Denver waved to John and said, "Thanks!"

"Good luck," he said with a small smile, adding, "To both of you!"

Denver took the lead along the side street and warned Clare, "Crouch low in the saddle!"

"I will," she promised, fear beginning to surge through her again as she realized that within the next few minutes both she and Denver could die from bullets from Blackie's gang.

Denver urged his chestnut along at a fast clip and she kept close with the dun mare. Then they were forced to turn out into the main street which led directly to the backwoods road and the trail beyond.

She bent low over the dun, knowing that each second their danger increased. She scarcely dared breathe as she urged the steed on.

Then from an alley there burst four riders, and just a glance told her they had guns at the ready and were going to follow.

"This is it!" Denver shouted, urging his chestnut all out.

Clare spurred the dun and cried out to encourage it to move faster. The horse responded as the first shots rang out behind them, and she was sure the bullets were whizzing close by their heads.

Denver turned in the saddle and aimed at their pursuers. He fired three times and shouted to her, "I've winged the leader! Keep moving!"

"Yes," she shouted, not certain he would hear her as two more shots came from behind along with the pounding of the horses' hooves.

"Follow me when I turn short to the left," Denver cried. And almost as he spoke he did this, reining the chestnut cruelly so that it reared up in shock and anger, then pounded off into the bushes.

Clare managed the same stunt with more difficulty and found herself beside him in the shadows. The horses were perspiring and stamping restlessly despite their holding them in taut rein.

Then two riders came clamoring by and Denver carefully aimed and winged them both. Seeing one toppled from the saddle and the other cling wildly to his arm as his frightened horse reared around in a circle, Denver nodded to her and urged his horse out onto the road again with her following. The two remaining members of the gang made no attempt to

halt them, too occupied were they in looking after
their own injuries.

Clare and Denver rode on swiftly, their horses'
hooves clattering through the silence of the night.
When they were a safe distance from town and their
pursuers, Denver brought his mount to a halt and
waited for her to come up to him.

He leaned forward in the saddle and taking her
hand in his, drew her close for a kiss as the horses
stirred uneasily. "You were wonderful!" he told her.

Her smile was bleak. "I nearly fainted from fright."

"There was no sign of it."

"What now?" she asked.

"I'll have to get you to the construction camp," he
said. "I think it best to follow the trail we took last
time. We can stop at the shack in the woods for the
night and proceed in the morning."

"You know best," she told him, filled with triumph
and joy at their survival.

"I wonder," was his somewhat gloomy reply.

They continued on at an easier pace and within
two hours were at the same shack they had stopped
at when he'd rescued her. They dismounted, tethered
the horses, and watered them. Then they took the
blankets from the saddles and went into the low-roofed
structure.

"I remember this place," she said as he found a
candle, lit it, and set it out.

"There's always a cache of coffee and tinned meat
here," he said. "The ones using the camp make it a
point to leave some food for whoever comes along
next."

"We won't be able to do that."

"No," he said. "But I'll leave double when I come by next time. And we won't be using much of the supply, not like a crowd of cowboys."

He built a small fire outside and made them coffee, and they sat and relaxed as they enjoyed it. Denver glanced up at the dark sky.

"We were in luck. No moon or stars showing. That could have made the difference."

She marvelled, "We really escaped them!"

"And left them with something to remember," he said dryly.

She stared at him, her eyes bright. "I have never known such a night!"

Denver looked worried. "Don't tell me you relish danger."

"In a way," she said, "yes."

"I don't recommend it as a way of life," was his reply.

They finished the coffee, put out the campfire, saw that the horses were all right, and went into the make-shift shack to sleep. Clare knew they would not sleep immediately. The tension of the night had stimulated her so that she longed to feel Denver's arms around her and join her body with his.

The blankets were spread out and with a shy smile she removed the outer clothing she'd borrowed from the stableboy, then her undershift, so that finally she knelt there in the faint glow of the candle, a young woman of beauty in both face and body. Denver had already shed his clothes and he pressed her to him as they kissed hungrily. Then his hand caressed her breast and lowered to that place in her body which ached for him. They stretched out as they became one and were lost in the ecstacy of loving.

Again it was Denver who prepared breakfast in the morning, as Clare bathed in the nearby spring. She donned her rough stableboy's outfit and joined him at the campfire, enjoying the hardtack, canned bacon, and coffee as much as she'd relish a gourmet breakfast at the Pembrook Hotel.

The sun was shining and she wore a smile to match it as she sat next to him and said, "It's so wonderful to be alive."

Denver smiled. "Especially when it didn't seem we would be."

"I was sure Blackie would kill you. You should never have gone into that room with him."

"I would have broken the code."

"I call the code stupid, and all that happened last night a kind of madness."

"It's not your world," he told her.

She gave him a pleading look. "I don't want you to make it your world any longer."

"I have to go back to Mame's."

"No!"

"She'll expect me. Everyone will. Otherwise they'll think I'm hiding out afraid."

"I don't care what they think, you mustn't go back to that way of living again. This is your chance to make a break."

He sighed. "I wanted to get you out of danger. I really should have stayed and shot it out with them."

"You did," she said. "You probably killed one or more of them and the others were wounded."

"They'll still expect me to return."

"And I want you to come to the camp and take over the job of leading the guards."

"Do you think your father would really welcome me?"

She said soberly, "If we don't get better security we'll fail. They keep undoing the work we've completed."

"I'll think about it," he said. "First, let us get there safely."

Her eyes met his. "After last night do you still want to leave me?"

"No," he said. "I want to marry you. But it wouldn't be fair."

"I think it would be as fair as expecting me to go on giving my heart and myself to you without any prospect of our having a future together."

He said, "What about this new fellow?"

"Larry Brand?"

"Yes. Isn't he anxious to marry you?"

"He's proposed to me."

"That would be a good match."

Clare rose indignantly. "Is that your plan to be rid of me?"

He got to his feet. "I'd like to be with you always."

"You can be!" She went close to him.

He took her in his arms. "Temptress!"

She smiled. "Sometimes it's a woman's only weapon."

"You frighten me," he said and then kissed her.

Within a half-hour they were in the saddle again and heading through the wooded highlands which would eventually bring them to the construction camp.

The sun was blazing but the tall evergreens protected them as they rode along the twisting trail at a steady pace, halting only to water their horses and drink from the springs themselves.

At one of the stops, she asked, "When do you think my father will reach the camp?"

Tin cup of water in hand, Denver said, "I'd imagine he'll have to wait a few days before he gets enough supplies together and hires the workers he needs."

"So we should get there first?"

"Likely."

"He'll worry about me," she sighed. "But he knows I'll be safe with you."

Denver gave her a knowing look. "He may think you're safe but I don't see his dancing with joy because you came with me."

"I'll explain when I see him. He'll understand."

The handsome gambler smiled. "You have more faith in his generosity than I do."

"Because I know him better," she said.

"I can't picture him giving you away to me at a marriage ceremony," Denver warned her.

She laughed. "You needn't worry! I'll plan the whole ceremony and Jefferson Myers can give me away if Father refuses."

"I guess you would settle for something like that," he said, a little in awe of her.

"The easiest trail isn't always the best one. I like to blaze my own paths," she said as they got back up on their horses.

It was warming that when they finally reached the railway camp late in the afternoon, Old Hank was the first to greet her. He uttered a shout of joy and threw his hat in the air when she and Denver came riding up.

279

"You look like a boy in that outfit, Miss," Hank told her with delight as he helped her down from the dun.

She said, "You remember the Denver Gent?"

"Yep, I sure do," he said heartily as he took the bridles of both their mounts.

"Good to see you again Hank," Denver said cordially. "Take care of the horses. They've had a hard ride."

"Don't worry," he said. "I'll take care of them."

"What's been happening?" she asked him.

"Not much," the old man said glumly.

She sensed from his manner that he was concealing something. "Is Larry Brand keeping the work schedule?"

"Sort of," Hank said. "Not like when you and your father were here. But then none of us expected it would stay like that."

"Any more raids?"

"Nary a one," Hank said. "I guess they're waiting for you and your Dad to return."

"Probably," she agreed. "Does Larry return here each night?"

"About every other night," Hank said. "Most of the time Pedro is with him. Those two are as thick as thieves."

"Well, we do want them working well together," she reminded him.

Hank gave Denver a look of interest and said, "You reckon to be leaving with your mount tomorrow morning?"

"I'm not certain," Denver said. "You probably should have him ready."

"No," she broke in sharply. "You must stay here at least until my father returns."

Then she and Denver walked up to the executive car. She showed him to a guest compartment while she went to her own to bathe and put on new underclothes and a favorite yellow sateen dress.

It was time for the evening meal when she went out to meet Denver. He looked rested and refreshed. He told her, "I've been checking the camp again. It's an interesting setup."

"And it needs protection," she reminded him.

"I think four men who knew what they were doing could take care of most of your problems," Denver said.

"You must share your ideas with my father."

As they talked, Larry Brand came riding in. He left his horse at the corral and strolled slowly up to them. She could see his face take on a grim expression at seeing her with Denver. She hoped to make it easier for all of them by running forward and greeting him with a smile.

"Larry! I've been waiting for you!" she exclaimed, kissing him on the cheek and bringing him up to Denver. "You've met Denver, of course."

"Yes," Larry said shortly. Then he asked her, "What are you doing back ahead of your father?"

Embarrassed, she said, "I decided to ride here with Denver."

Denver spoke up, "I had some problems in town. I had to leave. She came with me."

"I'm aware of that," the young man said with some impatience. "Do you mean you were in trouble with the marshall?"

"No," she spoke for Denver quickly. "Nothing like that. I mainly took the opportunity to ride with him to bring you the latest word first."

"What is the word?" he asked.

"The project is going on," she said. "We've won."

Larry looked only modestly pleased. "The backers decided not to abandon the line?"

"Yes," she said. "And my father is rounding up materials and men now. He should be here with them tomorrow or the next day."

Larry said grudgingly, "That's good news. We need materials and we've been short of workers."

She smiled in Denver's direction and went on, "I have hopes that Denver is going to remain here and organize a protection group."

"We've had no more raids," Larry said.

"But we're bound to," she insisted. "Oh, I met one of the lawyers for the Great Western. He's very nice. His name is John Carter."

Larry looked uninterested. "It wouldn't mean anything to me. You should have told him to keep his raiders away from the camp."

"I talked to him about that and he denied any knowledge of it."

Larry was scornful. "You'd expect him to deny all knowledge of it."

"I think he was being truthful," she replied, fearing that Denver's presence was going to make him especially difficult for a while.

And she was right. Dinner that evening was an ordeal with a sullen Larry silent much of the time. Clare was grateful to him for all he'd done for her and her father, but she did not think he should be behaving so childishly. She wished that her father would come back soon as he had the authority to keep everyone in line.

She tried to make conversation at the table by asking him questions about the project. "Is the track all laid in the gorge area?" she asked.

"Pedro is finishing the last hundred feet or so of it now," Larry replied.

"He's turning out to be a good worker despite his ugly looks and evil reputation," she commented.

Larry frowned. "Who says he has an evil reputation?"

Caught off guard, she said, "I'm not sure. One of the workers."

"There are few of them whose pasts would bear checking," he said sourly. "Pedro is no worse than most of them."

"I'm sure my father is satisfied with your picking him," she replied.

Larry gave Denver a pointed look and said, "If he were a known outlaw that would be something else. There's no big price on his head."

"Nor on mine, I hope," Denver shot back with a sour smile.

Larry touched his napkin to his lips and stood up. "I wouldn't know about that," he said. And he strode out of the dining compartment.

"I'm sorry," she said to Denver. "I didn't think he'd resent you so much."

Denver smiled. "You can see that he does."

She sighed. "I suppose it is because it's so obvious that I'm in love with you."

"That could be."

"He'll have to get used to it."

Denver reminded her, "He's important to the project now that Harris Trent is dead."

"I think he'll remain with us no matter what. This has been a great opportunity for him and could lead to other jobs."

Denver said, "I think I'll take a stroll and talk to Hank about the boys he thinks might make good security bets."

"Do you want me to go with you?" she offered.

"No," he rose and kissed her on the cheek. "I think I might get better information if I talk to Hank on my own."

She smiled. "That could be."

He left and she remained sitting at the table. It seemed she might have won her point. That Denver might be going to remain as chief of security after all. She had to be careful that Larry didn't spoil everything with his jealousy.

A moment later Tom Lee came in wearing his apron and looking rather drawn; he had been doing the waiting as well as the cooking following his sister, Dora, being shot down by the raiders.

"Will I clear up now, Miss Clare?" he asked.

"Yes, please, Tom," she said, smiling.

As he gathered up the dirty dishes, he said, "Good to have you back, Miss."

"I'm glad to be back," she said.

He had the dishes stacked to take out but he held back. Then somewhat awkwardly, he said, "I've been waitin' for you to get back to tell you somethin'!"

"What is that, Tom?"

"I ain't been restin' good since what happened to Dora."

She sympathized. "I can understand that. I liked Dora very much. She's a loss to the camp."

He nodded glumly. "The fact is I'm goin' to leave."

"To leave?"

"Yep," he said. "I've thought it all out and I guess I'll head back to Denver."

"But why? We need you here."

He hesitated. "I ain't happy here."

"Because of Dora. But you'll remember her death wherever you may go."

"I know that," he said. "This is different."

"I'm afraid I don't understand," she said.

Tom eyed her unhappily. "I don't like the way it happened. I still don't understand it. I think something went wrong. I can't imagine Dora going out there like that. It weren't like her!"

Clare was startled, and staring at Tom, she asked, "Are you suggesting she may have met her death through some foul play on the part of someone here in the camp?"

"Mebbe," Tom said. "Anyways I don't feel so good here now. I keep wonderin' if someone got her out there where she'd be in danger. And who it was."

It was a devastating revelation. If the forlorn Tom was right, it meant someone in the camp had wished Dora dead. At once the name of Larry Brand flashed through her mind. He had wanted to be rid of her. But Larry was not the sort to kill over a thing like that. And he had made his peace with the girl before the raid in which she was killed. That ruled him out.

But maybe in the meanwhile Dora had taken up with another of the workers.

"Do you suspect anyone in particular?"

"No," Tom admitted. "That's part of what makes it so bad."

She sighed. "Were there any men in the camp she saw a lot?"

He shrugged. "She used to see Mr. Brand. But they broke up."

"I know that. Anyone else?"

"There could have been," he said, miserably. "Dora was a girl who liked fun. She wasn't one to sit around and mope. I expect a lot in the work crew knew her well enough to talk to her."

"So if there is any blame to place, it could be on almost anyone's shoulders."

"That's why I don't want to stay."

She said, "I understand your feelings, Tom. But I'd like you to remain until my father gets back and you talk to him about this."

"All right, Miss," Tom said. "I'll do that."

Clare felt sorry for the man, knowing how much his sister had meant to him. But the more she thought about it, the more certain she was that he was wrong in his suspicions. Dora was, like herself, an adventuresome young woman, and when the raiders had struck she'd gone out to help defend the camp. And she'd been unfortunate enough to be struck down by an enemy bullet.

She felt her father might be able to persuade Tom to remain, but only time would tell. She left the dining room and went out to stand on the grassy embankment in the fading light. It was then that Larry Brand came up to her.

His smile was sour. "I see Denver has managed to tear himself from you long enough to visit the corral alone."

Clare reproached him. "Larry, you mustn't show such jealousy."

"I don't like seeing you with an outlaw and a gambler, that's all," he said.

"Let me be the judge of whether he's fit company."

"If that's how you want it," Larry said. "But I don't think the workers will want him as head of security."

"I don't see why they should object."

"We'll find out if you appoint him."

"I hope you'll be on our side."

He spread his hands. "I try not to take sides."

"Yes," she said. "I seem to remember that's true. By the way, there's another complication."

"What now?"

"Tom Lee is threatening to quit. He has an idea someone here in the camp framed his sister so she went out to meet her death."

"That's mad enough to sound like Tom," Larry said with contempt. "He's not a good cook anyway. We might be better rid of him."

"I don't agree," she said. "I'm sure my father won't either."

"Then let him settle it when he returns." Larry said. "I'm wondering about us."

She stared at him. "Don't mention such things."

"And don't you play important lady to me," he harangued her. "If I were to pull out now, your father would never get that viaduct finished. No matter how many men or how much money they sent him."

She stepped back. "I don't know! I think he could manage!"

Now he took the opposite stand. "I didn't mean that, Clare. But I go a little crazy when I see you bringing Denver back here."

"I agree you're not being sensible," she told him.

"I'm not an easy mark like Harris Trent! You can't play games with me!"

"You're not above a few games yourself, Larry," she said firmly. "If you know what is good for you, you will make the most of this opportunity. It could open up a whole new world for you."

He eyed her with resentment. "You're still thinking of me as a worker because I came here as one."

"I'm telling you this is your big chance to lift yourself up permanently," she said. "Like others you suffered through the war. Father has given you a chance. Make the best of it."

Larry listened and then said quietly, "You're right. I'm sorry. I'll try to do better."

That night Denver came to her sleeping compartment and they were together again. Being with him helped ease her nerves which Larry Brand had badly upset. It seemed she moved from one scene of tension to another. She warned Denver that they could not openly sleep with each other when her father returned. He agreed that he had too much respect for her and her parent to bring about such a situation.

Larry rode off to the viaduct the following morning and Clare went down to the office and marked out the progress that had been made in her absence. While she was bringing the records up-to-date, Denver dropped by.

She looked up from the map she'd been marking and smiled at him. "Well, how are you making out?"

"I had another talk with Hank," he said. "And according to him, we need two security outfits. One here at the camp to guard main supplies and one at the viaduct where the bridge is being completed."

"What do you think?"

"It sounds sensible. I'd say you ought to have at least two guards on either side of the viaduct and three here."

She said, "Seven men, including yourself."

"That's right. And in addition to me, one of the men at the viaduct would need enough experience to be a leader."

"Did Hank suggest anyone?"

"He's given me a dozen names, but he warned me some might not want the guard work, and some I'd probably disqualify for one reason or another."

"Then your next step is to interview these prospective guards?"

"Yes," he said. "I guess I'll talk to the men here on duty at supplies first. Then I'll talk with some of the workers at the viaduct and at the gorge."

"Excellent," she said with a smile. "That means you are going to stay here."

His smile was wary. "For a while."

She went to him and kissed him and held him close. "I want you here always!"

"That's a long while," he teased her as he held her

in his arms. "But I will stay until the project seems in good shape. I don't like to leave you so dependent on Brand."

"And we will be if you go," she assured him.

"That's my chief reason for remaining," he said. "I don't like the way he behaves toward you or his general attitude around the camp."

"I gave him a lecture last night," she said. "I have an idea he's going to be better."

That afternoon she and Denver rode out to the site of the viaduct. It was coming along well with the spans on either side of the marshlands complete and only the more difficult arches out over the river and very high above it waiting to be completed and joined.

They sat on their horses and watched the men on the bridge far above working. They seemed the size of ants at that height. And the manipulations of giant timbers into place seemed nothing less than the engineering feats of the same clever insects. The derrick had been repaired and hoisted up again where it was once more serving them well.

Larry Brand was directing operations from an area near one of the main supports. Seeing them, he came over and said, "With the new steel arriving we should get the center span completed on time."

Clare nodded. "You've done well."

Denver asked him, "Is the major part of the construction timber of the sort you're placing now?"

"Yes. It is vulnerable to age and fire but it's easier to work with and quicker to come by. But we must have steel for the strategic points."

Clare told Denver, "You know we had one accident

here earlier. This end of the structure collapsed. It had been tampered with so that when we moved the derrick out over the weakened spot the next day it collapsed."

"That's why we should have twenty-four-hour guards here," Larry said, continuing to behave remarkably well in view of his surly attitude the previous day.

Clare had noticed this quality in him before and hoped that it was a good sign, not merely an example of his cleverly covering up his true feelings. She said, "That's why Denver is here. He wants to screen some of the present men for guards."

Larry frowned slightly. "You'll have to confine yourself to the ground crew. The workers on the bridge are specially picked and trained. I can't afford to lose one of them."

"I understand that," Denver said. "Do you mind if I chat with a few of the ground workers now?"

"Go ahead," Larry told him.

So Denver got down from the chestnut and went over to the work crew with Larry. Clare also decided to stroll around for a while. She tethered the dun and found herself heading to the small cemetery where the workers who'd been killed at the site were buried.

She stood by the rough marker over Harris Trent's grave and was amazed at how the green grass covered the mound as if it had always been there. How much had happened since they had all arrived at the construction camp to complete the railroad line! Who could have dreamed then that Harris would be dead now and she deeply in love with a man who'd recently come into her life. Or that Larry Brand would have risen from the ranks to make himself a principal in the project.

So lost was she in these thoughts that she didn't hear the footstep behind her. A hand touched her arm and when she turned it was to look into Larry's taut face. Without a word he drew her to him and kissed her.

She suffered the kiss and then pushed him away. "What does that mean?" she demanded.

His eyes met hers. "You should know! It's not the first time we've kissed."

"Larry, I can't encourage such conduct. We're working. I'm technically your boss. What if some of the men saw us just now?"

His lip curled in a smile. "Aren't you worrying mostly about the Denver Gent seeing us?"

"I wouldn't want that either!"

"And I know why," he told her.

"Larry, don't spoil it all, please!" she begged.

He raised a placating hand. "I'll behave," he promised. "But I want you to know I still haven't given up. I love you and one day you'll marry me."

She said, "Larry, I'm not in the mood for this!"

"I know," he said laconically. "Just remember, I can wait." And he walked away, leaving her alone amid the graves.

She was more thankful than ever that Denver was going to remain. Although it seemed to bring out the worst in Larry, at least it did not leave her at his mercy. With her father and Denver around, Larry wouldn't dare try to force himself on her, though he might if they were alone.

She was worrying about all this when Denver came striding up the hill to join her. She managed a smile and asked, "Have you finished?"

He nodded. "I've talked with most of them. So far I have about three good prospects."

"And you need three more?"

"Yes," he said. "Larry suggested we ride by the gorge on our way back to camp. Pedro has about a dozen other workers there. Some of the old hands."

"Fine," she said. "I'll show you the way."

They found their horses and set out on the shortcut to the gorge line by the back trail. It took them no more than twenty minutes this way as the crew were working on the end of the line nearest the viaduct.

They came out on the cliffs high above the spot where the workmen were putting down the final rails. Clare showed him how the ledge along the cliffs had been joined by manufactured ledges to form an even surface for the rails to follow.

As they leaned over the edge gazing down the dizzying depths to the ledge and the stream between the cliffs far below, she said, "This is where I almost tumbled to my death."

"And Larry saved you?"

"He acted quickly enough to grasp me. It was a miracle."

"No wonder he seems to think he owns you!"

"I am grateful but I don't think I need be that grateful," she said.

"It's a remarkable feat of engineering," he marvelled.

"My father's conception; Harris Trent carried it out against his will. But he was a major part of it."

"I remember him," Denver said. "Nice fellow."

"He was," she agreed. "Now we'll ride down the trail to the level where Pedro has his gang working."

When they reached the scene of activity, the fat Mexican was standing over his men. On seeing them he came up to greet them. He bowed in his usual fashion and showed his broad smile, but for all that Clare felt the chill along her spine which always came whenever she had to converse with him.

Sombrero in hand, he waved towards the crew. "The men are working hard! We're ahead of time!"

"So I understand," she said, forcing a smile. And then she explained what Denver wanted.

The fat Mexican nodded his thick head of coarse black hair vigorously. "There is no problem! You will come with me!"

Denver followed the broad-shouldered Mexican over to where the crew were working. Pedro gave them some instructions and they lined up for Denver to query.

As she waited, the foreman came slowly back to her and stood smiling in his menacing way. He said, "The Denver Gent is turning into a lawman?"

She nodded. "Yes," she said tautly.

He chuckled. "That is very funny!"

And she knew that beneath his overdone respect and his genial smile there had to be hostility. Just as she now felt that Larry Brand was barely concealing his mad ambition to take over the project and her along with it. The two men who remained so close were bound by ties of evil.

Chapter
Thirteen

When Clare and Denver returned to the camp that evening, they discussed the business of selecting the guards and this was the chief topic of conversation at the dinner table. Larry Brand did not show up for the evening meal, and Clare learned from Tom Lee and some of the others that he sometimes stopped overnight in the workers' camp at the viaduct site, particularly when some construction problem had to be worked on later than usual. Thus it did not strike her as of any importance that he was not there. In fact, she felt much less tense without his presence. And Denver seemed more at ease.

"How many likely men have you found?" she asked.

"Five," said Denver.

"And you need six?"

"We should have that many. And we need another

leader. I haven't found a man suitable for that role."

"There may be someone among the men my father brings from Denver," Clare said.

"I hope so," Denver replied. "I'd like to organize the guard right away. I can see how vulnerable you still are."

"And we've been lucky," she said. "There have been no raids lately."

"That's fortunate," he agreed. "But I think a little strange. I suspect they'll start again soon."

"The dangerous time has to be after the new supplies arrive. The Great Western will know about that from their Denver spies."

A smile crossed Denver's handsome face. "Meaning John Carter?"

"No," she said. "I trust John."

"He does work for Great Western."

"I don't think he betrays his principles for them," was her opinion. "I believe he acts as their lawyer and that is that."

"You're probably right," Denver agreed. "But there are lots of others with no such fine convictions."

"I know," she sighed. "What do you think of Pedro?"

"The fat Mexican boss?"

"Yes, that's him."

"The sort that could slit your throat and smile at you while he did it," Denver said.

"Exactly the way I feel about him," Clare agreed. "And yet he's Larry Brand's right hand man. Larry trusts him completely."

"A strange alliance," Denver mused. "The southern gentleman and the Mexican scoundrel!"

"I'm afraid of Pedro and I'm not sure I'm not also also afraid of Larry Brand."

Denver took her hand in his. "I wouldn't expect a spirited girl like you to have such thoughts."

Clare smiled weakly. "You think I'm imagining wrong where there is none?"

"I do. Pedro can't help his villainous looks and he works hard."

"Yes, that is so."

"Larry is obsessed with you. I can't blame him. So am I. And he thinks he should have special consideration because he saved your life."

The rest of the evening passed quietly and Clare went to bed earlier than usual. She lay awake for a time thinking. Denver seemed to be organizing the safety patrol they needed so badly, and perhaps her father would be returning in the morning with men and supplies.

At last she fell asleep and did not waken until the early morning. She washed and dressed and went to the dining area to have breakfast. She found Denver standing there and no sign of the table having been prepared for their morning meal.

She gave him a questioning look. "Where is Tom?"

"I don't know," Denver said. "I've only just arrived. He's not in the kitchen. I looked."

Clare sat down at the table. "He's left without telling us."

"You think so?"

She glanced up at him. "I'm sure of it. He told me he didn't want to remain here."

"Because of his sister's being killed here?"

"Yes," she said with a frown. "He felt very strongly about it."

"You can't blame him."

"But there was something else," she went on worriedly. "He seemed to think that Dora being shot wasn't the accident it seemed."

"Meaning what?"

Clare looked at Denver with troubled eyes. "He suspected that someone in the camp, I mean of the camp, deliberately exposed her to the raiders' bullets."

"Isn't that far-fetched?"

"I think so," she said. "But he got it into his head and so he wanted to get away."

Denver smiled. "And he has."

"Yes," she said. "Well, it won't take me long to make a breakfast for us. I don't know what the others will do."

"While you're getting our food ready, I'll go out and tell the boys they'll have to fend for themselves until we appoint a cook."

"They're not going to like it," she predicted. "Better say if we don't find anyone for the job I'll take it on temporarily."

Denver's eyes widened. "Isn't that a pretty big chore?"

"I'll manage!"

"Even with a new lot arriving? Plenty of mouths to feed!"

She smiled. "I'll locate a helper." And she stood on the car steps to watch him go the short distance and hear what he said.

Denver strolled to the spot where the workers had

their campfire and saw that coffee was being made. The dozen or so veteran workers showed curiosity on their weathered faces as they waited to hear what was going on.

He told them, "I'm sorry. It appears Tom Lee left the camp after dinner last night. Until we get matters straightened out, we will have someone else do the cooking. For this morning you'll have to fend for yourselves. I see you already have."

"We have plenty of coffee," a white-haired man by the fire said. "Can we pick up some bacon and eggs from the kitchen?"

Denver nodded. "Go get it. Miss Clare is there and she'll give you the food you need."

His news delivered, Denver started back to join her in the cook's quarters. Looking out the window, Clare saw Hank shout to him from down at the corral and gesture that he wanted to talk with him. She knew it would be about the missing cook and the old man's breakfast so she went into the kitchen and pulled out a slab of bacon and filled an iron dish with two dozen eggs. When Hank appeared at the door, she gave him the food and said, "I hope this will do."

"Will more than do, even though those cowpokes have powerful hearty appetites," he said, smiling, and went on his way.

Clare then began to prepare bacon and eggs for herself and Denver. Her back was to the car entrance and suddenly hearing someone come in, she turned and saw Denver and a shocked-looking Hank.

Denver came to her soberly. "Hank has some news."

She rubbed her hands on her apron and stared at the old man. "All right, Hank, what is it?"

"I just found Tom Lee," Hank said, nervously licking his lips.

"Where?" She had an onimous feeling as she put the question to him.

"I found him hanging from a tree back of the corral," Hank said. "He must have hanged himself sometime in the night."

Clare felt ill. Denver came to her and put an arm around her for support as he said, "You claimed he was depressed."

"Depressed," she agreed. "But I never dreamed he would take his life."

"That's what he's done," Hank said.

Denver turned to Hank. "I'll have coffee and then be down to help you with the body. Meanwhile you go to the boys and tell them and have something to eat and drink."

"Yep," Hank said. "I'll do that. Tom was mighty well liked by the boys. They'll be sorry." And he went out.

Clare gave Denver a resigned look. "What next?"

"It's too bad," he said. "Do you want anything to eat? A little coffee is all I need."

"I've made it," she said. And a little later they sat in the dining area with their coffee discussing the tragedy.

"You said he was talking wildly, blaming someone in the camp for his sister's death?" Denver asked.

"Yes," Clare said, her lovely face shadowed. "I suppose that was a warning of his coming mental breakdown."

"Likely. But you couldn't be expected to know that."

"I tried to reason with him," she said. "I begged him not to make any decision until my father came home."

"What did he say?"

"He said that he wouldn't."

Denver drummed his fingers on the table top and considered. Then almost casually he asked, "What if he didn't commit suicide?"

She frowned. "Hank found him hanged from a tree."

"He might not have done it himself! He could have been murdered."

Her hand came up to her lips and she murmured, "No, not that!"

"I don't say it happened," Denver said evenly. "I say it is a possibility."

"That would mean he was right in his suspicions," she said, feeling that chill sweep through her again. "And he was murdered to keep him quiet."

"It could."

She shook her head. "I can't believe it. He must have gone insane."

"That's just as likely."

Clare looked at him with eyes wide with fear. "When you let the body down, make a thorough examination of everything. See if there is any hint of foul play."

He nodded. "I will."

She was trying to think who might have a motive for such a crime. Inevitably she thought first of Larry Brand. But he had not returned to camp last night. Nor had Pedro Reilly. Both were away at the construction sites. With them eliminated she could only suppose that Dora may have had another lover among

301

the workers. Someone who'd kept quietly in the background, perhaps a spy in the camp working for the Great Western. And this unknown had decided he must kill Dora, who knew his secret, and then her brother, in whom she'd likely confided the information.

Clare was stunned by the way the pieces of the jigsaw fitted. The only piece missing was the identity of the murderer. She decided she could not keep thinking about such things and began preparing one of the enormous beef stews which Tom had regularly served the crew at noon. She was still working over the steaming pots when Denver came back.

She went outside to hear what he had to say. "I'm almost dead from the heat in there. Did you find anything?"

Denver looked frustrated. "I had a bad break. Hank let the body down before I got there so I wasn't able to check as I wanted to."

"Have you come to any conclusion?"

"From what I've been able to tell," Denver said, "it was a suicide rather than a murder."

She gave a relieved sigh. "I'm glad to hear it."

"No use making a case when it can't be proven," he said. "I was probably wrong in my conjecture."

"What about the burial?"

"Hank is fashioning a rough coffin now," Denver said. "We'll bury Tom right after the noon meal. Two of the boys have dug a grave near where Dora is buried."

"My father will be shocked," she said. "I do hope the supplies train reaches here before the funeral."

But it did not. Denver presided over the simple

service and the workmen stood by silently with saddened faces. When the grave was filled they walked away slowly and returned to their various duties.

Hank remained to mold the earth over the grave and as he went about the task he told Clare and Denver, "Sometimes it looks as if none of us is ever going to get out of here alive."

"I know how you feel," she said. "But we've almost finished and the work should go better after Father shows up with his reinforcements."

Denver and Clare were in the office when she suddenly looked up and standing very still, said, "I hear it in the distance!"

"The train?"

"Yes! Let's go out to meet it!"

They were standing cheering with the other workers when the supplies train came chugging to a halt just to the rear of the construction train. There were four cars on the engine, two of them flatbeds stacked with wooden timbers, and more importantly some gleaming steel rails and support beams!

The new workers hung out of the front cars and waved to the cheering group on the grass. After the train came to a full halt they streamed out the rear door of the second car.

Clare counted and had finished with about two dozen when her father stepped down from the first car entrance. She ran to throw her arms around him.

"Father!" she exclaimed happily.

"My dear! So you are alive and safe!" he said, holding her in his arms and kissing her on the forehead.

She smiled up at him. "Denver is here organizing our security patrol."

Her father turned to Denver, looking somewhat less happy. He said, "I wondered where you'd gone."

Denver said, "It was not my wish that Clare go off with me that night."

"I gathered as much from John Carter," her father said.

Clare spoke up in defence of Denver. "I gave him no alternative. I made him take me."

Her father nodded. "I know how determined you can be. It was foolish of you! You could have been killed!"

She said, "But as a result we have Denver here to work with us."

Milton Thomas gave him a look. "I'm glad you're here, Denver. I actually brought along someone with whom you should be able to work."

Clare asked, "Who?"

"Another fast man with a gun," her father said. "Wild Bill Hickok."

Denver showed surprise. "I thought he gave up gunfighting to travel with a circus."

Clare's father smiled. "Evidently he discovered that life too tame for him." As he spoke, a tall rangy man with a drooping mustache wearing a black frock coat and Stetson, brown trousers, and high brown shoes appeared on the steps of the front car carrying a suitcase.

The Denver Gent hurried up to him and pumped his hand. "Bill!" he exclaimed happily. "You're the right man, here at the best possible time."

Wild Bill Hickok's lean face broke into a smile. "Didn't reckon to find you here, Denver."

"I'm organizing a guard for the camp and the construction site," Denver told him. "I need another leader for the patrols. You're the answer!"

"I might as well be toting gun for Intercontinental as anyone else," Wild Bill Hickok said, looking pleased.

Clare went up and after Denver had introduced her, she said, "We are so lucky to have you two!"

The news of Wild Bill's joining the camp completely overshadowed the arrival of the supplies and new workers. Clare took her father aside and told him about Tom Lee at the first opportunity and he was duly shocked. But they had to move forward, so a query was made among the new men and one of them turned out to have cooking experience. He was installed in the kitchen at once.

Late in the afternoon Larry Brand rode into camp. He immediately went over to the supplies train to check the materials on the flat cars.

Clare saw him from the office door and crossed over to the train to join him. "We have almost everything we need and more promised," she said.

Larry turned to her. "I can see we've done well. That steel is exactly what we want for the central bridge span."

"Guess who Father rounded up to help Denver with the security?"

"Who?"

"Wild Bill Hickok! Isn't that great?"

Larry looked less than impressed. "He's an over-the-hill gunfighter who's been riding around firing blanks in some circus!"

"He's back to gunfighting now and he's going to join up with Denver to ward off raiders."

"What if there aren't any?"

"It's good insurance," she said.

He glanced around him. "The camp is lively. How many new men are there?"

"About two dozen not counting Wild Bill," she said. "You didn't come back to camp last night."

"I thought it would please you and the Denver Gent. I didn't want to intrude."

"Don't talk like that!"

"I had a problem come up late in the day. We worked until it was too late to leave."

Clare said, "That makes more sense. Something happened last night."

He stared at her. "What?"

"We had a suicide. Tom Lee hung himself."

Larry Brand looked startled. "Tom did that!"

"Yes. Hank found him this morning."

He sighed. "So both Tom and Dora are gone."

"He was very depressed about her death," Clare said.

"I know," Larry said. "He mentioned it to me several times. He seemed not to be able to accept it."

"We buried him this afternoon."

"I wish I had been here to pay my respects."

"The grave is easy to find. We buried him next to Dora."

Larry looked sad. "I'll visit it after I wash up."

"A lot of changes," said Clare. "I wonder how many more there will be."

Larry said, "I liked those two. In spite of what you think, I tried to let Dora down easy. We had things settled before she was killed."

"I remember your telling me that," Clare said, knowing that she had never been convinced of it.

306

Larry went on, "If you think she was hurt by my turning from her to you, why can't you understand how I feel about your giving yourself to the Denver Gent?"

She stood stunned by the bluntness of his question as he moved away. More and more she was understanding what a complex person Larry Brand was. She believed that as an officer of a defeated army he still felt a resentment about Northerners. The majority of the camp had been on the Union side, so he was cast in the role of loner. Further, they gave him no credit for the rank he'd held in the Confederate army. This made him more insecure and easy to make angry.

The new cook was not as good as Tom but he managed a fair meal for them that night. Wild Bill Hickok was the latest recruit to the dining table in the executive car. And the veteran scout was a good talker and apparently enjoyed telling stories. Larry Brand was the only one who did not take much part in the conversation or the questioning of the famous gunfighter.

"I know you have a notorious reputation as a gunman, Mr. Hickok. Would you mind telling us how many white men you've killed?" Clare asked.

The rangy man deliberated, "Well, to the best of my knowledge I guess I must have done in over a hundred."

She asked, "Did you kill them without cause or provocation?"

He shook his head. "No, by Heaven! I never killed a man without a good cause!"

Milton Thomas spoke up. "Bill, how old were you

when you killed your first man and what was the cause?"

Wild Bill said, "I was twenty-eight years old when I killed the first white man. If ever a man deserved killing, he did."

"Who was it?" Denver asked.

"Jim Stair! A gambler and a counterfeiter. I was in a hotel in Leavenworth City then, and seeing some rough characters around, and since I had some money on me, I thought I better get to my room as soon as I could. I was in bed about a half-hour when I heard some men at the door. I pulled out my revolver and bowie knife and had them ready but concealed. And I pretended to be asleep."

Clare listened with excitement. "What happened then?"

"Well, miss, it isn't pleasant to tell. The door opened slow-like and five men came into the room. One whispered, 'He's drunk and he has money! Kill him!'" Wild Bill paused.

"What next?" Denver asked.

"It was a bad time," Wild Bill said. "I kept perfectly still until his knife touched my chest. Then I dodged and buried mine in his heart. Then used my revolvers right and left!"

"Did you kill many of them?" Clare asked.

"Only one was wounded besides the one I killed. I dashed out of my room and to the forest and told the soldiers on duty there. They came back to the hotel and captured the whole gang, about fifteen in all. We searched the hotel cellar and there were eleven bodies buried down there, all killed for money by those villains."

Larry Brand said with some reason, "Of course that justified what you did."

Will Bill Hickok gave him a sharp look. "Wouldn't you have done the same? I've never been sorry I did it."

Clare tried to cover up Larry's hostility by asking another question. "You served in the army didn't you?"

"Yes, miss, I did. I served as a scout for the Tenth Cavalry. I near cashed in my chips in the winter of '69."

"What happened?" Milton Thomas asked.

"I was delivering dispatches between Fort Lyon and Wallace. I was attacked by a Cheyenne war party. We had a running fight and I got it in the thigh from an Indian lance."

"No dainty weapon," Denver explained for the scout. "Those spearheads can be mighty broad of blade."

"Right, Denver," Wild Bill said. "It was a dirty wound and refused to heal. I spent weeks at the fort recovering and then I went back to Troy Hills to get my strength back."

Clare was impressed by the famous man. She asked, "How old were you then?"

"Over thirty," he said. "I got tired of all female company so I up and travelled to Chicago to visit a boyhood friend of mine named Herman Baldwin. I met him at the La Salle station. You ever been there?" he asked Denver.

Denver smiled. "Many times."

"Well, he took me over to a saloon just across from the station and we had a few drinks. I was wearing buckskin and moccasins. A bunch of thugs gathered at the bar making fun of me. One of them began fingering my clothes and calling me, "Leather Britches."

Clare said, "Of course he was asking for trouble."

Hickok said, "And he got it, miss, he and his pals. There was a pool cue on the bar and I yanked it up and went at them until they were all on the floor beaten and bloody."

Clare nodded to the two ivory-handled guns which he wore and asked, "Where did you find them?"

"I didn't find them, miss. They were given to me by Senator Henry Wilson. He gave me them and five hundred dollars for guiding him and some of his friends. I've worn these beauties ever since. I reckon until the last shoot-out!"

Larry Brand got up from the table, saying, "I read all that long ago in the *Police Gazette* and they told it a lot better!" And he clumped out.

There was a moment's silence after he vanished and then Wild Bill said, "I reckon that young man doesn't like me."

Clare's father said, "You mustn't mind him. He's been promoted lately and he's feeling his power. If he isn't careful he may be demoted just as quickly."

"I take no offense at those who don't approve of my way of life," Wild Bill said mildly. "Not everyone understands what makes a gunman and what keeps you at it."

"I'm sure we're all delighted to have you on our side," said Clare.

"I don't know whether it will make a mite of difference," said Wild Bill. "But it's a pleasure to be riding along with the Denver Gent."

"I think we can organize a posse to keep any raiders at bay," Denver told them.

"It's important that you do," Milton Thomas said. "We can finish if there are no unexpected delays from the outside. But it will be touch and go."

"When I finish here," Wild Bill said, "I'd like to wear a marshall's star and take over keeping law and order for some town."

Clare said, "You should have no problem getting offers."

Wild Bill smiled. "Nope. I've had a heap. The big thing is to know which one to take."

They all chatted for a little longer and then Clare and Denver went out for a short stroll before they turned in for the night. Most of the new workers were sitting around a campfire by the construction car, but she didn't see any sign of Larry Brand.

Arm in arm with Denver, she walked away from the fire, saying, "Larry wasn't very polite. I wonder where he went?"

"Does it matter?" Denver asked bitterly. "I think he hates Wild Bill because Hickok's a friend of mine."

"He seems to resent everyone but Pedro," she worried.

"Two of a kind," he said.

"I liked Wild Bill's idea of becoming a marshall. That's what I hope you'll be one day."

"I'm not as famous as Bill."

"You're famous enough," she said. "And also you're younger!"

He laughed softly. "You're never satisfied unless you're planning some future for us."

"What's wrong with that?" she asked, halting and

looking up at his handsome face framed by the starry sky.

"Nothing," he said. "But it may all come to nothing. One day I could get the urge and just ride away."

Her eyes met his filled with love. "Somehow I don't think you will," she whispered.

The busy days that followed were filled with progress. The new workers helped move the materials to the viaduct, and the entire force now concentrated on that mighty span across marshlands and river. The Denver Gent and Wild Bill Hickok drilled the guards and taught them the fine points of gunslinging. Clare went down to watch the recruits at target practice and was amazed that in a few days most of the men had become crack shots.

Best of all there had been no raids! She reminded her father of this as they stood with plans before them at the construction site, saying, "Now that we have Wild Bill and Denver no one is bothering us."

Her father smiled. "I guess the Great Western people don't want to tangle with those two gunmen!"

"That's probably true," she agreed. "So just having them here keeps the peace."

"This is the way I'd rather have it," her father said. "Even if we turned away any raiding parties there would be men and material lost. This way there's none."

With outside danger at a low ebb Clare became more involved with the engineering and construction of the bridge. Larry Brand and Pedro had already gone ahead with a work crew and were laying rails beyond the viaduct to tie with the line being built out of Cheyenne.

Jefferson Myers journeyed out on one of the work

trains and stayed for several days. He talked to Clare and her father privately in the office back at the construction camp.

The fat man said, "We've had new offers from the Great Western people."

"No need to worry about them," Clare said proudly. "We're way ahead of them."

"I told them that," Jefferson Myers said. "They didn't take it well and hinted we might be sorry before it was all over."

"I can't think why we should be," Milton Thomas said.

"Nor I," Myers agreed. "When I tell those bankers the wonderful construction you've done on that bridge, they'll be behind you more than ever."

Clare said, "It's too bad you can't bring them out here."

"Not them," Myers said. "They're too busy figuring the profits they're going to make." Then he changed the subject and asked, "Where is the Denver Gent?"

"He's out riding patrol," Clare said. "They scour the country around here every day to be sure no raiding party is gathering."

"Excellent," said Myers. "He and Wild Bill make a great team."

"They've given us a free hand to work," Clare's father said. "And that is what has made our progress possible."

Jefferson Myers frowned, "I have a message for him. Mustn't forget to give it to him before I go back."

"He'll be back before dinnertime," said Clare. "He's living here at the camp." And at the same time she wondered what the message might be. Perhaps some warning that the remaining members of Blackie Mason's gang were hunting for him. But she made no enqueries, thinking it might be better to wait until Myers talked with Denver.

With his moving on to lay the advance line, Larry Brand had changed his custom of returning to the camp every night or two. Now he sometimes returned only on the weekends. He avoided Denver and Wild Bill whenever possible and gave Clare the impression he was still in a sullen mood. But he was doing a wonderful job in getting the steel rails down, so Milton Thomas was pleased.

"Brand has a lot of ability," was his comment to Clare. "When I go on to another project I'd like to take him with me."

"You probably can," she said. "His one problem seems to be his disposition. He's not friendly towards most of the others."

"I know," her father said. "I hope he'll get over that."

But Clare was not so optimistic. She knew that much of Larry's frustrated behavior was because of her. But she could not pretend that she loved him when she didn't. He had seemed to be less upset about her rejection when Denver wasn't around. But when he saw her in Denver's company and it was clear she was in love with him, Larry seemed unable to bear it. So much of the time he remained sullen and away from the camp.

When Denver rode in that evening, Clare saw him and Jefferson Myers having a serious conversation and Myers giving him an envelope. She intended to ask Denver about it after dinner, but before she could, something unexpected and alarming happened, and the letter was forgotten.

They had just finished dinner and were chatting around the table when a rider from the viaduct construction site arrived. Grimy and covered with soot, he burst into the dining area with a message. "There's a big brush fire. It's threatening the viaduct!"

"When did it start?" Milton Thomas asked jumping up.

"About an hour ago," the messenger said. "We saw the smoke first and then it began to move like wildfire!"

Now they were all on their feet. "Is there a wind to fan it?" Wild Bill asked.

"Yes. And it's blowing the wrong way, straight towards the timbers set into the bank."

"Is there a crew fighting it?" asked Denver.

"Yes," the messenger said. "Brand is fighting it with his men; it's on his side of the river. But he doesn't have enough men! He needs more to beat back the flames!"

Clare's father said, "Go back and tell him we'll be there with every possible man!"

Pandemonium took over the camp. Wagonloads of men with shovels and dynamite rumbled off towards the fire with Denver, Wild Bill, and a number of others on horseback. Jefferson Myers insisted he wanted to see the conflagration and so Clare had Hank hitch two stalwart mares to a chuckwagon and she, Hank, and the fat Myers followed the main party.

Clare was able to smell the fire and see the smoke trailing up into the darkening sky long before they reached it. Once there, they had to use a small makeshift bridge to cross the river as the main bridge of the viaduct was not yet completed.

When they finally reached the scene of the fire Clare was aghast. The flames had raced down towards the bank and the viaduct's foundations and even some tall trees were engulfed in flames.

She told Hank, "You stay here with Mr. Myers. I want to get closer!"

Hank shook his head in warning. "You shouldn't try that, Miss! Easy to get caught in that dry bush and not be able to escape!"

"I'll be all right," she shouted over her shoulder, already on her way.

When she reached the firefighters who were more or less organized in a line, she wet her scarf in a bucket of water and tied it over her head. Then she found a shovel lying nearby and joined the choking, coughing band of workers who were desperately attempting to contain the flames.

Her eyes were soon smarting and she was having trouble seeing. The men around her kept shouting new orders to each other and changing their formation. She dug away and crushed down any small burning bushes, feeling that she was gaining little with her efforts.

Her arms and back ached and she was becoming aware of the heat. The thick clouds of smoke had spread everywhere like a sinister fog, making even breathing difficult. She went on with her exertions and twice had to stop as she was racked with coughing attacks.

All at once she glanced around and found she was alone—alone and surrounded by walls of smoke and barriers of flame! Somehow she had become detached from the others and now she was isolated in what seemed to be a circle of fire. She stamped out a hungry flame licking at her skirts and hastily brought the shovel down on another.

It was plain that she could not carry on much longer! Her strength was ebbing fast, and she was having more difficulty breathing every moment. The heat was appalling and she was lost! Terrified, she cried out for help, her shouts sounding like the hoarse croaks of something not quite human.

She kept turning this way and that, weakly fighting off the flames as best she could. Her full skirts threatened to be caught up in flame, turning her into a living torch within minutes. She began to sob and even the tears in her smoke-filled eyes brought their own agonizing hurt.

"Clare!" She heard her name called.

"Here!" she cried, cupping her hand at her mouth. "Here!"

She waited and nothing happened. She began to feel it was all over. She tried to stamp out the flames around her again; her arms and hands were numb. She stumbled and fell down on the singed earth, convinced she would soon die.

As she sobbed out her fear she became vaguely aware of another presence. A figure was groping by her and again she called out, "Here!"

"Clare!" The voice was Denver's and now he bent down and helped her up and took her in his arms. She pressed close to him, coughing into his strong shoulder.

She wasn't aware of the moment they emerged from

the thick of the fire. But she was conscious of being tenderly placed on a grassy bank and of the air being less acrid and easier to breathe and of looking up into Denver's handsome, begrimed face bending over her.

"Are you hurt?" he asked anxiously.

"No," she managed in a strained voice. "I was a fool to wander so far alone."

"Not your fault," he said. "It happened to others as well. The fire kept moving about in a circle."

She glanced up at the clouds of smoke still rising from the bank above them. "Have they managed to contain it?"

"Just," Denver said. "It will burn for a while longer. But the viaduct is safe."

"You came just in time," she said.

Denver raised her up a little and kissed her. "They told me where you'd last been seen. And I knew you couldn't have gone far. The fire had trapped you!"

She let him help her to her feet and sent him back to see if he were needed. Then she made a somewhat shaky descent to where she'd left the wagon with Hank and Jefferson Myers.

Hank came running to meet her. "Miss Clare, you look as if you are in blackface!"

"I imagine," she said with a grim smile. And she removed her wet scarf and used the inner side of it to cleanse her face as well as she could manage.

"You was caught up there!" Hank said. "I saw the Denver Gent bring you out. I told you it wasn't any-place for you!"

She gave him a playful push aside. "Hank, be quiet!"

She went on to the wagon where Jefferson Myers was standing watching the fire.

"As far as I can tell the viaduct is unharmed," he said.

"Denver says so," she assured him.

"You might have lost your life," Myers said. "You ought to have stayed here with us."

"I'm safe," she said, lightly. "That's all that matters."

Myers gazed up at the smoking cliffs again and said, "There's been so little rain! The brush was tinder dry!"

Hank nodded and then gave her a strange look. "No doubt it was the worst time ever for a fire. What I'd like to know is how it got started."

Clare nodded. "Yes, so would I."

Chapter Fourteen

The following morning Clare's father called a meeting at his office to discuss the fire and its effect on the project. All the executive members of the construction crew were there along with Jefferson Myers, Wild Bill Hickok, and Denver.

Milton Thomas opened the roundtable discussion, directing his first question at Larry Brand who sat glumly on his right. "Larry, how many of our workers were incapacitated by the fire last night?"

"One man was killed by a combination of the fire and smoke suffocation, half a dozen more were burned badly enough to be off work for a few days, and one man broke his leg in a jump to escape the flames. All the other injuries were minor."

"Serious enough," Clare's father said gravely.

"Yes sir," Larry said in a low voice.

Jefferson Myers leaned forward and said, "You were

in charge of the crew near the fire. Why didn't you notice it earlier?"

"I don't know," Larry replied. "It started without any warning."

Myers pursued his line of questioning. "You mean to say you saw no smoke or flame until the whole area was a burning mass?"

Larry's jaw firmed and he said, "I wasn't aware of it until the wind blew some smoke and cinders in the direction of our camp."

Milton Thomas asked, "And did you begin to fight the fire at once?"

Larry nodded. "Yes. And I sent for aid. I knew we'd need it."

Jefferson Myers praised Larry's action. "You were right in that! For a time I thought the whole bridge was going up in flames!"

Milton Thomas said, "It was a close thing." And he asked Larry, "Have you made a thorough check of the damage?"

Larry said, "Not yet."

Clare felt it was time for her to speak up. "I knew a report would be wanted, so Denver and I rode out this morning." She was aware of the glare she was receiving from Larry.

Her father said, "That was thoughtful of you. Please continue."

"Some of the timbers closest to the cliff are charred but not deeply. None have been harmed enough to require replacement."

"Excellent," Myers said. "That means that we have not lost much."

Clare's father again queried Larry, "You will be able to resume operations later this morning?"

"Yes," he said "Little time will be wasted."

Myers asked, "How do you think the fire may have begun?"

Larry shrugged. "That's difficult to say."

Wild Bill Hickok spoke up. "May I offer an opinion?"

Clare's father encouraged him, "Please do, since you are an expert on the woods."

Wild Bill said, "It has been much dryer than usual for the season. It would take very little to start a fire. It could have been the rays of the sun, spontaneous combustion."

Clare's father said, "I suppose that danger always exits under such conditions."

Wild Bill nodded, nervously tugging at his slim, drooping mustache. He said, "Then there is another possibility. It might have been due to someone's carelessness. A worker making his way out into the woods and having a smoke. A pipe full of ashes, or a cigar half-burned, could leave a fuse to smoulder for a little and then burst into flame."

There was a silence in the room. Clare and Denver exchanged glances. Wild Bill looked a little embarrassed that he had brought up the matter. Larry again looked angry.

He turned to Wild Bill and said sharply, "Are you suggesting I have so little control that my men wander off at will and take smokes in the woods?"

"I didn't say that," Wild Bill protested. "I simply pointed out what could have happened."

"I'm sure Bill meant nothing personal, Larry," Milton Thomas said in a placating tone. "We know you can't personally watch every man every minute. I suppose it is possible some careless person might have done as Bill has suggested and innocently caused the blaze."

"I very much doubt it," Larry said angrily.

"So be it," Clare's father said. "And now, Bill, what is the other possible explanation?"

"The one I like the least," Wild Bill said. "That someone began the fire deliberately to try and destroy the viaduct. This could mean neglect on the part of the patrol, for which I must take blame. That would be the case if some intruder got close enough to commit arson, in site of our efforts. Or, and this would be beyond our responsibility, it could be someone within the camp is guilty. In short, there may be a traitor among us working for the Great Western."

It was another bombshell and brought another long silence to the drab office. Finally Jefferson Myers spoke up. "I must say I don't think that's the case. I can see Bill's first two possibilities but not the third."

Clare's father nodded. "I'm inclined to agree. I saw the way all of you fought the fire last night. I can think of no traitors among us."

Larry's face was dark with anger. "I need hardly tell you I will take responsibility for all my men."

"Agreed," Milton Thomas said. "I think we have gone over all the pertinent facts. The most important thing now is to get on with our work. I call this meeting dismissed."

The first to get up and leave was Larry Brand. Clare followed him out and stood with him in the bright sunlight, saying, "Bill didn't mean any of that personally."

"I wish I believed that," the young man said bitterly.

"He was only trying to sort out the truth," she said. "We know your men have worked hard and you have done wonders with them."

"It seems I'm getting shortchanged on the credit for it," Larry said. "You'd think the Denver Gent and Wild Bill had taken all the risks and laid the rails!"

"You're reading that into it," she told him. "No one is against you!"

His eyes met hers. "What about you?"

Startled, she asked, "What do you mean?"

"You rode out to the viaduct this morning with Denver to be able to report on the damage. Why didn't you ride over and get in touch with me to check it with you?"

"I didn't know where you were. You didn't come back to camp last night."

He said, "I was busy checking the last of the clumps of burning bushes. I worked half the night!"

Clare said, "I'm sorry, Larry. I didn't mean to hurt you. It just worked out that way."

"It always does," he said. "Since Denver came back you have worked with him against me."

"No!"

"I won't argue about it," he said. "And I'll stay on the job until this project is completed. Though I don't know any good reason why I should!" And with that he strode away to his tethered horse, mounted it, and rode off.

"What's wrong with him now?" Denver had come out and was standing behind her.

She turned to him, saying, "He thinks Bill, you and I, that we're all against him."

Denver looked grim. "I could see that in there."

"He's so unhappy," she said worriedly. "He makes me feel guilty when I know I'm not."

"That's what he's trying to do," Denver warned her. "He's attempting to bully you into allowing him to make love to you."

"It hasn't worked."

"That's why he's so angry."

She looked in the direction Larry had ridden off. "It's too bad," she said. "All that ability and he ruins it. He's harder to deal with than Harris Trent ever was. And I thought *he* was impossible."

"Maybe if I hadn't come back," Denver said.

"What's that got to do with it?"

"You know Larry's jealous of me."

"I'd still be in love with you whether you were here or back in your gambling hall. Nothing can change that!"

She was stopped from speaking further on the subject by the appearance of Wild Bill Hickok, who had come over to join them. The veteran scout rubbed his chin thoughtfully and said, "I let them overrule me in there. But I have to admit to you two, I still think the fire was deliberately set."

"Do you really?" Clare asked.

"Yep," he said.

Denver said, "I think I'm with you, Bill. The flames began in exactly the right spot to cause the greatest conflagration. It was in the area where the wind would surely carry it to the viaduct."

"And it did," Bill pointed out.

"Then who?" Clare asked.

Bill sighed. "Could be some Indian or paid renegade from the outside. If that was it, Denver and me didn't do a very good job scouting the woods."

Denver said bitterly, "It hints of a diabolically clever mind. One lone agent sent in would be harder to find than any raiding party."

Clare said, "And the fire could do the job just as well."

"Maybe better," Denver said. "I think that's what happened."

Clare turned to Wild Bill and asked, "What about the other thing you mentioned? That there might be a traitor in the camp."

Wild Bill said, "I think Brand covered that well. His men have done fine work and they risked their lives against the flames last night. But...."

Denver stared at him. "What else?"

"I could be wrong," Wild Bill said. "But I'm suspicious of that Pedro Reilly. I know he was in prison for murder and robbery. I saw his picture on the wanted posters."

Clare nodded. "They say he escaped and made his way here."

"I think he could do a thing like that," Wild Bill said. "And he'd be the kind of renegade the Great Western would hire to be a spy."

"He's worked very well," Clare said. "And Larry trusts him because he's such a good foreman under him."

Denver pointed out, "He would do that to have

Larry guarantee him. Be sure to speak up for him."

"He's to be watched," was Wild Bill's opinion. "And from now on, I'm going to watch him close. If he makes another wrong move I want to know about it."

Clare nodded. "If you could get evidence against him Larry would have to accept it. That's your best hope."

Denver and Wild Bill left Clare to ride out with their patrol. She went back inside where her father and Jefferson Myers were still at the desk conferring. When Myers saw her he smiled and said, "It seems to me you've got that young Larry and the Denver Gent feuding over you!"

Clare blushed. "I won't admit that."

Her father said, "I believe Jefferson is right. Those two never miss a chance to attack each other. And Larry has been sullen since Denver returned."

"He's acting childish," Clare said.

Myers chuckled. "Well, you better soon pick one of them!"

"I have," she said, with a small, defiant smile.

Her father looked pained. "Clare!"

"Well, why shouldn't I be frank?" she demanded.

"I think I know who it is," Myers told her.

"I'm sure you do," she replied. "It's Denver. And it has been for a long while."

Her father raised a protesting hand, "Please, Clare, this is a personal matter."

"I think of Mr. Myers as family," she replied.

Myers looked pleased. "You bet I'm family. And I'm on your side. If you want to tie up with that gambler I can only say you could do worse."

"Thank you," she said. "Now I think I'll ride out to the viaduct and get to work."

Her father protested. "After last night, you ought to be resting today."

Jefferson Myers rose. "I'm going back to Denver on the work train this morning. Come along with me and I'll stake you to a wedding dress!"

Clare laughed. "I'd love that. But I have no use for it yet. Denver hasn't let me set any date for our marriage."

Myers pointed a warning finger at her. "You better get after him before he slips away from you again."

Clare left right after that. And it wasn't until she was on the dun on her way to the viaduct that she thought of his words. And she also recalled the conversation he'd had with Denver the night before and the letter he'd given him. Then news of the fire had come and everything else was forgotten.

But now she found herself filled with curiosity about that letter. What had it contained and who was it from? Had it anything to do with Jefferson Myers warning her that Denver might decide to leave her as he had before? It was a worrying thought and she decided to challenge Denver about it as soon as she had a chance.

The chance did not come until after dinner. Clare and Denver went outside and strolled towards the workers who had gathered around a campfire. One of the new crew was a fiddler, and he came up by the fire and played a succession of lively dance tunes. Two of the younger men jumped up and began to do the figures of a square dance.

Clare laughed and taking Denver's hand drew him closer to the fiddler. Then she began to dance, forcing him to join in.

The fiddler was enjoying the fun and he played faster and faster. The two young men swung themselves around until they collapsed laughing on the grass, with the other workers clapping them for their show. Clare, her face flushed and hair awry, managed to keep going around, her arm linked with Denver's. It seemed they would have to wind up on the ground with the others, but finally the fiddler took mercy on them and brought the music to an end.

Clare stumbled into Denver's arms laughing as the workers gave them a round of applause. She gasped, "I didn't know it would go on that long."

He smiled at her and said, "Let's get away before he begins again!"

"Oh, yes!" she exclaimed. And they moved off into the darkness so they were a distance away when the fiddler began playing again.

Clare stood and gazed up at the quarter moon and the stars. "So peaceful after last night."

"Yes. I had an eternity of torment when I thought I'd never find you."

"It wasn't that much a picnic for me," she said.

"You don't know what a close call you had."

"I'd rather not think about it," she said, holding onto his arm.

He glanced back to the dining car where a yellow glow emanated from the windows. "Looks as if your father and Bill are having another go at cards tonight."

"Father enjoys playing cards. Jefferson Myers always joins in a game when he's here."

Denver nodded. "He'll be back in town tonight."

Clare looked up at him. "There's something I wanted to ask you about. I'd almost forgotten."

"Oh?"

"Last night before the fire, I saw Jefferson hand you a letter."

Denver's face betrayed nothing as he said, "I planned to tell you about it later."

"Later?"

"Later tonight."

Clare felt a nervous apprehension, the sort she'd known before when he sprang some sort of unhappy surprise on her. In a taut voice, she said, "Well, tell me now."

"The letter was from the city."

"I guessed that."

He sighed. "It was an appeal for aid."

"I'm afraid I don't understand you."

He sighed. "The letter was from Mame."

"Mame?"

"Yes. She's in bad trouble."

"What could that possibly have to do with you?" she said, feeling a slight anger.

"I'm the one responsible for her being in a spot."

"Go on!"

"When I left she looked for someone else to take over the gambling. A fellow from Chicago offered to handle it, sharing the profits with her as I did."

"And?"

Denver said, "He hasn't paid her anything."

"Well, surely the marshall can look after that," Clare said.

He shook his head. "No marshall mixes up in that kind of row. He's not using his star to help a brothel owner when half the good women in town are raising cain about her."

"It's not fair for her to involve you."

"This man isn't only not paying her. He's threatening to have her killed and take over the operation of the brothel himself. She's afraid for her life."

Clare said, "I still think it is none of your business."

"She's my friend. There's no one else to help her."

"What can you do?"

"There's only one way. I'll have to go back there, rout him out, and find somebody else reliable to take his place. I should have found someone before I left."

"You can't mean it," she said. "You'd leave the project just like that?"

"Bill is here," Denver said. "He can do a good job without me."

"I don't think that is true. And even if it were, what about me? What about us?"

"I'd come back as soon as I get things settled."

Clare stared at him, aghast. "I can't believe it! Do you know what you're saying?"

"Yes. I said I'd come back to you."

"If you're not shot down!"

Denver frowned. "That doesn't worry me."

Clare flared up at him. "Do you know the pain you'll cause me if you go back there to help that creature?"

"Mame is a decent woman," he reproved her gently.

"Perhaps by your terms. Why do you feel so obligated?"

Denver pleaded, "It's partly my fault. If I don't help her, I'll never be able to live with myself. I'll have no honor."

"You have a funny idea of honor!"

"Maybe," he said. "But I've lived by a code for a long while I can't change now."

Clare stared at him as they stood facing each other. "I hoped you might soon set a date for our marriage."

"This has nothing to do with that!"

"I think it has," she said, wearily. "If you plan to go off on insane crusades like this for the rest of your life, forever risking your life, I don't think I want you for a husband."

"Clare!" he pleaded.

"It's true," she went on. "Why be your wife when only too soon I'd find myself a widow? Loving you has caused me enough pain now. I don't want more." She walked away, her back to him.

Denver came up behind her. "When you think about this more you'll know I'm right."

"Never!"

"I love you, Clare," he said. "But you have to understand you can't change me. I have to live by my standards, even if they seem stupid to you."

"All right," she said quietly. "If that's your choice."

"If I go," he said, "it's because I can't help it!"

Clare turned to him. "No," she said. "If you go it's because you are choosing that woman over me!" And she turned and began running back to the executive car. She heard him follow her for a moment and then give up.

Her father and Wild Bill were too busy with their

card game to notice her run inside the car. She made her way to her compartment and shut and locked the door. Then she threw herself on the bunk and cried herself to sleep.

It was no surprise to her the next morning when Denver did not appear at the breakfast table. Her father, unaware of the happenings of the previous night, openly showed his concern.

"Where's Denver?" he asked.

Wild Bill, who was seated with him at the table, eyed Clare unhappily and then told her father. "I talked with him early. He's left. He had to go back to Denver for something."

"Back to Denver?" Milton Thomas said angrily. "At the time when he is most needed?"

"He asked me to take over," Wild Bill said. "And I promised I would until he gets back."

Clare's father turned to her and demanded, "Did you know about this?"

"I didn't know he was leaving this morning," she said with some truth.

He persisted. "But you knew he was thinking of returning to town?"

"Yes!" She held her head down.

"Why?"

"He had some business to complete, I understand."

Her father sighed. "So he had business to complete in town. Just as I was beginning to have some confidence in him. We are paying him a salary to be here, not move out any time he gets the urge."

Wild Bill said, "I reckon it was important to him. He wouldn't have gone otherwise."

Clare's father gave her an angry glance. "Well, I hope this opens your eyes, my girl. After the way you talked to me and Jefferson yesterday, I would pray that this is a lesson for you."

"It is a lesson for me, Father," she said in a low voice. "And I'd rather not discuss it."

"I can well understand why," her father said bitterly. And breakfast went on in silence for the three.

Clare ate only a little and even that little choked her. She left the table as soon as she could and went down to the corral where she asked Hank to get her horse saddled. While waiting for him to do this she saw Wild Bill Hickok coming down to talk to her.

She steeled herself, knowing the veteran scout would try to defend Denver. As he came up to her she greeted him with, "Well, now, you have two men's work to do."

"I don't mind that," Wild Bill said. "I understand what Denver has done and I think you ought to try to as well."

"It's an old story," she said unhappily. "We argued it out last night. Mame won and I lost."

Wild Bill said, "Denver and Mame are old friends. You don't let down old friends."

She held her head high. "What about deserting the girl you promised to marry?"

"Miss, if Denver told you he'd marry you he'll be back."

"If he lives to come back. You've forgotten there is some risk in what he's planning to do."

"I reckon there's a risk in most everything," Wild Bill told her. "Denver is doing what he must do, whether you understand it or not."

"I expected you to side with him."

"It's not a question of taking sides," Wild Bill said. "It's a question of having a reputation and living up to it. If Denver turned his back on Mame in her trouble he'd be disgraced all over the West."

Clare smiled at him grimly. "You brave gunmen! You build up your codes and live by them until somebody puts a bullet through you. I'd think you'd learn how futile it all is."

Wild Bill shrugged. "You're seeing it from the outside, Miss. I see it Denver's way."

Hank was bringing her horse up and she had only a moment left so she asked the question which was bothering her most. "Do you think I should follow him?"

Wild Bill shook his head. "You'd only complicate it. Let Denver handle it in his own way. He'll be back safe before you know it. Wait and see."

She knew that Wild Bill was telling her this so she would not worry so much. But as she rode off towards the viaduct she could not bring herself to have any confidence in his prediction. Wild Bill only knew what she knew, that Denver had gone off on a dangerous mission and might or might not return.

When she reached the viaduct, Clare saw that work was under way to join the central arch of the bridge. She rode on across the lower makeshift bridge and caught up with the rail-laying crew which Larry Brand was heading. She saw him watching Pedro yell at the workers to put more energy into their work. No wonder he wanted the man to work under him—he was a hard-driving foreman.

She dismounted and tethered her horse and went over to Larry. "Isn't he pushing the men too hard?" she asked him. "They're apt to react by deliberately slowing down in their work. You can see they resent him."

Larry gave a small smile. "They're also afraid of him; if you have eyes you can see that as well."

"I don't like it," she told him. "And neither will my father when he finds out the way Pedro is going on."

Larry squinted at her in the sunlight. "Did your friend Denver tell you that before he rode back to Mame?"

Clare pretended not to hear him and rode on along the line. The work was getting done—she could not deny that. If nothing of consequence took place they would finish their part of the line and see it joined on with the Cheyenne road. But something told her it still was not going to be easy and many things could slow them. Most of them unpredictable hazards.

Back at the viaduct she walked far out on the almost-completed structure and watched as her father guided the men in bringing the all-important central arch together. They still had a distance of at least twenty feet to span before the two projecting sections would be joined.

She held her breath as her father went as far as the timbers were in place and gave careful directions on the closing of the wide gap. Her relief was great when he came back to where she was standing.

He removed his Stetson and mopped his perspiring brow. "How is it ahead?"

"Larry was doing well," she said, deciding her views

of Pedro's behavior had best not be mentioned at this time.

Her father replaced his Stetson and eyed her grimly. "Just about everyone is doing well except your friend, the Denver Gent. I should never have let you talk me into hiring him."

She retorted, "You wouldn't have made this much progress if he hadn't been here as a guard."

"I guess Wild Bill would have managed all right," her father snapped. "You'll remember I brought him with me when I came back from town. I was prepared and didn't need that no-good gambler."

"He's gone now. You're not apt to be bothered by him again," she said tautly.

"He better not come here for work when he gets tired of catering to his fancy woman back in that brothel she runs. I'd think you'd have more pride than to mix with his kind!"

She gave him an angry look. "You may be my father but you are a fool when it comes to judging men." With that she abruptly walked away from him.

She took lunch with Larry's crew, but she did not sit with Larry. Instead, she joined Wild Bill and three of his patrol riders. The scout was in a troubled frame of mind.

As they sat eating on the top of a grassy hill, he told her, "I've been checking on the burned section this morning. We are just lucky we didn't lose everything up here."

"I know," she agreed.

Wild Bill scowled over where Pedro was seated with Larry and some workers. The fat man was wolfing his grub in a disgusting fashion. "I'd like to have a rope around his neck and then question him about where he was and what he was doing when the fire started. If he didn't answer prompt, I'd give his neck a little stretch every time!"

"You do think the fire was set deliberately?"

"I never seen a neater job," Wild Bill told her. "It was no accident, I'd swear to that."

They finished with the noon break and everyone went back to work. Clare was busy taking stock of the number of lengths of rail left and how many more would have to be sent up the next morning. The crew were back at laying rails and Wild Bill was riding up and down the line watching them.

For some reason this seemed to raise the ire of the burly foreman, Pedro. The Mexican gave Wild Bill a nasty look each time he rode by. Clare could feel the tension between the two building under the hot sun.

As Wild Bill rode by Pedro again, his rifle laying across his saddle in front of him, the horse moving at a leisurely pace, the Mexican suddenly let out an angry roar and blocking the way of the horse, he grabbed it roughly by the reins.

He glared up at Wild Bill and said, "You got some business with me?"

Wild Bill looked unperturbed by the outburst. He swung the rifle a bit and quietly ordered, "Just let go of the rein."

Pedro held onto it defiantly. "I'll let go when you answer me!"

"If you want an answer real bad I'll give it to you with this," Wild Bill said raising the Winchester.

It called the Mexican's bluff. He released the reins of Wild Bill's mount and stumbled back. Then he pointed a thick forefinger at him and yelled, "You're after me! You're trying to rile me so you can use that rifle!"

Wild Bill reined his uneasy horse and gave the burly foreman a look of contempt. He said, "There are a lot of questions I'd like to ask you, and maybe the most important one is how you got out of that prison in Cheyenne."

Before Pedro could react to this, Larry Brand came marching up and stood between the man on the horse and the angered Mexican. "You're interfering with one of my men, Bill. I suggest you keep to your patrol work and make yourself scarce."

Wild Bill gave the younger man a look of contempt. "Don't worry," he told him. "I'll do my job!" He made it sound like a significant warning as he rode back towards the woods.

Clare did not see Wild Bill again until the early evening when he turned up for dinner. She had changed into a bright cotton dress with a pattern of red and green leaves and she was feeling better after having had a dip in the pool. As they waited outside for dinner to be announced, she had a chance to talk further with him. She gave him a knowing look and said, "What about this afternoon?"

Wild Bill who also looked as if he'd freshened up, smiled faintly. "You mean when I nettled Pedro?"

"Yes. That was deliberate."

"It was, miss. An old trick. Rile them up and let them guess you know more than you really do. It usually brings the varmints out into the open."

"Isn't it a dangerous game?"

"I reckon it's part of my job," he said, exhaling two streams of blue smoke from a thin cigar.

"You believe he set the fire?"

"I do have opinions on the subject," the tall man drawled. "Later on I may have the facts."

"I hope so. Pedro hates you. He'll not miss a chance to get at you."

"I know."

Clare gave him a warning look, "And Larry Brand is determined to protect him. Pedro acts as his strong man to keep the crew in line."

Wild Bill puffed on his cigar again and gave her a wise smile. "I think I can handle the situation."

"If only Denver hadn't left us!" she said.

"Well, that's another matter."

"You are having to carry all the responsibility."

He shrugged. "Well, I guess in the same situation Denver would take over for me."

Clare gave him a look of disbelief. "I can't think you would ever let any female influence you. You'd never change for anyone that way!"

Wild Bill raised a protesting hand. "Now wait a minute, Miss Clare. Are you presuming that I'm not attractive enough to have a female interested in me?"

"No. But you are too strong to allow them to make you behave as they wished."

He chuckled. "Don't you believe it, miss. Ever hear of Agnes Thatcher?"

"I can't say that I have."

"Fine-looking woman," Wild Bill said. "Married a circus man before the Civil War. Was an actress as well, a real looker. Her husband was killed by a desperado named Jake Killeon and she decided to manage the circus on her own. She took a shine to me and wanted me to join her show."

"Did you?"

"For a little while. She decided she wanted to be a slack-wire artist, so she practiced on the wire and she became so good she was the star of her own show. One night after we had a big crowd and I was given an ovation for my sharpshooting, she took me aside and told me she was thinking of getting married."

Clare smiled. "What did you say to that?"

"I asked her who the lucky man was."

"And?"

"Would you believe it? She said it was me. Well, I darn near jumped out of my skin. And I told her right there I wasn't a good prospect for marrying!"

"Did that discourage her?"

"Not much," Wild Bill said. "So I just rode away one day and didn't come back."

"What happened to the widow?"

Wild Bill chuckled. "Well, she was so riled about my running out on her she sold the circus and put all her money in a firm making posters for shows and such. In no time the company went broke and she and her daughter had to join the Great Eastern Circus. She starred on the slack wire and her daughter was an expert horsewoman. Far as I know they're still travelling with that show."

The cook came to the door of the dining car and said, "Food is on the table."

"Thanks," Clare said, and turning to Wild Bill she asked, "Is there some message for me in the story?"

"What makes you think that?" Wild Bill asked.

"You ran from Agnes Thatcher because you're not the marrying kind. And Denver has fled from me, probably for the same reason."

Wild Bill smiled. "You're giving what I said a meaning I didn't intend. It's my opinion Denver loves you a heap and he'll be back."

Clare stepped up into the dining car ahead of him saying, "I wish I could be as certain of that as you."

Milton Thomas and Larry Brand soon joined them at the dining table. Little was said between them, and the conversation that did go on was concerned with the construction problems. Larry glanced across the table at Clare several times, but she tried to avoid direct eye contact with him. When the meal was over he got up and came to her.

"I'd like to talk with you, Clare," he said in a friendly way. "Can we go for a short stroll?"

She hesitated, not wanting to be too stiff towards him. Then she said, "All right. But I don't want to go far. I'm in the middle of a new book and I want to finish it."

Larry smiled. "I won't keep you away from it too long."

They took the path she and Denver had taken so often and as she walked with the attentive Larry she could not think of anyone but the handsome gambler. She worried that even now he might be dead, the victim of a gunfight with the gambler who'd been holding Mame a hostage in her own place.

So she walked slowly and said nothing. Larry broke into her reverie, saying, "I guess you're fed up with me."

She glanced at him. "What do you mean?"

He shrugged. "You're sick of my complaints and jealousy. I've shown you the worst side of myself."

"I'm afraid that's almost true," she said quietly.

He looked at her worriedly, "It has only been because I care so deeply for you and I feel I've lost you!"

She halted and faced him. "Larry, this is futile. We've been all over it before!"

"No," he said, looking directly at her. "Things are much different now. Denver has left you and I don't expect he will be back."

"How can you say that?" she asked.

"Because it is all very likely," he went on intensely. "And so you will need someone to protect you. Someone who loves you. I've remained and I've always been faithful to you, Clare. Let yourself love me!"

And he capped his pleading by taking her in his arms and hungrily caressing her lips.

Chapter
Fifteen

In the ten days which followed, the construction project went forward without any delays. There were no attempted raids nor were there any problems within the camp. The last section of the bridge had been joined, and now gleaming rails were being placed all across the viaduct, joined to the railway tracks on either side. By her father's reckoning another month would see them joined to the line coming out from Cheyenne.

For the final days of the work, the railway camp would be moved along the tracks, over the river to a more convenient location. But they were not ready for this big move as yet. If everything went according to schedule they would finish the contract before the snow came.

Larry Brand was a different person with Denver

away from the camp. He and Wild Bill Hickok became fairly good friends and he went out of his way to redeem himself in Clare's eyes. She could not deny that he was charming in his own way and he'd surely worked hard to get to the responsible position he now held. If only he'd not behaved so badly when Denver was around. She found that hard to forget.

It was as if the earth had opened and swallowed the Denver Gent. The passage of time made it more difficult for Clare to believe she would ever see him again. It seemed that he should have been able to straighten things out at Mame's and return by now, but still there was no word of him. The fear of what might have happened continually nagged her. She knew it was possible he was dead, but she didn't dare tolerate the thought for longer than a moment.

Clare kept busy in the field, seeing that supplies were moved forward as needed. She also supervised the grading of a hill some distance beyond the viaduct. Its incline had to be reduced to the point where a heavily laden train could safely pass over it. This called on some of the engineering skills she'd learned from her father and which none of the men or Pedro, who was in charge of this gang of twelve laborers, possessed.

When she rode back to camp after a day's work she was often tired and perspiring. At the end of one warm afternoon she stopped by the railroad car, picked up a cotton dress and underclothes, stockings and towels, and then made her way to the pond which had been a makeshift bathing place for them since the camp had moved to this spot.

The men almost never went there before they had their evening meal so she felt perfectly safe in enjoying the pond on her own. Sometimes she had sad thoughts of Dora who had often come along to bathe with her. She had liked the girl and still was distressed every time she thought about that awful night when she had been shot down.

On this particular evening Clare quickly undressed and with soap in hand waded into the pond. Because the water was so delightful she lingered there longer than she meant. And suddenly the brush around the pond parted to reveal Larry Brand. He walked out onto the rocks where her clothes were piled neatly and offered her a teasing smile.

"I arrived here just in time!" he said.

Careful to stay in water deep enough to keep her breasts safely covered, Clare said, "I've been here longer than I intended. If you'll leave I'll come out and quickly dress. Then you can have the pool."

On his haunches Larry continued to smile at her. "Do you really want me to leave?"

"I think it would be more gentlemanly of you if you did," she told him, just a touch annoyed.

"I don't get to see me a beautiful young female stepping out of the water that often. Should be a treat," he gloated.

She pulled her wet hair back over her ears and gave him a disbelieving look. "You can't be serious! You're just trying to torment me!"

"No," he said. "I'm sincere. I love you and I'd like to see your beautiful body as it comes dripping out of there."

Her annoyance increased. "Are you really that childish?"

He remained where he was. "May as well give up and come out."

With her cheeks flaming with rage, she said, "All right, Larry, Brand, I will!" And she noisily splashed her way to the edge of the pond and boldly stepped out of the water, her body nude and glistening. Her eyes flashed angrily as she glared at him.

It was Larry's turn to show embarrassment. He quickly said, "Sorry! I'll turn my back to you until you can dry yourself and get dressed."

Her anger not decreasing, she said, "Turn your back or not as you please!" And she picked up the towel and dried herself, noting that he had turned with his back to her.

He said, "It was just a joke, Clare. I didn't think you'd get angry."

"I call that a weak excuse for inexcusable behavior. Not the thing you'd expect from a former Confederate officer!"

"I thought you'd understand I was playing a game," he went on, distressed.

"It's a type of game I'm not able to enjoy," she said. She slipped on her underthings, then donned her cotton dress and sat on the rocks to pull on and adjust her stockings. All the while Larry stood there unhappily with his back to her. When she had stepped into her shoes and was picking up her work clothes, she spoke to him again. "No need to stand there like that now."

Larry turned, shamefaced and contrite. "I didn't expect you to be serious about it."

She held her chin haughtily. "You insisted I come out and remained there. So I did as you asked!"

"I turned right away!" He pleaded.

"I'm amazed that you'd have that much good taste."

He suddenly made a lunge for her. "Clare!"

She neatly eluded him and ran across the rocks and through the bushes. As she walked back to the railway car by herself she was still indignant. It wasn't so much that she minded being seen naked by Larry as that he'd taunted her and made her do it. Once again she was forcefully reminded of the difference between him and Denver. With a sigh she stepped into the railway car to put away her things and get ready for dinner.

Larry took his place at the dinner table still looking ashamed and uneasy. Clare kept up a conversation with her father and Wild Bill, deliberately excluding Larry from her remarks. This became so obvious to her father that he turned to the young man with a puzzled stare.

"You're mighty quiet tonight," he said. "I don't think you've said two words since you sat down."

Wild Bill Hickok laughed. "Worse than some Indians I've known. They can sit for hours and do little else than grunt."

Clare was enjoying it and seeing that Larry's face was crimson, she took her turn at teasing, asking, "What have you been doing to make you so quiet?"

Larry looked as if he wanted to leave. But he wound up by gazing down at his plate and telling her, "There are times when it is better to be silent."

"Now that's the truth," Clare's father agreed. "I

guess we all have plenty on our minds now that we're getting to the last days of work."

Larry darted Clare a knowing look and said, "I've been wondering where Denver went and what is keeping him away."

Clare's father frowned. "The way time is passing by we'll be finishing without him."

Clare looked directly at Larry and said, "I only wish he'd been here this afternoon."

Her father picked up on this. "Why this afternoon particularly? He was hired to be here all the time. He had no right to leave."

"I agree with that," Larry said, looking pleased with himself.

Clare glared at him. "So you can speak when you like."

Her father brought up an engineering problem and soon they were all deep in a discussion. After that the conversation around the dinner table ended.

Wild Bill and her father remained in their places to resume the endless card game which occupied them during their hours of leisure. Clare knew if she went outside, Larry would pursue her with a lot more pleading and apologies. She wanted none of it so she ignored him and went straight to her own compartment and shut the door. Then she picked up the book she'd been enjoying and commenced reading. It wasn't long before she heard Larry's footsteps outside her door.

He knocked and she coolly answered, "Yes?"

"Mind if I come in?" he said.

"I do," she said. "I'd mind a great deal."

He stood there in silence on the other side of the compartment door. Then he said, "All right, I'll go. I'd like to hear that you still aren't angry with me."

"I'll be more pleased with you if you do as I asked. Go!"

He remained there a moment longer. Then left. She felt he'd been properly punished and there need be no more mention of it. She only hoped she could get it out of her mind. There had been good relations between her and Larry since Denver's leaving, and she would prefer to keep it that way. But not at the expense of her self-respect.

That night she had strange dreams of emerging from the pool naked and having Larry spring out from the bushes and take her in his arms. While she was crying out and beating him off with her hands another figure appeared. It was Denver! Larry saw him and quickly released her. Now the two men faced each other on the rocks. Denver's Colt was in his hand pointed directly at Larry, who began to abjectly beg for his life. Denver's reply was to fire! With that she woke up in a muddled state of thought and drenched in perspiration.

When she went out for breakfast the next morning, Larry was just leaving. He hesitated in the doorway of the dining car to ask, "How are you this morning?"

She managed a smile. "Very well. And you?"

"I didn't sleep too well last night."

"Nor did I," she said. "But I expect that's only a passing thing. I don't see it as anything to worry about." She felt he would listen between her words and know what she was suggesting.

351

His face brightened. "Yes," he said. "It doesn't pay to give too much attention to anything in the past. Only to remember our mistakes and correct them."

She nodded. "Just so long as we correct them."

"I'll see you out there," he said, referring to the work scene.

"Yes," she smiled. "I'll be along soon."

He left and she felt that they had overcome the awkwardness resulting from his stupid behavior the afternoon before. And she hoped there would be no further such confrontations.

Milton Thomas came into the dining room next and joined her at breakfast. He said, "I suppose Wild Bill and Larry are both on their way to work?"

"Yes," she said. "Larry left just a little while ago."

"What was wrong with him last night?"

She shrugged. "He seemed to be in one of his moods. You know what happens."

Her father frowned. "I had the impression it was something to do with you. That you two were fencing about something."

"Really?" She pretended innocence.

"I hope you're getting on. That has been one of the benefits of the Denver Gent being away. Larry Brand has behaved in a much more reasonable manner."

"Yes, I know."

"Well, do try and get along with him."

"I will," she promised.

Her father consulted his watch and said, "This is the day the work train gets in. They're bringing us some new spikes we need badly and some other materials. I think you should be there to meet it."

She said, "You want me to remain here?"

"Yes. I'll be riding back in time for lunch. The train ought to be here around twelve or a little earlier. That way you can get the mail and have it ready to be distributed. Also you'll know if there's any word from Denver. Not that I expect any."

"All right, Father," she said. "I'll wait for the work train to arrive. I'll tell them you'll be here later."

She was in the office when she heard the train. Running out to greet it, she was pleasantly surprised when Jefferson Myers stepped down from the passenger car. He crossed to her with a warm smile on his broad face.

"Clare! What a pleasant surprise," he said. "I was afraid there would be nobody here to get me a drink."

She laughed. "I can get you one and I might even have one with you. What about the mail?"

He held up a leather pouch in his right hand. "I have it here," he said. "And I have some special news for you as well."

All at once she was on edge. "What is it?" she asked. "Nothing too bad?"

"No," he said genially. "It can wait until I have my drink."

"Father is riding in so you can have luncheon together," she said, and they started walking across to the railway construction cars.

Puffing slightly from the exertion of walking up the steep embankment, Myers said, "A lot of things have been going on. That John Carter talked to me again about us selling out. But I refused again."

"The Great Western haven't given up then?"

"No. They still want to buy us out."

"Which means their construction can't be going all that well."

"That's the rumor. Any more raids here?"

"None," she said. "I guess the reputation of Wild Bill Hickok and the Denver Gent combined has kept the outlaws away."

"You said that it would work," Myers wheezed. "And it has."

They reached the dining car where she found a whiskey bottle and poured a large drink for Jefferson Myers and a small one for herself.

Sitting by him, she raised her glass, "To the project!"

"Success!" he said, echoing her toast and downing his drink in a gulp. He pushed the glass forward for another.

As she poured it for him, she asked, "What is your other news?"

His eyes met hers. "About the Denver Gent."

"What about him?"

"He's still at Mame's. You could say he's trapped there."

"I'm not sure what you mean."

The fat man sighed. "Well, you know Denver went to clean the place up. Get rid of Chicago Sam, who was taking over everything from Mame."

"I know all that."

Myers said, "Things didn't work out as Denver figured. He expected to find Chicago Sam and shoot it out with him if he had to or settle it some other way."

"And?"

"It didn't happen like that. Chicago Sam got word

Denver was coming gunning for him and he got out of Mame's quick. So Denver just moved in and took the game over like he'd never left."

"Why hasn't he written to me? Or come back?"

"I reckon he's waiting," Myers said. "You see, Chicago Sam is still in town and he's talking big, telling folk that he's just biding his time to get Denver. Meanwhile he keeps out of Denver's way."

"So Denver is still really waiting to have it out with him?" she said.

Myers finished his drink, smacked his lips, and said, "That's the picture. He's living at Mame's and operating the game. And he's waiting for Chicago Sam, who I doubt will ever dare face Denver. He's more apt to try and have someone shoot Denver in the back some night."

The old fear took over and in a tired voice, she said, "It's back to the old principle. Those who live by the gun die by the gun."

Myers looked apologetic. "I think Denver really meant to leave the life. But he couldn't walk away from this one. Maybe when it's settled he'll be back."

"Or someone will send me word of his death," she said bitterly.

"I'm sorry, my dear," he said. "I wish I could have brought you better news."

"At least I know what has been going on."

Her father arrived a little later and he and Jefferson Myers went into a huddle about financing. Clare kept herself busy listing the supplies which had just arrived and ticking them off against the orders she'd sent in. When she completed this she went down to the corral and asked Hank to saddle up the stallion for her.

Hank was in a good mood. He said, "I remember the day you brought that black beauty here. It was just after the Denver Gent rescued you from those outlaws."

She smiled as she leaned on the top log of the corral. "That seems a long while ago."

The old cowhand nodded. "You're right, Miss Clare. A lot has happened since then."

"And soon we'll be moving the camp and the construction will be over."

"Don't seem possible," Hank said. "And where's the Denver Gent?"

"In town," she sighed. "I doubt if he'll be coming back."

"Sorry to hear that," Hank said. "I sorta thought you two..." he stopped.

"So did I, Hank," she said. "But I guess it was a foolish dream. He loves his freedom and the life of a gambler."

"He seemed happy enough here," Hank argued. "He and Wild Bill got along fine."

"I know, but Wild Bill is still here and Denver has gone."

Hank frowned. "I hope that doesn't mean you're going to turn your attentions to that Brand fella!"

Startled by the strong emotion behind his words, she asked, "Why do you say that?"

"He's not good enough for you," Hank said and spat on the grass. "Him and that Pedro!"

"The men seem to work well enough under him."

"They don't like him," Hank maintained. "It's just

that Pedro keeps them cowed. He's given a couple of them brutal beatings when they got out of line."

"I haven't heard anything about that!"

"Larry Brand sees to it that neither you nor your father hear about anything like that," the old man said grimly. "But I hear about most all of it."

"If there are any new incidents please tell me as soon as you hear about them," she asked.

"All right," Hank said. "And if I was you, I wouldn't give up too easy on Denver! You two made a great team!"

Having delivered himself of this opinion, Hank limped away to saddle the stallion. Clare stared up at the mottled blue sky as she waited and speculated on all the things they had just discussed.

She rode out to the ledge and inspected the rails along the gorge. It was while this precarious section of the line was being constructed that Larry Brand had saved her life and so started up the path which had led him to the post of assistant to her father. He had shown a great aptitude for engineering, so much so it seemed he must have had some formal training, though he had told her his education before the war had been law.

Leaving the cliffs overlooking the ledge she went on to the viaduct, the most impressive engineering feat of all. It ran across the marshlands, then high above the river, to finally end on hills on the opposite side. It was complete now except for a few small problems with the rails, and a crew of a half-dozen were working on that now.

Further ahead Larry Brand and Pedro would be urging on the remaining workers as they placed the line along fairly even terrain. When this section of railway met the section from Cheyenne, the project would be at an end, the contract completed.

She had no desire to go on where Larry was working. His behavior at the pond had left her with new feelings of uneasiness. There were times when he was very much the southern gentleman, and he did not lack either ability or courage. And he insisted he was in love with her!

On the other hand, he had been Dora's lover and repudiated her when it suited him. If Dora hadn't been killed she would have remained an awkward reminder that he could be devious when it suited him. He also could not keep his emotions fully under control; during his sullen, jealous times it was a misery to be near him. And to top it all, he had this unholy alliance with the criminal, Pedro.

As she rode slowly back to the construction camp, it seemed to Clare that she must be wary of encouraging Larry in any way. She knew she did not care for him enough to overlook his shortcomings. While he might think he had some claim to her love because he'd saved her life, Denver had earlier done the same thing, and at a much greater personal risk.

And it was Denver that she loved. The tragic thing was his dedication to a way of life which left no room for a female to share it with. With this thought something suddenly clicked in her brain. She asked herself, why not? Why shouldn't she go to Denver now and try to save him, just as he'd earlier put everything aside to rescue her?

It all came together as she reached this conclusion.

He had deliberately not been in touch with her as he did not want her to come to town and face the danger that surely awaited her there. He was attempting to protect her. And with this thought, she knew what she would do. She urged the stallion on towards the camp.

She left the horse with Hank who gave her an admiring look and said, "I reckon the ride did you a lot of good! There's a flush in your cheeks and those eyes are brighter than when you left."

Clare nodded happily. "I feel much better, Hank." Then she walked briskly across to the office.

Her father and Jefferson Myers were seated and enjoying cigars with their afternoon whiskey. She smiled at them and sat on the edge of her father's desk.

She said, "You don't really need me here now."

Her father raised his eyebrows. "What has brought you to that remarkable conclusion?"

"The work is almost over."

"I still need someone for the books," he protested.

Jefferson Myers raised a pudgy hand. "Don't neglect the books; you know those bankers want everything accounted for."

Clare said, "Well, at least you can spare me for a few days."

Her father stared at her hard before he said, "I'm almost afraid to ask why."

"I want to return on the supplies train tomorrow with Jefferson," she said. "I want to see Denver and talk with him."

Milton Thomas gave Jefferson a gloomy glance. "I told you I was afraid this would happen."

Myers looked upset. "Things are going to break there one day soon! There'll be shooting and Denver will be in the middle of it."

"I know all that. But I happen to love him and I think my place is with him."

Her father raised his hands in despair, "What can I say?"

She went over and kissed him on the cheek. "Give me your blessing!"

Myers chuckled and said, "I'll do the same thing for the same reward." And so she gave him a kiss as well.

Clare did not intend to discuss her trip to Denver City with Larry Brand. But Jefferson Myers made some reference to it at the table and the news was out. For a while she avoided glancing at the young man, giving all her attention to Wild Bill.

"I guess Denver would like to see you. Too bad you can't come along," she told him.

Wild Bill smiled. "I reckon he'll settle for you, Miss Thomas. Though I don't mind saying I'm itching to go to town. As soon as this job is finished, I'm moving some place where there's a running poker game and plenty of girls."

Larry spoke up coldly, "Then you should have gone to town instead of Denver. You'd have had the poker game and Mame or one of her girls."

Wild Bill said, "It wasn't my business to go. Denver had to make the trip."

Jefferson Myers changed the subject to the coming

visit of the bankers when the line was finished. Clare hoped that Larry would not bother her when they broke up in the dining car. But she was almost certain that he would.

And he did. He followed her outside and stood facing her, his face shadowed with anger. "Why are you doing this?" he demanded.

She was ready for him. "Because I love Denver and I think my place is with him."

"So you've been making a fool of me," he said bitterly.

"In what way?"

"Leading me on, allowing me to think I had a chance with you!"

"I don't remember doing any of that."

"You wouldn't," he snapped.

"Larry," she pleaded, "let us continue to be friends. Surely we can salvage that much. I'll never forget you saved my life."

"Saved you for him!"

"Does that matter?"

"I'll tell you what matters," he said. "You are going to step into the kind of situation that always ends in gunplay and bloodshed. This will likely be the finish of the great Denver Gent and there's a good chance if you're with him you'll be shot down as well."

"I know all that," she said quietly.

He eyed her in gloomy silence. "If you do this and he is cut down, don't think you can come to me. I'm not going to be your second best."

She smiled ruefully. "Isn't that strange talk for someone who claims to love me? Love often entails

361

tolerance and sacrifice. I think the only person you love is yourself!"

It was almost as if she'd slapped him hard across the face. He winced and then with clenched hands, told her, "No wonder they call you the vixen!" And with that he turned and walked away.

The supplies train was nearing the town and Clare and Jefferson Myers sat together in the small passenger section. Clare sat next to the window, sometimes looking out as the train moved along swiftly and sometimes talking with her companion, who spent much of the time with his pudgy hands folded over his stomach dozing lightly.

At one point he stirred beside her and said, "I had a dream. You were in it."

Clare smiled. "Was it a pleasant dream?"

"I'm not sure," the fat man admitted. "It was very confused but I saw you clearly. You were wearing the same pearl-gray suit you're in at this moment. I even noticed the flounces in the skirt."

"I made this myself from a pattern," she told him. "It's the latest-style walking suit and I covered my parasol with the same material."

"You have a talent for it," he said, admiring the outfit again. "It could have come from the best Chicago emporium."

"You haven't told me what happened in your dream."

He wrinkled his brow. "It was very much of a mixture. Full of confusion. But Denver was there and a lot of other people and it seemed to me you were trying to get through to him and tell him something.

But you couldn't. Someone was there to prevent you. I was standing beside you and telling you not to be afraid."

She said, "That's a sobering dream. It sounds as if either Denver might be in danger or someone was threatening me."

"I woke up in a sweat," Myers admitted.

"We'll soon know what's happening when we reach town," she said.

Jefferson Myers warned her, "I don't want you going to Mame's alone. You promised your father you'd let me come with you."

"Why place you in danger?"

"As long as I'm around the chance of trouble is less," he explained. "You mustn't be headstrong in this."

"Very well," she said.

"I'll see you safely to your room at the Pembrook Hotel," he told her, "and I don't want you to go out until I join you again."

"I want to see Denver as soon as I can," she said, glancing at him.

"Your father tells me you always carry a small, loaded pistol in your pocketbook."

She held the pocketbook up. "It's in there now."

"You should always keep a weapon like that with you. You never know when you might need it."

"I hope not to use it," she said. "The last time I would have tried to save myself, my attacker took the pocketbook from me and tossed it away."

"It is an obvious hiding place."

"Do you think somewhere in my suit?"

Jefferson Myers was deep in silent thought for a moment, then he said, "Years ago I saw a stage play. The girl in it was in a tight spot. So she made a pocket inside her parasol and when she felt she was in danger, she slipped the pistol inside it ready to use."

Clare smiled. "It is a clever idea!"

He nodded. "No one would think of a tiny parasol like that as a weapon. If you hit anyone with it they'd not be hurt and the parasol would break in two."

"But as a hiding place for a weapon?!"

"First-rate," he said. "Entirely unexpected. It worked out well in the play."

She laughed. "Between your dream and your memories of the play I'm becoming confused."

"I'd think about making that pocket and using it," he said seriously. "I don't expect it would take you long."

"A half-hour or less," she estimated. "I'd have to use material from the hem of my dress to match the parasol."

"Well, it's just a thought," he said.

By now they were rolling into the Denver railway depot, a long brown building with a half-dozen sections of tracks. She and Myers made their way out of the car and headed for a row of carriages which were waiting for passengers. Jefferson Myers told the driver to take them to the Pembrook Hotel and they were at once on their way through the dusty streets. There was the usual mixture of noise, confusion, and traffic, and the wooden sidewalks were crowded with people, while wagons, stages, and carriages clamored for room on the too-narrow streets.

Jefferson Myers glanced out the side window of

the carriage glumly. "At least back at the camp you have some peace and quiet."

Clare was thinking that she liked the excitement though she worried about possible danger. She said, "It's a wonderful change for me."

The usual idlers were in the lobby of the hotel. Since the opening of the new Denver Hotel, it was apparent that the Pembrook was getting less of the family trade and more of the transient workers and cowpokes. Jefferson Myers saw her safely registered and up to her room.

Before he left he said, "I will be back at seven. We will dine here and then go over to Mame's."

"Thank you so much," she said, sincerely grateful. It was clearly to her advantage not to embark on a visit to Denver alone.

The wait for his return—a little more than an hour—was a long one. She freshened up and was waiting when Myers arrived. After a better-than-average meal in the dining room, the moment for which she'd been waiting arrived; her pulse beat faster and she was tense from head to toe.

As they walked out on the sidewalk in front of the hotel in the early evening's darkness, Myers asked, "Are you sure you want to do this?"

"Yes," she answered quietly and confidently.

"Very well," he said and lifted a hand to summon a taxi.

Clare and Myers were silent as they were driven through the honky-tonk section of the city with its numerous saloons, brothels, and cheap hotels. The air was filled with noise—laughter mixed with angry shouts, the tinkling of piano music, the splintering of bottles. It was the busy part of the drab, growing town after dark.

Clare looked out the window of the cab again and saw the red lantern hanging in front of the house she recognized as Mame's place. "We're almost there," she told Myers.

"Doesn't make me any happier," he said nervously.

"I can go in alone," she volunteered.

"Your father would never forgive me," he said. The carriage came to a halt and he helped her out and paid the cabby.

Clare leaned on Myers' arm as they entered the brothel, carefully avoiding the leering smiles and lascivious glances of the men lolling about the entrance. Once inside she breathed a little easier.

Piano music came from the back of the house, and within a moment a familiar figure came strolling out to greet them. It was Mame wearing a tight black gown decorated with black ostrich feathers and smoking a cigarette in a long holder. Her naturally well-shaped features were caricatured by the heavy make-up she wore.

The blonde eyed them with an unconcealed look of annoyance. "I thought you might be customers."

"Not tonight, Mame," Jefferson Myers said.

"Nor any night for you," Mame said. "You know as well as I do, Jefferson Myers, if your wife ever heard you were visiting here she'd not let you inside your door."

He laughed nervously. "You know Miss Clare Thomas."

"We've met," Mame said.

"I've come to see Denver," said Clare.

Mame looked bored. "I guess you mean the Gent, not the town."

She blushed. "Yes, of course."

"You might have picked a better time," the older woman said.

Myers looked worried. "What do you mean, Mame?"

"The word is out that Chicago Sam is coming here to blast Denver tonight."

Clare and the fat man exchanged glances. Then she asked Mame, "Isn't that an old story? I mean, this Chicago Sam has been hiding out and making threats for days!"

Mame said, "He's done that about as long as he dares. I think he'll be here tonight."

Myers said, "Don't worry. Denver is the better man and he'll be ready for him."

Clare said, "I'd like to speak to Denver alone if you can arrange it."

Mame gave her a not-unkindly look. "I understand how you must feel, kid," she said. "You know that Denver is doing all this to help me."

She nodded. "I've heard about it. Under the circumstances I don't see how he could have acted otherwise."

"Thanks," Mame said. "I stand to lose a lot if Chicago Sam gets the drop on him."

"I think we should really leave," Myers urged Clare.

She turned to him. "If I do and Denver is killed tonight, I'll never forgive myself."

Mame said, "He's in the gambling room getting set up. I'll tell him you're here and you can talk to him in my own little parlor down the hall."

"Thank you," Clare said.

"I'll wait for you," Myers. "I'll stay right here in the hallway."

Mame gave him an amused glance. "You'll ruin my business! Go into the main parlor and listen to the piano music and talk to the girls. Who knows? You might decide to pick one out for yourself."

Clare told him, "I'll meet you there."

Myers' face was crimson as he said, "Very well, then. But don't be long!" And he went off to the doorway from which the piano music was coming.

Mame showed Clare into a small, neat room with some tintypes on the walls. She nodded to them with pride. "The big one is of my parents. And that innocent young girl in the oval is me just before the war."

"They're very nice," she said,

"This is my special retreat," the brothel keeper said, as she glanced about at the sparsely furnished yet pleasant room. "You've got a lot of spirit! I like that. Now I'll go get Denver for you."

She left and Clare sat nervously on a love seat with cushions at each end of it. Looking up, she saw the tintype of the bearded man and buxom blonde woman opposite her on the red and yellow papered wall.

The wait was almost unendurable. She tried to think of what she'd say. Whether she could persuade Denver to leave with her and avoid the threatened showdown. That was a dream, she knew; he would never agree to anything of the sort.

Then she saw the white porcelain handle of the oak-panelled door turn and the door opened and it was Denver. The sight of the familiar handsome face brought her to her feet with a smile on her face and happy tears in her eyes.

"Denver!" she said, going to him.

He looked pained. "Clare! I told you never to come here!"

Chapter
Sixteen

"I know where I belong now," Clare said. "With you, I'm not allowing us to be parted again!"

"You shouldn't have come here," Denver insisted.

"If you're in danger, I intend to be at your side!" Clare said, her lovely face determined.

A weary smile crossed Denver's handsome face and he took her in his arms. She crushed her lips to his and pressed her body close! It was a moment which she'd waited for too long. Just now there was no past and no future, just the tumultuous passion of these precious seconds!

Then he held her back at arm's length. "You couldn't have arrived at a worse time."

"I know," she said. "Mame told me Chicago Sam is threatening to come here tonight."

"He will come," Denver said. "I've been tipped off to that."

"Then you'll be ready!"

"As ready as possible. It has to be settled. I hope for Mame's sake I get the first shot in."

"What about me?"

He shook his head. "All I can do is try and protect you. I'll send you back to the hotel."

"No!" she protested. "I'm not alone. I came here with Jefferson Myers."

"He is a fool to have brought you to a place like this," Denver said angrily. "I'll talk to him and he can see you safely back to your room."

"Sorry, Denver, I won't go," she told him quietly.

"You must!"

"No! I want to stay here with you! I want to be at your side whatever happens."

With a grim expression, Denver said, "You've never been a spectator at a shoot-out. If Chicago Sam shows, either he or I will be shot down."

"I know that," she said, hiding the panic she felt.

"Does your father know you came here to me?"

"Yes. I told him."

"And he allowed it?"

"He and almost everyone else seem to understand that I love you and nothing can ever change that!"

He stared at her, then took her in his arms and held her to him. "I don't deserve you," he said in a whisper.

"Let me be the judge of that," she replied, her eyes gentle as she offered her lips to him.

They went out to the ladies' parlor where Jefferson Myers was enjoying a drink and some amusing repartee with the girls. He quickly left the rouged and garishly dressed females to join them.

"I hope you've talked some sense into her," he said to Denver.

"We've come to a decision." Denver said heavily. "I'll allow her to watch the game, providing you stay with her and get her out safely if anything happens to me."

Myers protested, "But it's a shoot-out! Anyone could be killed."

Denver gave him a bleak look. "She wants to stay."

Denver escorted them into the gambling room and Clare noted the two armed guards posted on either side of the single entrance to the room. A few poker players were already seated at the table and there were some couples at the bar, the girls from Mame's entertaining customers. Otherwise the room was strangely empty.

Denver looked at her and said, "Whatever happens, stay back by the bar with Jefferson. Don't move! No matter what!"

Clare nodded and Denver left her to take his place at the round gaming table. The other chairs were quickly filled and the game began. From a distance came the faint sound of the piano from the parlor. The few couples by the bar were talking in muted voices. There was a feeling of tension all through the big room.

She knew her own nerves were strung tight. In a low voice, she asked Myers, "Are there any rules, any code for this kind of battle?"

Myers nodded. "If Chicago Sam shows up alone, the guards will let him by, since this is a personal thing between him and Denver. We'll hope Denver sees him fast and gets to his feet, his hand on his gun. Then Sam should come into the room until he's only a few feet from Denver and facing him. At that moment when he stands still it's the signal for the shootout. And whoever gets his gun out first and plugs the other one is the winner. And the feud is settled."

Clare frowned. "You mean no one will try to help Denver? That he could easily be killed by this bully if his luck fails?"

"That's it," Myers said. "It's all a matter of luck."

"So that's why almost every gunfighter in the West has died by violence. Sooner or later their luck is bound to run out."

Jefferson Myers nodded morosely. "I sure hope it's not the Denver Gent's turn tonight."

"Maybe Chicago Sam won't turn up after all," she said.

"Maybe not," said Myers. "But if he does and the bullets start flying wildly, just throw yourself down on the floor."

They had drinks, Myers gulping several down in quick succession. The ominous quiet in the room along with the scant few gathered there made her sure that something was going to happen.

Meanwhile Denver and the men at the round table went on quietly playing poker. But she could see that like herself, most of them glanced towards the entrance nervously.

Then it happened!

The door slowly opened and a burly, ugly-faced man in a flat-topped black hat and a loud checked suit came slowly into the room. The fierce green eyes under heavy black brows were fixed on Denver, who stood up and took a step away and to the left of the table so he and the intruder faced each other directly.

The total silence told Clare this was Chicago Sam and that this was the moment of reckoning between him and Denver. With a quick movement she got up and walked slowly and calmly across the room to take her place at Denver's side.

Denver's cheek twitched but he did not dare look at her. The glaring Chicago Sam warned her softly, "You have twenty seconds to step back, Miss, or get blazed down with your friend the Gent!"

Chicago Sam's burning eyes were on her. Denver's lips were tightly compressed, his body rigid. And she prayed for the control she needed at this moment. She had planned it, prepared for it, and now she was ready. With no suspicious show of movement she held her tiny parasol to her. Then in a flash she whipped out the pistol she'd concealed there, aimed at Chicago Sam, and fired!

It was all so fast, no one seemed to be aware of what had happened. Chicago Sam's glare changed to a glazed look, and a small, round hole in the middle of his forehead spurted blood. He wavered for just a moment, then collapsed on the floor.

This was the signal for pandemonium to break out in the room. Some rushed to see if the big man was truly dead, while Denver took Clare's trembling body in his arms.

Myers came up sputtering, "Why did she do such a damn-fool thing?"

Denver said quietly. "To save my life."

"I know that," he protested. "But you would have got him anyway. You're a lot faster on the draw!"

"Who knows?" Denver sighed.

The barman came up to Denver and said, "He's dead! Bullet went right out through the back of his thick skull!" And he then raced to the bar to serve the dozens of patrons who were suddenly pouring into the place. The room that had been empty before was now filled with laughing, joking, noisy celebrants.

"Well, I didn't expect that." It was Mame who had made her way through the crowd to come up to Denver and Clare.

Clare handed the pistol to Denver and said brokenly, "Take it! I don't want to look at it!"

Jefferson Myers said, "I'm afraid you'll be seeing a lot of it. I'm sorry I told you that trick of putting your gun in your parasol!"

"Is that how she managed it?!" Mame turned to Clare with a smile. "Congratulations, kid. You did us all a service."

Denver asked Mame, "Where's the marshall?"

She jerked her head. "He came in with me. He's looking at the body right now."

Myers asked Clare, "Have you ever been in jail?"

Clare gazed at him in amazement. "No! Why?"

"The chances are you will be," he warned her.

Mame nodded. "We have some funny ideas about the law here. If Denver and Chicago Sam had drawn on each other and one of them was killed, there'd have been no fuss. Self-defense with plenty of witnesses!"

Clare said, "But Chicago Sam came in and threatened to kill me!"

Denver explained, "He said he would kill both of us but he hadn't drawn his gun. You caught him unawares. He was expecting the gunplay from me, but you shot him first."

Jefferson Myers spoke up. "And that, dear girl, is going to mean you're facing a charge of murder."

As he spoke, a large, gray-haired man with a lined face and a marshall's star prominently displayed on his chest came up. He gazed at her compassionately and said, "I'm told you shot and killed Chicago Sam."

"Yes," she said in a small voice.

The marshall spoke firmly, "Then I much regret, Miss, I shall have to arrest you for murder."

Denver burst out with, "You're not taking her to jail!"

"Denver, you saw what happened," said the marshall. "She just shot a man down! She admits it!"

"He meant to kill both of us!" Denver said angrily.

"She'll get a fair trial," the marshall promised. "But I have to take her in."

Jefferson Myers moved to face the tall marshall. He said with great authority, "I will personally be responsible for her appearance in court and pay any required bail. And I offer you the word of the Intercontinental Railway Company, along with my own, that she will appear."

The marshall rubbed his chin and considered. Then he said, "Bail will be twenty-five hundred dollars."

"I'll have it in your office within the hour," the fat man said.

The marshall turned to Clare, "You're a lucky girl to have such good friends. I want your word that you'll not leave town and that you'll be available for trial."

"I'll remain in my room at the Pembrook Hotel," she told him.

The marshall nodded and turning to Denver, said "I'm going to appoint you temporary deputy-marshall to watch over this girl and see she gets to court safely."

Denver smiled and placed his arm protectively around Clare again. "I'll be happy to take on that task."

Myers turned to the marshall once more. "The trial should be quick," he said. "Better to get this settled as soon as possible."

The marshall nodded. "We'll round up a jury to-morrow morning and have the trial at two in the after-noon."

With that the marhsall left them. Chicago Sam's body had been removed, and the crowd had thinned to a few stragglers.

Mame shook her head. "This has ruined my busi-ness for the night. My girls and the customers can't think of anything but what happened here."

Myers said, "Well, it's over. And Chicago Sam won't bother you or anyone else in this town ever again."

"It's not likely," the brothel owner said with a gleam in her eyes. To Clare, she added, "Thanks, kid. I never thought any female would rope the Denver Gent, but believe me you're different!" And she hur-ried off, the ostrich plume banded to her blonde hair wavering in the draught from the door.

Myers told Clare dismally, "I'll never be able to explain this to your father."

"I think it's going to be my privilege to do that," Denver told him.

"Why you?" Myers asked.

"Because she's going to be my wife," Denver said with a smile and took her in his arms again.

The law had appointed Denver to be the officer in personal charge of her. So it followed that he could not leave her at any time. Nothing had been stipulated as to how close he should keep, but the two lovers interpreted that for themselves. So it came about that on this night when one or both of them could have died, they were locked in each other's arms in her bed at the hotel.

Once again she knew the joy and love he offered her. And when their passion had reached a peak they lay happily, side by side, their nude bodies glistening with perspiration. Nothing was said between them to spoil the spell of the perfect love which they'd just experienced. Nor did they think about the trial to be faced, though that could shut out all their happiness like a fast-moving dark cloud.

After they had washed and dressed the following morning, they had an ample breakfast sent up. Towards the end of their meal there was a knock on the door and when Denver went to answer it, the familiar figure of the well-dressed John Carter was standing out there. In a brown plaid suit and brown derby, he was the epitome of the smart eastern businessman. He smiled and said, "May I come in?"

Clare jumped up. "John Carter! How nice of you to call."

Carter came to her as Denver closed the door. He took her hand and kissed the back of it, saying, "It is good to see you again, despite the unhappy circumstances."

Standing by Clare, Denver said, "Then you've heard all about last night?"

"Yes," the lawyer said. "I have actually gone to the extent of involving myself."

Clare stared at him. "Involving yourself?"

He smiled again. "It seems to me you need the best legal advice possible."

"That's certain," Denver agreed.

"So I have informed the court that I shall be acting as the counsel for the defense," John Carter said.

Clare gasped. "But you can't do that! We work for rival companies. They wouldn't let you!"

The nattily dressed lawyer raised a hand to silence her protests. "I'm merely a legal representative for the Great Western. They do not have my sole services. I'm free to take on any other clients for whom I have time. And I have chosen to have you as a client."

"It certainly makes me breathe a lot easier," Clare said happily.

"Me too," said Denver. "You are truly a friend. But you know it will not be an easy case."

"We shall see," John Carter said. "May I have some coffee as we all sit down and discuss this?"

When Clare had poured his coffee and they were all gathered around the table, she said, "I have killed a man before witnesses."

John Carter said, "Your plea will be self-defense. It will serve best."

"I agree." said Denver. "But how do you propose to manage that?"

John Carter looked confident. "It will be fairly easy.

The late Chicago Sam will be my chief witness for the defense."

"With Sam dead," Denver said, "how are you going to manage that?"

"It won't be as difficult as you might expect," the dapper lawyer said. "Before Sam came for his confrontation with Denver, word was leaked out to him that you were in the bar. He was told you were Denver's girl."

"So?" Clare asked.

"Before he entered the place Sam bragged before a number of witnesses that he would not only shoot Denver down, but you as well. I have a half-dozen men who heard him and will come forward."

Denver looked delighted. "It *will* work," he said. "It has to. Simply because it is the truth."

"Exactly," John Carter agreed.

Clare sat back in her chair with a sigh. "It makes me feel less guilty. Knowing that he would have finished me if I hadn't managed to get the first shot."

"You should be heading back to your construction camp in no time," the lawyer promised.

"I hope you're right. I don't know what my father will think of all this."

"If the jury frees you, you ought to be able to tell it all to him yourself," he said.

An hour before the trail began, the courthouse was filled. A white-haired judge presided over the bench; the prosecuting attorney was a bald man with a tic in his right cheek. He recited the facts briefly and told the jury that what had happened was on the record. Clare Thomas had shot and killed Chicago Sam.

John Carter began his defense by calling Jefferson Myers as a character witness. Myers' first statement was: "Miss Thomas is just about the most nonviolent lady I've ever known."

After dismissing Myers, Carter called six bystanders who had heard the big man swear he would kill Clare along with Denver.

When the lawyers were finished, the judge, a crusty veteran, scowled at the jury and told them, "You have several choices in your verdict. If you think this young lady wilfully and without provocation shot the victim, killing him, it is a charge of murder and should be so dealt with. On the other hand, if she suspected he might draw his gun and use it on the Denver Gent and perhaps on her, she had some right to defend herself. But, if Chicago Sam went into that room with the avowed intention of killing her along with the Denver Gent, the defendant had full right to defend herself. The shot she fired was in self-defense and she should be freed of any charges."

Denver was seated with Clare and he squeezed her hand as they heard the judge's summing-up. The jurors filed out, but it did not seem likely they would take long to come to a decision.

The atmosphere in the overcrowded courtroom was tense. John Carter leaned forward and told them, "After the way the judge summed up, I can't think we'll lose!"

Clare nodded. When she looked back over the crowded room she saw Mame prominent in the second row. The blonde waved a hand at her and showed a confident smile.

But minutes passed and the jury remained out.

Clare began to wonder what their verdict might be; surely they were going to give her some sort of sentence since they were taking so long.

John Carter whispered, "It's normal for juries to do some arguing. They feel it is their duty, and so it is. That's likely going on now."

"The case is so clearly in Clare's favor," Denver worried. "What would they find to argue about?"

The lawyer shrugged. "I can't tell you that. But I know this is what usually happens."

At last the jury returned and there was a loud murmuring from the spectators as the foreman rose to read the verdict. He was a small man with a pinched face and a precise manner of speaking. Very carefully, he said. "After due deliberation, we have agreed the defendent acted in self-defense and therefore should be given her freedom!"

He sat down to cheers from the courtroom and the thumping of the judge's gavel as he attempted to restrain them. John Carter smiled at Clare and Denver kissed her. When the melee was ended and the crowd under control, the judge asked her to stand up for sentencing. He said, "The jury has found you not guilty, Miss Thomas. So you are free to go."

Clare stood up and John Carter held her in his arms for a moment. "I have never wanted to win a case more."

"Thank you," she said fervently.

Denver smiled and shook hands with him. "We must have a victory dinner tonight in the private dining room at the Pembrook Hotel."

"When will you be returning to the Intercontinental camp?" the lawyer asked.

"In the morning," Clare said. "The train will be taking supplies out then."

John said, "Then we'll meet for dinner."

They agreed on a time and he left them as others crowded around to congratulate Clare on her victory. Finally Mame, resplendent in a red bonnet and green sateen dress with plenty of flounces, made her way to them.

She kissed Clare on the cheek. "You should be given a bounty for ridding the town of a varmint!"

"Just now it's all like a nightmare that's ended!" said Clare.

Mame turned to Denver and asked, "Will you be running the game tonight?"

He shook his head. "Sorry. I'm having a small dinner party for Clare. You're invited if you can manage it."

"Why not?" said Mame. "I'll close the house for a night. Give the girls a holiday!"

When Mame left, Jefferson Myers came up with his equally plump wife, Maudie, to congratulate Clare. Myers said, "You've become a heroine!"

"I hardly see myself in that role," Clare said. "I'll be glad to get back to the camp."

After they left the courtroom, Clare and Denver went directly to the hotel where they had sandwiches and coffee in her room. They sat side by side on a divan and after discussing all that had gone on, she asked, "What about you?"

"I'm not sure what you mean," he replied.

"After tonight. I know you're closing the room tonight. But what about after that?"

Somewhat amused, Denver said, "I knew you'd get around to that."

"It's important to me," she said.

"I can open the room again. Or I can go back to finish things at the camp with you."

"And which do you choose?" she asked.

He took her hands in his and gently kissed her. "My choice has to be to go with you."

She felt completely happy. "You really mean it?"

"Yes," he said, his eyes studying her with a deep sincerity. "You risked your life and freedom for me. The gamble paid off. You have broken the link! I need not meet any gunfighter friend of Chicago Sam's to live up to the code. You killed him and you are not a gunfighter by profession. In other words, your courageous action has freed me."

"Denver!" she said softly and pressed close to him.

Dinner was at eight and in addition to Denver and herself, there were four others present: John Carter, Mame, Jefferson Myers and his wife, Maudie.

In some ways they were an incongruous group, but they all had one strong feeling in common; they were staunch friends of Denver and Clare. Toasts were offered and enjoyed and it was a decidedly pleasant occasion. Denver was careful not to mention his plans at the table. But afterwards when they were all standing around with after-dinner drinks, Mame came up to where Clare and Denver were standing and challenged him.

"What about the room?" she asked. "Are you coming back?"

He smiled and shook his head. "I'm afraid not."

Mame said, "So I'll have to look for someone else to operate it."

"Be careful," Denver warned. "You don't want to wind up with another Chicago Sam."

"Not after what we've all been through," Mame said. "I have another idea if you approve."

"What?" he asked.

"I'll take over the table myself. I play good poker. And a woman in charge of the game ought to make for less challenges."

"An ace of an idea," Denver agreed. "But what about the house?"

"I've a girl who can handle that," Mame said. "I've been grooming her for when I retire. And then I'll always be around to supervise."

Denver said, "I think this is a wise decision. It makes it easier for me to leave."

Mame said, "You're going back to join Wild Bill and the patrol?"

"Until the contract is completed." He smiled for Clare's benefit. "After that we'll do what seems best."

Mame gave them an admiring glance. "You two make a great team! You'll do just fine wherever you go!" And she left to return to her house.

The next to leave were Jefferson and Maudie Myers. Maudie said little, but beamed at them warmly, and giggled at almost everything her husband said.

Myers said, "Maudie and I will remember this night for a long while. I'll see you both again when the railway line is completed. I expect to be out there when the final spike is driven."

With the exit of the couple only John Carter was

left with them. Clare thanked him once again. "We surely are grateful to you," she said.

"No need to be. I enjoy using what small talents I may have for my friends. And also, this makes a fine exit from the town for me."

"Exit?" Denver asked.

John Carter nodded. "Yes. I've submitted my resignation to Great Western. I'm tired of this town and I distrust their way of doing business. I'm returning to my law practice in Chicago."

Denver said, "I think you're wise. From all I hear Great Western is having big trouble."

"Do you think there is any truth in the rumors?" Clare wondered.

The lawyer's narrow face showed a frown. "Yes and no. They are not making the progress they should in order to beat you in the race to Cheyenne."

"My father thinks we'll have no trouble from now on," said Clare.

"Tell him to be wary," the lawyer said. "There still seems to be a confidence among them that they will win."

"Perhaps it's just a bluff," Clare suggested.

"That is possible," John Carter replied. "But be on your guard."

"I'll warn my father," she promised.

The lawyer bade them goodnight shortly after and Clare and Denver were able to enjoy another night together. Only on this night there was not a shadow of a prison sentence over her. There was nothing to mar their lovemaking or keep them away from the camp any longer.

They packed and made ready to leave the next morning. Then Denver went out to settle some financial matters with Mame, promising to be back in plenty of time for the noon supplies train. Clare filled in her wait by reading the latest copy of *Scribner's Magazine.* She was deeply engaged in an essay on the uplifting influence women could have on their husbands, fathers and brothers when there was a knock on the door.

Somewhat surprised, she put down the magazine and went to answer it. "Who is it?" she asked.

"I have come to speak with you on business," a pleasant male voice said. "I represent the Great Western railway builders and I have an important message for your father."

Clare quickly opened the door and saw a well-built, good-looking man in a gray suit. He was of early middle age and had a small mustache. He carried his black Stetson in one hand and a brief case in the other. He looked very much the railway executive.

She said, "Come in. I had no idea that Great Western had any representative in Denver other than John Carter."

The man smiled suavely as he entered. "Mr. Carter is no longer with us."

"I only just heard that."

"It is true."

She indicated a chair, trying to decide what she thought of him. He was surely very poised and confident. She invited him, "Do be seated."

"Thank you," he said, selecting the nearest armchair.

She sat opposite him on the end of the divan. "You said you had a message for my father?"

"Yes."

"I'm leaving in an hour or so. I'll see my father at the camp this evening," she said. "I can give him any message you may wish."

"Yes, I heard you'd be leaving on the supplies train," he said. "It is rather a difficult subject for me to broach."

"Really?"

"Yes. I much admire you. I think you did the right thing in killing that swine, Chicago Sam."

"I hadn't much choice," she said. "But aren't we getting away from the subject?"

"We are," he agreed at once. "I only wished to make my own attitude clear to you. I consider you an astute and superior female."

She smiled. "Is that what you came here to tell me?"

"No," he said. "I'm here to deliver a final warning to your father."

"Surely not another one?"

"This is not a matter to be taken lightly," he said in a firm tone. "I hope you understand that."

"We have had a number of veiled threats, and some actual raids on the camp," she said. "But we have settled all that with an active patrol group to guard us."

The man looked amused. "Your feelings of security are reflective of a false state of mind. You have built too much line, extended yourself too far for any man or group of men to be able to guard it."

She said, "They have done well so far."

"I'm here to warn you against stretching your luck," was the stranger's reply. "Not to threaten but to warn."

"I see little difference what term you may use," she said with equal firmness. "It is still a threat."

"If you wish."

"My father is really not interested in such warnings," she said. "Your company would be smart to desist in them."

His eyes fixed on hers and she saw the hardness in them as he said, "We cannot afford to lose. Tell your father that."

"I'll tell him."

"I'm sure he's willing to take a chance only because he is not aware of the odds he faces."

"My father is not frightened easily," she said. "But I promise to give him your message. By the way, I don't think I have your name."

"Of course, forgive me," he said. And he reached in an upper vest pocket to produce an elaborate business card and pass it to her. "My card," he said. "As you will see I'm an engineer with Great Western."

Her attractive face registered surprise as she read the card and then looked at him. "I don't understand!"

His eyebrows raised. "My name," he said, "It disturbs you?"

"Yes," she said, trying to quickly appraise him. She indicated the card. "It says here your name is Harris Trent."

"And so it is," he acknowledged smoothly. "And I'm an engineer. A specialist in railway construction."

She gasped. "But you can't be!"

He was clearly enjoying her shock. He said, "You say that because your father employed a young engineer by the same name."

"You *knew* that?"

"We are well informed at Great Western," he promised her with a mirthless smile.

"Harris Trent is dead!" she protested. "He was killed in an accident."

"I also know about that," he said. "But I must inform you it was not Harris Trent who died in that accident but man named Donald Moffat."

She was now on her feet. "You are telling me that Harris Trent was an imposter?"

"I fear that to be the truth," he said, also rising.

She began to pace. "It's not possible. Harris Trent was no criminal. He was a fine, upright man. Honest beyond belief!"

The man with the blond hair said, "I agree with all you say. But I tell you that I am Harris Trent. The man you knew was an army officer with the Union named Donald Moffat."

"But why?" she asked.

"It's a rather interesting story," the man said. "Moffat and I were officers in the same company. Towards the end of the war we were each assigned to clean up a certain amount of territory in which were suspected spies. I had one party and he led the other."

"So you knew him?"

"We were friends."

"What happened?"

"Moffat always worried about being in the army.

But he was strongly against slavery and so convinced himself he was doing his moral duty."

"That sort of thinking describes him well," she agreed.

"Some of the men in his party went ahead independently and by the time he reached them, the half-dozen who'd gone on their own had come upon an Indian family. The sergeant in charge had shot down the man as a supposed spy, raped his wife, and then sent her wandering wildly out into the woods with a babe in arms and another trailing at her skirt."

Clare found herself shocked at this horrible tale he told so calmly and sank back down into a chair. "What then?" she said.

The man sighed. "You can imagine how a man like Moffat would feel in such circumstances. He raged at the sergeant and shot him dead before the men. Then he sent out a search party for the Indian woman."

"Did they find her?"

"At the bottom of a cliff over which she'd blindly stumbled or thrown herself; both of the children died in the fall as well. Moffat was inconsolable and brought the search party to an end and marched his men back to camp. There he surrendered himself to his commanding officer."

She understood now and nodded. "To face a court martial."

"Yes," the man said. "I think when the facts were brought out he would have been vindicated. The sergeant he killed had a record for cruelty. But Moffat chose another way."

"What?"

"He deserted. Deserted in time of war. That is, as

you know, a most serious offense. I heard no more of him until after the war ended."

"Did they find him?"

"No," he said. "Moffat used a number of false identities. He came out here. And I suppose because he knew me so well, and could fill in the details of my family and my life, and he was also an engineer like me, he took on my name."

"You're not saying that Harris Trent, the one I knew, was actually this Donald Moffat."

He nodded. "When I came out here by a remarkable coincidence the Great Western people told me that a Harris Trent was already here and working for your company. I intended to confront him but he was killed before I had the opportunity."

Clare sat there for a moment in stunned silence. It didn't seem the incredible story could be true. Yet this young man who'd told it appeared perfectly honest. And nothing he claimed was beyond the realm of possibility. Indeed it seemed to help explain the enigma of Harris Trent's character. That he was sometimes courageous and kind and at other times confused and neurotic. It was only because of meeting Denver that she had not married him. Married an imposter.

At last she said, "I will tell my father what you have told me and he will take steps to confirm the truth of this tragic story."

He nodded. "Tell him to go ahead, Miss Thomas. He need only to get in touch with army headquarters in Chicago. They will have all the records on Donald Moffat, including his desertion and his next of kin."

She said, "If your story is correct, I would want to send a letter to his family and let them know of his death. And of his excellent service to my father and the company."

"That would be a kindness. I wasn't going to burden you with this since it really doesn't matter to me any longer."

"I'm glad you decided to tell me."

"Yes, I'm sure it is for the best," he said. He smiled. "I suppose it is difficult for you to think of me as Harris Trent."

She stared at him. "It is."

"Well, I will not intrude on you any longer," he said, picking up his briefcase and hat and going to the door. "You will not forget the other matter? Make your father understand that Great Western, even at this late date, is willing to strike a deal with you. We could amalgamate to the benefit of both companies."

"My father has no authorization to consider such deals," she said. "Nor would he if he could."

He looked sad. "That is too bad, Miss Thomas. At least I have delivered my message. Goodbye."

"Goodbye—Mr. Trent," she said awkwardly as she showed him out.

Chapter
Seventeen

Clare did not have time to tell Denver about the visit of the man who claimed to be Harris Trent until they were on the supplies train heading back to the railway construction camp. Denver showed a keen interest in her account.

"I wish I had been there to meet him," he said as they sat side by side in the small passenger area of the train.

"So do I," she said. "Do you think he was telling the truth?"

"Yes," he said. "I'm inclined to think so. I always felt there was some mystery about the Harris Trent we knew. This goes a long way to explain it."

She shuddered. "It was almost like talking to a ghost!"

Denver said, "The thing that bothers me most is his continuing to offer veiled threats against the project."

"That puzzled me as well," she agreed.

"I don't see how Great Western can win now. They should be making overtures of peace, not threats," Denver went on.

Clare sighed. "He seemed sure that the trouble he was warning me about was real."

"I suppose he would be bound to sound convincing," Denver told her. "Bluffing us into surrender would be the best way out for them."

"It won't happen," she said confidently. "We have too large a lead at this very moment."

"And they have to know that," Denver said. "I guess it's a variation of the poker game, tricking us to throw in our hand."

As the train gradually made its way deep into the wilderness, Clare sat back and idly watched the long procession of forest outside the window. Her mind was on what had taken place in the town. And it seemed to her she could not be sure of anything. The hectic adventures of the last few days still seemed unbelievable. She had shot and killed a man. She had been tried for murder and acquitted. And at last the Denver Gent was coming back with her!

She had no idea what might be ahead. Surely there would be problems. She could only trust that things were still going well at the camp.

But when they arrived at the construction cars they were told that her father was in his office and Wild Bill Hickok was with him.

"They've been down there talkin' for some time," Hank said as he met them when they stepped off the train.

"What's been happening?" Clare asked.

"Some trouble in the gorge," Hank replied. "But I don't think it's serious."

"Is that what Wild Bill is discussing with my father now?" she asked.

"I reckon so," Hank said. And he greeted Denver with a broad smile. "Things ought to be safer now that you're back."

Denver shrugged and turned to Clare. "I think we should go straight to the office and see what is going on," he said.

Milton Thomas and Wild Bill Hickok were standing in earnest discussion just inside the office door. When Denver and Clare presented themselves, her father's troubled face brightened and he came and put his arms around her and kissed her.

"I've been worried about you," he said.

She smiled for him. "I'm back, completely safe."

Her father then gave Denver a stern glance. "I see you have decided to join us again."

"That's right, sir," Denver told him. "My business in town is over."

"I warn you I won't stand for your running off whenever you like. If you leave again you needn't return."

Denver's handsome face showed a flicker of annoyance but he rapidly controlled it and said quietly, "I'm not likely to leave until the job is finished."

Wild Bill Hickok held out his hand to Denver and said, "Sure am glad to have you back. Did you settle things for Mame?"

"The account was squared. Chicago Sam is dead. Mame is taking over the game herself."

"Ought to have done that in the first place," Wild Bill said.

Clare's father gave Denver a sharp look and asked, "Did you kill that Chicago Sam?"

Clare held her breath wondering what to do. Should she speak up and let them know she did it? Or would it be best to let Denver handle it? She decided to let Denver take care of it.

And he did, saying, "No, sir. As it happened I wasn't forced to look after him. He was shot by someone else." And he let it go at that.

Happily, Milton Thomas accepted this partial explanation and said, "I'm glad you weren't implicated since you are still our employee. And I do not want my daughter running off to the city to persuade you to return every time you get the whim to leave."

"You needn't worry about that, Father," Clare said. "There's no reason for Denver to leave now."

"And every reason for him to remain here," her father said. "We've had an act of vandalism which might well cripple us."

Clare's heart missed a beat. "What sort of vandalism?"

Her father turned to Wild Bill and said, "You tell her."

The scout tugged at one end of his long mustache. "Me and the boys were making a routine patrol of the gorge when we heard a sound like an explosion. We rode in the direction where the noise came from and sure enough, several hundred feet of rails were upheaved and twisted out of place. Someone had put a charge of dynamite there."

Denver asked, "How bad is the damage?"

"Not as bad as it was meant to be," Wild Bill said. "Only part of the charge went off. There was enough dynamite there to blow the built-up ledge away at that point. When part of the charge failed, only the rails and a little distance of ground was heaved up."

Clare's father said, "Just good luck or the culprit didn't know enough about dynamite to properly set up the charge."

Clare asked, "Is the damage enough to hold us up long?"

"No," her father said. "We have Larry Brand and the main work crew doing overtime to get new rails installed."

Clare remembered what the Great Western agent had told her and said, "I think I know who was responsible." And with that she launched into an account of her meeting with the Great Western engineer who claimed to be the real Harris Trent.

Her father looked amazed. "A most remarkable story," he said.

"I think it is true," she told him.

Her father considered, then said, "It's very likely to be. You will remember we searched through the supposed Trent's things after his death and there was nothing to show us where he had lived, or who he was. All identification had been removed or destroyed."

Clare said, "He would have done that deliberately. His real name was Donald Moffat."

Her father asked, "What else did this man have to tell you?"

"He warned me that we should sell out. That we couldn't win against the money Great Western is paying out to have the project wrecked."

"They almost managed," her father said.

"It makes it seem more likely that he was telling the truth," Clare said, addressing everyone. "We will have to arrange even tighter security."

"That will be easier now that Denver is back," Wild Bill said.

Clare's father said, "One spot must be guarded more than anywhere else." He let this sink in and then added, "The viaduct."

Clare saw the sense of this and agreed, "That would be the end of us."

Wild Bill rubbed his chin as he speculated. Then he said, "Maybe from now on we'd better split the patrol into three outfits. I'll lead one and guard one end of the viaduct. Denver can lead another and watch the other end, and the third lot will do general patrol of the area."

"I like that idea," Clare's father said. "When can you put it into action?"

Wild Bill looked at Denver questioningly. "When do you say?"

"Tonight, at the latest," was Denver's opinion. "And we should divide the bridge teams so we have guards there day and night with the emphasis on the night."

Wild Bill nodded. "We can work that out."

So the meeting broke up with everyone determined to share the responsibility for protecting what had been built. And Clare felt they all were more confident. She and Denver left her father and Wild Bill going over some of the details of the patrol and went outside.

Denver carried her bag up to the executive car and halted to say, "I hope you don't mind."

She looked up at him. "What about?"

"I didn't tell your father it was you who shot Chicago Sam."

"I know," she said, amused. "My heart was in my mouth. I'm just as glad you didn't."

"He's almost certain to hear about it," Denver warned her.

"Not until later," she said. "And by that time many of his other worries will be over."

Denver said, "For a moment I was afraid he wouldn't have me back."

"He needs you," she said, her eyes bright as they fixed on his, "I need you!"

"Which is a lot more important," Denver said. He gave her a brief kiss and promised, "I'll see you at dinner. I want to set up the patrols with Wild Bill just now."

Clare was happy to be back in the tiny compartment which had been home to her for so many months. Having Denver back with her also made a big difference. Her hope was that he'd find no reason to leave her again. She had no idea what her father's next project might be, but she knew there would be one. And without a doubt he'd be able to find work for both herself and Denver.

The big question was whether Denver would be able to settle for this style of living. But she knew he wanted to marry her and have a family life, all of which would never be possible if he went on living as a gunfighter.

She changed into her working uniform of breeches and blouse and made her way down to the corral to fondle the muzzle of the black stallion and chat with Hank.

The old man asked her, "You heard about what happened at the gorge?"

"Yes. It seems we were lucky the blast didn't fully go off."

He nodded. "You know who I think did it?"

"Do you have an idea?"

"Yep," the old man said with a knowing look on his lined face. "I think it was Pedro."

"Why?" she asked, knowing it could well be true.

"Well, the boys told me the day before it happened, him and Larry Brand had a terrible argument. First they just stood snarling at each other and then Larry started to pummel him and sent him to the ground."

Clare was startled. "He and Pedro were close friends."

"They sure worked hand in glove," Hank agreed. "But they had a bad falling out. Nobody is sure what is was about. But I think it was because Pedro told Larry he was an agent for the Great Western and wanted Larry to go along helpin' him!"

Clare said, "If that were true Larry had only to report Pedro to my father."

The old man thought about this. "I dunno," he said. "Brand might be afraid of incriminating himself. He's been so thick with Pedro and went out of his way to keep him on the job."

"That's true."

"I think Brand told him to lay low but Pedro went ahead and planted that dynamite anyway."

"Is Pedro still in the camp?"

"No," Hank said. "He was gone the next morning. No one has seen him since."

"Then it must have been him," she said. "My father didn't mention him just now. But no doubt he and Wild Bill suspect him."

"I reckon so," Hank said. "Worst is, he may still be around. Hiding to do some more damage."

"Wild Bill and Denver are going to organize special patrols," she told Hank.

"Time they did," the old man said dourly.

Clare went back to the executive car and freshened up for the evening meal. And she made it a point to be standing on the grassy knoll in front of the car when Larry Brand came strolling up. She saw his face harden at the sight of her and knew he was angry.

When he came up to her with a sullen look, she said, "Hello, Larry. I hear you've been busy repairing the ledge."

"You're back," he said.

"Yes."

"I don't think I should discuss anything with you. We're not friends any longer."

"Wrong," she said. "I'm still your friend."

His smile was twisted. "Sure, that's why you ran off to join Denver."

"That's something else."

"Sure," he said with a jeering note in his voice. "Well, the job here will soon be over and I won't have to stay around and be tormented by you."

"I'm sorry," she said.

"We could have been happy," he told her. "Instead you want to throw your life away on him. He'll wind up leaving you alone and then a widow!"

Clare bit her lip. It was too close to truth to be comforting. She said, "Where's Pedro? I hear you had a quarrel with him. Then the ledge was blown up and he hasn't been seen since."

Larry looked mildly startled. "You've picked up a lot of news in the short time you've been back."

"All I need to know," she said. "What about Pedro?"

"He's like a lot of others," Larry said. "He doesn't know what loyalty means."

She gave him a meaningful look. "Maybe you're wrong. Maybe he knows where his loyalty pays best. The Great Western, for instance."

He stared at her. "I'm not saying anything. But if he shows his ugly face around the camp again I'll drill him."

"You really did come to a parting of the ways," she said.

"From now on I'm playing a lone hand," he told her. And he gave her a grim look and walked away.

Conversation at the dining table lagged somewhat. Larry spoke only when a question was put to him directly. He finished his meal and left without saying a word.

Clare glanced across the table at her father. "How long has he been acting this way?"

Her father sighed. "He's been in a mood ever since he had the quarrel with Pedro. Instead of reporting back to me he tried to deal with it himself. And to pay him off, Pedro undoubtedly blew up the ledge."

Wild Bill Hickok said, "I figure Pedro was sent here

by Great Western. I figured that from the start. Brand didn't get wise until it was too late. Now he's mad at himself for keeping the Mexican on."

"At least he's left the camp," Clare said.

Denver looked at them all. "But how far away has he gone?"

"A good question," said Milton Thomas. "That is why we must have a strong patrol for the rest of the project."

After dinner Clare and Denver took their usual stroll. It was closer to twilight than on the other evenings because the days were getting shorter. Hand in hand they walked among the tall evergreens.

Denver said, "Larry Brand didn't go out of his way to hide his hostility to me."

"He was in a dreadful mood."

"He didn't even speak to me," Denver said. "He blames for me spoiling his chances with you."

Clare smiled at the man beside her. "The truth is he never had a chance with me. But he refuses to believe that."

"We'll soon have the project completed," Denver said. "Then the camp will break up. He'll go on somewhere else."

"That's what he said. I think he once planned to follow Father and me to the next project but he won't do that now."

"Not likely," Denver said. "The West is opening up fast. He'll have no trouble finding another job."

"His experience on this one will serve him well," she said. "I'm sure Father will give him a good reference even though he has behaved so sullenly. He's done his work well."

"He was a southern officer," Denver teased her. "You could have done worse."

"I know," she said, picking up his teasing mood. "I fell in love with the wrong man!"

Denver halted under the branches of a towering pine and his handsome face looked a little sad as he asked, "What if you decide that one day?"

Clare reached her hands up and clasped them around the back of his neck. Eyeing him lovingly, she whispered, "Never, my darling!"

Denver took her in his arms and held her close as their lips met. She was still in his arms when the sound came. A rustle in the woods not far from them.

Denver was instantly on the alert, his hand on the gun at his hip as he quickly released her. He gazed around trying to be sure in which direction the sound had come.

Clare's face had taken on a shadow of fear and she was also looking and listening for some repeat of the movement in the bushes.

She finally turned to him. "Some animal, perhaps?"

Denver was frowning. "I don't think so."

"What do you think?"

His gun still in hand, Denver placed an arm protectively around her and in a low voice said, "Let's start back!"

They did, and Clare was fearful at every step. But there was no other sound nor did they see anyone. When at last they came out in the open within sight of the camp, some of her fright drained away.

She asked him, "Do you think someone followed us?"

Denver nodded grimly. "Yes."

"Who?"

"Most likely it was Pedro. He's surely hiding nearby."

Clare shuddered. "I'm terribly frightened! I feel something awful is about to happen."

"Not if we manage things properly," Denver said with confidence. "The viaduct is the most vital link in the line and the easiest to destroy. Our main object must be to guard it. I'm taking this side and Wild Bill and his men can look after the other."

Clare touched his arm. "I want to go with you."

Denver frowned. "That's not necessary, nor even wise."

"I don't care," she said stubbornly. "I have a definite feeling about this. Please don't refuse me!"

"Very well, if it means so much to you. But you're letting yourself in for a long, cold night. I'm sure you'll regret it in the morning."

"I'll risk that," she said.

The patrols set out an hour later. By prearrangement, they would search the entire structure and meet in the middle of the bridge. Then, secure in the knowledge that there was no one out there, they had only to guard each end. Because Clare was going to be with him Denver let the men who'd normally be with him go on a general patrol of the gorge line, which was the other most vulnerable area.

It was close to eleven when Clare and Denver walked out on the viaduct in the darkness. He carried a lantern and guided her along carefully. The footing was treacherous and an unexpected fall could result in death thousands of feet below. After a while they saw the two lanterns of Wild Bill Hickok's patrol approaching from the other side. They drew gradually closer as each group advanced until they met.

Wild Bill joked with them, telling Denver, "I wouldn't mind doing guard duty alone either if I had an assistant like you."

Clare smiled at him and promised, "One night I'll do guard duty on your side."

"I'll look forward to that," said Wild Bill with a chuckle. "Not that the bridge will get much attention."

It was an awesome experience standing out there so far from the land at either end and with the greatest drop to the river directly under them. Clare tried to visualize trains running over the structure with the passengers entirely at ease and unaware of what engineering magic had erected this frail span.

Denver said, "We'll be at the other end. If there is any trouble, fire a shot and we'll be on the alert."

Wild Bill nodded. "We'll be watching close. Especially with that Pedro on the prowl."

Clare said, "Even Larry Brand knows he's dangerous now."

"Problem was he took a long while to get around to it," the veteran scout said grimly.

They chatted a few minutes more and then went back to their stations at the ends of the bridge. Denver found a comfortable boulder behind some bushes on which they could sit, concealed. He put out the lantern and they began their vigil.

An occasional bird flew near them uttering melancholy, squawking cries which vanished in the eerie darkness. Overhead the stars seemed to be brighter than usual. But there was no full moon to throw its silver searchlight over their surroundings.

Denver put a protective arm around her. "Cold?"

"No," Clare said, though she was actually not all that comfortable.

"Hint of autumn in the air," he said. "We've got about five weeks more to meet the line from Cheyenne. I wouldn't want it to take longer."

"It gets very cold later on, doesn't it?"

"If we're bogged down by anything we could find ourselves brought to a halt by the winter. Once the snow and freezing starts there's nothing to be done."

"Great Western must be in much the same position," she sighed. "Otherwise they wouldn't be so worried about us."

"You're probably right," Denver said. "That's why they had Pedro come here as a spy."

"Larry was very angry with me."

"I can imagine."

"He accused me of leading him on and then turning to you. And that is one thing I didn't do."

"He showed he wasn't happy to see me back," Denver said. "Things were pretty awkward at the dinner table."

"I know. My father gave him several sharp looks. I'm sure he's tired of his sulky spells."

"Well the project should soon be over and he'll move on somewhere else."

"So will we all."

"Yes," Denver said, sounding a little uncertain about the prospect.

Then from the woods behind them came the sound of a gunshot followed by a human cry. Denver jumped up and stared in the direction from which the scream had come. Now there was only silence.

Clare, who was also on her feet, whispered, "What do you think?"

"I'd say someone was shot back there," he said. "I'd judge maybe two or three hundred feet straight through the woods behind us."

"What will we do?"

Denver hesitated. "We shouldn't leave here but we ought to find out what has happened."

"Let me go," Clare begged.

"No," he said. "You stay here. I'll go. If you see a shadow, any moving thing, challenge it, and if there's no reply, shoot and shoot straight!" He handed her his Winchester.

She took it and realized what she'd let herself in for. She begged him, "Be careful!"

He nodded and vanished into the darkness. Now her true ordeal began. The night which had seemed so normal before now took on a sinister atmosphere. She felt a menace in every branch which swayed above her in the cool breeze. Something between a shiver of cold and a shudder of fear rippled through her as she knelt behind the bushes with the Winchester pointed at the guard point by the end of the viaduct.

An eternity seemed to pass. Her arms began to ache. And she began to worry that the shot had been a trap to get Denver out into the woods where he might be easy prey for an attacker. The thought of this only increased her alarm.

Then she heard measured footsteps through the brush and swung around quickly with the Winchester pointed in that direction. Her eyes hurt from the strain of peering into the dark shadows. Then she saw the moving figure coming straight towards her. Coming very slowly.

"Stop!" she challenged the phantom intruder.

"Clare! It's me!" It was Denver's voice.

She lowered the gun with a small prayer of thankfulness and waited for him to come up to her. It was then she saw he had a body slung over his shoulder.

"Who?" she asked in an awed voice.

"Light the lantern," he told her sharply. "I'm not certain whether he's alive or dead."

She quickly turned, fumbled for a match, and lifted the lantern shade and touched the flame to the wick. With the lantern working she turned, holding it up over the man Denver had stretched out on the ground. It was Pedro!

Denver looked up, "He's wounded bad. But he's alive!"

She knelt down and brought the lantern closer. "Where is the wound?"

"In the chest. Near the heart," Denver told her as he tried to staunch the flow of blood from the Mexican's chest with the bandana he'd taken from his neck.

The yellow of the lantern gave the face of the wounded man a ghastly tint. But the intrusion of light somehow alerted him to the extent that his eyelids twitched slightly. Then he opened his eyes to stare up at them in horror.

His lips moved and in a low, harsh voice he managed, "Killed me! He's killed me!"

Denver bent close to be sure to hear him. "Who?"

Pedro stared up at him, his eyes glazing over. "Wanted my share! He refused!"

411

"Who did this to you?" Denver repeated his question.

Pedro stared up silently for a moment then said, "Brand! Great Western paid him—" But he didn't finish; a gurgling muffled his words and choked them off. A great bubble of blood emerged from his mouth and his head dropped limply to one side.

"He's gone!" Clare said, gazing at Denver.

Denver nodded grimly. "At least he lived long enough to tell us what we need to know."

"Larry Brand is the spy for Great Western," she said in an incredulous voice.

"Yes," Denver said. "Apparently Pedro tried to blackmail him so Brand finished him off."

"That means that he is somewhere close by!" she gasped.

Denver nodded and stood up. "Yes. No question of that." Then he suddenly froze and stared straight ahead at the viaduct. "I think I see something moving out there!"

"He's managed it while we were busy with Pedro," she said.

He grabbed the rifle from her and fired a shot into the air. Within seconds there was a corresponding shot from Wild Bill on the opposite end of the viaduct.

"You stay here!" he told her and ran out onto the viaduct.

Clare had no intention of doing that. She followed Denver as quickly as she could, remembering to pick her steps and avoid stumbling. She heard another shot and more shouts from far ahead in the middle of the bridge. Denver had managed to get so far along that she couldn't even see his shadow.

She followed on, grimly aware of her danger; then from out of the shadows a figure sprang and grasped her. She let out a scream of terror as she struggled to free herself. Almost at once a hand was clasped around her mouth, making it impossible to utter a second scream!

A voice grated in her ear, "The charge is set! It only needs me to get it and detonate it! You'll be my shield and we'll see the bridge, Denver, Wild Bill, and the lot of them into the river!"

Clare clawed at her attacker frantically and found a vulnerable spot near his eyes. With a curse, he struck her violently.

"Little vixen!" he said in her ear. "Tonight will see you tamed!"

Ahead she heard Denver's voice as he challenged, "Stop! Whoever you are!"

Brand laughed malevolently. "You know who I am! And I have a hostage! Your precious lady!"

"Don't be a fool, Brand, you're finished! Let her go!" Denver shouted.

Larry Brand's reply was to fire in the direction from which Denver had shouted. "Now we'll move on, just a little way to go!" And he somehow kept hold of her and made progress along the bridge in the darkness.

Terrified and tormented by the thought that Denver was dead, Clare fought on wildly. Larry's hand moved from her mouth; she was fighting with the mad strength of a cornered animal. His gunhand came within range of her mouth and she sank her teeth deep into it. He howled with pain and automatically let the gun fall. She struggled even more and at the same time screamed.

413

"Denver! His gun is gone! Denver!" she cried.

An instant later Denver loomed out of the darkness, his Winchester in hand. He faced them and told Brand, "Let her go."

"Drill us both!" was Brand's taunting cry. "You can't get me without her!"

"Not with this!" Denver said grimly. And in the same second he dropped the Winchester and leaped forward. It was a move Brand hadn't expected, and startled, he released her to defend himself.

Clare dropped to the tracks with a groan as the two men now grappled in the darkness above her. She heard the voices of Wild Bill and his men as they approached and was vaguely aware of the struggling Brand and Denver veering dangerously over to the very edge of the bridge.

There was a loud, high-pitched cry of terror and then one of them went over. It was only a matter of a few frantic seconds after she'd fallen on the tracks before Denver was bending down to help her to her feet.

"It's over," he said grimly. "He's gone."

The construction of the line could now go on without further interference. In the daylight they discovered the charge of dynamite in place and ready to be set off. The charge was safely removed and that afternoon Larry Brand and Pedro Reilly were buried side by side in the makeshift burial ground where Harris Trent and the others had been buried. But the bodies of these two were set a distance from the others, to separate them in death as they had been in life.

The camp took on a sober tone, and it was not until the main line came within sight of the line being built ut of Cheyenne that there was any celebrating. When hat happened, the two crews joined in a night of riumphant revelry.

Standing by one of the campfires with Denver and er father, Clare said, "Well, was it worth it?"

"I'd say so," her father said with a bitter smile. 'We've all lived and learned a lot. Part of the frontier xperience. I'll go on further west."

Denver nodded. "The West is changing. Some of s have to change as well."

Milton Thomas gave him a relieved look. "I'm glad ou've learned that lesson, Denver."

Clare felt a warmth in knowing the two men had rown much closer in the final days of the railway uilding. It was what she'd hoped for but never ex- ected. And now her hopes had come true. She still vorried about the future and what it might offer her nd the handsome gunman, but she'd noticed that ately he'd become much more reserved and thought- ul. She interpreted this as a good sign.

Her father spoke above the sounds of the distant iddles, shouts, and laughter, saying, "Our next big noment will be the day the first train moves here and ve drive the last solid-gold spike into place!"

This day came about three weeks later and not efore a small snowstorm had warned them that they'd ompleted their task just in time. The train was formed n Denver where it was widely circulated now that the reat Western had given up their line and was in ankruptcy. It was Intercontinental's plan to later buy he unfinished stretch of railway and incorporate it nto a second line to Cheyenne. Her father was ap- roached to do this the following year.

Jefferson Myers and his wife were members of the party to take the first regular train ride from Denver to Cheyenne. And at Clare's insistence, Mame and several of her girls were invited along for the trip.

It was in Denver that they said goodbye to Wild Bill. He had an offer to join the Buffalo Bill Show again and decided it would be a pleasant change.

"We're going to Europe," Wild Bill said with some excitement. "I've never been over there so I think this is my chance."

Clare smiled at him as they stood in front of the Pembrook Hotel, offering their goodbyes to the tall mustached man who had become their friend.

She said, "You must write us about your adventures."

He nodded. "I reckon I'll have lots of time. Playing the show with Bill is easy."

Denver shook hands with the gunfighter in farewell. He said, "Maybe Clare and I can find a place in Bill's show one day. She's an expert shot."

"I'll tell him," Wild Bill promised. "Bill has a warm spot for the ladies; you're liable to have an offer from him."

He rather shyly kissed her on the cheek, mounted his big chestnut mare, and rode out of their lives just as casually as he had entered.

Two days later the first train slowly pulled out of the railway siding in Denver City and began its first run to Cheyenne. The mood was a jubilant one but subdued compared to the celebrations the workers had held.

Mame came to Clare in the train, dressed in a

ew blue walking dress. "The latest thing from Paris.
Madame Ouida rushed to alter it for me in time."

Clare smiled. "You can always depend on Madame
Ouida."

"And on you," Mame said with sincerity. "I know
why the girls and I are on the train. And I'll not ever
forget your kindness."

Clare patted Mame's hand. "You're a friend of
Denver's and you're a friend of mine. This is where
you belong."

Mame smiled. "I'm almost as happy about you two
as if Denver had picked me. When are you going to
be hitched?"

Clare found herself indulging in an unaccustomed
blush as she said, "I can't tell you that."

"He hasn't set a date yet?"

She shook her head. "He hasn't actually proposed
yet."

Mama gave an indignant glance down the car where
Denver was sitting with her father and Jefferson Myers
and his wife. She turned to Clare again and told her,
"Don't you worry, dear. First chance I have I'll tell
him a few things."

Clare laughed. "Don't worry about it!"

Of course it was bothering her. But she hoped that
as soon as the trip was over and they reached Cheyenne, Denver would ask her to marry him and they'd
make plans for the future. She daren't think it wouldn't
happen.

It was late afternoon and the sun was beginning to
set when they reached the point where the last spike
was to be driven before the train moved on to Chey-

417

enne. Jefferson Myers was to drive the golden spike and her father carefully instructed him and remaine with him to guide him.

All the local dignitaries from both cities were present, as well as Mame and her girls, a scattering c workers, and the members of the train staff. It was triumphant yet solemn moment.

Jefferson Myers drove the spike slowly in place an then looked up triumphantly. "That's it, boys! She finished!"

There were cheers and general rejoicing. Mam and her girls were hugged and swung about happil by the workers who'd shown up, and Jefferson Myer planted a kiss on Maudie's lips.

Denver and Milton Thomas exchanged a siler handshake and then Denver came to her where sh stood alone, remembering the trials and the losse which had made the day possible. The face of Larr Brand was momentarily vivid in her mind. Larry Bran who had saved her life and later tried to take it.

"You're not joining in the celebration," he said wit mild amazement. "You're standing here alone and los in your thoughts."

"I'm remembering," she said. "I think Harris Tren would have been happy about today."

"I'm sure he would," Denver agreed. "Too man good men died for this."

She linked her arm in his and as they began walking back to the train, he said, "By the way. I've had a offer from Laramie, Wyoming. They want me to g there as marshall."

"That's wonderful," she said smiling. "You'll b staying on the right side of the law."

He nodded and then frowned. "There's just one complication."

"What?"

"They want a marshall who's a solid family man. A married man."

Her eyes met his. "I can do something about that!" she said.

To the delight of the onlookers Denver let out a happy whoop of laughter as he picked her up in his arms and swung her around!